You're the One for Me

A novel by Solange DewBerry

This book is a work of fiction. All names, places and events are fictional and are products of the author's imagination—and what an imagination it is. No portion of this book may be reproduced without permission from the publisher except by a reviewer who may quote brief passages in a review.

Published in the United States by Spilled Ink Press
Newington, CT

Copyright © 2020 Tina Kane
You're the one for Me

First Edition, January 2020

ISBN: 9781734227604

Dedication: To my dear, loving husband, and wonderful, patient children. I love you all for putting up with me all those hours I spent locked away.

And to all those voices that have been whispering to me for so long—I'm glad to have met you and found you belong to Berry, Moe and the gang. Welcome to my world.

Acknowledgement: to all those who helped me along the way, my deepest gratitude: thank you. And special thanks to Sloane Moore, artist, and to my dedicated editor, Liane Larocque of Edit Expert.

Prologue

My Perfect Hero

My perfect hero must be very good looking. He should be tall (more than six feet?) and very trim and athletic but not one of those muscly guys who only think about body-building. He will have perfect hair (dark, wavy) and deep brown eyes. Green eyes are also acceptable. His eyes must smile all the time, and he has a good sense of humor. He has to be very macho, but accept that the heroine can be moody and not tease her about that. He understands her. My hero is very strong and must be rich. When he sees the heroine, it will be love at first sight and he knows at that moment that he will do anything he has to in order to win her love. He will never, ever be mean or leave her. Or fight over stupid stuff.

By ~~Berry Samuels~~
~~Selina DeLonge~~
~~Selina DuBurry~~
~~Selma DewBerry~~
~~Sondra DewBerry~~
Solange DewBerry, age 15

Chapter One

Berry/Solange, 15 years later

My newest lover turned to me with his soulful brown eyes. His hand snaked over the sheet to hold mine lightly. A moment later, his fingers twined with mine, and he gave them a little squeeze. A wry smile graced his sculpted lips as he said, "All this sex all the time, as great as it is, it doesn't seem right."

What's this? Had my lover transformed into a boy-toy with scruples? I made myself take a deep breath and reminded myself that things are not always as they seem. He didn't mean it, even if he was right, in a manner of speaking. My lover lived for sex. He was very good at it. And I, well, I'm not kidding myself—that was the reason we were together.

This contemplative lapse was new for him. I needed a moment to decide what he was about. I looked at him as he lay on the bed, the sheets pulled up just so. As usual, he was looking like a Greek god, all muscles, and dark, thick, curly hair. His body was mostly smooth, hairless, and tanned. That was kind of funny when I considered how heavy his beard was, but of course, since he really did want sex, he'd shaven so I couldn't object on the grounds of probable beard burn. Not that I normally objected to sex, unless it was to allow him an opportunity to convince me. His seductions could be unbearable fun.

At the moment, he wore nothing but the bedclothes. All the good stuff was hinted at—the thin line of belly hair discretely trailing down his six-pack abs, so I couldn't miss his package. I'd put my oldest sheets on the bed that morning, the soft ones that were so thin, they were practically transparent. As a result, although he was covered, I could still see what was down there. Even if I couldn't, I've got a pretty good imagination. A bronzed hunk of a man. All testosterone all the time. All mine. Yum. Right?

But maybe he was right. I wasn't in the mood for sex but thought I needed to do this. I turned away to collect my thoughts. It wasn't easy to think when he was front and center, and especially when he was looking at me that way. You know, undressing me with his eyes, so he could eat me alive. You can't trust a man like him, so I couldn't turn away completely. This wasn't like him. Was it a new game? Points for him to think up something like that all on his own. Disconcerting, actually.

He gave me a sleepy smile with those bedroom eyes and ran his fingertip down my spine as I sat on the edge of the bed. "What's wrong, baby, afraid you can't keep up?"

I knew it. His fit of principled behavior didn't last. Or was he speaking metaphorically? That would be a first. Still, shivers followed his touch even through the thick flannel I wore, so naturally, I lay back in his arms. They were warm and strong, just what I needed in this melancholy mood. He pressed a kiss to my brow as he stroked my arm softly. Of course, his fingertips brushed the side of my breast. They wandered from there. I swear the man was insatiable, no matter what he'd said earlier.

But the truth was, I simply wasn't in the mood for sex. Not at that moment. Later. Maybe.

Had he sensed my mood and echoed it in a moment of weakness? I turned my eyes to look at him again.

You want to know something? Greek gods are Greek Gods. They're beautiful enough to break your heart, but to be honest, I wanted something more than physical attraction and passion, something harder to define. I wanted, well, companionship. Conversation. Someone who would do the dishes when I was too tired or bitchy to do them, or run to the vacuum cleaner—you know, something spontaneously romantic. I wasn't certain this guy could deliver those goods, no matter what he'd said earlier, but I tried anyway.

"It's not that. Sex with you is great. But it's just so, I don't know, empty."

I caught my breath, not believing I actually said that to him. He might have been a pussycat most of the time, but I didn't trust his moods. My lovers tend to be temperamental, and he was no exception. I bit my lip, waiting for the explosion.

Either he didn't hear me, or he was still processing my words. He might look like Apollo, but honestly, if I didn't put the words in his mouth, he didn't have a clue. But then his arms tightened around me, and I felt the love. He sighed and kissed the top of my head. His big hands started that rubbing thing again. I glanced up at him. Was he angry? I was prepared to be mortified and backpedal if I had to. No need. He looked at me as if I had two heads, and two-headed women were a serious turn-on.

"Empty?" he asked, his incredulity evident not only in his rumbly tone but by the lift of one eyebrow. He didn't believe me. Instead, he smiled that seductive smile, the one where his mouth quirks up on one side and usually melts my heart.

And it was in that moment I realized he was all wrong.

You see, every single one of my guys seems to be born with the ability to lift one eyebrow at will. And they all do it all the time. I mean, it makes me feel like an idiot when they express their skepticism so easily. And silently. But they never say anything doubtful aloud, oh no. Instead, they always have something else to say and know when to say it, like perfect automatons. And that's on top of perfect hair, perfect skin, perfect teeth, perfect bank accounts, perfect lips, perfect cars, perfect bodies, and perfect lawns for crying out loud. It gets old fast. Not that I'm complaining, mind you. A perfect man, wanting me? And when I tire of him, another is waiting to take his place? Come on. I'd have to be an idiot to say something bad about the deal I've got. Right?

Maybe I'd best explain.

I'm no one special. I'm not perfect, far from it. I do have a few things going for me. I've got a job I tolerate and a hobby (it's more than a hobby, but that's what my family calls it) that I love. The job pays the bills and leaves something left over at the end of each month. I own my own home—well, a condo. My car's paid off, and it still runs fine. I bought a new laptop, the first is hooked up to the internet in the spare bedroom, but this one I keep off the web to keep it safe from viruses. That's important, so I don't lose anything. Oh yeah, I've also got a few terrific friends, coworkers who rely on me, and a family that mostly adores me. Mom and Dad are still around, and I've got an older brother too, a very successful up-and-coming guy. He's helped me a lot.

But that's where the good things kind of end. I'm not ancient, but I'm about to hit thirty, and I have to admit, it's getting to me. The sly comments, or so-called 'hints' from my mother and aunts, really burn me up. I'm not married, have never had a proposal from a guy I considered marrying. Add to that the fact that I'm, well, not exactly a model, in stature or figure. Hell, I'll say it. I've got curves, okay? Natural ones that cling no matter how much I diet and exercise. And I'm not tall either.

I haven't even gotten to the bad stuff. My hair's okay,

pretty normal, brown with light highlights. Yes, they're from a bottle, but they're pretty close to what my hair did naturally when I was a kid. And I've got one blue eye and one that's hazel. They're good eyes, color-wise, but it's weird having two, even now when I should be used to it. They call it heterochromia. I never could get used to contact lenses. I squint like anything when I don't wear my glasses, and that causes wrinkles. So, I wear them.

And the worst part: I'm shy. There, I said it. I'm socially awkward, an introvert. A late bloomer who's still waiting to bloom. They used to call girls like me wallflowers. Isn't that quaint? These days, with all these confident, kick-ass heroines around, I'm an anomaly. I hate that. People don't understand, and I'm simply too inhibited to explain. How's that for a conundrum?

Except in the proverbial bedroom. In there, when it's just me and my lover, I can tell him what I want and what I need. Kinky, straight up, light bondage, and almost anything in between. When it's my lover and me, no problems talking. And tonight proved it again. To wit: I just told this Adonis of mine that his lovemaking was empty.

I'll bet you'd think someone like me would be worried about a man like him walking out on me since I'm no bargain, and he's, well, like a Greek god. Funny thing, isn't it? So back to that.

Yeah, sex with this guy was fabulous. Every night, as much as I wanted. I mean, he never got tired, never flagged. But it got, how shall I say this nicely, predictable. First, he'd make sure I was happy, you know? Any number of ways to do that. Then I would be happy again. And maybe a third time. Then we'd assume one of several standard positions, and he'd slide in perfectly, and hold me tight and then we'd both be happy. And then he'd cuddle me all night long. No snoring, oh no. His nasal passages were as wonderful as the rest of him.

And there's more. My perfect guy always left the toilet seat down *and* dry. Never a single beard hair in the bathroom sink, or blobs of toothpaste. No mud on the floor. His boots always stowed neatly under the bed, whether they were motorcycle boots, construction, or ski. One time, they were cowboy boots. Those weren't under the bed. I made him wear them while we did it. He wasn't happy about it, but because he was my perfect lover, he agreed.

I never once had to clean up after him, other than the odd scrap of paper that would drift down on an errant breeze. And he was always gone in the morning, so there was no messy morning breath or pillow-creased cheeks to worry about. My hair can be a mess, and I don't care. I didn't have to worry about what kind of coffee to buy, no one to argue with about who gets the last onion bagel. I never had a single thing about him that I could complain about.

On paper, he was simply perfect.

But he *was* predictable. Bordering on boring. Right up to the line. Sometimes a toe crossed over. Sometimes the whole foot.

Regardless, I knew it was time for someone new. I hadn't been with a blond for a while. Maybe green eyes, or an eyepatch… a pirate. I'd never been with a pirate. Or perhaps I'd try voyeurism. Never done that either.

So, right then and there, I got rid of my Greek god. Gave him the old heave-ho. No tears, barely a fond farewell. Maybe some other time, Buster. But he wasn't coming back to my bed, at least in that form. There wasn't anything different enough about him, nothing that set him apart from the others. Perfection has its price. Who knew it was boredom?

Just like that. Gone clinging white sheet. Delete. Gone

deep, probing brown eyes. Delete—backspace. Gone, perfectly raised eyebrow and large, warm hands. Delete. Delete delete delete delete. Gone slender line of dark hair pointing to a perfect groin. Click, drag, drag, delete. So sorry, but it wasn't working out for me. *Tonight*, I told myself, *I'm sleeping alone.*

Chapter Two

Berry

I've never been the kind of woman who goes to bars. Or singles groups, or visited dating sites. What I mean to say is I didn't go out much, no more than was necessary. To the grocery store, the post office, the bank. I went to work five days a week. I frequented the office supply store and the drug store. And the bookstore. I made myself go there instead of buying online. I had *some* pride. Besides, there's something about being among those shelves, smelling those new book smells, picking them up and putting them down—but I don't want to get too carried away. Suffice to say, that was the extent of my social life. The sad thing is, it was by design. I had a mild, self-diagnosed case of agoraphobia, or so I thought since I didn't have the nerve to go see a doctor about it. I mean, what if I was wrong and was just a stick in the mud?

Don't get me wrong. I like people. I love being with them, but the thought of forcing myself to go out and do things was sometimes too much. Okay, often too much. I had friends (I still do), but not the type who have large, wild parties. No one who drinks to excess, or says or does things they later regret. I've had boyfriends but no one recently. With all my perfect imaginary lovers, I'd gotten pickier about the real ones. To be honest, there hadn't been anyone for quite some time. It always takes me a long time to get to know a real man.

I knew something was missing from my life but hadn't quite worked up the energy to fix that. It's so much easier to fix imaginary relationships.

I wasn't exactly desperate for actual human contact, but that was on the horizon. I guess you could say I'd lost the thread on how to achieve that. Pathetic? Not really. My life, in many ways, was pretty good. You see, besides my day job, I was a writer. Not that I made much money at it, but I planned to someday. I wrote romances. Still do.

But I digress.

What is it writers say to themselves to get motivated? Butt In Chair, Hands On Keyboard. Got that. Got my herbal tea, and a plate of cookies too. I treated myself and got the vanilla swirls with the candied cherries on top. There's something about the dry cookie crumble and the squishy, sticky cherry chew that makes me want to write. They weren't always easy to find, so I ration them for those days when it seems the words seem stingier than others. Days like that day.

So, I'll set the scene. It was autumn—late September, and it was cold. My feet were tucked into toasty slippers and rested on top of the radiator. I simply cannot write with cold feet. As I waited for the laptop to boot up, I began to nibble around the edge of my first cookie, and as soon as the screen lit up, I popped it into my mouth. As I swallowed the last of the crumbs, I opened the file of my latest story.

I'm on my sixth manuscript. The last, the fifth, sold—amazing. It has been on bookstore shelves and in e-readers for a few months, and I still couldn't believe all those years of slaving over the keyboard had paid off. Or paid for my fancy new laptop. My agent predicted modest sales. I was a newcomer after all and had no budget for a promotional tour. I shuddered at the thought of all that travel. But I was willing to take whatever fame and small fortune I could grab.

So, there I was. My butt was firmly in the chair, hands (free of crumbs) most definitely on keyboard. I've reread the last page I'd written. My heroine and hero—Svetlana and Conrad—were at last alone, after many trials and tribulations, and chasings of each other around the globe. All their flirting and grand gestures were finally coming to a climax. Literally. I closed my eyes and began to type.

    She looked at him with her dark, sultry, welcoming eyes. At long last, this was their moment. He'd moved mountains for her, followed her on a merry chase for far too long, but ~~at last~~ now he had her exactly where he wanted her, and nothing, or no one, could ruin this moment. They were alone on his ship and would be for days. The ~~raging~~ storm ~~raging outside~~ would assure their privacy. Nothing could stop him now.
    The ship rocked gently on the waves, and he ~~smirked~~ grinned, thinking how the movement would enhance their lovemaking.
    Not taking his eyes from ~~her~~ Svetlana, he took a sip of bourbon from the crystal tumbler. Its sweet, smoky flavor flowed down his throat. But he didn't want anything to ruin this moment. He set the drink down and reached for the buttons…

Damn. Would he have buttons or ties at that time? I made a note to look it up later and kept writing.

    …buttons/ties of his shirt. The flames in the fireplace were reflected in her eyes.
    From her prone position on the mattress, Svetlana rose to her knees, pulling at the

voluminous fabric of her skirt to free her movements, and as he neared, she took the fine lawn fabric of his shirt between her hands. Urging him closer, she kissed him hard, her sharp **(really? Maybe rethink that)** small tongue thrust~~ing~~ its way into his mouth. He groaned and pulled her closer, feeling the silky blouse slide against her skin. Soon it would be him doing the sliding. His hands gripped her tighter.

With a <u>sharp</u> cry **(ugh, that word again)**, she pulled away from his seeking mouth and yanked the sides of his shirt out and down, hard. Buttons **(Please let there be buttons)** pinged away into the cabin. She gave a throaty laugh as she tore the tattered garment from his body.

Gently, she pulled away and eased back ~~down~~ onto the bed, her long fingers playing with the strings ~~at the neckline~~ of her peasant blouse.

Undeterred, he placed first one knee ~~on the bed~~ and then the other on the bed, stalking her like a tiger. With his teeth, he pulled one ribbon loose and listened to her gasp of pleasure. His strong fingers spread her knees, and he crawled further onto the bunk. It would not be much longer before he sank into her, the first of many, many times he would love her that night. His teeth gently grazed her earlobe, and he felt her shiver. She threw back her head, urging him wordlessly to caress her long, white neck.

With a groan borne of desire, Conrad submitted to her unspoken command and pressed warm lips to her throat. His hands swept down the length of her body, more than anxious to ~~finally~~ consummate this love and longing he'd suffered for months, nay, years. He heard her whimper of surrender, and ~~his eyes~~ with his closed eyes, savored this moment before his conquest was complete.

She draped an arm across his broad shoulders and…

From the screen before me, Svetlana looked up. Conrad froze as she pushed him away. He fell to the bed with a thunk and lay there senseless as she sat up.

"Is wrong," she said.

Damn. The mood was broken.

She pushed her hair behind her ear. "You change location. Are we on ship or in remote cabin?"

Svetlana rolled further away from Conrad and pulled the ties of her white silk peasant blouse together, hiding the tops of her breasts he'd been at such pains to uncover. Of course. She was a professional who wanted to be fully dressed for the story conference.

From his position on the bed, Conrad frowned. I heard a groan from this throat, but with my focus on Svetlana, he was stuck where he was. He didn't give a damn where they were. He wanted her naked. He wanted her silky skin rubbing against his manly body. He wanted most of all to sink deeply into her. Who the hell cared where they were?

Svetlana did.

Who put you in charge? I asked myself.

"I make comments to you. For own good. Would be good for you to be more like me," my heroine sniffed. "A little more bust, a little more energy, zip, zest and zing for life and adventure."

She rose from the bed and walked toward me. In the background, I could see Conrad sit up and rub his head.

"I show you how if you like?" she offered.

I shook my head, and with apologies, scrolled back to reread the beginning of the scene. Damn it all. They were on a ship. I'd have to lose the fireplace and replace the bed with a bunk. So much for my plans to have them roll over and around a bit later. But if I couldn't have an open fireplace, then how can I show the fire reflecting in her eyes? She's been all about fire up until now. That's been her symbol from the start of the novel.

My index finger tapped the mouse lightly. I slowly scrolled back through the story to see where I'd gone wrong. To place them in the woods would mean I had to rewrite most of the prior chapter. I really was looking forward to using the roll of the ship to punch up the sex scenes. Maybe later? I checked my notes but didn't see how I could fit that into my plot.

On my first published effort, my editor had been all over me about continuity. Other than her edicts to tone down my hero's character and sweetening my heroine, most of my rewrites were to get the details straightened out. I didn't want to have to listen to her lecture me about that *again*.

"I don't care about the darned fire in her eyes. I just want to bed the wench," Conrad cried from page 276. "I've already been waiting too long."

I scrolled back to find Svetlana pacing the floor, one

hand on her face to help her concentrate, the other waiving at Conrad to shut up. He was on the bed, frowning. Actually, he was pouting.

When he noticed I was back, he rose up and glared at me. "Can't you write the flipping scene and fix the details later? I've been carrying this boner for ten pages, and if I can't get rid of it, my head's going to explode."

"Not head, you idiot," Svetlana snarled from the corner. "And how you think I feel? You think it's easy for me to be such a tease all the time and not get any?"

"Sorry," I muttered. "But if I don't fix it now, I'll forget. I planned for the two of you to spend a few days trapped together, naked."

Conrad smiled at that.

"But I have to make sure you have enough provisions to get you through a few sex scenes. If I don't, someone's going to complain."

"If you don't get on with it, I'm going to complain," Conrad groused.

"Like you aren't already," I said under my breath.

I needed to regain control of this moment and fast.

"If all the same to you, I prefer a ship to a cabin." Svetlana looked at me. "Ships more romantic."

"No scenery," Conrad muttered.

"Not need when I'm around." She stood proudly and thrust out her breasts.

How can a woman have such big ones and not need a good support bra?

"Is fiction," she proclaimed and pushed them out further. "You should know."

Conrad looked at them and looked at me. His hands spread at his hips. I could see the tent in his pantaloons. `"Do you mind hurrying?"` he asked. `"I've got things I need to do."`

"Keep your shirt on," I said under my breath.

`"Too late,"` Conrad said.

I forgot they could hear me as well as I could hear them.

`"She just ripped it off me. I can't find the buttons. And I'd prefer a cabin. It would let me go out and hunt for our food. That's a manly activity. Fishing in a harbor—that's for wimps."`

I was getting annoyed with this hero and heroine. They'd been nothing but trouble right from the start, complaining about everything. "If you two don't get a grip, I'm going to start backspacing," I threatened.

I've never seen a man switch from infuriated to contrite so quickly. `"Don't do anything drastic. Things have been good until now. Splendid, in fact."` Conrad sat on the edge of the bed and crossed his legs, his hands pressed between them as he started rocking forward and back. `"A little more time, no problem. You were heading in the right direction."`

`"I prefer ship."`

Svetlana had a lot more control right from the start of the novel. Conrad then whispered something to her, and I heard the words `'reduce'` and `'erase'` come up more than once. Svetlana shot me a dirty look and clamped her jaw shut, but she sat next to Conrad and patted his back.

"I'll tell you what. You guys decide where you want to be. I can make either work. You two, alone, say for three days? No one else? Hard to be on a ship that long without the crew making an appearance."

"`Ship`." Svetlana stood and folded her arms over that magnificent bosom.

"`Cabin`." Conrad stood as well, his back to hers.

These two had no real memories past the last few pages. I still wasn't certain exactly what they saw in one another, other than sex appeal. Well, for lovers in a romance novel, maybe that was enough. I'd leave them in another seventy-five pages, after the wedding so they could work out the rest of their happily-ever-after for themselves. But I had my doubts that readers would go for it. If I wasn't convinced, how would my agent or editor feel about it? That's what final drafts were for.

"Hey," I yelled, at least I did in my head. "You two work it out and let me know. I'm shutting down for now."

A look of pure horror was on both their faces. "Noooooo," they wailed together. "`Don't leave us in the dark!`"

"`Don't make me wait another day to bed her.`" Conrad was practically begging. "`I implore you.`"

I looked at them as sternly as I could manage. "If I leave the program running, will you two promise to work it out and tell me later where you want to be?"

"`And how I'm going to make love to her and make her my love slave for the rest of our lives?`" Conrad bellowed.

Svetlana tossed her long curls over her shoulder. "`Love slave? This is first I hear of love slave. If anyone will be slave, will be you. Readers love to see big man brought to knees.`" She closed her eyes and looked imperiously away.

Conrad looked at me, murderously. "This is all your fault."

I nodded. "Yup. And if you don't like where this story is going, you'd better come up with an alternative. And I mean a good one. Something that will sell."

Conrad rubbed his chin at that. "You mean commerce." He rubbed his chin again.

Did I really have him do that all the time? Eww. I'd have to think of another mannerism for him. At least he wasn't always up with one eyebrow. Way too much of that in the genre, if you ask me.

"Maybe a turn-around in the sex roles would be a good thing?" he mused, obviously warming to the idea. "Maybe she ties me up and then reverse things later in the story. Much commerce from that."

"Right," I told him. "And selling will mean you and Svetlana get to do this a lot, in many, many bedrooms across the country. Around the world," I added, getting ahead of myself. I'd hardly made a dime off my first novel, and here I was, making grandiose promises to my hero and heroine. "Make it good. I want much commerce."

Svetlana's eyes opened to slits. "And for us?"

"Commerce for me. Fortune. Fame for you. Many fans and admirers."

She smiled. Svetlana liked when people noticed her. She was a little too smug for her own good. I could hear my editor now, "make her a little more likeable, Berry. You know, sympathetic."

Svetlana would have none of it. Still, she was a heck of a lot wilder than my first published heroine, Trista. Not by choice, mind you. That one I'd really had to clamp down on to keep her under control. Svet was a little more intriguing, I thought, and I had more leeway, what with it being a historical and all.

"So, make it good," I reminded them. "I'll be back as soon as I can." I rolled away from the laptop, leaving it open. A moment later, the screen saver began to thrash across the monitor. It was ridiculous to leave it open because my characters demanded it, but every once in a while, giving in to their demands led to interesting plot twists. It wasn't as if they'd come up with something that would scuttle my entire story. They *were* figments of my imagination, so they couldn't possibly go that far astray.

So much for a productive Sunday afternoon of writing. I turned to my work PC. I'd neglected the real world long enough and needed to face what awaited me tomorrow. Not the cabin in the woods. Not the captain's quarters on the ship. Commerce awaited me. I logged in to my emails.

"Berry, are you there? We have to finish the presentation for tomorrow."

Duncan's plaintive tones came through all too effectively, even via email.

Chapter Three

Moe

<u>My Search for the Perfect Burger</u>
My dad's best food was hamburgers. He'd always pull me outside and whisper to me, "Hey Moe, a new burger joint opened down the street. Let's go grab one. Hurry up before your mom finds out." It was just the two of us, me and my dad. I love hamburgers too.
    I really miss my dad.
by Maurice Conrad, grade 3

Yo. Moe here. That's short for Maurice. Maurice Conrad. Not the world's sexiest name, but maybe in the top ten. That's fine with me, but I think my folks were thinking about a great uncle of mine, and not my love life in mind when they named me.

    So anyway, it's my birthday and my youngest brother, Sam, thought it would be a good idea to get me one of these personal recorders, so I could talk to myself while I'm driving around. Fewer buttons to push than a cell phone. I promised him I'd try it. So, here I am talking to myself, feeling stupid. But it's only me here in the truck, so maybe it's okay, as long as no one else is around.

    Like I said, it's my birthday. Thirty-two today. Never thought much about my age before, but this one's getting serious, in a manner of speaking. The "oldest of the brood," as mom likes to say. What she doesn't say is that my dad was thirty-two when he died. She wouldn't look at me much this morning when I went to her place for my birthday breakfast. I guess it's hard on her, even after all this time. The old man's been gone a lot longer than I ever knew him—longer than she knew him—but she still worships his memory. Gotta love her for that. Gotta think he'd love her right back if he was still around. Lord knows, all us boys do.

No sense in getting maudlin. And yes, little brother, I know all sorts of ten-dollar words. First one in the family to go to college, and I was the one who saw to it that the rest of you bozos went too. Not that it matters since we're all in the building trades. Still, having a degree in business management made it easier for me to start and run Conrad Brothers Restoration and Construction Company; make sure no one's going to rip me off. Hell, I'm doing great if my bottom line means anything.

Yup. Since I'm all alone, I'll admit to being proud of that. As far as I know, I'm the first from the old neighborhood to make it this far. And as soon as I close on that house next week, I'll be the first to own a home in a fancy zip code, too. So, what if it's a fixer-upper. Once me and my brothers are done with it, it's going to be the most beautiful place in the neighborhood. Those 'before and after' pictures are going to be great for business. And then I'll sell that puppy for a pretty penny. It'll probably take a year 'til it's ready since we can only work on it in our downtime, but something tells me that old house is going to be the key to taking me from where I am to where I want to be. Doing renovations is okay, even the occasional addition, but restoring one of those old places, doing all that fancy work like they did it back then—now that's satisfying work.

Anyway, back to my house. I want to be sure it will be the showplace of the neighborhood, so I'm heading over to meet my brother Paul at the bookstore to get some books on ideas to decorate it. See, I can use a backhoe, pour concrete, do any kind of rough or finished carpentry, basic electrical, and plumbing. I can make a wall out of anything you hand me, but once that wall is standing, I don't have the damndest idea of what to do to make it look good. There must be a book or two to help me figure that out. I won't be able to use it as a spec house unless it looks as good as it is solid under its skin.

Of course, I could hire a decorator, but that would be my last resort. I don't think I could stand one of them and their snooty ways. My buddy married one, and that was the last I saw of him. It put me off to the whole profession. Not all women, mind you, but a select portion of the local population.

Speaking of women, and keeping this just between me and this here machine, it's been a while since I had a woman in my life I'm serious about. Not that I don't like the ladies—I like them fine thank-you-very-much. But I can't seem to get into the ones I meet. Most I encounter on the job are too young, or too old, or too married, or they're looking for a good time. Joey, the next to oldest, tells me I intimidate them because I'm so tall. My buddy Frankie-who-married-the-witch always said it's because I joke around too much and never talk seriously to the girls. I wish to hell I knew what it was, but I wouldn't mind having one to settle down with. I can picture it, some evening, and she's drinking a glass of wine while I have a beer. Put our feet up and watch some TV. You know, a girlfriend. Maybe even get married someday, have a kid or two. I wouldn't mind that with some soft-hearted, soft-skinned, soft-bodied woman. One with some curves on her who's not worried what I'll think if she has a plate of lasagna once in a while, or will let herself have something besides a salad on the weekend. Someone smart, so we could talk stuff over at night in bed when we're not doing other things in bed.

Yeah, I'd like that—a lot.

Maybe my saying all this stuff into this recorder isn't the best idea in the world. Wouldn't want one of the other guys to hear it and get the idea that I've gone soft. I'm still the boss and their oldest brother. As soon as I figure out how to use this thing, I'll erase it. When I get home from the bookstore. Hey, it's my birthday. Maybe I'll meet someone today. Best be careful, though. The men in this family tend to turn into idiots when we're in love.

Chapter Four

Berry

Let me explain about my boss, Duncan. His first name is Conrad, but he liked his last name better and demanded that's what we call him. And just so you understand—I'm pretty much at the bottom of the food chain in my work life, so what he demanded is what I did. It was kind of charming in a quirky kind of way. I'd never gotten up the nerve to ask him why he did that. As far as I know, no one else knew either. He wasn't the type to chit-chat in the hall.

In Duncan's mind, it was very clear that I existed to serve him. I was there to make him look good. He knew nothing about my secret identity as a romance writer. All he cared about was the work I did for him. Day and night. Weekends too. He thought that because he liked to work twenty-four seven, I did as well. He didn't get the whole work-to-live thing as he lived to work—poor guy.

It was a good deal for him because I was very good at what I did and worked well under pressure. That I had in spades. Truthfully, I didn't always work half as hard as he thought I did, so please don't let on. If I had, I never would have finished any of my manuscripts, and if I hadn't, Svetlana and Conrad would have languished in their cabin/ship with their buttons/ties for months without seeing the light of day. Either they'd have perished for lack of food, or exhausted themselves with sex because I wasn't there to put on the brakes and build tension.

Besides, my editor said for my first book no really dirty stuff until I'd established a fan base, and that fan base said they wanted raunchy. That would've been tough for me to write. I'd *read* a few books featuring rough sex, but never, how shall I say this, engaged directly in anything approaching coarse. I couldn't push my imagination quite that hard. I liked all the regular stuff just fine, but anything that involves pain or torture—I'm definitely not your gal.

So, you might be wondering how the hero of my story came to have the name of my boss. When I first started writing *Loving a Rogue*, Conrad and Svetlana's story, I was stuck for my hero's name. I was noodling around, and I came up with 'Conrad' as a joke to fill in until something better came to mind. My pirate hero was nothing like my boss, not physically or emotionally. On the other hand, Svetlana's name came to me early, and there was no doubt that was who she was destined to be. She sprang from my head, fully formed. And as she liked the name Conrad, that was that.

I sometimes worried about that in the middle of the night. If this book sold, and if the real Conrad discovered I named this swashbuckling captain hero after him, he'd make more of it than he should. I mean, it started out as a joke, even it if was a private joke I had with myself. The fact is, you can't reach my age without encountering a lot of names that have associations tacked onto them. I always figured if I ever had kids, I'll probably have to name them something really odd like Hepzibah or Nesbit, so they don't make me flashback on someone who pushed me down on the playground in third grade or stood me up for the prom, or dated me because they wanted an in with my brother.

As I mentioned, the two Conrads are nothing alike. My hero was rich and tall, strong and tanned, and very sure of himself, a real charmer. He's a man's man whom women adored. Close your eyes and imagine George Clooney in the 1700s. He's got longer hair, of course, and he's clean-shaven most of the time, especially when he thinks he's finally going to get Svetlana in bed. (Note to self, wherever they end up stuck for three days, have shaving equipment and a mirror available, so he doesn't chew her face up with his beard). But he's got those same brown eyes that exude confidence and make me shiver whenever I see George on screen. Oh, and a deep voice and booming laugh. It's all part of the alpha-male shtick. And you should see him in a sword fight. (Another note to self, watch a film with sword fighting to help with that upcoming scene where he must save Svetlana from his chief rival. Swinging from the rigging not required but nice to have. Basil Rathbone?).

The real Conrad could have been good-looking, but he was totally focused on his work and not so much on personal grooming. I don't think the man thought about anything but work and certainly didn't pay attention to much beyond it. He wouldn't have noticed a woman with a crush if she banged into him. Not that I ever did, but there was this woman in accounting who seemed to. She was very nice and attentive. I don't know what's wrong with the man.

To illustrate: a few months earlier, this new analyst was hired. Darlene. A real femme fatale. All the guys in the area were falling all over themselves to get her to notice them. I watch things like that, not that I'm jealous or taking lessons or anything, but because I'm a writer and a student of human nature. I like to observe how women like her control men, so I can make my characters do the same. Or learn to. It depends.

Darlene was supposed to be the rocket scientist of analysts, but really, she didn't do much except file her fingernails and delegate. It was astonishing what a cliché she was. In fact, she turned out to be an expert at delegation. And she got away with it. I don't say this to be mean or to tear down another woman to make myself feel better, but I think it was mostly because she was pretty, and she traded on that rather than skill. Not Svetlana larger-than-life beautiful, but pretty. Blond. Blue eyes. Skinny but with a lot on top if you know what I mean. You know the type. And (at the risk of sounding jealous, which maybe I am), she had a hell of a lot of confidence and could work a room. All skills, as I might have inferred, I lack. Did I mention it was mostly men in the department?

Anyway, my brother Rocky noticed her. But because he's the big boss and he's already under a microscope because he arranged for me to work under him, he couldn't ask Darlene out no matter how much he wanted to.

So, I'd sit there in meetings with Darlene, Duncan and the rest of the team; and Duncan never noticed her. Better yet, he never cut her a moment's slack when she didn't get her stuff done on time (in other words, when her delegation skills fell a little short). Not like the rest of the guys did.

I have to admit, aside from welcoming all the good theater she provided, I appreciated that about Duncan. I was such a workhorse in that office that people didn't notice me much. They depend on me, sure, but see me? Nope. No one cut me a deal or gave me an inch of latitude because I'm built, which I'm not, at least not like her. Or was pretty or had blond hair like Darlene, or even because my brother's a big deal in this company. Which he still is.

So, Duncan expected Darlene to perform her job pretty much the same as he expected it of me. You should have seen her face the first time he let her have it when she didn't meet a deadline. I don't think anyone had ever held her accountable before, and she sure didn't appreciate the learning experience. Come to think of it, Duncan's exact words were, "Darlene, you ought to use Berry as your role model. She really knows how to get things done." That was the only compliment he ever paid me, and it wasn't even to me.

Not to surprise you, but Darlene didn't care for that. She transferred to another department a few months back. No doubt she's got it a lot easier there, but that's okay because I don't have to see it. Naturally, they didn't hire anyone to replace her, so my workload went back to being too much for one person.

My brother Rocky was responsible for that. He's Duncan's boss, by the way.

If you thought that makes my work life complicated, you'd be right.

Rocky is really something. And he's not all bad—I owe him a lot. I wouldn't have this job if not for him. He took all kinds of hell for getting me hired in the first place. Of course, he knew I was more than up to the work, but nepotism isn't looked upon kindly at Bi-Teck Associates. Due to the circumstances, everyone knows he's my brother, and I've had to bust my butt to prove to everyone that he was right in hiring me despite the fact we're related. And I've had to keep on busting it because around here, it's a culture of "nice job last week, but what have you done for me lately?" We're all subject to it. Rocky's a master of it. He's risen high enough in the food chain that he's the one often doing the asking about what people have done. Don't get me wrong, he's being judged every bit as much as the rest of us, but to him, it's like a game. He thrives on it.

I hate it.

At work, I don't think he's got a caring bone in his body. I've seen him fire people. I mean, I've been there when he walks up to their desk and tells them oh-so-nicely to follow him, and you never ever see them again. An hour later, he's got someone packing their things into a box. If I ever see that person again, say at the grocery store, they won't look me in the eye. I don't know what goes on in those closed-door sessions, but it must be brutal if they won't talk to me. It kind of hurts—that guilt by association.

You see, well, I care. That's part of the problem. I'd seen too much, and instead of getting hard-hearted, I've gotten all soft and squishy, but not in a good way. Instead of adversity making me stronger, it reduced me to a simpering puddle. Especially when there was nothing I could do about it. But I didn't dare quit. Remember—that wallflower bit I mentioned earlier? Job interviews slay me.

On the other hand, from watching my brother, I learned to be brutally mean to my characters. To make a better story, of course. Don't tell them I cry right alongside them while I'm doing it.

Enough feeling sorry for myself. I had to switch gears from Conrad and Svetlana, who were hoping to reduce each other to a single puddle of pleasure and focus instead on Duncan, who never takes a day off and thinks no one else should either.

"What up?" I emailed him back. I can take these liberties on a Sunday afternoon, and he can't complain about it. He did once, but I got up the nerve to bitch to my brother that if I'm going to spend my Sunday on company business, it's going to be a casual day, so to speak. To my everlasting surprise, Rocky agreed with me.

Conrad must have decided my attitude wasn't worth an argument. "Where is the presentation you are giving tomorrow at 2 o'clock? We are supposed to go over it."

See what I mean? The man can't relax long enough to use a contraction on a Sunday. To him, casual means using a numeral instead of spelling out the number two.

Grumbling under my breath, I went in search of the presentation materials and shot them back over the web with my coup de grace, "You mean <u>your</u> presentation. I'm sitting this one out."

I know I must have given him pause, or he was ignoring me. Regardless, it would take him a few minutes to pick it apart, so I checked in on Svetlana and Conrad. Those two were napping in the same positions I'd left them in, her standing there, him sitting on the side of the bed. Her side was decorated like a ship, and his looked like a cabin in the woods. So, they'd been discussing this while I was away—before the laptop went into sleep mode. I could have told them that would happen. Like always, it was up to me to figure things out and make it right. I figured they could nap until dinnertime, and then I'd rake them over the coals for sleeping on the job.

My work laptop beeped. Duncan was done reading. I glanced at my watch. Either he hated it and wanted to start from scratch, or he loved it as he tore through it and didn't have much to change. The later was so unlikely, I snorted at myself for even considering it.

"We need to talk," was what he wrote. "Call me." Of course, he was efficient enough to give me his number.

Oh damn. I didn't want to talk to him. It was Sunday.

I dialed his number slowly, considering what my voice should convey. Irritation? Exhaustion? Did I dare?

"Berry?"

"Yeah, it's me. Did you hate it?"

I liked the silence on the other end of the line. It let me know I made him think. "No. It was not what I expected," he said at last.

That Duncan really knew his way around a compliment. I huffed a sigh. "Is that good or is that bad?"

There was another one of his pregnant pauses. "Did I catch you at a bad moment? Your brother said you would be working all weekend."

Of course, he'd expect it would be for him.

"Rocky must have misunderstood. I'm working on something personal. But this is okay," I added quickly. Rocky might have gotten me the job, but Duncan had more input into my continued employment than anyone else, and if he thought I was being snippy, I'd be unemployed again. Not a good prospect. I started to sweat thinking about it. "Was there something wrong with it? I put it together, like the last one."

"It is adequate." I heard his nose whistle on the other end of the phone. Not creepy, like he was thinking hard. "Berry, you usually throw a little more creativity into your presentations. You did not this time."

Whoa. Did I fall off the earth into an alternate reality? "You usually take the creative bits out, so I held back. I didn't want to do a lot of work just to undo it again."

"That is rather ironic." He laughed. I settled for experiencing a small tear in the space-time continuum. "Rocco mentioned that my presentations are rather stodgy. I thought this time I might use some of your embellishments."

It was my turn to laugh.

"Do you think maybe we can work on it, together, that is? Instead of my seeing things when you're done, I thought perhaps, if I could watch your creative activity, I might get the hang of it."

It's a good thing I vacuumed earlier because a dust mote might have bowled me over. "You mean come here?" *Not going to happen.*

"Oh, well, if you'd rather I didn't, I thought maybe we could meet at an internet café and if you brought your laptop…"

His voice trailed off as if he were having second thoughts. I thought of him, sitting at his kitchen table, all dressed up with nowhere to go. Was he asking me out on a date? That sweating thing I mentioned earlier—it started in earnest now. I didn't want to date Duncan. I didn't want him to even consider me in that regard. A man like him would never approve of my 'personal' writing, and I refused to give it up for anyone. He wasn't my type, and I sure didn't want to be his.

"I wasn't planning on going out today," I told him. Oh, there was a lot more I could tell him, but wouldn't.

"Can you make an exception?" he asked. Clearly, he was desperate—well, desperate for him. "Just for an hour."

I heard myself agreeing to this, all the while cursing inwardly. The bookstore I like had free internet. I was comfortable there, and I could always use a new book—the stack by my bed was down to five, and I liked to be stocked up, just in case. In case of what, I'm not sure.

Duncan sounded relieved when I agreed, and broke the connection.

I hung up and forced myself to take some deep breaths. I could do this. It would only be for an hour with someone I knew at a place I was familiar with. Other people did stuff like this all the time. I could be one of them.

What does one wear when one is meeting one's boss on a Sunday afternoon to do work in public? When it wasn't a date, but one needed to look one's best to feel normal. I didn't have a girlfriend I could call and ask about this specific thing—they'd all laugh at me.

So, I did the next best thing. I turned back to my other computer and called up a file I hadn't opened in a long time.

I scrolled to the end.

"Trista," I muttered. "Wake up. You have to help me." I tapped on the mouse impatiently. "Come on, come on…"

I finally found her shaking the rice from her hair. She looked up. "Oh, it's you! I didn't expect..."

"Yeah. I need some help. Fast."

"Brad and I were just about to drive away." I imagined her beaming at her dreamy husband of a few hours. In my world, it had been over two years since they first came together, but I wasn't about to tell her that. She'd be aghast if she found out, and I'd spend unnecessary time getting her caught up.

"Listen, I need your help. I'm about to meet Duncan for coffee and to talk about work, but it doesn't feel like work. What did you wear when you and Brad first met? I know it was something classy, but understated. I don't have time to search."

"You're going out with him?" She wrinkled her nose as she handed her bouquet off to a bridesmaid walking by and stood there with her hands on her hips. "I thought you hated him."

"Never mind that. He wants me to meet him to do some work, and I need to figure out what to wear, so I don't look like a total slob but still look like it's the weekend. Like I'm not trying too hard." I didn't need to tell her more. Trista knew me almost as well as I knew her. She'd been a part of my life for a long time.

I could see her eyes narrow as she began to plan. I'd have to remember not to have Svetlana do that. It wasn't that attractive. It didn't matter for Trista now that she was launched. My readers would probably never notice.

"How much time before you have to leave?" she asked briskly.

"Forty minutes."

"Where are you meeting him?"

"The bookstore café," I replied.

She nodded smartly. "Okay. This is what you need to do. Shower. Don't wash your hair—it will take too long. Let's hope he showers. I can't forget how you told me about his greasy hair.

Your best jeans and black twin set. Light on the makeup. Gold hoops. Flat soled shoes. You won't run, but you'll be more comfortable if you know you can."

"Okay. Got it. Thanks."

"We'll be there as soon as we can..."

I shut the laptop. At least she made me laugh while she allowed me to focus. I think she was getting ahead of herself if she thought she could step off the pages and into real life. If such a thing were possible, there'd be all sorts of interesting characters out there in the world.

I was still laughing about it, imagining what would happen to sci-fi writing in that regard when I undressed and stepped into the shower. What would it be like if Conrad and Svetlana were suddenly to appear in the real world with me? They'd probably be arrested, the way I had them behaving in the first draft. Not to mention their costumes.

Trista and Brad, on the other hand, would be perfectly at home. Being a couple of over-achievers in a contemporary chick-lit novel, they were larger than life, but in an understated way. Of course, they were more beautiful than real people, and the regular rules of give-and-take, even time and space, didn't quite apply. When they got the sniffles, their noses might get a little red, but chapped? Never. No big honking sneezes or runny eyes. No money worries ever, and come to think of it, I never once had them stop and gas up their cars. But that's what's so great about writing fiction—you can make the world as you want it to appear, not as it is. That's why I write. To escape. Never made any bones about that goal. I don't care to talk about it with everyone I meet.

Chapter Five

Berry/Solange

You might think it a little bit odd that I consulted a fictional character on what to wear that afternoon. Despite my difficulties with Trista and Brad, I'd loved writing their story. I'd rewritten parts of it umpteen times, and I still cried during her black moment when she and Brad break up, and he never wants to see her again because he thought she didn't love him and that she deserved someone who could give her the world instead of a huge cattle ranch out west. It still breaks my heart. The whole idea of unrequited love, misunderstandings from which there was no recovery, gets to me. And I'm not the sort of writer who needs to come up with fantastical ways to reunite my characters. They have to come together through believable circumstances, like Triss and Brad did. You might not believe it what with my imaginary lovers and all, but my feet are firmly planted in the real world. And, unless the book I'm reading is clearly in the paranormal or fantasy camp, I won't accept any of that *deus ex machina* stuff. I don't like that sort of book, so it's strictly off-limits when I'm in control.

Instead of magical or spiritual intervention, I made sure Brad and Trista ran into each other at a club six months after they'd broke up. Triss came on a double date with friends, and Brad was there with a gal-pal since he didn't have it in him to make love to another woman after he broke up with Triss. So that friend overheard Trista crying in the ladies' lounge that she can't stand to see Brad so happy when her heart is still breaking over him. The gal-pal, who is currently my favorite candidate for my next contemporary heroine, goes and tells Brad, who then overcomes his pride and finds Trista, punches her boorish date in the nose, gets a black eye himself, and takes her away. They then declare their undying love forever and ever and have fantastic, mind-blowing make-up sex. Then the wrap-up and epilogue, which is where I found Trista with rice still in her hair (I wanted birdseed, but my editor overruled me). A happily ever after. The End.

I couldn't stop thinking about it the whole ride over to the bookstore. It kept me from worrying what Duncan was up to or what other calamity might strike. Triss and Brad had been a huge part of my life for the past couple of years, and if I was lucky, they'd make me a bit of money. They'd certainly led to another book contract.

I had the weirdest feeling when I got to the bookstore. It wasn't an Oh-My-God-I'm-out-in-public sensation, more of a what-in-the-world-is-happening-around-me surreal kind of weird, sort of like right before a thunderstorm when the air is charged. But it was a gorgeous October day with a blue sky. Perfectly normal.

The reason was apparent as soon as I stepped out of my car. There was this great-looking guy getting out of a big truck two spaces down. He had light brown hair that was sun-streaked, and his face was tanned as if he worked outdoors. It was long and lean, and the rest of him—oh mama!

He looked at me and smiled as if he liked what he was looking at. A great guy like that, thinking dumpy old me was okay? I had the strongest urge to look behind me to make sure he wasn't flirting with someone else and instead forced myself to smile and nod back. I wanted to fan myself.

Two points for the shy girl.

But it didn't last. It never does. I must put off strange vibes because just as he looked like he was going to meander over and mention what a nice afternoon it was, there was a terrible racket behind me. Someone was loving the sound of their car's horn. The guy from the truck kind of grimaced before he hurried away. I turned to see what the commotion was about and was dumbfounded to find Trista and Brad pulling up next to me.

Seriously. I know how that sounds. I blinked. "Oh no." I think I whimpered. "Tell me this isn't happening."

"Surprise!"

Trista was out of the car and hugging me before Brad came to a full stop. "When you reached out to me, I simply knew we had to come to help you." She wrinkled her nose. "We'll get rid of Duncan and then find you someone who can show you a good time."

You want to know something? In the real world, her voice was a little squeakier than I imagined it would be. And louder.

I tried hard to express my sincerest delight in seeing them, but dread descended like an acid tide in my stomach. This could not be good. Hell, it couldn't be real.

"You shouldn't have," I fluttered as Brad jumped out of the car (he didn't use the door of his convertible) and came to hug me. He was as good-looking in person as he was when I dreamed him up. Rather too, I thought in retrospect. He might have been more interesting if I'd have given him a scar, or maybe a broken nose. And he was so tall. Who knew six-foot-three would cause me to strain my neck? Then again, I'm not as tall as I made Trista, the fashion model.

"My plum-dumpling said you needed us, and off we came," Brad announced to the world in his deep baritone, looking like the hero he was. "If we couldn't do one thing for you after what you did for us..." He lowered one eyebrow meaningfully. "I don't need to tell you..."

Was I really that free with the ellipses when I wrote his dialogue? And that eyebrow thing makes me cringe inside. I made a mental note to search and obliterate it anywhere it appeared in my new manuscript.

"You really shouldn't have come. I mean it. You should be off on your honeymoon and not worrying about me. I'll be fine. I come here all the time."

Trista frowned. "Well the thing is, when you stopped by, we realized we didn't know what to do or where to go. You only hinted at a fabulous honeymoon but didn't tell us what it was. The story ended with us getting in the car." She looked at Brad and smiled. "I wouldn't have minded repeating the reunion scene on page 314," she confided, "but we can do that any old time. It seemed it would be a fine adventure to come see your world for a change."

Oh crap, I thought. She was right. I hadn't been able to decide where I wanted them to go, so I left it all mysterious and up to the reader to fill in the blanks. I was clean out of ideas at that point. Exhausted really.

"I'm speechless," I told them. It wasn't true. I had all sorts of words going around in my head, but I wasn't about to share. For all I knew, I was cracking up, and then I saw Conrad looking at me through the plate glass window. He must think me an idiot for standing there talking to myself. Oh, my mystique was getting better and better.

"Listen, why don't the two of you go in and browse. But I need you to leave me alone until he and I are done, okay? Maybe you can look at the travel books and get some ideas for that honeymoon of yours. Then you can tell me all about it, and I can write a scene in a new book that takes place there." I glanced at Conrad again. "I need to go meet my boss."

Brad's brows lowered. Both of them thank goodness. "I think we shouldn't leave Solange alone. Who knows what sort of riffraff she might run into."

Trista snuggled in close and kissed him hard. "Bradley darling, I think you need to leave the thinking to me. Solange is a big girl."

Trista clapped her hands together before she grabbed Brad by the wrist and dragged him into the store. "Come find us as soon as you're done," she tootled.

I looked at them as they entered the store, expecting them to disappear in a puff of pastel smoke. No such luck. They didn't walk through the glass doors either but opened them as you or I would. I'd put enough chivalry into Brad that he knew to open the door for her. The problem was, a stream of other customers chose that moment to arrive, and he was holding the door longer than he anticipated. I saw a look of panic come across his face. This wasn't real, was it? But I also realized that all those people were seeing him and thanking him for holding the door. If that was happening, this whole fiasco couldn't be a figment of my imagination.

I reached into my car and grabbed my laptop and portfolio. Locking the car, I took a deep breath. Best to get this over with and back home as soon as I could.

With determination girding my loins, I marched into the store.

"Hey, Duncan."

He looked a little startled, but I figured if he was going to get me out into the world to work on a weekend, he could put up with a little casual talk from me in person, not just online.

"Berry," he acknowledged as he moved his laptop to make room for mine.

"I take it you know what you want changed."

His face focused on his screen. "Yeah. I'm opening it up now. Why didn't you bring your friends over?"

What? Could he see them too? I gulped. "Who?"

"Those people in the parking lot. They seemed to be friends of yours."

I bit down an expletive. "Well, I don't like to mix work and fun. I'll get together with them later." I pulled my laptop from my case and set about booting up and logging in.

He shrugged. "Whatever. Here. I found what I wanted changed."

We went back and forth for the next hour. For the life of me, I found it hard to concentrate. I could see Trista and Brad flitting around the bookstore, talking too loudly, looking too beautiful. People were staring at them, including the hunk who smiled at me in the parking lot. Damn, but he was big and good looking. Not like my fantasy boyfriend last night. This one was real. Broad in the shoulders, he was probably a few inches shorter than Brad, lean and muscled. His white tee-shirt was stretched just so under a worn bomber jacket. I wish I had better words to describe it, but the only thing I could think of was that I wished that jacket was chocolate so I could eat it off him. His jeans fit just right, not too snug as to constrict anything, but molded to his tight butt in a way that made me want to sigh. And the work boots. I'm a sucker for a guy in any kind of boots.

I took a quick glance at Duncan's feet. Loafers. What a bore. That's what Brad wore when he wasn't on the ranch. I thought myself so clever with that, thinking he could step out of them when he and Trista were going at it. It wasn't until then that I realized all that time spent unlacing could build the tension in a scene.

I was salivating. I looked at Duncan to ground myself, but my eyes were in rebellion mode. It was no use. I had the truck guy firmly stuck in my brain.

I forced myself to focus.

Duncan was reviewing my edits when I looked around. The truck guy had his face in a book, so I figured I'd take a moment to soak in his atmosphere before I returned my attention to work. My memory was fine. Later on, I'd write what I was seeing. That's when I noticed a small patch of chest hair showing at the opening of his V-neck tee-shirt. So, he wasn't a smooth-bodied guy like the ones I wrote about, the kind I thought I preferred. On him, that chest hair worked. I looked him over again. Damn, but there was no need for embellishments with this one.

Nope. Mr. Muscles was fine from the top of his wavy hair down to his good, worn boots with the top eyeholes undone. They seemed to be splashed with paint or mud or something. That's when I caught him looking at me again—grinning like he knew what the sight of those boots was doing to my insides. Did he have to have such an appealing smile?

I looked away. I needed to finish up and fast, so I could get away before I felt totally out of sorts and out of control. Home. Safe. Back to the ship with Conrad and Svetlana, or the cabin, or an eighteenth-century manor house. Or maybe they could do it on a wild carriage ride. The possibilities were endless with a historical.

Just then, Trista caught my eye and held up a copy of my book, pointing at the cover with a huge smile on her face. Oy. My heart started to pound. I had to get out of here, fast.

"Duncan, are we almost done? I've got things to do."

He nodded distractedly and waved his hand. I was packing up when he looked up at me and then at Trista. "Berry, before you go, would you mind doing me a favor?"

I braced myself. "What is it?" I know better than to

agree to a favor before I hear it.

"Can you introduce me to your friend? The blonde?"

Oh, crap. "Um. Why?"

He looked at me like I was an idiot. "Because she's a babe."

I had to blink a moment. Was that the Duncan I knew and...knew? I zipped up my case. "Duncan, she's a newlywed." *And she'd never look twice at you even if she were single. Beauty, passion, brains aplenty. A little low on compassion. That's how I wrote her.*

"Oh." He looked crestfallen, but then he perked up. "I thought that guy might be her brother."

I looked at Brad and back at Trista. There *was* a resemblance. I wished I'd noticed that when I first saw the two of them together in the sample photo in the picture frame. Don't laugh. That's how I first pictured them.

"Doesn't matter." Duncan met my eyes calmly. "I like talking to beautiful women. That's why you and I get on so well."

Well, damn. Would wonders never cease? "As long as you don't get your hopes up, I'll bring her over."

I gestured to Triss, and she came prancing over. I took a deep breath. So long as Duncan didn't want to get involved, I could survive this introduction.

"Trista Johnston-Harding, I want you to meet my boss, Duncan. Do you know where Brad is?"

"Duncan," she purred and held out her hand. I hoped it was warm. I couldn't recall if I ever mentioned her body temperature other than when she and Brad were naked. At that point, it wouldn't have been her hands I was describing. I focused all my energy on sending 'warm' to that hand of hers.

"Trista? It's a pleasure to meet you. Berry hasn't mentioned you to me before."

"Berry?" She wrinkled her nose. "Who's that?"

"Me," I said softly. I turned to Duncan. "Trista and Brad know me as Solange."

It was his turn to look quizzical.

"My pen name. The three of us know each other through my writing."

I don't think he understood, but I wasn't about to explain he was calmly salivating over a fictional character. Trista didn't help matters when she held up the book with her face on the cover. I hope the picture frame manufacturer never puts two and two together. "See. Solange DewBerry. She wrote this."

Duncan took it from her hands and turned to the back cover. His eyebrows lifted as he read the copy.

>Trista Johnston has it all. Fame, fortune, good looks. She's come a long way from the sheltered ranch she lived on as a child with her grandparents. Now her face is recognized the world over, and top designers scheme to have her wear their creations on the runway or the covers of top fashion magazines. But she can't forget her roots, nor the boy she left behind all those years ago.
>
>Brad Harding is a hard-working rancher. His parents' tragic deaths in a hot air balloon excursion across the Rockies left him a wealthy young man, but alone on his enormous spread. He's got plenty of friends the world over due to his position in the World Cattleman's Federation. But he has no one to share his spacious house with, no one to help make it a home.
>
>Though beautiful women plot to meet him and fall into his bed, he can't forget the girl he once knew.

What happens when a globe-trotting supermodel meets the boy she left behind while on a photo-shoot for a new perfume? Will sparks fly, or will their disparate lifestyles keep them apart forever?

"Solange?" He looked at me. "Berry, you wrote this?" He turned to Trista before I had a chance to explain. "Wow, so you're a model for book covers?"

She snatched it back from him with a frown. "No. I *am* Trista Johnston-Harding. This book is about me."

Duncan turned to me, a look of consternation clear on his face. "Oh, um, very nice."

Double crap. I looked around to see if Brad might join us. Might as well make this nightmare complete, but he was reading by the magazine racks. I swear, his lips were moving. How was I going to end this?

"Solange, I met the nicest guy," Trista tittered. "I was over reading the decorating books, for my new career since I gave up modeling to marry Brad and live on his ranch, and he was there looking at books with me."

She waved at someone over my shoulder, and her nose wrinkle indicated she caught his eye. "I told him that I was in your book, and he wanted to meet you."

I swear I'm not making this up. The hairs on my arms stood at attention. I peeked out the window to make sure there wasn't a thunderstorm heading our way. That's when I heard a throat clear behind me. It could only belong to a deep voice. Which had to originate in a deep chest. I closed my eyes, and I think I started to pray. I'm not sure I did, because I'm fairly certain my brain was shutting down. I know I *wanted* to pray. That was my intention.

"Solange, meet Moe. Moe, this here is my best friend in the world, Solange DewBerry."

I turned and looked. It was the guy from the parking lot,

and his smile couldn't have been sunnier if he tried. I think my heart wanted to jump out of my chest and chase him around the store. The rest of me was longing to go along for the ride. Except for my feet. They were made of clay.

He reached out a hand and took mine. "Solange. It's my great pleasure to meet you."

Chapter Six

Moe

Trista may have had a model's good looks, but she had nothing over the woman whose hand I held in mine.

She had eyes like an autumn sky—one of them at least. Maybe it was the reflection from the lights on her glasses, but the other looked like the color of storm clouds. Regardless, they were very wide. I mean, they had to be for me to notice, right?

Not exactly on the tall side, but she had enough inches to reach my shoulder. Great if I was hugging her and wanted to rest my chin someplace. And she wasn't one of those willowy blondes. Nope, she was stacked, with curves in all the right places. Her hair was the color of burnished light oak but looked so soft, I wanted to reach out and touch it. I managed to mind my manners and do nothing more than hold her hand until even I knew I had to let it go, sooner or later. She was just so pretty I almost forgot to speak. And what the hell kind of name was Solange? I thought that was a made-up name from that singer.

"Aren't you going to say something?" Trista asked her friend.

"Nice to meet you," Solange stammered. Ah. So, she'd noticed me after all. Good. I wasn't sure if she was with the guy next to her, but he was starry-eyed over Trista, so I made up my mind they weren't a couple.

There was an awkward silence. "So, you and Trista know each other?" she asked.

"We met over in the decorating aisle," her friend gushed before I could say a word. "Just got to talking. I never did that before, Solange!"

What an airhead. I turned to Solange. "My brothers and I are fixing up a house, sort of as an example of what my firm can do—you know, renovations. We've got the construction covered, but I was looking for some ideas on how to decorate it once we're done."

"I can help you. I'm starting a decorating business. You can be my first client."

I wished Trista would shut up and let her friend talk.

The little beauty leaned in. "Maybe Moe wants to shop around, get some advice from someone with a little more experience." Ah, so she was smart too. I liked her. Liked her a lot.

Trista took my arm, ignoring the other guy. Everyone was ignoring him. What else could he expect if he didn't wash his hair? "Of course he doesn't," she said, giving me a little shake.

The other guy cleared his throat to try to get her attention. "I might need your help," he said. "I'm Duncan, by the way."

I smiled and tried to disentangle myself from Trista, but it wasn't easy. "I'm flattered that you want the job, but it's going to be some time before I'm ready. I've yet to close on the house."

"Oh." Trista's face fell, and she let go of my arm. Lord, but she looked like she was about to cry. I didn't need that. I can't stand it when a woman swaps her emotions in and out like that. Makes me kind of crazy.

"What's that you have there?" I took the book Trista was hugging, and a weird zing ran up my arm. Not a good one either. Made me wonder if I'd sprained something on Friday and didn't notice. "Maybe I can buy you this as a consolation prize." It looked like one of those romance novels my mom's always buying and lending to her friends.

Not that I have anything against reading, I love to read. But honestly, it gave me the willies to hold that book for her.

"That's the book Solange wrote about me and Brad."

I looked at the beauty next to me and darned if a blush didn't cross her face. "You're a writer?" Hot damn. She must be pretty smart then. Even Duncan looked at her funny as if he'd learned something surprising about her.

"I didn't know you were a published author, Berry," Duncan said.

"I, um..." she scratched her nose, and I think I nearly lost my mind—she was so cute. "It's not the kind of thing that comes up in everyday conversation at the office."

He called her Berry. Sweet. Was Solange her pen name? I kind of liked that. But it probably meant DewBerry wasn't her real last name. I took another look at the book and noted the publisher. Maybe, if she was reluctant to call me, I could seek her out that way. Regardless, I needed to get control of this conversation back and pronto. "Listen, Trista. If you want to give me your card, when I'm ready to decorate, I can give you a call."

"My card?"

There was an awkward pause. I couldn't help but feel I'd put my foot in it, but for the life of me, couldn't figure out how.

"Trista hasn't printed any cards yet," Solange—or was it Berry—said at last.

Finally, I had an excuse to look at her again. I gave her what my mother calls my killer smile. I have to admit, she looked a little faint. Or panicked? "Maybe you can give me your number, and when I want to get in touch with your friend, you can hook us up."

She glared at Trista. As much as she had looked at me like she was interested earlier, I could tell the idea of giving out her number wasn't what she had in mind. Yeah, she was smart all right. It made me like her even more.

"You're in construction, right?" Trista asked, blissfully unaware of what was going on inside my head. She turned to her friend. "All that time you were writing about Brad and me, you were complaining about your den. Maybe Moe can help you fix it up!"

"Oh, I—"

"Oh, go ahead, *Solange*," Duncan encouraged.

She glared at him only to have him wink at me. That set her back on her heels. Maybe he wasn't the nerd he appeared.

Somehow the conversation ran away, and it looked like it would have to be me to rope it back in. "Okay, why don't I give you my card?" I reached into my pocket and pulled out a few. It never hurts to hand them around. You never knew what might come of it.

I placed one in Solange's hand, pressing it slightly. "If you want work done at your place, call me. No job is too big or small for Conrad Construction."

Her fingers curled around it then, and the funniest smile crossed her face. "Conrad?" she asked and looked askance at the skinny guy. "Your name is Moe Conrad?"

"Maurice," I admitted. "Ma had grand plans when she named me."

That's when my brother Paul walked up and ruined everything. "Moe, come on. Julie's making that party for you. You don't want to be late and piss her off."

A birthday party, as if I was turning six instead of thirty-two. Did he really have to say that in front of these ladies? This one lady?

I looked at Solange—I mean Berry. What I would give to have her walk through Julie's door with me. "It's my birthday. My cousin's making a cake. If you'd care to join us—"

Trista looked like she was up for a party, but Solange had one of those deer-in-the-headlights looks. "I'm afraid I have things to do later. Triss, you and Brad were coming back to my place, remember? We've got some things we need to discuss."

Trista looked crestfallen but gave in without a whimper. "Right."

I looked at the book in my hand. What kind of hot, sexy stuff must go on in Berry's mind? More than anything, I wanted to know if she would like someone to try her ideas out on. "I'll get this for you."

Solange raised her head, "Oh, you don't need to do that—"

"Nonsense. I insist."

Now it was her turn to look disappointed. Or maybe worried? "I wish you wouldn't—encourage her," she said under her breath.

What in the world did she mean by that?

"No problem. And I mean it. If you're ready to get a quote on your place, call me, and I'll come over."

Paul was looking at me like he knew what was going on in my head. My brother knows me pretty well, knows the type of girl I usually date. Solange—Berry wasn't one of them, but I knew he knew I was interested. Oh yeah, I'd be hearing plenty about it when we got to my cousin's place. I didn't really care. One way or another, I was going to get to know Ms. Solange DewBerry, and maybe get to know Berry-whatever-her-real-name-was even better. A lot better if I was lucky.

Berry

I was so mad, I was ready to spit. But of course, that was impossible. Mom brought me up the old-fashioned way, so women in my family don't spit, don't curse, don't talk back.

We've mastered the silent snub, however. Oh yes, and the brittle smile. It's second nature to hold my elbows in, to cross my legs at the ankle when I sit. In fact, other than leaving in a few kick-ass characteristics, I had to clamp down hard while writing until Trista became a refined lady too. The thing is, when I began to write her, that polite inner lady was pretty quickly overtaken by someone who had both the desire and the willpower to say whatever was on her mind. In the book, I managed to make it humorous and work to her advantage. In real life, it wasn't that easy. Out here, there are no rewrites, so I mostly kept my mouth shut. Thank heavens, my new heroine Svetlana wasn't held to the same standard.

I was still thrown by the fact that Trista and Brad were even *here*. Now I'll admit while I was writing them, they'd seemed real to me. I'd thought about them day and night, and any time I wasn't working, I was busy on their story—while I was driving, at the grocery store, getting my hair done, when I was falling asleep and when I woke up in the middle of the night because I thought of something that would be *just perfect* for their story.

But since I'd sent in my final draft after the edits were made and *You're the One for Me* was out of my hands, I honestly hadn't given them much thought other than to check my royalties, and what I'd do to promote the book, which was entirely different. I'd worked on another story for a while. I'd abandoned it as soon as Conrad and Svetlana's story came to mind. It really wasn't until today that I'd given Brad and Triss much thought at all since the book hit the stores a few months back. Why had they come to life now? Was it because I called them up on my computer to ask that dumb question about what I should wear? Had I imagined them into real-life now that they were out and about across the country?

And if I stopped thinking about them, would that mean they'd fade away? I wanted to give it a try. Having them around could get complicated, and my head hurt thinking about it.

"It was nice meeting you, Moe. Happy birthday. I'll keep your card on file." I turned to Duncan. "I'll see you tomorrow in the office. We can go over the slide deck again before the meeting if you want, but I will *not* be the one to present. Rocky doesn't like it, and I don't want to cross him."

I looked across the store to see Brad still reading the same magazine. If he and Trista didn't evaporate back into the ether soon, she was going to get awfully bored. I didn't have time to write them a new scene. I had Conrad and Svetlana to bring to life. Crap. I didn't quite mean it like that.

No one had moved. Moe was looking at me like he was amused. Was I being too bossy? I needed to watch that. I waved and heaved my computer case to my shoulder as I grabbed Trista's arm. Maybe I could leave before Moe remembered to buy her the book. Who knew what would happen if Triss had a copy of her own to carry around?

"Well, see you around," I said as I headed for the door.

"Wait," Moe called.

Damn. I turned and forced a smile.

"I promised I'd get this for your friend," Moe told me as he sauntered over to the cashier, this time with me in tow. "I like to keep my promises." He winked at me, and I swear, his eyes twinkled. I thought that was something that only happened in fiction. It was so trite, I never dared write it. But twinkle Moe's eyes did.

It occurred to me then that perhaps I was in a dream and that he was no more real than Trista and Brad, Svetlana and Conrad. That would certainly explain a lot.

This seemed too real, though. I could feel myself blushing and that never happened in my dreams. The smell of new books was too strong in the air. And I never, ever conjured up a handsome man with chest hair. I looked at it again and swallowed hard. I hope that little sound I made was audible only to me. But when he smiled again, I knew he'd heard it too. Crap. But it was a nice smile, like he knew I was attracted to him but that he understood that I wasn't an aggressive sort of person. Or I was imagining the whole thing. Or something. *Don't let him think I'm an idiot,* I thought.

"I meant it. Give me a call. I'd be happy to give you a free quote," he told me. "And if you change your mind and want to come to my birthday party..." his eyes did that twinkle thing again, "... give me a call. My cell number's on the card too."

"That's very nice of you," I said. "But really, I have to finish up what Duncan and I were working on. And I do need to talk to my friends. They're a—new to this area and aren't familiar with it."

He leaned in closer. "Yeah, I noticed that they're a little odd," he said. "Like they're from another country."

Another dimension is more like it. "They'll only be around for a short while, and I want to make the most of their visit. I haven't seen them in over a year."

"Got it." He smiled again, and I could feel my insides turn to soft butter. "To be honest, if you want to get together for a drink or a movie or something other than construction, call me. I don't often get to meet nice girls like you."

What sort of girls are you used to meeting, Moe? thought I. "Girls?" I said instead.

He grinned then, a sort of a boys-will-be-boys and sorry-you-caught-me kind of grin. "Slip of the tongue. I'm usually more of a sensitive male than that."

He paid for my, I mean Trista's, book and one of his own, and we walked back to where my 'friends' were standing.

"I meant it. I'm mostly harmless," he said. "And I wouldn't mind getting to know you better."

I shook my head. I'd always fantasized about getting picked up in a bookstore by a handsome, sensitive man. Wouldn't you know I'd be babysitting two fictional characters when it finally happened. "See you around, Moe."

"See you, Solange."

God, but he gave me shivers the way he said my name. And it wasn't even mine.

Chapter Seven

Moe

Paul leaned back on two chair legs and set his beer on his belly. "That girl in the bookstore was kind of cute."

Annoying kid brothers turn into annoying bigger kid brothers. I wanted to swat him, but though he was a few inches shorter than me, he had me outweighed by twenty pounds. That and the fact that he wrestled throughout high school and college kept me from it.

"Woman," I corrected, recalling Solange's amused grin when I'd called her a girl.

Paul gave me a funny kind of smile before he tipped his bottle back and drained it. "I stand corrected. She was still damned cute."

From across the table, my mother smacked him on the shoulder for using the cuss word.

Coming from Paul, 'cute' was a compliment. To him, women were either hot or dogs. At a mere twenty-six years of age, he still had a bit of growing up to do.

"She was," I agreed. "I hope she calls."

"You didn't get her number?" Pete asked. "That's a first." Pete is brother number three, right after Joey and before Paul and Sam. He's usually tolerable, except when he isn't. He's my foreman on some of my biggest jobs, and I'd trust him with my life, but not with my girlfriend. I didn't have one at the moment.

"Nope. But I gave her mine."

"Where did you meet this girl?" my mother asked.

None of us dared correct her usage of the female noun. She'd just as soon whack our heads or our bottoms as not.

So, I explained about the pretty girl, the bookstore connection, the writing, the weird friends—all of it.

"I bought that book when it first came out," mom said. "Pretty good. Kind of predictable, but that's what a lot of first-time authors do. I suspect she's got more in her than that. She must be smart. Since when are you going for smart girls, Maurice?"

I shrugged. I always liked smart girls, not that anyone noticed. "Just thought I'd try something different this time."

"You're not getting any younger. Time to settle down and get me some grandchildren. Girls if you don't mind. After you five boys, I want to buy someone a pretty pink dress for a change."

I'd like that too. If Miss Solange DewBerry would call me. "Sure, ma. I'll get right on it."

Everyone laughed, and we went on to talk about something else. Mostly about the house I was about to buy on the corner of Maple and Elm. It was a run-down Victorian that the realtor thought should be razed and replaced with a McMansion, but I saw gold in that beat-up old place. A lot of living went on in there, and it still had the bones to withstand a lot more.

The outside was a mess, and the yard hadn't been cared for in a decade, but the original stained-glass windows were carefully stored in the basement. The foundation was sound. Even the plumbing was halfway decent. It needed some TLC, care of Conrad Brothers Restoration and Construction, Inc. I was going to go all out with this place and re-plaster the walls rather than replace them with wallboard. That house was going to be restored to its original glory. If it was half the job I thought it would be, I wouldn't have time for a girlfriend for the next year and a half.

I expected my brothers were all going to pitch in

whether they wanted to or not. They all work for me in addition to the rest of my crew. With winter coming, I didn't know if I'd have enough outside work to keep them all busy with other jobs, but I had enough in the bank that I could pay them to work for me. Since there were plenty of other bargain houses like this in the area, I figured we could all practice our restoration skills on my place before we started to bid on the others. Nothing like a little on-the-job training. If it worked out well, I could flip it and start again.

The party was a pleasant distraction from my afternoon, but driving home that night, I couldn't get Solange out of my mind. It was hard to figure out exactly what it was that drew me to her. She was pretty enough—cute like I said. I can be a hound, and that stuff matters. She was not a stunner, but there was something else about her that suited me just fine. She was refined. Ma would probably say she outclassed me, and she'd be right too.

But it was more. I had watched her working with that skinny, geeky guy, and liked how she was so focused on what she did. It was a privilege to watch her think, to see the ideas popping out of her head. She kind of wiggled each time that happened. Really. It was like she sat there quiet, not moving. Then I could see something cross her face, and her whole body gave a little jiggle before she looked up with this darling smile and said something. Duncan—I think that was his name—more often than not would shoot her down, but then she'd go after it again and think a little more, do that dance in her seat and try again. I couldn't imagine ever getting tired of watching her. She was dressed kind of plain. I think she was pretending to be plain, but when she smiled, it was like a whole other woman was sitting there. Man, if she were mine, I'd spend half my day plotting ways to unleash that smile and the other half enjoying it.

I wondered if it was the same when she was writing her books. I've glanced at one or two of the romance novels in my mother's vast library, and to be honest, some of them made me sweat, and a few of those scenes made me wince. I couldn't image Ma reading that stuff. She's my mother, for crying out loud. So, riding home that night, it got me to wondering what kind of wicked smile Solange had on her face when she wrote a sex scene. Or was it a dreamy look? I pulled up to my apartment building and sighed. I'd probably never know, but damn, it was fun to speculate.

Her friends though—they were kind of out there. I'd had no idea those romance novels were based on real people's lives. I guess there were a lot of things I didn't know.

Berry/Solange

This conversation wasn't going well. I'd tried hinting, and I'd tried suggesting all evening, but Brad and Triss were not buying my plan that they return to the world of fiction. To be honest, I couldn't blame them. With each passing moment, they became more solidly real.

I hadn't dreamed it would still be a problem at bedtime. I'd hoped that somewhere along the drive from the bookstore to my place, they'd vanish. I mean, they had no reason to continue. Their mission had been accomplished, their story told. Fashion advice had been delivered. Yet, they followed me home. Hours later, I began to despair they'd ever leave. And as long as they were around, I couldn't help but think about them, which made them all the more real to me. The complications posed by their existence were beyond scary. I had to convince them to return to wherever they came from, or I was afraid I would go mad.

And entertaining them meant I couldn't get back to my

work in progress. After dinner, It was time to be frank.

"Listen, you guys. I don't know how to tell you this, so I'll be blunt. You're not—well, not really real."

"Well, I know I am," Trista said with that perfectly reasonable tone of hers. "All afternoon, I've been here and not pressed between the pages of some book. We met people and talked to them. I ate dinner. We drove in a car. Brad even read a magazine."

I was starting to despise her logic.

"And everyone we met thinks we're real... You're the only one who doesn't," Brad pouted. "That Moe guy who gave us his card... Never occurred to him we weren't born here."

No, this wasn't going well. I hadn't been able to get any work done. Poor Conrad and Svetlana were languishing betwixt and between while I was dealing with my completed literary creations. As far as I knew, nothing like this had ever happened to anyone. At least, no one mentioned it on any of the writers' chat groups I frequented. I considered holing up in my den to pose the question, but in the end, I was afraid to mention it and be labeled a freak. Besides, I was afraid to turn my back on my guests.

Then I had an idea. "Maybe we could all sleep on it. I'll pull out the sofa bed for you. Maybe things will be different in the morning."

Ha! They'd hate that uncomfortable bed. Because of that awful piece of furniture, I never had an overnight guest for more than one sleepless night.

"But I have to work tomorrow. We'll have to figure out what we're going to do when it's light out again."

"And we can go to work with you!" Trista exclaimed. "That would be so interesting."

Oh, no. That would not be a good idea. "Let's talk in the

morning, okay?"

I made up their bed as they gazed on in fascination. I must not have mentioned sleeper sofas in their story. I'd created my characters so wealthy, such a thing would not have been necessary, what with all their spare bedrooms, guesthouses, maids, and the like. As if I knew what I was talking about when I wrote it.

Not me. I had exactly two extra towels and one spare toothbrush they'd have to share. Being newlyweds, that shouldn't have been a concern. I mean, their tongues were always in each other's mouths. And they weren't real. So germs weren't a problem. Right? It was getting so bad, I had to remind myself of that fact.

Once I settled into my bed, I heard them laughing softly in the living room. Actually, Brad laughed. Trista giggled. Then she giggled some more. Crap, did I really have her do that? I heard them throw some numbers around, which made no sense. Then they began to go at it—each other I mean. Damn. I'd forgotten that I'd written them to make noisy, uninhibited love, and had to suffer through a protracted, wild session on the other side of the wall. It was almost embarrassing. No, scrap that. It *was* embarrassing even though they were my own creations. That bar under the mattress didn't seem to deter them in the least.

After a long while, they finished with a bang. Or a scream. Or something. I was afraid to guess. I was going to have trouble meeting my neighbors' eyes for a while, and that's if they weren't complaining to the condo association about the noise. At least now, I could sleep.

I rolled over and made myself comfortable only to hear Brad call out a number, and then they started again. With a groan, I realized that they never stopped after one go-round, except one time when they were interrupted by Trista's grandmother when they were in the backseat of an old Chevy. Even then, they'd more than made up for it as soon as I had the old lady called away for a neighbor's casserole emergency.

I pulled a pillow over my ear and screwed my eyes shut. It was going to be a long night. I could only hope they'd exhaust themselves into oblivion and disappear when it was over. I swore, I'd delete their file from my computer, so I would never be tempted to open it again. At a minimum, I'd relegate them to a flash drive that I'd then lock away in a safe somewhere.

I'd had a terrible night's sleep. I dreamed I was writing a sequel, but things didn't go quite as planned. It was hard to recall exactly what transpired, but I do recall that Trista, my innocent, trusting, sensual heroine, had turned into the opposite. Brad, the alpha male I'd slaved over, turned into a wuss who couldn't find his way out of a paper bag. It was terrible. I was ashamed to call myself a writer.

What I should have dreamt about was Conrad and Svetlana and how the heck I was going to resolve their conflict, but who was I kidding? What I really wanted to dream about was Moe of the bulging biceps and terrific smile. Not that I could see those biceps under his leather jacket, but I do have an active imagination, and I knew they were there. It occurred to me that I might remake Conrad into Moe's rugged self. I could almost hear my buccaneer protesting from the PC, where he was locked away two rooms over. I sighed and rolled over. Maybe not. Moe and Svetlana—I wasn't in a mood to share.

Maybe my next book would feature someone like him, an outdoorsy, windblown, tall, handsome hero with dark brown hair and bright brown eyes—no, topaz eyes. Not like mine. Someone once compared them to the two sides of my personality: one common and the other mysterious.

Pshaw. Freak is more like it.

Anyway, the alarm went off at the regular time, and I had to start moving. I crept out of my room to find Triss and Brad sprawled on the sofa bed. The sheets barely covered them. Crap. It must have been all those dreams I had that prevented them from fading.

I didn't want to linger. Maybe work would get them from my mind, and I'd return to find them gone. Permanently.

I didn't wait, just showered, dressed, grabbed my purse and computer case, and got out of the condo fast. I wasn't going to leave them a note or money or anything. *Focus, Berry*, I commanded myself. *Think about work and nothing else. They'll be gone by the time you get home.* I didn't dare let myself think about the consequences of leaving them alone.

The problem was, I couldn't stop thinking about them the whole ride in, imagining the passion going on in my nice quiet condo. I frowned. Why didn't I ever get to have any fun—I was just the writer who invented it for others. I could almost imagine what was going on in my absence. The scene was writing itself in my mind...

Trista blinked open one eye. She heard a rustling noise in the bedroom and quickly lay down.

"Can we do it again?" Brad whispered.

Triss shook her head. "She's awake. Go back to sleep until she's gone."

He obeyed, falling back into the dreamless void. Trista listened hard. Solange could move quietly when she wanted. Minutes later she was out the door, locking it behind her.

Brad's hand came exploring.

"Not now. I've got things to do," Triss complained. Brad frowned and tried again, but she swatted his hand away. She'd never done that before. He had a boner and she'd never, ever before said no.

"Triss," he whined, but she shook her head and climbed from the bed.

"Give me a few minutes. I want to see if I still have that card from Moe. He liked her, and she liked him. But she won't call him."

"What are you planning?" Brad asked, one brow rising suspiciously as Trista searched the living room for stray bits of paper.

"A little matchmaking," Triss smiled slyly. "Turnabout is fair play, don't you think?" She held up the card in triumph. Only was it Solange she was matching, or someone else? She wasn't about to let Brad suspect.

"Come'ere woman," he grinned. "Once you've found that card. We can make love until it's late enough to call."

"You bet," came her happy reply, and she bounded across the room and into his arms. "Do me like that scene in chapter seventeen, you know, where I'm being coy, and you're angry, and we really go at it. Page one-sixty-four."

"I was in the mood for chapter twenty-four, page two-forty-three. No Two-fifty-two, that was even better," he said with a leer. "I like it when you're the aggressor and go down on me when I don't expect it.

When I'm sleeping."

She frowned. "But, you're expecting it now."

"Nope." He wiped the smile from his face and lay back on the bed. "My mind's clear."

Trista thought a moment and nodded. "Okay Brad. Here I come." And she did.

I heard it all in my imagination as I drove to work.

No. There was no way those two could possibly take that much initiative. They were fictional characters. It was impossible for them to do anything but what I imagined they could do. Of that, I was absolutely certain. Or at least I hoped I was. And all that stuff I imagined... Oh crap.

And no way was she calling Moe.

It was a Monday with a vengeance, followed by a Tuesday of horrors, Wednesday of despair, and the rest of them in descending states of wretchedness. My boss's presentation was delayed, and it took most of my time to convince him to keep things the way they were. Finally, late on Friday, I reneged on my promise and sat in the room while Duncan spoke. My brother scowled at me, but I didn't care anymore. I was doing my job. I swear, that man can't stand it when anyone besides him receives praise. Naturally, he found a way to grab any given to me, reminding everyone that he was the one who had hired me. Thanks, bud. I owe you yet again, in a never-ending stream of gratitude. Nope.

Not that I'd ever say so to his face. Long story. I'll tell you sometime when you've got time.

And of course, my house guests lingered. I was really getting worried.

That night, I trudged home exhausted. To be honest,

for the first time that week, I hadn't given my houseguests a thought all day, not until I put the key in the lock and wondered what I would find.

The night before, as I'd waited for them to finish banging away (again), I wondered if this connection between us might have something to do with proximity to me. If I could get far enough away, maybe they'd fade. But what if it was proximity to their origins, or to their book, the one Moe purchased? The one that Trista kept in her purse, or under their mattress, as if she knew that was the key. The whole thing gave me a headache.

I opened the door to find the sofa still down, the sheets a tangled mess trailing on the floor. Okay, that didn't mean much. Everything was silent though, which was a good sign. I put my stuff down with a sigh of relief. Maybe now I could get back to work on my new story. My agent wanted it done by February. To accomplish that, I'd need to devote every minute I wasn't working or sleeping.

That's when I heard the sound from my bedroom. Crap. Was it them or a burglar? I was almost hoping for the latter.

I made for that room. "What the heck?" I stopped dead in my tracks as I saw Brad going down on her. On *my* bed. The two of them had all day to do it (again). Why were they still at it at six o'clock at night (again)?

"Oh hi, Solange," Trista waved from the bed. "We were finishing up. We need to get ready. Moe's going to be by in a little while."

"What?" I nearly screeched but caught myself. "I didn't give him my number."

"No, I did." She closed her eyes to concentrate on Brad's work. A moment later, she opened them and looked at me. "When I called, he was able to get your address off the internet since he had your real name. I didn't know you had two names. Can I have two names too?"

"No," I scolded. "You're set in stone now. No more changes." *And get the hell out of my bed, damn it.*

"Okay," she grinned as she surged upward. Brad was doing delicious things to her with his tongue. I should know. I wrote this scene. But without conversation.

"Um, I think I'll wait out here. Can you two hurry it up and get out here? Dressed?" I shut the door and sat in a chair before I popped up and started to tidy up the room. How dare they use my bed? How dare they call Moe? Why the hell were they still here?

Wait. What? Moe?

I'd just finished stripping the sofa and folded it up when they came out of the bedroom, holding hands. They were fully dressed and perfectly coiffed, and if I didn't know better, I would have thought they'd stepped from the pages of a photoshoot.

"Mind helping?" I grumbled. "Can you bring those dirty dishes to the sink and put them in the dishwasher? If you're going to be here, you may as well learn to be good houseguests."

"Sure," Brad agreed cheerfully. He kissed his bride and did as I asked. Maybe he could stay awhile. Meanwhile, Trista stood there doing nothing but looking beautiful.

"I read one of your cookbooks this afternoon, so I'll prepare the cocktails and canapés," she announced. "Where do you keep your caviar and crème fraiche?"

I glared at her. I didn't need to be nice. In fact, a book I'd read on writing fiction told me I needed to torture my characters, make them really suffer. Sounded good to me. But shoot, it was too late for that, they were already published.

I heard the phone ring, but Brad picked it up before I could tell him not to.

"No. No canapés. No cocktails. You can call Moe and cancel the appointment. I am not ready to redo my den. I have a deadline to meet."

"Another book?" She almost pouted. "You mean, you're writing another one? Without me?"

"Yes," I shot back. "And I have to finish it, so make your call and then disappear for a while."

"I can't." She looked positively sorry. "He was so happy that I called. He really liked you, Solange. Or should I call you Berry?"

"Berry. I'm only Solange for my writing." My heart sank. "Why can't you cancel Moe?"

That's when the doorbell rang.

"Because he's here," she announced. "Can I at least offer him a beer?"

"You can offer him water," I snapped. From the number of dirty dishes, I wondered if I had any food left in the house. Or a clean glass. Besides, I didn't keep beer on hand.

I pulled the door open and took a step back. Moe stood there looking tall and handsome, and hell, I'll say it: robust. No. Delicious. Deliciously robust. Yes, my heart skipped a beat. This was not good, not good at all. I firmed what little resolve I had and opened my mouth.

"I'm afraid Trista took a little too much upon herself," I said by way of a greeting. "I'm sorry to waste your time."

He smiled at me, and all that fine determination of mine became mush. "Hello to you too, Solange."

There was something about the way he said it that made me want to change my name permanently.

"She prefers Berry," Trista whispered from behind me. "Solange is her pen name."

His grin grew even wider if such a thing was possible. "Berry. I like that better. But since I'm here, maybe I can take a look at your den? The quote's free and is good for a year."

I sighed. I didn't know what would be ruder, to send him away for nothing, or send him away after wasting more of his time. And damn it, he was wearing those worn construction boots. And a tape measure was clipped to his belt. I nearly salivated when I saw it. So, I opened the door wider. I really did want to redo my den. Just not immediately.

"Fine."

I glared at my guests. "If you could stay out of the way for a few minutes? The room is kind of cramped. Maybe you can go for a drive?"

"No." Triss sounded wistful. "We tried that yesterday, but we kind of faded."

Ah. I'd have to explore that later. "Well then, you can finish cleaning up in the kitchen."

Brad nodded cheerfully and headed back, dragging an unwilling Trista with him. I hoped they wouldn't start in on each again. I mean, every guy reaches a limit sometimes, doesn't he? I think the kitchen was the only room where I never had them make love, and only because Trista seemed to have an aversion to doing anything but cook in there. I prayed they weren't feeling inventive. My kitchen wasn't that big. And didn't have any doors. Then I heard a laugh I recognized, and I cringed. *Crap*. I could only hope they'd be quick, even if I never wrote a quickie. Maybe for this next novel...

"This way," I said to Moe.

I opened the door onto my cramped writing area. The place was a mess, with papers and books open on every surface. Cheap bookshelves were sagging against the walls, overloaded with novels and reference materials. My PC and printer were crammed into a tiny space along with my broken desk chair. I can't remember the last time I cleaned in there. And dusted—maybe never.

"Wow. The writer's warren," he whistled as he picked up an empty picture frame. Not exactly empty—I'd never replaced the fake photo—all right, it was the one of Brad and Trista—the original one. At least he was focused there and not on the titles of the books in my collection.

"Yeah," I agreed. "This is where the magic happens."

There was another giggle from the kitchen. If he heard anything, Moe was too much of a gentleman to mention it.

"So, what were you thinking of doing, other than gutting it and starting over?"

"I thought built-in shelves, for one thing, so I can get at my reference books. And a desk for the computer and printer. I'd like to build the shelves around the window, you know, framing it. This room gets kind of cold in the winter, so I thought the books would help insulate it."

"And the floor?" he asked, looking down at the shabby shag carpet that was there when I moved in.

"Vinyl tile maybe? Something where I can roll the chair around. And drawers so I can put my supplies away."

"Do you want pretty, or functional or both?" he asked as he walked around the tiny space with is tape measure.

"I hadn't thought that far," I admitted. "It was just a passing thought. I mentioned it to Triss, and she ran away with it. I'm sorry she called you. I'm not ready to do anything right now."

He nodded as he took a few notes. "I'll tell you what, let me make up a few drawings and put some numbers together. This sort of thing is nothing much. If you decide to do something, you'll have more work than me packing this stuff up for the duration."

"I really can't do anything for a few months. I have a deadline."

"Not a problem." He gave me another grin, and rational thought became a little bit harder to process.

There was an unmistakable sound from the kitchen. I know I winced.

"What do you say you and I talk about it over dinner? Give your friends some privacy?" He winked.

I can't believe I said yes. On second thought, how could I not escape for one evening? So I could remember what normal felt like.

Chapter Eight

Moe

When we got outside, she hesitated. "Why do you drive such a big truck?"

It wasn't the first time a woman had asked me that question, usually as a come-on. Not Berry. She really wanted to know.

I put on my best straight face. "Well, obviously, darlin', I'm compensating for something."

I'd used that line before. Mostly it either shuts up the questioner or leads into some interesting follow-ups.

"What are you compensating for?" she asked. Seriously, she did.

I could no longer hide my grin. "Maybe you'll have to get to know me better to find out."

She looked at me then, as if trying to puzzle that out. Imagine that, her thinking me complicated. Didn't she know flirting when it was in her face? Hmmm. I'd have to work on that with her.

Still and all, I could not believe she agreed to dinner. She didn't seem like a burger-and-fries sort of woman, at least not on a first date, so I took her for pizza.

The fact was she had whacked-out friends who were totally committed to acting like the proverbial newlyweds. It was confirmed by the sounds of their doing it in the kitchen with the two of us standing not ten feet away. Maybe she agreed to go with me so she could get out of her place for an hour and let them finish up. That's what I would have done if it was a buddy of mine, even a married one.

Her friends were awfully good looking, and if I were

Brad, maybe I'd'a been clawing Trista's clothes too. But in private, you know? They didn't seem to have much in the way of common sense. Or decency for that matter. You'd think they'd have the manners to get a room of their own. Or a door.

I didn't really care. All that mattered was that here it was a Friday night, and I suddenly had a date. Not that I planned on sleeping with her. From her serious face, I knew she wasn't the type to have a go on the first date. But she was there, and despite the fact that it looked like her teeth were clenched, she'd picked up her purse and followed me out the door. She might have grabbed a book on the way out and stuffed it in her purse. I wasn't about to ask. If she was as weird as her friends, I'd find out soon enough. I sure hoped not. Besides, I'm not so boring that she'd need to read while we ate dinner. She just didn't know that yet.

Berry was awfully quiet on the way to the restaurant. It was a place she knew and said was good. Other than giving me directions, there wasn't a lot to talk about. It had started to rain, and being fall, it was dark. The city was busy this time of night, between commuters leaving and locals looking for dinner.

We parked in a crowded lot across the street from the restaurant. I hopped out of the truck and went to get her door, but she'd already climbed down and was walking around the end before I could help her. I didn't think she was helpless, but I wanted to show her I had some manners.

"Nice evening," I said as the rain beat down harder. I flipped up her hood for her. "Think we'll have to wait for a table?" I took her arm, and we made it across the lot and street.

"We can always eat at the bar."

Be still my heart. "Whatever you want," I said. And I meant it. "Maybe we can have a beer while we wait, get to know each other a little better."

She gave me her first smile of the evening. She even looked a little relaxed. "Sure." She ducked under my arm as I held the door open for her.

As we stood in line, I noticed how prim she looked, despite all her curves. Her feet were placed together, and she held her elbows in tight. I think she was biting her lip but stopped as soon as I glanced at her. I gave the hostess my name. She said it would be an hour before a table was ready, so we went to the bar and found two stools. I helped her up, and we ordered. Beer for me, red wine for her.

She took a big sip and closed her eyes. "I needed that," she laughed lightly. "It's good to get out. Having house guests can be a trial."

I'll say. Especially newlyweds. "I take it they're unexpected company?"

"You might say that." I think she was about to laugh again but covered it up.

"Can't you ask them to leave? I would've."

The look on her face was priceless. "That wouldn't be polite." She looked down as she swirled the wine in her glass. "I've been dropping hints, but they don't get them." She gave a small shiver. "Do you think our taking off like this without telling them might work?"

"Well, you know them, but if it were me, I'd get the message." I put my arm around her. I saw it as a friendly gesture. She was wet and cold, and I, well, I was right there, and warm. "Maybe when I drop you off, I can give them a hint or two myself."

She looked up at me with so much hope that I felt like a heel. I didn't have a clue how to help her with her strange friends. "In the meanwhile, let's relax and have a nice time.

We can talk about your condo. And I want to know more about your writing. I mentioned it to my mother, and she said she'd read your book."

Berry's eyes lit up. "Really? Did she like it?"

"Yeah. She said it was real good, and wanted to read another."

Her face fell. "I can't write when they're around."

What could I do but hug her again. What can I say? I'm a great guy. "Okay. We'll see what old Moe can do to get rid of them."

I'll never forget the way she looked at me or the way it made me feel inside. Like I was one of her heroes. Hell. I don't think anyone'd ever looked at me quite like that before. Maybe since…

She'd finished her wine by the time we were seated, and she had another with her meal. The pizza was good, better than average, and she didn't balk at my wanting to load it up either. And she was very nice by offering to pay half—not that I'd let her. By the time we were done eating, we were laughing as if we'd known each other for years. Forget the prissy woman. She was warm and funny, and her eyes shone, and it all made me a little hot under the collar, not to mention elsewhere.

Maybe turning thirty-two wasn't such a bad thing. And best of all, she seemed to like me back. Not that I like to brag or anything, but girls usually do. They like my size and my biceps. They like that I treat them to dinner and drinks. They say they like my smile. More than one's dropped hints that she wanted to make things a little more permanent. Things always came up to ruin that though. Can't really understand why. It's not like I've got something against marriage, but it never felt right. Either that or I had rotten taste in women.

Case in point: a few years ago, when I was getting my

business started, I made the mistake of entering a contest for the sexiest contractor in the county. It seemed like a good, cheap way of getting some exposure. I got it all right. I was the second runner up and had to pose shirtless for a calendar in front of my truck. Mr. November. I didn't know what the hell I was thinking at the time, but once it was published, I realized how they'd had me pose, with a hammer placed, shall we say, strategically? Yeah, I got plenty of publicity for that. Lots of girls called me up, and I could have had as much tits and ass as I wanted. But I didn't, not after the first few. Yeah, I like sex, but the reality of being a sex symbol wasn't nearly as much fun as I thought it would be. Talk about pressure.

But Berry didn't know any of that. I doubt someone like her would ever have heard of it, and I wasn't about to tell her. Certainly not right then. All I could think of was how pretty she was sitting across from me, how she took my breath away when she smiled and laughed. And she seemed to like me for who I was.

I ordered her another glass of wine. "No. Two's my limit," she protested, but the deed was done, and it appeared in front of her.

"I shouldn't. I get the worst headaches," she said as she took a sip. "I won't be able to tell you how to get back to my place."

Never let it be said I needed to get a woman drunk to like me. I'd finished my third beer by that time, so I reached across the table. "I'll help," I said and took a swallow. The stuff wasn't bad, but I wanted to be able to drive, so I pushed it back at her. "Have as much as you want. I can find my way back to your place and deliver you safely."

"The longer I stay here, the longer I'm away from Triss and Brad." She gave a happy sigh and took another swallow and closed her eyes in pleasure. At some point, she'd taken off her glasses to rub her eyes and hadn't put them back on again.

"Do you mind if I ask you a personal question?"

Her peepers popped open. I was able to confirm that they really were two different colors. What do you know about that? One for Berry, the other for Solange. "Shoot," she said with a little smile.

"Aside from the fact that I'm glad they're there, because they're responsible for my coming over tonight, how in the world do you know them? Aren't they from way out west somewhere?"

She shook her head. "You wouldn't believe me if I told you."

"Try me."

She got this skeptical look on her face and then started to say something before she stopped and shook her head. "No. It's too bizarre."

I took her hands and rubbed her fingers. "Come on. It's been a long time since I heard a good story."

"Okay." She took another sip of her wine, and then a deep breath. "I made them up." She sat back and waited. Her mouth was set something fierce like she was expecting me to react somehow.

Truthfully, I didn't have a clue what she meant. "What?"

"I made them up," she said a little louder. "For my story, my book. They're not real. They're fictional."

Wow, she was good. I laughed.

Berry leaned closer. "Have you ever had trouble separating reality from fiction?" she asked in all apparent seriousness. "I mean, do you ever find yourself in a situation and just wonder?"

Was this a come-on? If so, it was the most original I'd ever heard. The trouble was, she looked totally serious and not whacked out like her friends. Or was it the wine? I didn't know what to say, but that didn't seem to matter.

"Sometimes, when I've been writing for hours, fiction seems to bleed over into reality. Or if I'm at work and sitting in a boring meeting, my mind starts to wander. If I don't pay strict attention, I imagine I'm with my characters."

She gave me a beautiful smile that looked both sad and amused at the same time. "My own life isn't always what I would have chosen for myself, you know? I sometimes take something that happened to me, and rewrite it to make it better, more interesting."

What could I do? This was all a whole lot deeper than I usually wanted to go on a first date, but hell, it was fascinating.

Still, enough was enough. I managed a straight face to say, "Well, I live very much in the here and now. We're here, let's do this now."

She looked startled for a moment, then shook back all that hair and laughed, really laughed.

It was my turn to smile and shake my head. Okay, maybe she'd had enough to drink, or she did have a really good imagination. Or both. Those two we left at her place were as real as she and I, if not quite as civilized. Regardless, it was time to get her home. I had already paid the bill, so I got up and held out my hand for hers. She placed it there readily, and I helped her to her feet.

"You don't believe me, do you?" she asked as she slipped her arms into her coat.

"I think either you really *should* stop at two glasses of wine, or you are pulling my leg on purpose to see how I'll react."

She cocked her head to one side, and I could see her jaw un-tense a little. "You really think that?"

"Sure. It's clear to me that you fall into the category of 'nice girls,' so this isn't a tease. You're testing me. So, now you know my sense of humor is fine."

She sighed. "Yeah, you found me out."

She turned, and I put my hand on the small of her back as we left. The place was hopping. The pizza was pretty good, but I noticed they had burgers on the menu. I'd have to come back sometime and sample them. One of these days, I'd write an online review. Maybe my new writer friend could help me.

I held her arm as we made our way back to my truck. "Will you let me be a gentleman this time, and help you with the door?"

She grinned at me. "Since you asked me so nicely, sure. Most of my dates don't involve car doors." She giggled. "Or trucks. I don't think I've ever been in one before."

"You haven't lived unless you've dated a man with a pickup," I told her. I wrapped my arm around her, and she didn't protest. Not that I was angling for more than a goodnight kiss, but she was a heck of a lot friendlier now than when the evening started.

"No," she sighed and leaned her head against my arm. "I guess I haven't."

She wobbled a little bit as we walked. The rain had let up, but the air was cold, so I kept her close. Believe me, it wasn't a chore.

I unlocked the truck and was about to open her door when she leaned against it. "Before I forget, thanks for the pizza, Moe. And the wine." Her voice had gotten low and sexy. "I had a really nice time."

"Me too."

She stood there looking at me, smiling. I didn't want to be rude, but we weren't moving anywhere either, so what could I do? I leaned in and kissed her.

Let me tell you something. Miss Berry Samuels had

some very nice lips, soft and warm, still tasting slightly of red wine. I intended it to be a quick kiss, but she surprised me and wrapped her arms around my neck. Then she kissed me back. Yes, definitely, there was action on her end, and wow, what a kiss it was. Are all lady romance writers such good kissers? Who the heck had she been practicing on? A little voice in my head said, *let it be me from this point forward.*

What could I do but wrap her up in my arms and hold her closer. It's not like it was some big sacrifice to hold her, all soft and curvy as she was even with my bomber jacket and her raincoat between us.

I have to say the kiss didn't stay mellow for long. Berry sure had me fooled. She wanted me and wanted me bad. As much as I liked her and wanted to take things slow so I could see her again, I guess my baser instincts kind of took over at that point. I held that girl so tight, she didn't need her own legs to hold herself up. And she was the one who started with the tongues, not me. I'll put this out there. That woman tasted as sweet as she was pretty. That last glass of wine was definitely a good idea.

"Can we go back to my place now?" she asked when we came up for air.

"Uh huh."

I'm sorry to say it wasn't the most sophisticated answer I've ever given. You'll have to forgive me as I was being driven mostly by hormones at that point. I think male hydraulics were involved. I did manage to pull her away from the truck, hoist her up, and shut the door. I ran, I think, to my side and got in, only to have her start kissing me some more.

I took a break long enough to start the engine and get out of there. She lived five minutes from the restaurant. At least she did that night. Her hand was on my knee the whole time, and I was glad she didn't decide to move it because I would have crashed for sure.

I pulled her out of the truck, and we got past the security guard and into the elevator. I couldn't help myself but haul her into my arms again and kiss her all the way to the eleventh floor. We kind of stumbled into the hall, and I managed to get her to her door, kissing the whole time.

Yeah, Berry sure had me fooled. Not much on talking once she got her mind into the physical, I'll say that for her. I do believe her eyes were closed most of the time, so it was up to me to navigate. Good thing I have a memory for directions.

It crossed my mind to wonder what would happen if her friends were still there, but figured that would sort itself out once we got the door open. After all, if they were uninhibited enough to go at it in the kitchen, she and I could retreat behind a closed door. And I knew how to be quiet. It remained to be seen if she did.

It took a while to get the door open. She kind of hauled me down to her height while I was trying to get her key into the lock, and we stayed that way, kissing and rubbing and generally getting to know one another very well. I will admit to being hot and bothered, and my anxiety about getting inside was growing. I'd pretty much resigned myself that we were going to have sex on the first date, and that would mean a second date was going to be rather awkward (not that I minded *that* much), but I do draw the line at any sort of intimacy in public. I was *not* going to so much as touch her boob as long as we were out in the hall where anyone could see us.

Despite her kisses, and some very nice little urgent sounds she was making, I eventually managed to get the door unlocked, and we stumbled through to find the living room dark and quiet.

That brought her head up. Were her guests in bed? What if they were asleep on the sofa? I didn't think they'd be going at it again. During the course of the evening's conversation, she mentioned they'd been indulging when she got home from work. I'm not bragging, or anything, but not every man had enough endurance for three shots in a few short hours. I'd been through enough of a drought that I thought maybe I could manage it, but I wasn't about to say anything to her about that.

Berry held on to my arm and glanced around. She must have known what she was doing, for she switched on a small lamp by the door as she peeled off her coat. The lamp cast enough light for us to see that the living room was empty. In fact, it looked a whole lot tidier than it had when I'd been there earlier. Her guests may very well have taken off, but if they did, they did a good job cleaning before they left.

She grabbed my hand and tiptoed to what I assumed was the bedroom. I hadn't thought of that. Maybe Trista and Brad had commandeered it. I hadn't thought much of Brad's balls in that regard (seems he saved them all for Trista), but Trista was bold enough to do something like that. Apparently, Berry thought so too.

That room was empty as well. It was as tidy as the rest of her place, and that was the only signal I needed to haul her back into my arms and start kissing her again.

She didn't seem to mind much. In fact, she dropped her purse with a thunk and wrapped her arms around me. "They're gone," she whispered in excitement. "It must have been when I took the book. I have my home back."

Yeah, except for me, and I wasn't going anywhere any time soon.

I back-walked her into the bedroom until the backs of her knees were at her bed, never letting go of her lips the whole time, other than when she threw her head back so I could start on her neck. Now, I'm somewhat a connoisseur of women's necks, and Berry's was about as fine a neck as I'd ever come across. Long and slender, her skin was soft and warm. She wasn't wearing any perfume, which was fine with me. Have you ever tasted cologne? Bitter.

No, her sweetness was all her own, and she was offering it to me, as much as I wanted. I prayed she'd let me see her again, and not just for this. I wanted to take her out for pizza again and again and again. Maybe a movie sometime. The occasional wedding…

As I was kissing her neck, I decided it was time to put my other moves on her. It sounds like a good plan, right? I mean, here we were in her bedroom and all systems were go. I brought up one hand to touch her, you know, her boob, as I'd been wanting to do all night, really wanted to do since she started this whole kissing thing in the parking lot. And she didn't say boo, didn't squeak or squawk or react much at all.

It was a nice one too, soft and pliable, the right size to fill my hand, but not obnoxiously large. I gave it one more squeeze, just to see. Nothing.

I broke from my kissing her neck to see what was going on.

My dearest Berry, despite all her urgency, had fallen asleep.

She let out a small huff of breath. Not quite a snore. Not exactly not one either. It was the cutest breath I had ever heard.

I was so frustrated, I nearly cracked a tooth. Hell. This was not fair.

If I left now, it meant that despite a little personal agony, I could see her again without all the sexual baggage the night would otherwise bring. Without shame, without fear. If we went about this courting business in a little less of a rush, it might mean I could make her a steady girlfriend. Who knew what could lead from there?

All this ran through my mind as I stood with her sleeping in my arms.

I could have laid her down, covered her up, and left. I knew I could do that, and leave her a note to tell her I'd call. Yeah, that's what I'd do.

I pulled back the covers of her bed and lay her down. She had on this dress with a long zipper down the back, so it wasn't too much trouble to get her out of that. It was at that point I realized the flaw in my plan. If I went any further, I was going to have to see her naked. Yes, that was the general idea going into this, but with her out cold, it didn't seem exactly right. Especially since I was the one who pushed her past her limit of two glasses of wine. As I said before, I'm a hound, but a principled hound.

Women's underwear didn't seem very comfortable for sleep, so I managed to get her out of most of her things and under the covers without peeking at her more than I absolutely had to. Scout's honor. Except that my hands were shaking pretty bad before I had her all tucked in for the night.

My brain may have been applauding what I was doing, but my body was protesting every step along the way. I swear though, I didn't touch her, though my gaze may have lingered a little longer than was exactly polite. Let me tell you, it was worth all the chastising my conscience would give me on the ride home. All in all, I considered myself a perfectly frustrated gentleman.

I closed the bedroom door on my way out and nearly tripped over her purse. When I picked it up, the book she'd grabbed earlier fell out, and I stooped to pick that up too. It was the one I'd bought for Trista last weekend. I thumbed through it and found all sorts of handwritten notes inside.

That's when I did stop to think. If Berry had written the thing, chances were she had a copy or two around the house, so I might as well borrow this one. It's not like I hadn't bought it. In fact, the sales receipt was still tucked inside. I wanted to read it, find out what my Berry could do. I'd be damned if I was going to embarrass myself by buying a second romance novel.

I figured, if I was going to see much more of her under conventional circumstances, then it would be a good idea for me to read her book. It wasn't as if I could ask my mother for her copy. For one thing, she probably loaned it out to someone. For another, she'd look at me sideways if I suddenly took an interest in that sort of literature.

I sat down on the sofa and read the first few pages. They weren't bad. Before I knew what I was doing, I'd laid back and got comfortable and finished the first few chapters. Shoot. It didn't take long before I was hooked.

That's when I glanced at the time. It was closing in on one in the morning. I needed to get home.

I tucked the book into my back pocket and made for the front door. It wasn't until the lock clicked into place that I realized I'd forgotten to leave her a note. Damn. Well, I'd call her in the morning. Late morning. She was probably going to sleep in with a whopper of a headache from all that wine.

With any luck, I could see her again tomorrow night. I sure hoped she liked bowling.

Chapter Nine

Berry

Have you ever woken up with a pounding head, a thundering heart, and the worst imaginable taste in your mouth? What's worse, you can't remember how you got there? Yeah? Well, it was a first for me.

I won't even guess how long it took before I had the courage to open my eyes. Then it took a while longer before I had the energy to keep them open. I wish I hadn't. The room was dark, but it was spinning. That's when I began to remember bits of last night. The trouble was, I couldn't figure out what was real and what I made up.

Moe. Dinner. A loaded pizza that should have revolted me, but the wine had given me the courage to try. It was quite good. Sitting across the table from that man had also been good. Very good. Better than very good. Very better than very good.

I remembered the wine in the bar, then the wine with dinner. I remember feeling warm, then comfortable, then happy, then chatty. But was there a third glass? I knew better than to drink more than two, especially if the first was on an empty stomach. Especially when I was out with someone I hardly knew. But the memory persisted. The feeling of rightness remained. Of laughing and glowing and wondering if this is what normal felt like, and could I have some more please. Not wine. I don't think I finished that last glass. I wanted more of the rest of it.

I couldn't recall much beyond snippets of conversation.

He wanted to know about Trista and Brad. Oh god—them. I think I groaned aloud then, but when I stopped, the condo was silent. Had I really told him they were fictional? I remember confiding that, but things were pretty hazy from that point forward. I seem to recall some kisses that made me lose my mind. Kisses in the parking lot. Kisses in his truck. Kisses in the living room and the bedroom, but everything after that was a blank. That later part had to have been my imagination. I wouldn't have let Moe kiss me, let alone kiss him. I wasn't that sort of girl. Out in the real world that is. At least that's what I tried to convince myself.

I rubbed my face then, to find that my arms were naked, that my face was still wearing makeup. I sat up, despite the spear of pain in my head, to find my clothes neatly folded on a chair rather than on me. What the hell happened last night?

I forced myself to get up and put on a robe. On the positive side, my bed didn't look like anyone but I had slept in it. The covers were still tucked up under the pillow to my right, and there wasn't a crease in the quilt or dent in the pillow. I mean, you didn't need a whole bed to have sex, but Moe was a big guy. He struck me as the type to…well, never mind. And I was still wearing my tights.

I wobbled my way into the living room. Everything looked like it always did, neat and tidy. Not a speck of dust, the chairs were arranged just so with the cushions smooth.

That's when I saw the sofa. It was a mess. The cushions were mashed down, the throw pillows piled up to one side, and some scattered on the floor. Yes, a tussle could have taken place there. I groaned when I saw a streak of dirt on one end. He made love to me with his boots on? On my sleeper sofa? I was going to kill him the next time I saw him. Assuming I didn't die of embarrassment first. I mean, it's one thing in my imagination—and another on my clean sofa.

No more red wine for Berry Samuels. I idly wondered if Solange DewBerry could hold her liquor better than I could. God, but I'd rather be her right now. She had ovaries of steel. Not like me.

A small part of me began to wonder if I'd had a good time. I didn't feel any different, minus the headache, of course. My body felt pretty much as wound up as it normally did, not the slightest sense of lassitude that I used to get when I had made love. Not that I had very often—you know what I mean. I remembered that feeling. But that morning, there was also no soreness from using any underused muscles. And the tights—no way would I put them back on.

That's when I realized that my condo was empty, save for me. No Trista. No Brad. No dishes all over the place. The sofa was a sofa, not a bed. I rushed into the kitchen and found it in its usual spotless condition. Opening the fridge, the food I thought they'd eaten over the past week was there—all of it, including the extra I'd bought.

Everything was exactly as it should be.

Except the copy of *You're the One for Me* was no longer on the coffee table. I recalled grabbing it on the way out last night. I checked my bag, but it was gone. Did Triss leave and take the book with her, or had my taking it away from her last night done the trick? Or had I been hallucinating all week? The thought worried me more than the date I'd had last night. Unless that too was part of my hallucination. After all, it had been Trista who introduced me to Moe. Maybe he was no more real than they were. And if that were true…

My mind simply could not reach the realm of higher reasoning right now. I settled on the fiction of my having caught the flu and left it at that. Just a nightmare that was thankfully over and done. There was no Trista. No Brad.

No Moe. I'd figure out how that streak of dirt got on my sofa another time. Or I wouldn't.

That being settled, I made coffee. I thought I might handle some toast too.

As I buttered it, I thought back to what must have been a dream. An imaginary man had kissed my throat. I'd given him a name. Moe. Maurice. Maybe I could work that into *Loving a Rogue.* Conrad had been very demanding and commanding, but what if I made him more tender with Svetlana? Would that win her over sooner? But if so, then what would the conflict have been through the middle section of the story?

Maybe he could start out the way he had, but ultimately win her over with a gentler approach. I snagged my mug of coffee and headed for my den. It took only a moment for the PC to boot up and for me to log into the story.

"Took too long," Svetlana complained as the file opened. "Have been wasting away, waiting for big sex scene."

"I must agree, young woman," Conrad said over her shoulder. "Have you any idea what it's like to support an erection this size for so long?"

"If you two will cooperate, we'll see the deed done in the next hour," I muttered. "Places, everyone."

Svetlana climbed back on the bunk—apparently, they settled on a ship after all, and loosened the strings of her top. She closed her eyes and threw back her head. She looked up again, and pulled her skirt from under her knees, widening them. Conrad was right behind her, about to clutch her breasts with his meaty hands.

"No," I told them. "Svetlana, you've got to be a little less eager. You want him, but you want him to work until you're ready to surrender to him. You still have doubts that he loves you. You think he's doing this for the sex."

"I *am* just doing this for the sex," Conrad growled. "And there's been precious little of that, you'll notice."

"Hang on," I told him. "Svetlana, close your knees and close your eyes. Throw your head back again. Good. Now, Conrad, listen to me and do exactly as I say. This won't be perfect, but we'll go back and smooth out the rough edges for the next draft."

Conrad sighed.

The phone rang. I ignored it.

"That one will go much faster, I promise," I told him.

At last, he had her where he wanted her, alone on his ship, anchored in the harbor. The crew was all off in the town and wouldn't be back for days. He had supplies to last them for a week if need be. Long enough to tame this woman for his own.

She was here at his mercy. Should he bind her wrists to have his way with her or would a more tender approach be called for? After all, he was in love with the fiery wench, wanted her as he'd wanted no other woman. And he wanted her to want him as passionately. Not only for now but for all time.

The binding could wait for another day when it would be done in play and not for power. No, tonight, he would use passion and tenderness as his weapons.

With a gentle hand, Conrad brushed the hair from Svetlana's nape and smoothed it down her back. He could feel her trembling, see the breath as it heaved her ripe bosom. Did she fear him? No matter, for after tonight, she never would again look at him with anything other than desire.

"Get on with it," **Conrad groused.**

"No. I like," **Svetlana purred.** "More words of love please.

He ran his large hands down her arms, slowly savoring the softness beneath her blouse until he captured her hands in his. With care, he pressed one of her open palms to her leg and held it there, the other he brought up to his lips where he placed a warm, lingering kiss.

"I am going to explode," **Conrad muttered between his teeth.** "Hurry up, woman."

"Keep your shirt on," I groused.

"My shirt is already off. Do you want me to put it on again?"

I'd never heard him so frustrated before.

"T' would do nothing to drive this scene forward."

"That's an expression. It means be patient. Remember, I'm in charge here. You can't come until I say so."

He let out a frustrated groan and pressed his erection to Svetlana's backside.

"I like that too," Svetlana said in a whisper. "Keep in story."

He turned her hand until he kissed her

palm, tonguing it in his passion. Of their own volition, his hips pressed forward to sooth the raging heat of his manhood against her soft bottom.

"Now we're getting somewhere," **he crowed. "Shhh."**

"I want you," Conrad whispered against her ear before he pressed those warm lips to her sweet neck. "I want you, Svetlana, more than all the riches of the Orient. My love for you is vaster than the seven seas."

His lips trailed behind her ear, where he took a little nip before he soothed it with more kisses and his tongue. "Please, my darling. Let me love you. Let me make love to you, and please you."

He guided her hands, still clasped in his, to her breasts. He would give her this pleasure first and deny himself a few moments more. Yet through her hands, he felt her softness, the luscious pillowy depths of her body through the thin silk of her shift. Of its own volition, her head lolled back on his shoulder, allowing free reign to her throat.

Conrad did not hesitate to take advantage of the bounty before him. His lips kissed and sucked in her sweet, salty essence until a groan escaped his tight control. He brought her hands to rest on his hips as he left them there to explore the wealth of her body, now his to freely claim.

"This neck kissing is good," **Svetlana** purred. "I like. You do more in later scenes? Worth giving up the hard passion. You bring that back though, right? I like when tossed on bed."

"I'll have him do that in a later love scene, I promise."

This neck kissing business was even better—once I started writing it—than I thought. You might think I'd experienced it myself. But of course, last night was a dream.

Svetlana turned her face and moaned as his large hands closed over the overflowing lushness of her breasts. He squeezed gently and in so doing, pressed her hard against him. She brought her hands up to clasp his face, to bring his lips to hers for a deep kiss of her own devising.

Conrad could hardly hold back his passion but clamped down with what self-control was left him to keep to this path and not throw her down, toss up her skirts and have his way with her. No, this first time, she had to want him as much as he wanted her. It was the only way he could ensure she was his for the rest of their lives.

"I see where this is going now," **Conrad** murmured. "I didn't like it much, but I see there will be much for me to profit from later."

"Atta boy," I told him through gritted teeth. "Now, stop

distracting me and let me write."

He pulled her shift up out of her skirts and slowly caressed the tender skin of her belly until his hands found that which they sought, the smooth, soft tips of her breasts. At the first contact, she thrust them into his hands, and he took them, rolling their tips in his fingers until they furled into tight, hard buds. She groaned as he pulled them, tortured them sweetly. A shot of moisture wet the entrance of her secret chamber, and she pressed back against him, wanting this waiting to be over.

"At last," **Conrad blew out.
I liked it, so I kept it in.**

"Svetlana," he purred into her ear. "Let me make love to you tonight, tomorrow, all the days ahead of our lives. Let me make you mine. Let me become your lover, now and forevermore."

One knee urged hers apart as he left the hollowed touch of her breast, and his hand made its way her leg. There, he gathered up the volumes of fabric of her skirts until he found her skin. With the same, gentle, slow pressure from before, his hand explored, rising ever steadily upward until he came close to the center of her glory, of her fire.

"Touch me," she commanded in a strangled

voice. "Conrad, touch me, make me yours."

The one hand still on her breast closed in triumph, heightening her passion until she cried out. But her joy grew to greater heights as his hand found that which it sought and closed over her soft, downy mound. He found her wet warmth and gloried in it. He had made her thus, and he would be the one to reap the rewards.

She gasped as his fingers found her, explored her folds and secrets. The breath caught in her throat as he found the one spot that, above all others, promised passion untold. "There," she whispered. "Touch me there. More."

And he obeyed her orders, for they were the same as his desires. As he pinched her nipple gently, one finger entered her, slowly, carefully. Svetlana nearly convulsed with the joy. "More," she gasped. "I must have more, and you too,"

Conrad seized the moment for he'd never have another like this.

He quickly tore the shift from her breast as he ripped his own billowy shirt from his body. His boots already shucked; it was quick work to peel his breeches from his muscular legs.

"His shirt off again?" **Svetlana whispered breathlessly.**

"Hush. I'll fix that later."

He kneelt on the bed, watching her. This

time they faced each other. His hands reached out and took her breasts. She watched as he kneaded them, pinched, and weighed them. He watched as the flush spread from her face down her neck until it consumed those beautiful globes of glory in his hands. She watched his hands until her eyes glanced down to see his wicked, engorged blade of love.

"Oh," she gasped in spite of herself.

"Do not worry, my love," he whispered as he came closer. "We will make this work."

He kissed her then, to close her eyes to the sight of his desire, and slowly lowered her to the bed.

"She's still got her skirt on. And you haven't adequately described how built I am," **Conrad complained.** "I think your readers want to hear about that."

"Shhh. Women like it when they still have some clothes on when they make love. It's sexier to them."

"Harrumph," **was his reply.** "Let's get on with this."

I didn't waste my breath telling him that was exactly what I was trying to do.

He lay down beside her, his hands still caressing, worshiping her body until he made the last of her worries flee from her mind. He pressed kisses to her lips, her throat before he moved down and took one rosy nipple into his mouth and sucked upon it, hard. Svetlana's body came off the bed, so great was the sensation. Her legs opened wide, and she eagerly pulled up the skirt that tangled in her legs. "More kisses," she demanded, hooking an arm around his neck. "All over, like you promise."

"I never promised that," **Conrad complained.**

I made a footnote to have him promise her that in an earlier scene. "Satisfied?"

"All in good time, my beauty." And time is what he took as he worshipped her body, tasting, kissing, loving each inch of her sleek form. At last, he stripped away her skirts and petticoats until she was as naked as he, writhing in her eagerness to be made one with him.

"I want..." Svetlana breathed. "I want you, my Conrad, my love."

"And you shall have me," he replied as his mouth pressed upon her very core. Svetlana shrieked as her head tossed on the pillows. Conrad had his way with her and did not stop until he was satisfied that she was mindless with pleasure. When he introduced a long finger, then two into her body, she thrust her hips upward, her beautiful neck straining with the urge to finish what it was he had started. "Oh," she cried as wave after wave of infinite pleasure crashed upon her. "Oh, oh," she cried when they came and would not stop.

Conrad took one last long, lingering lick before he heaved himself up her body and entered her in a flash. She cried out as her pain erupted around him, then eased as he began to move within her. She caught his rhythm and moved with him, up and down, in and out, pumping harder and harder as the waves built again.

"You did not say how long and thick I am, that she has trouble containing me!" **Conrad groaned between thrusts.**

He could feel her soft breasts against his wide, furred chest…

"I have no chest hair," **Conrad moaned.**

"I'll fix that too," I cried.

…gloried in how she rubbed herself against him to heighten her pleasure.

She cried out his name at last, collapsing beneath him as he pressed on until he too found the ultimate in satisfaction.

His hips continued to thrust in and out of her as her body squeezed every last drop from his manhood, and he sighed in complete contentment.

"That, my dear, is what we will have for the rest of our lives."

Svetlana sighed as she wriggled to a more comfortable position under his heavy, well-muscled body. "You promise me more love like that, Captain Conrad, and I shall be your woman for the rest of your life."

He wasn't quite certain her declaration of love was all it should have been, given his recent efforts, but he would take it for now. For he planned to live a long, long life, her plans to kill him notwithstanding.

Chapter Ten

Moe

I hung up the phone after leaving my message. It was only ten in the morning, but I figured that would be late enough to call. She didn't have *that* much to drink. And I wanted to see her again. Tonight if possible. Sooner, if she'd let me.

I'd been up early to inspect the job my brothers were working on. I had to get an extra-large tub of coffee for myself because I'd been up most of the night reading about Brad and Trista. Boy, the scrapes Berry'd come up with to keep their romance interesting really had me baffled. A bunch of missed signals, double entendres, conversations that were overheard and misconstrued. Was it really their story? The whole thing was a lot of fun but highly improbable. The Brad she wrote about was not the same as the stiff I'd met, except when he was in bed. Then he was stiff a whole other way. Except when he turned into a human pretzel. With staying power.

Trista though, was captured to a T. Beautiful and outgoing, somewhat ditzy, and very sexy. Appearance-wise, she was nothing like Berry, but inside, the fun, the excitement, that was like the woman I'd shared a slice with last night. Was Trista really like that, or had Berry written herself into the story more than she realized? One thing I knew, Berry had a whole lot more imagination than the woman on the cover of her book.

I couldn't believe that all those books in the romance section had actual events behind them. The story was a fun read, not too deep, but it sure got me worked up during the sex scenes. And when the hero and heroine were torn apart, I had to catch myself from caring too much about them and their troubles. Like I said, I was up late reading.

I couldn't wait to ask Berry what she was working on next. And exactly where did she come up with some of those scenes anyway? To be honest, if I ever saw those friends of hers again, I was going to have a hard time keeping a straight face knowing what they did behind closed doors—or in the back of a pickup truck. I've been driving one since I was sixteen, and I never ever did it with a girl in the back. There was always too much crap back there, or it was too hot or too cold. I mean, the beds of those things are plain old too hard on the knees or the keister.

I might be using my underworked imagination here, but something told me that a lot of that sex stuff was made up. It was just too..., too, well, too much. Berry didn't strike me as the sort who had that much experience—I mean last night before all the kissing started, I'd catch her looking at me, you know, and then blushing and looking away. Man, that did my libido a world of good. And last night, I know she was drunk and all, but when she was going after me like that, it was strictly the work of an amateur. An aroused, hungry, sexy amateur, but an amateur, nonetheless. Maybe if we ever got to that point again—and I hoped we would—I could teach her a thing or two, smooth out the rough edges if you know what I mean.

That brought me up short. What if we hit it off and we finally did the dirty? What if we did become a couple? Would I want my sexual exploits to be paraded about on the pages of a book? No, thank-you. Even if I could get a few pointers from her about what women liked, there was no way I wanted my face on the cover of one of those puppies. Or my name inside.

Remember that contest and calendar I told you about?

Well, one thing did come out of it. I hooked up with a girl I met at the ad agency that ran the contest, Carly. She was nice enough, and we got on fine. Good times. We were pretty exclusive for a few months, and I was starting to wonder if maybe she was the one.

It was a year after the contest. The business magazine that sponsored it did a follow up on those of us who won. They interviewed me, and I gave them all sorts of facts and figures about how my business improved since my picture went public. I even mentioned that I'd met Carly as a result. That was a mistake. The next thing I knew, some other paper in town, the kind that runs personal ads, interviewed her and a bunch of other girlfriends about how it was to date the sexiest contractors in the city.

She told them. Everything. Or close enough. I don't think my face burned that much since I was eight years old and was caught behind the garage with Susie Shepherd.

We had it out, Carly and I. I gave her what for. I wasn't going to drop her at first if she was sorry about the whole thing, but in the end, she didn't seem to understand what the big deal was. I guess she wanted her own fifteen minutes of fame more than she wanted me. Regardless, I haven't seen her since.

So, maybe I needed to rethink the possibility of dating a romance writer.

I thought it over.

Berry was too darned cute to give up on so easily.

I'd give her until this afternoon to call me, and if she didn't, I was going to find her.

Berry

Wow. I sat back and reread what I'd just written. It was crude to be sure, more a sketch than finished product, but it had the structure I wanted to convey—tenderness and urgency, love, desire, even desperation. And it had the all-important declarations of love, if not so baldly stated. And a cliff-hanging hook. Yeah, that banged out of my fingers before I really thought too much about it. Talk about an unexpected plot twist.

I didn't know how I'd come to be so inspired first thing in the day, sitting there writing in my robe with nothing else on but a hangover. But if it worked, it worked, and I wasn't going to argue.

"I think it needs work." Conrad lay in the bed with his arms folded behind his head, eyes closed. He had a look of utter bliss on his face. Svetlana nudged him with her foot and pulled the blanket over both of them.

"You don't explain much about what I'm feeling throughout that scene," he groused. "Nothing about how I exploded, how the lethargy stole through my body following this best of all sensations. I didn't even quirk an eyebrow up when she threatened to kill me."

"Oh man up, will you?" Svetlana whined. "I feel perfectly content. Maybe she flings more adjectives to you in next draft? Now, let me sleep. Solange, you go and write other scene, set up next round of lovemaking for us. Conrad, you come back down here and keep my back warm, yes? Maybe we come up with ideas on our own."

I shut my laptop. That scene had exhausted me, what with Conrad fighting me the whole time. I swiveled in my chair, and my elbow cracked into a stack of books, sending it to the ground with a whump. I really did need to do something about this room, or I might not make my deadline, contract and all.

When I reached over to pick them up, the coffee mug crashed into my picture frame, and both fell to the carpet. Now the burnt orange fibers had a wide brown spot. It was a wonder I could write in this place, let alone think.

I picked up the frame and set it back on the cluttered tabletop. The glass was cracked but not shattered, but coffee had seeped under it and stained the cheap photo below. It occurred to me that I should get the room redone. I could use the rest of the money from the first novel—it was still sitting in the bank, unspent. Moe thought it wouldn't take more than a week or two... But I reminded myself I had decided that Moe wasn't real. I was also starting to think, if he was part of my imagination, then I could start to formulate him into the hero of my next story. Hmmm...

That's when I saw his card. It hadn't disappeared when every trace of my visitors had.

But, if it was real, then Moe couldn't have been a figment of my imagination as Triss and Brad, Svetlana and Conrad were. What a cruel irony. But I could find another contractor—a real one.

But hang on. Hadn't Duncan asked me about my friend and her husband on Friday? How could he have unless they'd really been here? And that meant that if Moe was real, all that neck kissing thing had been real—and my clothes on the floor this morning, and the rest of it. So, maybe the whole week hadn't been a hallucination? Only parts of it. And what did happen last night?

My head started pounding again. The only thing I could come up with was to make myself another cup of coffee, seeing as there was no arsenic in the house.

That's when I saw the red light blinking on my phone. I pressed the button to hear the message.

"Yo, Berry. It's Moe. Just wanted to say hi. See how

you're doing this morning. I thought you might want to get together again, grab some dinner or a movie, or go bowling. Also, I worked up a quote for your den. Give me a call."

I felt faint. Moe was real. That meant something did happen last night, but what? I felt my face grow hot, thinking about the possibilities. Oh crap. Did I sleep with him, and was he looking for more? Never, ever in my life, did I give into a man so quickly. My last boyfriend waited months before I let him into my bedroom, and that was faster than my usual speed.

And this meant unequivocally that Moe was real. If that was the case, what happened to Trista and Brad? And that copy of my book that Moe bought for Triss?

I tore around my condo looking for it. There were no traces of my guests. No extra towels or sheets in the laundry. It was as if they had never been there at all. I wanted to cry. Was I going mad, or did this happen to all writers? Though they weren't in the same room as me this morning, Conrad and Svetlana had all but talked to me as I wrote their story. But the other two—they'd been like flesh and blood.

I checked my place again. Nothing. Not in the laundry, not in the trashcans. Even the extra toothbrush I'd given them was sealed in its wrapper as if it had never been used.

I listened to Moe's message again. Of course, calling him was out of the question. Whether I slept with him or not—the very thought that I'd been so forward was enough. How could I possibly face him again? It was why I was becoming a recluse at age twenty-nine.

I deleted the message and took a shower.

An hour later, I felt better. With my head cleared, I was determined to not think about certain subjects. I brought my garbage out to the compactor and then decided to go for a walk. The sun was shining, and there wouldn't be too many more days I could do this without bundling up so much as to make it not worthwhile.

The landline rang again as I was locking my door. I stopped a moment to listen. Moe again. I tugged the door shut, and speed walked to the elevator.

Moe

I was starting to get concerned. I was pretty certain Berry had fallen asleep last night, not passed out. But she still hadn't called back. It wasn't as if she hadn't expressed some affection for me. Maybe she was away—it was hard to tell, but I figured I'd drive by to see her, to make sure. I brought the written quote with me as an excuse.

I swung by the house I was buying first. It was a beauty, a diamond in the rough. Abandoned for the past few years, there was little about it that didn't need work. If I didn't know that I could do most of it myself, I would never have considered it.

The three-story house looked pretty much the way it had every other time I'd driven by—big and lonely and waiting for the right guy to get his loving hands on it. The yard was a mess. I'd leave that to Pete, one of my middle brothers, to work on in the spring. His specialty was landscaping.

If any other jobs came in during the slow winter months, this could be put on the back burner. All I wanted right now was to get the downstairs functioning and patch the roof. I planned to seal off the upper floors and live on the first level until I could do more. I had a furnace guy lined up and ready to work as soon as the ink was dry on the sales agreement.

I thought about the rest of the house. The first floor held

the kitchen, a large and small parlor, dining room, and a maid's bedroom. There was a full bath there, plenty of space for me until the rest of it was fixed up. One of the parlors had a turret that extended to the second and third floor. I thought it could be a nice place to look out at the neighborhood. I wondered if Berry would like it.

I gave myself a mental dope slap. Why the hell was I wondering that? For all I knew, she never wanted to see me again. But hell, I couldn't have been more of a gentleman than I was. Other than the undressing her part, that is.

Shouldn't have thought of that. The image of that body, even in the semi-dark room, was enough to get me going all over again.

I hopped on the highway and was in her neighborhood in minutes. I thought about calling again, but if she ignored my first two calls, she could as easily ignore a third.

I cruised down her street, looking for a place to park. Quite a few people were out in the sunshine, walking their dogs and going for runs. In the distance, I made out a form that might have been her. She was walking slowly toward me, her head down as she was scribbling something on some paper. Despite her hair being tucked into a pink baseball cap, I was sure it was Berry.

I pulled over to let the cars behind me pass and rolled down my window as I waited for her to approach.

"Hey lady," I called out the window as soon as she was close enough to hear. "Mind telling me where I can find the prettiest girl in the city? I think I lost her somewhere last night."

I must have startled her, for the pen and paper flew into the air. With a scowl, she reached down to pick up her things. That was the first sight I had of her backside. All I can say is, wow. If I wasn't already smitten, I was now. I'm a guy. I can't help it.

She waited as I parked the truck. "Hi," she said, but I couldn't tell if she was glad to see me. No, I'm lying. She wasn't. I was just flattering myself.

"I wanted to explain about last night—" I started, but she cut me off.

"I'd rather not discuss that. I behaved abominably—"

Abominably? "Aw, you weren't that bad," I interjected.

"—for which I am very sorry. I've been under a lot of stress, or I would never have agreed to it. I'd just as soon you didn't mention it again."

Whoa. She was apologizing to me? "I think we have our signals crossed, lady. I was going to—"

She held up her hand. "Really, no need. Let's forget it ever happened and move on."

She started to walk away, and I had to trot to catch up to her. Even so, I was at a loss for what to say, and for anyone who knows me, that's saying a lot right there. She might ask a lot of me, but the last thing I was going to do was forget last night. But she didn't have to know that.

"Okay. You call the shots. You're the boss."

That got her attention. "I am?"

"Sure. If you want me to work on your place, you give the orders. I'm the brawn you're the brain."

I wished I'd had a camera to preserve that look of utter confusion. With her face and figure, I thought guys would have been falling all over themselves to flirt with her, yet here she was at a loss with a little light teasing. Last night, after a glass of wine, she'd been giving as good as she got. I liked this Berry just fine, the one I'd met the first time. But I liked the other Berry a whole lot too.

"Oh." She tucked whatever she was holding into her pocket. "Okay."

"I called a couple of times. I wanted to make sure you

were okay."

"I was busy this morning," she replied as she looked at her shoes. "I have this deadline, and the past week was a bit of a loss for me."

"I know. With your houseguests and all."

I'm not sure why, but for she jumped and blinked. "Yes, them." Was it relief I saw on her face, or horror? "Anyway, I've been stuck on a scene, and this morning when I woke up, the answer came to me. I spent the morning writing, and then came out for a walk."

"As long as you're okay." I shoved my hands in my back pockets to keep from reaching for her. She didn't look like she'd appreciate a hug as much as she looked like she could use one. I may be a hound, but I know how to keep my distance. "If you have time right now, maybe we can talk about the quote?" I remembered then that I had her book and reached into my leather portfolio to pull it out. "Also, I wanted to give this back to you. I um—borrowed it last night."

She looked at the book as if it were a snake. A poisonous one. "If that's the copy you bought, you keep it," she told me, her hands still in her pockets. "I have others."

My arm fell to my side. What the heck was going on with her? "Can you at least autograph it?" I asked.

She hesitated before she nodded. I think she kind of smiled too. Maybe it was wishful thinking, or maybe she really did. "Okay." She took it with her fingertips and flipped through the pages briefly, her brows rising as the paged fanned by.

"Did you make these notes?" she asked.

I shook my head. "Nope. I think your friend Trista did. Most of them are about her character, though she ranks on Brad a few times."

"Really?" Berry read a few more of the comments

before she pulled out a pen and signed it. "Here you go," she said as she handed it back to me.

She had a big fancy signature. I must say I was impressed. My first autographed book ever. 'To Maurice, best wishes, Solange DewBerry.'

"Did you like it?" she asked. The sun was kissing her face then, or she was blushing? I didn't care which. She was making conversation with me.

"Yes. Very much. Well written. You have a way with words. I liked the funny bits and the sad ones too."

"Anything else?" I think she was smiling now, maybe a little.

"The hot parts made me sweat," I admitted. "I kept looking forward to those. Read the whole thing in one sitting." No need for her to know I'd put my feet up on her couch for the first hour. She looked like the type who might not like that.

"Really?" She looked pleased, like the Solange side of her was starting to emerge. "None of the readers who contacted me said that before." She looked at me sideways. "Two sittings at a minimum." She glanced down at my feet.

I couldn't help myself. I looked down too.

Damn, had I really put my boots on her couch last night? Did she know? I didn't know what to say to that, so I shoved the book under my arm and held out the envelope with her quote. "Maybe we can go somewhere to go over this? Somewhere quiet?"

She looked up at me then, with that big blue eye that matched the sky, and the other the color of clouds. That's when I realized I was holding my breath. I didn't want her to say no. I didn't want her to hesitate and worry and look at me as if I wanted to have her for lunch, which I did. And dinner. And breakfast the next morning. That image of the two of us sitting on a couch somewhere together came to me again. Holding hands. Her writing and me reading, and then my dragging her willing body off to the closest horizontal surface. Or vertical. God, I was starting to think like one of her characters.

Is this what it feels like when you've met the person who you want to spend the rest of your life? What would she do if I asked her to marry me right now?

"Okay," she said after what seemed like forever. "But you have to keep that book in your truck. I don't want it back in my place."

So, she was a little odd. Hell, everyone's entitled to be a little quirky. And even if they weren't, I wasn't about to argue with her. We hadn't gone far, so I tossed it in my truck and locked the door. "Whatever you say, boss."

Chapter Eleven

Berry

He didn't act like a man who had ravished me the night before and expected to ravish me again at will. And no, I can't help but use words like ravish.

I wasn't sure what would he would have been like if he had—maybe cocky and overbearing, maybe a little more sure of himself. Instead, he was nice and polite, and in fact, wholly charming while I was being a scared, shy jerk. It was stupid of me, but after my last boyfriend used me shamelessly to climb the corporate ladder, I hope you can understand that I was a little gun shy. Okay—I'm not the first woman to be used like that, not with her brother's tacit consent either. That wasn't a problem here. I'd never date someone from the office again, and I didn't think Moe would have much to gain by currying Rocky's favor. In fact, Moe didn't seem like the type to kiss anyone's rear end for anything. I liked that about him. But I wasn't about to trust him because of it.

And I wasn't about to let him back into my condo. Instead, I took him downstairs to the common room where some of the older residents played Scrabble all afternoon. I might be willing to give him a second chance, but I wasn't going to be stupid about it.

He didn't seem to mind. In fact, he remained a perfect gentleman, opening doors for me, smiling and agreeing with everything I said. He even charmed the Scrabble ladies, and they tend to be a grumpy bunch.

I won't bore you with the details other than to say he'd made some rather interesting drawings of the den and had added the built-ins that I specified. It all looked very nice and professional. Who am I kidding? I was drooling over the prospect of having that room become a writer's warren.

As I sat there listening to him outline the work, I couldn't help but daydream about him coming to my house each morning, outfitted in his worn-out jeans and work boots. Each morning, I'd greet him dressed in my work clothes, buttoned up and prim, and I'd give him a mug of coffee, and we'd sit at my little dinette as he told me what he was going to do that day. He'd smile his warm smile, and I'd melt a little, and we'd linger, moving on to other topics. By the second day, I'd be a little late for work, but I'd put my chin up and ignore my boss and my brother.

Each day we'd do this, and each morning he'd progress from a handshake to a kiss on the cheek, to a kiss on the lips, to a full-fledged lip-lock. Then, on the final morning, I'd be running late, or he'd be extra early, and I would be getting out of the shower when he arrived. I'd greet him at the door, wearing nothing but a towel and a smile. He'd take me in those big strong arms of his. The towel would fall away, and his tool belt would clatter to the floor. We'd do it right there in the small foyer of my home. Do it until we were incapable of moving more than a muscle, and once we'd recovered, we'd move to the bedroom, and do it all over again. I'd call in sick to work and make him stay in my bed all day. And he'd have to come back another time to finish because all he'd done the day before was finish me. But of course, a fresh day meant a fresh me, and he'd have to work his magic all over again. The job would never be done, and I'd have him, my love slave, for the rest of my life.

As I sat there in a stupor listening to his deep voice, I knew I didn't have all the details of this new fantasy down exactly the way I wanted them, but I'd refine it. Not too much. Like him, it was raw and earthy and suited me fine the way it was. Hot damn.

He cleared his throat as he gathered up the papers and shoved them into the envelope. "Of course, I wouldn't do the work myself."

Reality smacked me right in the face.

"When you're ready to commit, I'll have one of my guys do the job. I'd come by once in a while to supervise."

"Oh." And I call myself a writer. Was that the best I could do? Maybe he didn't want me after all, and this was his way of letting me down. "Why not you?" The words were out of my mouth before I could stop them.

I felt myself blushing, and he smiled. Crap, could he read my mind? Images of that tool belt on the floor were still dancing around in my head. Or was it the jeans next to the tool belt that did it to me?

"Because I make a habit of not mixing business and pleasure. If I worked on your place, it would mean I couldn't ask you out again until it's done."

I swallowed hard. Well, when one asks a question, one does hope to get an answer, doesn't one? Especially that answer.

"That all sounds good. Of course, the price is kind of high." *Good stall*, I congratulated myself. I'd never haggled for anything before in my entire life.

That's when his grin hit me with a thousand watts. "Seeing as we know each other and all, I can give you my ten percent friends and family discount."

What can I say? I melted. I suspect he knew how devastating that smile of his was. If he used it all the time, he'd be a wealthy man. "But I still need to think about this." Sales of my book were steady, so I expected to see another check soon. I did need to do this. The den was a mess.

"How soon can you have one of your guys start?"

He checked his calendar. "How does next week sound? As a bonus, we'll even help you pack up the room for nothing."

How could I say no to that? To him? How many other women had fallen under his spell?

"Give me a few days to think about it, okay?"

He sat back and flashed that smile one more time. "However long you need, Berry. I'll be waiting." He leaned forward and touched one calloused finger to my hand. "But don't keep me waiting too long."

He was good. Any more of this, and I was going to be in over my head.

If there is one thing I pride myself on, it's my ability to focus when I must. I put Moe and his offer firmly out of my mind. I dared not think too much about Trista and Brad. If they showed up again, I'd worry about them then, but I'd pretty much convinced myself that they had been self-inflicted torture, prolonged by the presence of the book Moe had purchased for Triss. I figured since they were gone, as long as I didn't pick up the copy on my shelf, or reopen the file containing their story, I would remain free.

At work, I was the detail demon I needed to be. Duncan's proposal was approved, which meant more work than ever, but that was okay. I put in my time and kept my head down. That kept both him and my brother at bay. At night, I rushed back to the continuing adventures of Svetlana and Conrad. My agent had called looking for an update, and I was able to report that the first draft was almost finished. Unless she or the editor absolutely hated it, the second draft would be a snap to complete. In fact, my agent was the only one I spoke to in the evening. I let the machine pick up all other calls. Including Moe.

Especially Moe.

I would not think about him, his strong hands, that large body. If I really wanted to, I could remember the way he kissed. No. Way too distracting. I needed to focus on my story.

Conrad was outraged. This woman he loved, the one for whom he had sacrificed his honor, his ship and crew, the one who meant more to him than anything in the world, had betrayed him. He'd done it all for her, sailed the ocean in the dead of winter, lavished jewelry and clothing upon her, furs, gold coins—and none of it was enough. She scorned him at every turn, even denying him his rights in her bed.

Ah, but her protests only lasted as long as her willpower, and he had learned the secret of using that against her. She was highly vulnerable to his lovemaking, once he got past the knives in her garters.

He looked across the small cabin. A fire roared in the corner hearth, warming the room. Slowing, he peeled off the layers of fur ~~from his body~~ until he was clad in nothing more than his thin linen shirt, his buff leather breeches, and Hessian boots. A ~~day's~~ week's growth of beard darkened his face, and he planned to use those bristles to their full advantage in making her wild.

Svetlana watched ~~him~~ warily from the corner. Despite the heat ~~of the room~~, she had yet to shed her fur-lined cloak. Her eyes moved with him as he prowled about the room, but she was otherwise motionless.

The wind howled outside the small cabin. It was her fault they were here in the middle of nowhere, because Conrad followed her, despite her threats and pleas that he leave her. Her assignation with her former master had come to naught. Oh, how she rued the day her stepfather had sold her to that man. It mattered not that he'd never laid a hand on her—not that way. Conrad was the only man who had ever plumbed her depths, unleashed her desires. But her master had violated her in other ways, far deeper and more deadly. It was because of him she'd never know the life-long happiness of being in Conrad's arms as his wife, mother to his children, in short, all she longed for.

"Come, my dear, get comfortable. From the sounds of that storm, we will be here for days." Conrad approached her openly, but she held up her arms to ward him off.

"I won't bite you. At least, not until you beg me to," he purred in his dark, silky voice. He made her nipples ache for his touch, her breasts swelled, longing for his large hands to engulf them. And between her legs, she grew wet at the very thought that he would soon, once again, possess her and bring her ecstasy. He chuckled, and the sound pierced her with desire. Why, oh why ~~did~~ had she fallen in love with this man?

With reluctant fingers, she loosened the ties at her throat and let the heavy cloak drop to the floor. She wore little beneath it but her thin blouse, her layers of skirt, and her knives, fleeing as they had with only time to grab their boots and cloaks. But the heat of the room was overwhelming and there was no advantage in not enjoying it. So Conrad would look upon her body and desire her. Perhaps for once, she would not give in and could use him to her advantage instead. Yes, she yearned to go to him, to take him in her arms without a fight. But that was impossible. She needed to kill him to win the terms of her release, and that of her younger sister. Those were the rules, and she was bound to obey them.

She heaved in a deep breath, straining the worn fabric of her blouse to its limits. She watched as Conrad's eyes lingered there. How she wished to throw herself into his arms and beg for mercy, but out there, somewhere, someone was watching her and would report back. She needed to kill Conrad, and soon.

Perhaps this time, she should let him approach her and then stab him in the back as she was instructed. It would be so easy. But if she let him have her without a fight, would he grow suspicious?

"Come, my pet. Sit before the fire and relax your aching muscles. The horses have been put away. We should eat, and then, perhaps, test this new bed we've found for ourselves."

Conrad kicked a chair to her, and placing

it before the fire, she sat. Suddenly weary beyond belief, she hung her head. Let him think her defeated by the cold, by the journey. It was not far from the truth.

He moved with the grace and speed of a cat. With a sharp cry, she found he grasped her wrists before she could reach for her knives. He twisted one, then the other arm behind her and tied them tightly. She listened in dismay as he laughed at his triumph.

"My beauty, you are mine until this storm ends. Mine to take any way I desire." He laughed and gave another tug to the ties on her wrists.

He squatted before her. Svetlana tried to kick him, but he grasped her ankles and tipped the chair back so far she was afraid he'd drop her and it. With a gasp, she ceased her struggles.

"That's more like it."

"You bastard," she hissed as he righted her chair. "I hate you."

"I wish that were true," he sighed softly. "And I wish I hated you in return. But I fear we are bound by love, and despite ourselves, by passion."

Note to self...change title to *Bound by Love*? Nah. Well, think about it. Maybe a sequel if this sells—her sister's story perhaps?

His hand slid up her leg until he came to her thigh, where he grasped the top of her boot and slowly pulled it down, caressing the bare skin of her leg ~~as he did so~~. She tried to suppress a shudder, but he felt it and smiled. Deftly tossing the boot away, he kissed ~~her~~ behind ~~the~~ her knee before he tied her pretty ankle to the leg of her chair.

Conrad made quick work of the other boot and leg, taking the time to caress her properly as he rid her of her knives, to make her chest heave with desire. She wanted him and this deadly love of his. In spite of it all, their passion was one thing they could never deny or tire of.

He sat down and loosened the ties of his shirt. "Now that we're alone, and for the moment safe, it's time you told me what is going on. Why have you been trying to kill me these past weeks? Are you displeased with the way I make love to you?"

She presented him with her fine profile. Conrad only chuckled and leaned back as he admired her from afar. "Let me guess. Someone by the name of Leonid wishes me dead?"

At her gasp, he smiled. "Ah. Now we are getting somewhere." He leaned forward and lifted her skirts to expose her spread knees. One hand caressed her fine calf before he moved away again.

"Tell me, my beauty, or it will go badly for you."

"You can do nothing to me," she spat at him. "I laugh at your attempts to scare me."

He picked up his saber and pointed it at her. Svetlana's jaw snapped shut with a clack. "You would not dare," she hissed.

"No?" He stood and unsheathed the sharp, glistening blade. With a quick slash, he parted the blouse until it hung in tatters, caught on the tips of her breasts. "Dare I not?" he whispered.

"So, kill me," she squeaked, unsure of her voice but determined to be brave.

With the tip of the blade, he caught the ragged edges of her clothing and moved them until she was bare before him. She threw her chin back as she laughed with a bravery she did not own.

Until the point of the deadly weapon was poised at her throat. "Tell me," he ground out between his teeth. "What does Leonid have hanging over your head that you would betray me like this?"

"I cannot tell," she whispered as traitorous tears slid from her eyes. "I dare not."

"Dare." His lips were on hers then, his large hand pulling back her wild tangled hair, his tongue invading her mouth. He pulled back. "Tell me," he begged her. "That I may kill him and win your freedom."

She wrenched her face away and shook her head. "He will kill her," she cried. "Before you or I can reach her. If he learns I have failed, he will kill her."

Conrad gripped her hair and forced her to

meet his eyes. "Who?"

"Anushka. My little sister," she wept. "My mother's husband sold us to Leonid. If I fail to kill you, he will torture her, and it will be my fault. When he is done, he will sell her to the slavers. She will then be worse than lost to me. I must slay you to free her."

Slowly, Conrad loosened his grip from her hair. "But you already have slain me, my beautiful Svetlana," he said sadly. "Each time we make love, I die a little more." He stood and re-sheathed his sword.

With quick pulls, he loosened the bindings at her ankles and helped her to stand, her arms still tied behind her back.

"Come. I will let you kill me a little more."

With gentle hands, he led her to the bed, untying her hands only to retie them to the two posts at the head of the bed once he had lain her down.

Her ankles he rebound, spread-eagled, and stood back to look at his handiwork. With trembling fingers, he separated the two sides of her blouse to expose her to his sight. His hands reached out and caressed that bountiful flesh as she squirmed and moaned on the bed. Her lips parted and she licked her lips, wanting him. He then lifted her skirt to see the pink, glistening folds of her desire. Yes, despite it all, she wanted him. He sank two large fingers into her and was rewarded as those delectable hips came off the bed to meet him, to make him thrust harder.

There was no reason to wait, no need for preliminaries. His manhood strained against his pantaloons, and he quickly loosened their confinement to have it spring forward. Her eyes widened at the sight, terrified and eager.

Conrad climbed to the bed and stood above her. Hands on hips, he was an imposing sight, and she moaned again in her passion, in her desire. Without warning, he dropped to his knees around her chest and quickly thrust his member into her mouth. This is what she wanted, what she loved to do. His eyes closed in the glory of her wet, hot mouth sucking him. He pulled up her skirts behind to ready the path for his invasion. She was his. That which she feared, he would defeat, and then they would in truth, be one.

His hips surged forward, filling her as she strove to take him as deeply as he wanted. The pleasure was exquisite, but it was not all he wished of her. There was no satisfaction like thrusting into her, that of spilling his seed deep inside, and he would not deny himself that pleasure today. Tomorrow, perhaps he would come on her breasts, watch as she rubbed his seed deeply into her skin. But tonight, he would make her his.

That ought to satisfy Conrad's need to tie up his lover. I

was fanning myself too. I'd never written anything remotely this hot. I could hear my agent now—"Too raunchy. Pull back!"

"Is good," **Svetlana told me.** "No pain for me. But have more fear, more desire. The bindings turn me on. Need say more about that."

"Those turn me on," **Conrad crowed.** "Come on, finish this. I want inside her, and I want it now."

"Yeah, yeah, sure," I groused. I wasn't sure I wanted to be tied up, but if I could write this scene, then maybe somewhere deep inside me, I wanted it too. But who could I trust enough for that?

Moe's face swam before my eyes. "No, damn it," I muttered.

"Oh, go for it already," **Conrad whispered.** "He's all right. Big and strong like me. He won't hurt you."

"Maybe make love conventional way first," **Svetlana counseled.** "Then try fun stuff like Conrad and me. And yes, want to finish scene. Am burning up here. Write, write!" **she commanded.**

He felt himself close to the edge. With care, he pulled from her mouth and kissed her deeply. "I love you, my Svetlana," he purred as he moved down her body. "I love you and will protect you and your family. You need to trust me. I will not harm you." He kissed a trail from her mouth, down her throat, stopping at each breast to suck and make her gasp before the trail led down her soft belly.

Oh, I was panting now. My fingers returned to the keyboard.

He inched his way down until he was between her widespread legs. Lifting her slightly, he brought his mouth to her very core and sucked gently, bringing her off the bed with a gasp. Gently, slowly, he laved until the sips became slurps **(must find another word)**, and his tongue invaded her. She screamed as he hit the center of her universe, screamed again as two long fingers thrust inside, and brought her to the very edge of reason. He laughed then, her gasps and heaves bringing him joy as she strained to find completeness. "Not so fast, my beauty."

With quick fingers, Conrad untied her ankles to free her legs. The bindings trailed after her as she bent her knees upward.

He slid up her body, and with his large hands, tilted her hips just so. He thrust inside with a grunt, pressing the air from her body. Svetlana moaned and wrapped her ankles around his slim hips. She strained against her bound wrists, but as he surged out of her and in again, she gasped again, thrusting her own hips upward to meet him.

"More," she whispered urgently. "Give me more, Conrad, my love."

His hands slid to her breasts and

tortured them as he pounded into her, and she cried out her joy. He slammed into her, and she began again, only to cry her joy once more. "I can't get enough of you," he panted as he heaved over her. "So tight, so right," he thrust again as a roar bellowed out of him, and then he fell over her, spent.

"Let's see if your Moe can do that," Conrad panted as he wiped the sweat from his brow. "Are you okay, my precious?" he asked Svetlana as he untied her wrists.

"Don't do that," I cried.

"Oh, he tie me up again when you begin writing again. I'm not really going to kill my lover, am I?" she asked as her chest heaved along with Conrad's.

I was panting along with them. This scene was going to need a lot of work in the rewrite, but I was happy with it. What passion! What drive! In the distance, I was aware of a ringing sound and without thinking picked up the phone.

"Hello?" I wiped my brow. This writing in my bathrobe was working out better than I thought it would.

"Berry, are you okay?"

"Moe?" Damn. Why did I answer the phone?

"You sound like you ran a marathon," he said. "Or are you writing another hot scene?"

Chapter Twelve

Berry

Please explain to me why I even considered asking for, let alone accepting the advice of fictional characters in the first place? They were figments of my imagination, right? At a stretch, you might say Svet (or even Trista) was my alter ego (though I'd deny the later, strenuously), but underneath it, they were still a part of me.

My only defense is that with Conrad and Svetlana panting behind me, with the memory of their wild sex fresh in my head, I was not right in the head. So, I accepted Moe's invitation to dinner.

"I promise this is not about business," he said at my front door a few hours later. "This is about having a nice time. And, no more than two glasses of wine for you," he said with a roguish grin.

I should have been angry about that, but there was something about him, the way he swaggered rather than walked, the lift of his eyebrow (on him, it wasn't, you know, so prominently done. I could live with it). I told myself I was being an idiot for avoiding him in the first place. Why not have some fun?

"I'll stick to two if you will," I challenged.

His smile quirked up on one side with that. "You're on," he agreed. "But I was thinking we'd go for Chinese tonight, then catch a movie. I never much liked beer with my Kung Pao chicken. Tea's more the thing."

"I love Kung Pao chicken," I said before I could lock my enthusiasm down. Something about writing uninhibited sex did that to me and gave me an appetite.

"Let me guess—egg rolls and glazed, boneless spareribs too."

I nodded. It seemed the stars were aligning tonight. "Like candied pork. And Moo Shu."

"Ah, a match made in heaven." He took my arm and led me to the truck.

I admit I checked behind the seat to make sure the book wasn't there. The last thing I wanted was for Trista and Brad to show up at the restaurant for a double date.

He took me to a place I'd never been before, but the staff all seemed to know him. The aroma almost had me salivating. "Nice to see you, Mr. Conrad. You're staying for dinner for a change? And you brought a pretty date this time."

"I'll have you know this is not just a pretty date. Tonight, I'm dining with a soon-to-be world-famous author." He placed his large, warm hand on the small of my back as we walked to our booth. "Miss Solange DewBerry has a novel climbing the best sellers list as we speak, and is hard at work on her second."

I felt my face grow hot, but he chuckled. "If you want to buy a copy, we'll be back next week, and she'll autograph it for you."

I opened my mouth to protest this foolishness, but Moe grinned and sat me on the bench seat. Instead of sitting across from me, he pushed in with his hip and moved me further into the booth. "Much cozier this way, don't you think?" He winked.

Then he did the craziest thing. He leaned over and kissed me. I felt him smile before his lips left mine. "That's to get the nervous tension out of the way. I'm going to want to kiss you when this date ends tonight, and I sure want you to want to kiss me too," he said. "I was getting all worked up thinking about it and thought you might be too. I figured unless I did this, one of us, probably me, would get all nervous and uptight later. I promise to use a breath mint."

I could not help it. I laughed. "You're not like anyone else, are you?"

His hand curled around mine. "I don't know how to be anyone but me," he shrugged. "How am I doing?"

"I'm considering falling in love with you," I told him with what I hoped was the right amount of levity. That was something Trista would say, or my next character. Regardless, it was Solange DewBerry talking, not Berry Samuels.

"But?" he asked, both brows clearly heading for his hairline.

I gave a small shrug. "I'm waiting. To see what that goodnight kiss is like." I tried to be snooty, but I ruined it by laughing.

"My charm is working exactly as I had planned." He leaned over and kissed me again. "I hope you don't mind if I do that. Each time I think about later, I get all anxious. This seems to be the best way to counteract that."

"I don't mind," I told him, which I didn't. "But you may want to hold off while we're eating. That could be a little unsanitary."

"Right." He gave me a little salute and picked up his menu. "Now, since we've established that we both like the same regular stuff, how about we get adventurous and try one of their specials? I promise, whatever you pick, I'm going to love, especially if it involves Szechuan peppers. And over dinner, you can tell me why you were panting so hard when I called this afternoon." Damned if his eyes didn't twinkle again.

Oh my. This was so much more fun than having one of those Greek gods in my bed. There was no way I would delete a single part of Maurice Conrad.

Moe

I had the distinct impression Berry was hiding something from me, and it wasn't another man unless he was of the fictional variety. I had a strong suspicion she'd been writing when I called. I couldn't wait to hear what about.

Sitting next to her had been a stroke of genius. As much as I wanted to sit across the table and gaze at her, being up close and personal was great in a whole other way. And it wasn't just that I got to sneak in a bunch of kisses before our meal came. Well, that was a part of it. But when I was next to her, I could tell if she squirmed or sat still, could feel how animated she was talking about something she was passionate about. My heart hadn't led me astray. I was, after two dates, seriously falling in love with her.

She ate like a bird. I don't think it was that she was nervous—I did my best to keep her from that. But she wasn't that big a woman. I think I probably outweighed her twice over. I did notice though, that she got very protective of her steamed buns after I snagged one from her plate. She retaliated though. She might have been small, but she was quick with her chopsticks when fried dumplings were at stake. I couldn't wait until we got to the fortune cookies. When she read hers out loud, 'you will be awarded a great honor,' I added, 'between the sheets,' she turned all shades of red. God, but I loved that.

We packed up the leftovers and headed out. I hadn't asked her about what movie she wanted to see. Nope. Had that all planned out. I figure most girls don't like action movies, but this one promised to have plenty of chase scenes and not a lot of blood. If she didn't want to watch, I sure didn't mind if she hid her eyes against my shoulder. Or chest. I planned to have my arm around her for most of the movie anyway, so hugging her close would be no burden. Yeah, I'm a sneaky dog. But if you were me and had her out on a date with you, I'll bet you'd be one too.

"Are you sure you don't mind seeing this?" I asked as I put my wallet back in my pocket. The tickets were bought, so she couldn't say no.

"I'm fine. I don't get to see this kind of movie too often. My friends prefer chick-flicks."

"You like action movies?"

She nodded. "Love 'em. Those that I've seen."

At that point, I think I died and went to heaven.

"Rocky used to take me to see them."

"Rocky?" I asked as nonchalantly as I could, all the while alarm bells were going off.

"My brother. When we were little, and he wanted to go to the movies with his buddies, our mother made him take me along."

"You must have been cute. Let me guess, pigtails."

She shook her head. "Braids. My hair's too curly for pigtails. Braids were the only way to keep it neat."

Curly? "Um, I don't want to contradict you, but your hair's straighter than mine."

She leaned in closer. "I spend a lot more money than I care to admit to get it to look this way."

I recalled the feel of her hair in my hand and couldn't resist stroking the back of her head. "As pretty as you are right now, I think you'd probably be a knockout with curly hair."

She shook her head and looked away, but I could see the smile by the curve of her cheek. "You have no idea what you're talking about," was all she would say. "So, tell me, are you always this charming?"

I puffed out my chest—how could I not? "Born and bred. My mother always said I was a handful."

She squinted her eyes and frowned. "I can picture a miniature version of you strutting around the playground with a group of boys and girls tagging along in your wake."

She had me pegged. "Pretty much. I'm the oldest. My dad died when I was a kid, so by default, I became the man of the house."

"I'm sorry to hear that."

I shrugged. It still hurts, but I've got my memories. That's more than my littlest brothers have. "Thanks. We survived. My brothers all work for me from time to time. The youngest is still in school, so he puts in hours during the summer and weekends when he's home. He'll be graduating this spring. I made sure they all finished high school and went to college. It was my father's dream."

She laid her head on her hand. "Let me guess. You were the one to prod them to do their homework and nag them to apply to school."

What can a man do but accept responsibility for his successes. I puffed out my chest again. "Damn straight. If I could do it, then they could too."

She smiled dreamily as if she were far away. "You must be proud," she said softly.

"Yeah." She had no idea. "I guess I am."

We found our seats, and as soon as she sat down, my arm was around her. "So, what are you writing now?"

"Contrary to what you told the hostess at the restaurant, I'm on my sixth manuscript. The first four didn't sell. It was the fifth that was published."

"Holy cow!" I had no idea. "It must take a lot to write one of those. Care to tell me what you were writing today? Since you were so out of breath, it must have been good."

She grew rosy at my question. Must have been a

passionate scene. If what I read in the paperback was any indication, that must have been something. The woman must have had a hell of an imagination to think up all that stuff. I could hardly wait to get her alone. "So, spill," I insisted.

Right then, the lights lowered, and the previews started. Damn.

"Shhh," she said with a smile of what looked like relief.

"You can tell me when I drive you home," I whispered as I slung my arm over the back of her chair. "Don't forget."

She answered by shifting to lean her head back against my arm. What could I do but drop my hand onto her shoulder and pull her closer? I leaned over to kiss her one more time as the previews began. "Once more, so we don't get all stressed when the lights come back on." I felt her smile beneath my lips, and it felt so good, I kissed her longer than I'd planned. She didn't seem to mind. In fact, it was her hand on my chin holding me in place that gave me hope that once we got there, our real goodnight kiss was going to be one for the record books.

Chapter Thirteen

Berry

I find action films a scream. Most of the storylines are pretty thin compared to a chick flick's plot, but with a lot more going on the screen. I could tell Moe was enjoying himself, laughing at all the jokes, even the corny ones, and holding me tight for the few tender scenes. He seemed to like it when I hid my eyes during the worst of the action, pressing me against his chest. In fact, I think he really liked that as much as I did. But he didn't kiss me again until the lights came up. I guess he didn't want to miss any of the chase scenes.

The only time it got uncomfortable was in the scene where the hero and his sidekick visited a strip bar. All those perfect naked bodies undulating on the screen were a bit of a shock, but I'm a trooper when it comes to stuff like that. You never know where you might pick up ideas for a romance novel—the more unlikely and unusual, the better. There's nothing more boring than a ho-hum courtship. Regardless, I made it through.

It was still early, and it was a Saturday night, so after the movie, we went to a bar Moe liked. It was nothing special, but everyone there seemed to know him, and that was nice. He ordered a beer on tap and wine for me, teasing me again about my limit. Moe introduced me to everyone he knew but managed to leave out the bit about my romance-writing career. From the way some of the guys were looking at me, I think he figured keeping that bit of information to himself was the wiser course.

Do you know what I liked best about that date, next to

the kisses, that is? Other than once in the restaurant, and again at the movie theater, he never checked his phone. Most guys these days have it in their hands constantly, like whatever is on that little screen is far more important than the person they're with. Not him. It made me feel special. Everything about the evening did.

As we sat at a large table in the center, a few of his friends came by. Then one of his brothers, Paul I think, stopped in with a bunch of his buddies, and Moe introduced me. The guys were all joking and flirting with me, but when they crowded around the table with their own pitchers of beer, Moe draped his arm around me to warn the others away. I really liked that. There was no overt posturing, no harsh words, just a quiet signal that I was with him. It had been a long time since anyone did that for me. In fact, I don't remember any time where it had been done with quite so simple and clear a gesture. It could have been worse. He could have distanced himself from me like... Nope. Not going to go there again.

He drove me home after that. There was something on the stereo that I'd never heard before, cool jazz he called it, from the sixties. It made me feel mellow and warm inside. I never expected he was so sophisticated. Maurice Conrad was full of surprises.

He pulled into my building's lot and parked the car. "Darn. You never did tell me what you were working on today," he said, his voice laced with disappointment.

I yawned to divert him. "I guess it'll wait until some other time. I'm sure you'll find it boring. Besides, it's only the first draft. By the time I give it to my agent, it won't resemble what I wrote today."

"You're stalling," he said with his grin. I was going to see that smile in my sleep tonight. There were a lot worse things to dream about.

"Yeah," I admitted. "I am. I'm not used to talking about my writing with anyone."

"Tell me this. Did it involve sex?"

I nodded, and he rubbed his hands together.

"Kinky sex?"

I frowned. It was borderline. Enough to make it awkward to talk about. "What would constitute kinky?"

"Whips and chains," he said without hesitation. "Forget that. You don't seem like that kind of girl to me." His grin faded. "Tell me you're not into that stuff."

"I'm not into that stuff," I was able to say truthfully. "It was run-of-the-mill sex." *For a romance novel.*

"But it was sex." His grin returned. "And it got you hot."

"Well, there was also a fight scene in there." No need to tell him who was fighting. "So, that got me out of breath. Do you have any idea what it's like to have all those people moving around in your head at one time and keeping them all straight?"

He shook his head. "When I was reading your book, I kept wondering how you managed to explain sex from the guy's point of view."

I bit my tongue to keep from laughing. Those were the most difficult parts for me to write if Conrad's complaints were any indication. "I take it I did an okay job?"

He shot me one of those lopsided grins. "I wouldn't say it was *exactly* from a man's point of view, but it was close enough to keep me interested." He rubbed his chin, and I could hear the bristly sound of his beard on his calloused hand. "But what really fascinated me was how you described it. That was an eye-opener. All those words, but they worked. I knew what you meant. I could almost imagine it was me." He squinted at me. "Tell me, if you and I were to make love, would you be taking notes? Would I see my moves published in one of your novels?"

I know I turned beet red, I could feel it. "That's a big if. There's no telling that anything I write will ever again be published."

"You're skirting the issue, lady."

It was my turn to smile. I was beginning to think that nothing had happened last night. "Let's say *if* you and I were to make love, I can honestly say I would not get up afterward and write a play by play. You would not see your technique outlined in one of my books." *Other than the kiss you gave my neck last night.*

He nodded. "That's good. I'd hate to have my privacy divulged like that." He gave me a funny look. "I had a problem with a girl a few years ago along those lines. I wouldn't want it to happen again."

"Well, assuming we someday have sex, your secrets are safe with me."

"Cool." He opened his door. "Don't move. I'll be right there to get your door."

"You don't have t—" He was gone before I could protest. All this chivalry was going to spoil me for all other men. God, but I hoped so.

He walked me into the building. The security guard buzzed the door open, not giving me a chance to say a quiet goodnight down here.

Moe slung his arm over my shoulders. He was a perfect height for that, and my arm just sort of naturally came around his waist. We fit well that way.

He pushed the button for the elevator and said, "Uh oh. I feel an attack of nerves coming on." He lifted my chin with his free hand. "Quick, kiss me so it doesn't get out of hand."

I didn't have time to laugh or panic—as soon as his lips met mine, I was toast. He turned, or I turned, or we both turned so that we were facing each other, and it was the first full face to face body contact we'd had all evening. Dare I tell you how good it felt? How wonderful he was? I had never before kissed such a tall man, nor one so wide, or strong. Or one so talented. It was spoiling me.

I know the elevator came. We must have gotten on it for the next thing I knew, we were on my floor, and he was kissing me out of the sliding doors and down the hall to my front door. He didn't stop until we were there, and then he paused only to brace his hands on either side of me, and leaned down to kiss me once again, this time touching me only with his lips.

"It's time," he said against my mouth.

"For what?" I whispered back.

"Time for me to give you that goodnight kiss we've both been so worried about all evening."

I gave a small burst of laughter. "Oh." *This wasn't a kiss?* "I'll brace myself," I told him.

He pulled back and looked at me, his eyes more serious than they'd been all evening. "There's lots of ways I can go about this," he said slowly. "I could dig right in, startle you and undo all the fun we've had all evening, or I can take you in my arms and bend you backward until you're afraid I'll drop you. Which I wouldn't. Or I could start in with a chaste kiss, all lips and no tongue. Or I could—"

I'd hear enough. I stood on my tiptoes and hauled his head down to mine. "Or you could shut up and kiss me," I said before I did just that to him.

"This works too," he agreed as his arms closed around me.

How do I describe his kiss to do it justice? Warm. No, not warm, hot. Skilled. Spirited. I don't know how much he thought about it, for the whole act seemed to come to him naturally. He slanted his face against mine, so our noses didn't bump. He worked up the right amount of suction to get me to open my mouth. There was moisture, but it wasn't sloppy. He was gentle; he was forceful; he was heaven.

That's all so clinical, so I'll tell you how I felt instead. Cherished. Wanted. Desirable. I felt like he'd been waiting all his life to kiss me, and that the kisses he'd given me all evening were a pale reflection of how he kissed me outside my door.

His arms were warm and strong and close. When I moved to hook an arm around his neck, he opened up and let me, before he closed in and resumed his embrace. He didn't stop moving, didn't stop kissing, but for as hot as it was, as much desire as it generated, he was chaste. There was no mashing of his body parts to my body parts. We hadn't spoken of our last date—not once. Those kisses had been pure madness, mostly because I had been too distracted by other things to appreciate them for what they were—the work of a master. This time, I had the luxury of enjoying his skill. But his hands didn't wander past my back. There were no gropes, no coy teasing cops. This kiss told me he meant business, and that he wanted me, that he wanted me to want him just as much.

Oh, but I did.

At last, he pulled back and resumed his stance against my door. His arms were outstretched as if he was doing pushups against the wall, and he was panting as if he'd sprinted a mile.

I wasn't in much better shape. "Give me your key," he said, and when I didn't act fast enough, he reached for my purse on the floor and began to rummage around inside. "Which is it?" he asked before he held up the ring.

I took it from him and picked out what we needed. He took it from me as he thrust my bag into my arms and swiftly undid the door. With a bow, he waved me through.

But then he stood there on the other side of the threshold. The wrong side.

I looked up at him in surprise. He gave me a weak version of his grin. "I'll say goodnight now." He leaned forward and without hands or arms, kissed me softly on the lips once more.

"Goodnight?"

He nodded, kissed me once again before he took the key from the lock, and handed it to me. "I'll call you. Soon," he said before he turned and walked away.

As he turned the corner, I heard him say, "And this time, make sure you answer the damned phone."

Chapter Fourteen

Moe

"I like her."

That was Paul's pronouncement Monday morning as we were hanging drywall.

"Yeah?" I challenged. "Enough to take her from me?"

He scowled as if I'd lost my mind. "I didn't say that. I like her. For you." That's when his brows lowered. "Why, you thinking of walking away from her?"

"Not exactly."

"You'd be an idiot if you did," he said as he put the screw gun to the chalk marks on the plasterboard. "I think even Ma would like Berry."

Really? Ma hated every girl I'd ever brought home in spite of her soliloquies about wanting me to settle down and start a family. I figured at the rate I'd been going with women I'd have to elope to get married. She could hardly object to a daughter-in-law of fact rather than probability. Oh, right. This was Ma I was thinking of. She could do anything she wanted.

That all flashed by in a moment. "You think?"

He nodded as he finished securing the board, and I stepped aside to lift the next one. "Yeah. Berry was quiet but classy. Good sense of humor and smart. You know how Ma likes smart women. Doesn't want us to be with anyone who'd dilute all that good Conrad DNA." He snorted his laugh.

That sounded like Ma, all right.

"What are you guys jawing about?" Pete came into the room, looking for my ratchet set.

"Moe's girl, Berry. I say Ma would like her."

"Damn straight she would. Then she'd be on my case about Debra all over again. "Why can't you get a nice girl like Maurice's?" he said in falsetto.

I laughed. "What, and spoil your fun?" Pete was the biggest hound among us five brothers. He had a new girl every month, each one prettier than the one before. I can tell you this, he didn't go out with women for their conversation, fool that he was.

"That's what I'm talking about. You gotta keep her to yourself."

I hefted the next sheet of drywall to the wall and waited for Paul to screw it in place.

"And if I don't?"

They both groaned. "You're going to ruin things for the rest of us."

I shrugged. It was my job as the eldest to set the standard for the rest of those clowns. Still, I was glad to hear that at least these two approved of my girl. They may have thought her meek and quiet, but they weren't the ones who'd kissed that spitfire Saturday night. I swear, my lips were still burning. It was the hardest thing I'd ever done in my life to walk away from her. But I'd done it and would do it again if it meant she'd start to trust me.

I knew what happened that first night still hung in the air between us. I had no idea if she remembered any or all of it, but she didn't mention it, and because she didn't, neither did I.

One thing was certain though, she wasn't like her friends. I don't think Trista would have let me walk away Saturday night.

I smiled to myself thinking about that look of confusion on Berry's face when I did.

"Ah Jeez, look at that shit-eating grin on his face," Pete

grumbled. "Cat who got the canary."

Hell, I didn't get that bird. Maybe a feather, but that's it. "If only you guys knew."

Joey and Sammy wandered in there to see what all the ruckus was about.

"You guys taking a break already?"

"No, I'm holding up the wall here," I said as I waited for Paul to screw it to the studs.

"Seriously, we were talking about Moe's new girl."

"B-berry? I like her," Sam said. He leveled a look at me. "You d-didn't break up with her, did you? Think she'll want to go out with me?" He had the good graces to look embarrassed. "After a few weeks that is. I wouldn't ask her r-right away."

"Never." I turned my back to him. "You won't ask her, ever. I'm not breaking up with her."

It was awfully quiet behind me. I turned back to see them all smiling. It was the same smile they wore the first time they realized they could gang up on me rather than have me wrestle them to the ground individually. "What?"

"You really like her." Joey said it.

"And if I do?"

One by one, they all shrugged.

"It's not like we've known each other for a long time," I explained.

"And?" Pete asked.

"I've only taken her out a few times. Twice, officially."

"And?" Sammy prompted.

"And nothing." I turned my back on them. "I'm going to take her out again. A bunch more times." I could hear feet shuffling behind me and the quiet snickers. "And after I've taken her out a dozen times, I'll ask her to marry me."

I heard a back slap or two before I heard Paul complain, "Crap. I knew you were going to ruin it for the rest of us."

Berry

It was Wednesday night, and that meant dinner with my family. Rocco was there, of course. What was different was that he brought his new girlfriend. Darlene. Yes, her.

In the first place, I could not believe he was dating that uh, woman, but what started to set me off, in a quiet, ladylike way, of course, was that he brought her here. Was he that serious about her? What really got my teeth on edge was how she sat there and smiled at me as if she was on top of the world. On top of Rocky, no doubt. Figure he'd want the woman to do all the work.

Ouch. Since when did I think thoughts like that? Truthfully, since when didn't I? What was different was that night, I wasn't censoring myself like I usually did, even internally. Normally, at one of these dinners, I'd sit there and say nothing, try to think nothing, just wait until it was over. That night, I was having trouble corralling my thoughts. After all, why bother? They were my thoughts. It wasn't as if I was going to say anything out loud.

Or was I? After last week, who knew what would happen. I played with my fork and pushed the food around my plate.

"So, Princess, what is new with you?" my father asked.

I cringed. I really hated that pet name. "Not much, dad. Almost done with my next novel."

"You write?" Darlene squeaked and opened her eyes very wide. "I had no idea. Children's stories?"

Rocky chuckled. "Not quite. Bedtime stories for grown-ups is more like it."

"I write women's fiction," I said and waited for it.

Darlene's eyes grew narrowed, and she gave a smirk.

"Porn?"

I hated her. I truly did. "Romance," I said between my teeth.

My mother was right on cue. "Sweetheart, when are you going to get tired of this hobby and get serious about your work? Or find a husband..." In case you didn't catch on, it was as if my mother was brought up in the fifties rather than having been born then.

"But I thought Berry was the pride of the off—" Darlene said, but she was cut off. I think Rocky kicked her under the table.

"She could do so well for herself, even rival Rocco in her success, if only she put aside this foolish idea of writing," mother continued. "Her father and I offered to loan her the money to go for her MBA, but she wouldn't take it. A young woman can meet lots of nice men in grad school."

My mother turned to me then. "Or at least get married. Give me something to brag about to my friends. I don't dare mention to them what you do in your spare time."

"With sex scenes?" Darlene asked.

I frowned at her before I turned back to my mother. "I went out last weekend—"

"Dad, hear about that new merger?" Rocky said over me.

"Who, darling?" Mom asked. "Someone from work?"

"But I don't see what the big deal—" Darlene started, but stopped abruptly.

From the way she glared at him, I think Rocky kicked her again. I didn't know if I should thank him for stopping her line of questions or ripping him a new one for even bringing her here. What would they say if I brought Moe home for one of these torture sessions—I mean dinners? A part of me—okay, a big part of me—wanted to know.

"Mom, I'm perfectly content with my job and my writing.

I made more than I expected from the book, and my agent is hounding me for the next one. If I keep this up, in a few years, I could quit my job and write full time. Go on the lecture circuit if I wanted to."

"Lecture circuit?" My mother laughed. "You couldn't put two words together to speak to my garden club about your petunias."

Nice. Nothing like a little ancient mortification to season the pot roast. I set my fork down.

"I was eight years old at the time. I'm sure I could manage now," I said quietly. *Heck, I could speak for an hour about making characters come alive, couldn't I?*

"I still think you should go back to school in the evenings, do something meaningful with your life. Why, Rocco tells me Darlene is taking night courses."

"Really?" I almost hurt my neck swiveling around to glare at her. "And what are you studying?" I asked.

She preened right there in her chair. "Right now, it's a Chinese cooking class. I've really learned how to handle a cleaver."

"I'm sure that will come in handy for your next presentation." *Oops. I guess maybe one of those catty remarks slipped through after all.*

My mother's mouth snapped shut, but she glowered at me. Oh, that was a good word. I'd have to remember to use it when Svetlana was looking at Conrad sometime.

"Well, Rocky thought it was a good idea. He's thinking of doing more entertaining. You know, bring clients home, his boss, the company president. Wouldn't it be nice if he could surprise them with a gourmet meal?"

"So, you'll be in the kitchen while he's entertaining all his important guests?" I smiled sweetly, so she'd know there were no hard feelings. "And cleaning up afterward?" From the look on her face, I could tell my barb hit its mark.

I looked at my brother. "For shame. You really ought to think about hiring a chef for that, or at least a maid to do the clean-up work."

"That's enough," my father said in his sternest voice.

"Wait, you said you were seeing someone?" Trust mom to pick up on that.

"Yes." I pulled my elbows in and crossed my ankles below my chair.

She looked at me, a patient smile waiting. "And..." she prompted.

"He's a contractor. I'm thinking of redoing my spare room to make it more functional."

"Oh honey, not a...a...someone who works with his hands," my mother groaned. "You can do so much better."

Shoot me now. "Moe's a contractor. He has his own business, with other people who do the work for him."

"Moe?" She wrinkled her nose.

"Maurice," I said, possibly through clenched teeth.

"But honestly sweetheart, someone in the trades...?" she shook her head. "Darling," she said, looking at Rocky. "Get your sister some information on that MBA program you did."

MBA indeed. No doubt it would be practical, but it if turned me into someone like Rocky, it was the last thing I wanted.

I put my napkin on the table and stood. "If you'll excuse me, I have some work to do tonight. And don't worry mom, it's not my frivolous hobby. I promised Duncan I'd start work on his next presentation." And wait for Moe's nightly phone call. That would be the highlight of my evening.

Chapter Fifteen

Moe

I saw her again last night. I forgave her for making me wait almost a whole week between dates because she picked up the phone every time I called. I didn't exactly tell her that, but regardless, it was a whole week of wondering, and wanting and pacing and planning.

You see, last Sunday morning, I was still elated from the night before. Monday, I was whistling while I worked. I think on Tuesday I still had a smile, but by Wednesday, I was starting to growl at my crew. Thursday was worse, and I don't even want to talk about Friday. But by Saturday morning, I was smiling again.

I took her out for a burger (she had the salad), and then bowling. Yes, I know, how blue-collar of me. Guess what? She loved it. The first time she struck a pin, she did this wiggly little dance that I don't think I'll ever forget. When she got a spare, she ran and threw herself into my arms. What's not to love about bowling?

After we were done, after a quick stop at the bookstore, she let me take her back to her place. I made some pretense of asking if she'd made up her mind about my taking the job, but I wasn't fooling anyone. As soon as she gave me the green light, I was right back where we ended last weekend, with me all over her, and she, well, she was doing a damned fine job of finding me to her liking.

And for your information, I was a gentleman again. Mostly. I did progress to second base if you must have the details. She didn't seem to mind too much, and in fact, she was downright accommodating. I thought about rounding third but stopped myself. We still hadn't discussed what happened that first night, and I still had the feeling she thought maybe a lot more happened than it did. I didn't exactly want to disabuse her of my intentions, but I also didn't want to scare her off by thinking I only wanted her for sex. That was part of the package deal I was interested in, but not a deal-breaker. At the moment. A ball-breaker maybe.

So, I left her place with my blue balls screaming. However, I had my dignity intact, and so did she. A little sexual frustration hadn't killed me yet, and I knew it wasn't going to last forever. And I wasn't the only one. As I was leaving, she kind of hesitated, as if she was going to ask me to stay. In the end, she reached up and kissed me on the cheek before she pushed me out the door. I drove home smiling, knowing she was having kind thoughts about me.

I made myself wait until Sunday evening to call her. I didn't expect she'd want to see me again so quickly—she had made a big point about how she was trying to meet her deadline, after all. But when I suggested that the next Saturday afternoon we take a ride in the country, she jumped at the chance. At last, we could spend some time together, just the two of us, without a lot of distraction. I might be able to work a few kisses in between our stops, and then, maybe—well, we'd see what happened at the end of the day. Not that I was trying to rush or anything.

I picked her up at eleven. The doorman made me wait until she came down.

Five minutes later, she came into view, looking about as gorgeous as any woman ever did. She had on a light jacket over her clothes, I think she wore boots or something. Although it was a clear fall day, I swear the sun shone brighter as soon as I saw her smile.

"Hey," I think I said. Clever of me, isn't it?

"Hey yourself." She kissed me on the lips, a quick one that made me want more. But we had an audience, and I don't like that much.

"Want to get going?" I asked. "I made lunch reservations for one."

"Sure. Am I dressed okay?" She spun around. I don't think she was looking for a compliment. She really wanted to know.

I thought she looked fine, but as I also remembered what she'd looked like without her clothes, I could only nod. Not that I was complaining about her wearing them. I'd already noticed the looks other guys gave me when we were out together. Berry seemed wholly unaware of what a knockout she was. My brothers hadn't given up ribbing me about her. Pretty soon, they'd tell my mother about her, and then I'd catch hell.

Ma liked to meet the women I dated—all the girls her boys dated that is. But it seemed as though she was singling me out, and not a single girl I'd ever brought home was good enough. In her opinion, they were either dumb as doorposts, or too good looking. One was lazy, and another had flat feet. I don't remember her ever criticizing the other guys' dates as harshly. But she was always nice to their faces. She'd always call me the next day and pick them apart in the very nicest way possible.

I wasn't ready for Ma to find fault with Berry. As far as I could tell, Ber's biggest fault was that she didn't give me nearly enough time. Oh, and she had weird friends who had a very hot sex life.

But I digress.

"You look fine," I told her.

She frowned. "You can tell me the truth. Am I overdressed? Underdressed?"

She was dressed. That was the main problem. "No. You look great. We're not going anywhere fancy." I kissed her again. "You'll have to coach me on what words to use, you being the word-meister and all."

"You mean it?"

What could I do but kiss her again? This time, I used a little tongue. So what if someone was watching? But I didn't go on for too long. I pulled away, and kind of had to catch my breath. "I mean it. I'm the kind of guy who would tell someone her ass—I mean her rear end looked too big in a dress. Not couth, but honest."

That made her laugh. "I'll have to think twice before I ask your opinion the next time."

"Well, I do like your rear end, so what you might take as criticism might be meant as a compliment."

She looked over her shoulder, and it was my turn to laugh. "You have a way to go before you even approach big. I'm not complaining. I like what I've seen."

Oh. Her face went all red. She took my arm and hustled me out to the sidewalk. "You have to watch what you say in front of the security guard. Next thing I know, it'll be all over the building."

I smiled. "I'm not afraid of a little gossip."

She looked at me sideways. "You don't have to live here. I swear, sometimes it's worse than the office gossip mill."

I helped her into the truck and kissed her again before I shut her door. A long kiss. The one we started two weeks ago and worked on again last Saturday night. I wondered if we'd get to finish it sometime today. Maybe start a new one.

I broke away to see a dreamy expression on her face. Yeah, that was the look I wanted.

"Where are we going?" she asked as I climbed in and

started the engine.

"I heard about some vineyards around the state. A few of them have restaurants, so I made a reservation. After that, we can do a wine tasting or two. Maybe stop at a farm stand and buy a pumpkin for Halloween? Since we'll be near the shore when we finish up, maybe a seafood dinner later."

Her smile was enough to make me glad I'd done my homework. If the day had been rainy, I'd have found something else to do. I'm not a man who likes to take his leisure lying down.

"It sounds like a perfect day," she said as we turned onto the main road. She picked up the map tucked next to my seat. Do you want me to navigate?"

"No need. I memorized the route," I told her. "Worse comes to worst...I'll turn on the GPS."

"That's a relief," she laughed. "I'm the world's worst map reader."

"Sit back and enjoy the scenery." I looked at her and found it hard to look away. "And so will I."

"Maybe I should drive then," she said with a smile.

Somehow, I couldn't picture her behind the wheel of my half-ton pickup. "Maybe later. You can pick out some music instead." I nodded toward the CD rack in the visor. "If you don't find anything there you want, I've got satellite radio."

Berry thumbed through the selections and picked out one of my favorites. I'm not a country-western fan by any stretch, but there's something about Lyle Lovett that I really connect with.

"I haven't heard his newest," she said as she plucked it from the holder and inserted it into the player on the dash. "Any good?"

"He's only the best," I replied. "I keep waiting for him to tour in this area. As soon as he does, I'm getting tickets."

"Can I come along?" she asked.

"Even if it's a weeknight?" I asked, keeping my smile to myself.

She sighed dramatically. "For Lyle, I'll make an exception."

"Maybe I'll get four tickets, and we can invite your friends."

"No," she said flatly.

"Haven't heard from them since they left?" I took a deep breath. "Not that I mean to be critical or anything, but it seems a little ungrateful that you put them up for a week, and they took off without so much as a thank-you note."

She shrugged and looked out the window. "I've put it behind me," she said in a small voice. "They were really kind of high-maintenance."

"I'm glad you said it, not me."

That got a smile from her.

We were heading into the country now. I spend so much time in the suburbs and the city, it sometimes surprises me how close we are to farm country. The rolling hills were golden with drying cornstalks. Farm stands had fall produce and scarecrows by the dozen, with signs promising hayrides out to pumpkin patches. Berry smiled as we passed them, and I could almost see her writer's mind soaking up the atmosphere, taking notes for her next book.

"You going to set a scene out here?" I asked.

She shook her head. "If I am, it won't be right away. My current novel is set in the early eighteen hundreds. I was going to set it earlier, but I was having a hard time matching facts to my fiction. Rather than spend a lot of time doing research, it was a lot simpler to change the timeframe of the story."

She did take out her notebook though. "It never hurts to

capture the atmosphere to save for later."

"I can't imagine how your mind thinks up all those stories. Of course, with it being set at that time, you can't use any real-life experiences, not like you did with your friends." I hadn't forgotten what she'd told me about their being fictional, but I knew it was the wine talking that night.

She was silent for a while. "Oh, I don't know. I sometimes think Triss and Brad became more like themselves once I started writing about them."

"I know you're going to think I'm a perv for asking, but did they tell you all that stuff about what went on in their bedroom—in the back of the truck and all, or did you make it up?"

She turns the prettiest shade of pink when she's embarrassed. "It would be like kissing and telling if I were to reveal all my secrets," she said at last with a nervous laugh. "If I told you what they said, you'd think them stranger than you already do. And if I were to tell you that I made it all up, you'd get the wrong idea about me."

"Oh no, darlin'. If you were to tell me you made it all up, I'd be hanging on every word. I'd even be happy to demonstrate a few moves of my own. Not for publication, of course."

She grinned but tried to hide it. She was so darned cute. "But then, you'd still be afraid that I'd use your stuff in my next novel. Sex is ageless. I think the biggest difference between a historical novel and contemporary, is that a contemporary writer is much more likely to mention birth control."

"Speaking of which—"

Her face went from pink to red.

"Well, maybe we'll talk about that when the time comes."

She nodded and looked out the window.

After a long moment of discomfort, as Lyle sang about learning about love, I said, "I did mention that I'm six one, and that my feet are a size thirteen, right?"

She looked at me, startled.

"That means," I continued, "when I put my foot in my mouth, it takes me a little extra effort to get it out again."

She covered her mouth then to hide her smile.

A few miles on I asked, "You like antiques?"

"I do," she replied. "My place is pretty well furnished, so I haven't let myself look for anything in a while."

"I'm making note of all the places down here. I recently closed on an old fixer-upper. I've got exactly three rooms worth of furniture to move into a ten-plus room house, and I don't think a single piece of it is suitable, style-wise. I figure one of these weekends, once we have enough wine to hold us, maybe we'll come back this way and start poking around some of these places, and you can help me pick stuff out."

She stared at me, a small smile playing around the corner of her mouth. "Let me get this straight, okay? You mean that you and me—we—are going to be a couple? Exclusive that is? The kind that makes plans more than one week out?"

It was time to be honest. At least she didn't flat-out ask me if her ass was too fat in her pants. Which it wasn't. "I'm sure hoping. That you'll reserve your weekends for me. I was kind of wanting you to want that too. Seeing as we get on so well and all. I figured I needed to take you out on a few more dates at least before we make the announcement."

Her head swiveled so fast I could swear I heard it creak. "Announcement?"

"You know, that we're getting married and all?" *Oh Moe, you are one smooth talker. Now you've done it.*

She shook her head, and my heart nearly stopped.

"I'm ... I don't know—flabbergasted I guess is the best word."

"You mean you don't like me?" *Was it time to backpedal? Nope. Couldn't recall those words.*

She looked at me then, and it was all I could do to force myself to look at the road. She was so surprised. "Not that. Not at all. I like you a lot. It's just that you're not what I expected."

I lifted one eyebrow. I'm proud that I can do that. It took hours of practice in front of the mirror when I was fourteen. I seem to recall her having Brad do that a lot too, so it must be a turn on for her. So why was she was suddenly scowling at me? "Exactly what did you expect?"

"That you'd find a reason to break things off like most other guys do," she said in a small voice. "Not propose on what, our third or fourth date?"

"What the...?" I pulled into the first driveway I found and yanked up the break. I unbuckled my seatbelt, tore off my sunglasses, and took her by the shoulders.

"What the hell do you mean by that?" I demanded. "Why would I run screaming from you? You're the cutest, smartest, most interesting woman I've met in a long time. Ever. Can't you tell I'm doing all I can to get to know you better? That I want you to like me back?"

I think I might have shaken her a little, for she got very pale. I let her go, ashamed of myself. "I'm sorry. I was so surprised to hear you talk down on yourself." I looked at my hands, clenched them together. "Since we met, I can't stop thinking about you. Good thoughts." I looked up to meet her eyes then. "If you want me to turn around and take you home, I will. I didn't mean to scare you." I paused. "Maybe all that talk about getting married was a little premature. I don't want you to think I'm desperate or anything."

She looked at me then, her eyes all big and wide behind her glasses, and there was something a little wild in them too. From the corner of my own, I watched her hand creep along the console until I felt her cool fingers on mine, curling in and loosening them.

"I'm sorry too," she said in a small voice. "I'm not used to men like you liking me."

"What do you mean, men like me?"

She met my eyes full on then. "I mean, men as interesting, fun, men as nice and sexy as you. They don't usually look at me twice."

That knocked the wind from my sails. I opened my hand and let her fingers in, holding them close. "Then, those guys are all dickheads."

Her mouth remained solemn, but a smile crept into her eyes. "You mean it?"

I leaned over and kissed the corner of her mouth until her smile reached in and took hold. "I mean it. I hardly know you, and I'm already crazy about you. In case you didn't notice, I want to spend as much time with you as I can. Why else do you think I want to do that work at your place, other than to have an excuse to stop by?"

There was no hiding her smile now. "Are you sure you're not saying all this, taking me out, to get my business?"

"Honey, I'm planning on spending more on you for lunch today than I'd make on that itty-bitty job of yours. And it'll be worth every penny."

I kissed her then, kissed her as best I knew how and then some. It kind of took a lot out of me to hold back and all. I can tell you this too. She kissed me back, like she meant it, like she meant every word she said, and some she didn't.

"Oh," she said when I'd pulled back. Her fingers went to

her lips as if they were still tingling. I knew mine were. "Okay then."

Chapter Sixteen

Berry

In my admittedly limited experience with men, I've learned that if something seems too good to be true, it usually is. In the past, it seemed the crazier I was about a guy, the faster he'd run from me.

So, what was wrong with this picture right now? Moe wasn't about to make a lot of money off me and the little job I still hadn't made my mind up about. He traveled in completely different circles than I did, so there weren't any advantages to him using me that I could see unless he figured he could parlay my job into some other, bigger ones given my parents' and brother's social standing. But as far as I knew, he didn't even know who they were or that they had money. Was it that he really and truly liked me for me? I tried to find a flaw with this, and other than the fact that perhaps he had terrible taste in women, nothing came to mind.

There was still the question about what had happened that first night when I'd had too much to drink, but he wasn't holding that over my head or taking advantage of it. Not the way he'd left me at my door the past two Saturday nights.

And the truth was, I was falling for him, hard. What woman wouldn't? From the top of his sun-bleached hair to the rugged face with the killer smile, down to those broad shoulders that went on forever—yes, and included those slim hips and the way he had of standing with one hip raised, totally relaxed and in control. I was a goner.

"So, where are we going for lunch?" I asked. My lips

were still zinging from his kisses. I didn't think I could handle any more of those right now. It was all I could do to breathe normally.

Moe dropped the shades back over his eyes before he pulled back onto the road. "We'll be at the first vineyard in soon. I figured we could start there, see how their stuff tastes with food." He looked at me as he shifted into a higher gear. "So, what kind of wine goes well with salad?"

I had to admit, I put my nose in the air about that. "I suppose I'll have to ask the sommelier for a recommendation," I sniffed.

"Hey, watch those ten-dollar words, lady. You're with a simple man, remember."

"A simple man with a business degree. Graduated third in your class. Don't tell me you don't know a few highfalutin' words yourself."

"Busted," he said with a laugh. "You been talking to my mother?"

"Nope. I Googled you. I know all your secrets. Including that Mr. November business. I saw the picture."

I think I might have sniggered as he winced. "That woman you dated wasn't exactly thinking long term with her tell-all interview, was she? What was she trying to achieve?"

He shrugged with a frown marring his forehead. "I've wondered myself. She was surprised when I confronted her about it. Maybe she figured anyone who'd take his shirt off for a few publicity pictures wasn't playing with a full deck."

"You're better off without her," I said, then laughed. "But those pictures were hot. Listen to me giving you advice about your love life."

"Who better?" He put on the turn signal, and we headed up a small country road. I soon saw signs for a vineyard and restaurant. We passed row upon row of vines draped gently over rolling hills. There were people in them, harvesting grapes into big baskets at their sides. If not for the sound of top-40 radio hits coming from the side of the road, I would have sworn we were in Europe.

"Think we can pretend we're in Italy or France?" he suggested as he turned smoothly into a parking lot.

"So, you'll order the cheese plate?" I teased.

"Nope. A burger. I'll concede to a cheeseburger maybe. I'm on a quest to sample the best burger in every joint in the state. As long as they have one on the menu, that's what I'm ordering."

"I'll bet you make a mean one yourself," I said, and we rolled to a stop.

He laughed that self-depreciating laugh I'd come to treasure. "Nope. Can't cook. It's the one thing my mother never taught me. I can do laundry and clean a house. Hell, I can build myself a house. I can even press my own shirts, but I burn water."

He got out, and before I could pull the handle on my door, he was there, opening it for me and holding out his hand.

"You know, you're really spoiling me for other men," I quipped as he helped me down. It was one big truck after all.

"That's my intention," he replied as he put his arm around my shoulders. "I want you so bamboozled by my charm, you'll never think to look at another guy."

We walked the few steps up into the chateau-style building. "So, how am I doing?" he whispered into my ear as we got in line.

I looked up at him and swallowed hard. "If I were to tell you now, you'd sigh in contentment and coast the rest of the day."

He threw his head back and laughed, his hand tightening on my shoulder. "For that, maybe I wouldn't mind seeing this date in a book of yours one day. But you have to promise to change the names to protect the guilty."

We stepped up to the hostess, and he said, "Reservation for Conrad."

I managed to suppress my wince. Dare I tell him that my newest hero's name was Conrad? Granted, the century was not like this one, but the two men did share certain characteristics: both were big and defined masculinity. They had big, booming voices and a sense of leadership. And in the past few weeks, my Captain Conrad had taken to kissing his heroine with the same skill and technique that one Mister Maurice Conrad exemplified. When this fantasy relationship ended, and I was sure it would, I was going to be a long time getting over him.

Lunch was superb. They did indeed have a white wine to go with the goat cheese and walnut salad I ordered, and Moe was more than happy with the full-bodied red that accompanied his gourmet burger. He had me laughing throughout the meal, and I was still smiling when we left the sun-dappled patio and went inside for the tasting.

We stood shoulder to shoulder with others who had wandered in, taking our time tasting a variety of wines, and talking about them. Moe surprised me by purchasing several bottles of the varieties I'd liked the most, and tucked them behind the seat of his truck before we got back on the road.

An hour later, we were by the shore, and though he hesitated for a moment, we went down to the water's edge. The sea was calm, barely a ripple to be seen. He kissed me there; boy did he kiss me. When we came up for air, I looked around, and in the distance, we watched a wedding being performed on the golden, autumn sand.

That's the most romantic thing I've ever seen, I thought as my heart fluttered in my chest. Try as I might, they were too far away for me to picture myself in that bridal gown.

"Hmmm, how can I top that?" he chuckled. "I don't think we're *quite* ready to get married yet, do you?" He took my hand and kissed it. "No matter what I said earlier."

"Did I say that out loud?"

His brows lifted. "You did. And I can see those wheels turning already, with you figuring out how you can work it into one of your stories."

"I'd have to build a whole story around that being the ending," I laughed. "I'm not sure how a romance novel could start with a wedding unless the hero and heroine were then ripped apart before they could consummate their wedding vows. I'll have to think about it." Most definitely not my current story. Conrad and Svetlana may have held off on doing any consummating for the first three-quarters of the book, but they more than made up for it in the last portion. I was rather proud of myself for heightening the sexual tension for as long as I did. Speaking of which...

He took my hand. "Come on. We've got another vineyard to see today, and then we're getting pumpkins before it's too late. And I want to take you to see my new place. I've finally got one room in decent enough shape to show it off. I want to know what you think. Just keep this wedding on the beach thing in the back of your mind. We'll get back to discussing it one of these days."

Just when I thought I had my heartbeat under control, he had to go and say something like that.

A half dozen more bottles of wine were stowed behind the seat before we were done. We stopped at a few antique places along the way, and Moe haggled with the owners over weathered old signs and a couple of mismatched kitchen chairs. There was a large partner's desk that he liked, but thought the price was too steep. "That's okay. I don't have a partner anyway," he laughed as we drove away. "Once you see my place, you tell me what you think will go best. Or should I call your friend Trista?"

Gah. I really wished he'd stop talking about her. "Oh, don't bother. I don't expect to see her any time soon." *And if you did, how would I ever get rid of her again? How would I begin to explain her when I'm sober?* "I'll do my best."

"Okay. You want to stop for that seafood dinner before we go any farther? There's a great clam shack not too far from here." He looked at me sideways. "You do eat fried clams, don't you? Or do you only eat the green leafy stuff?"

"I love fried clams as long as I've got onion rings on the side."

"Oh lady, I knew you're the one for me." He leaned over and kissed me before he put on his signal and headed down another road I'd never seen before.

It was almost dark when we pulled up in front of a huge home on a corner lot close to the university. Some of the asphalt shingles were missing from the exterior, and the sagging wooden porch that ringed the house was missing balusters, but there were enough gingerbread carvings and gables for even the most imaginative. The overall effect was, 'Wow.'

"What do you think?" he asked in his low baritone. There was a touch of doubt in his voice I'd never heard before.

"This is your home?" I asked as I scrambled down from the truck. "You live here?"

"You like it?" Nerves seemed to give way to

astonishment.

"Like it?" I turned to him. "I want to set my next novel here."

"Yeah?" His face lit up in the fading light. "I can't say as I live here yet. Soon. Come on in, let me show you around."

Who would have thought someone as solid as Moe would pick such a fanciful house in which to live? I figured him for a placid ranch style, certainly not something that had decorative brickwork on the many chimneys.

"I can't wait," I told him.

I could feel his eagerness in the touch of his hand on my back. Never before had he pushed me, but it seemed he wanted to get inside as much as I wanted to be there.

"Watch your step. As soon as I get some of the rooms ready to live in, I'm fixing the porch. I think it makes the whole house, don't you?"

"I don't know what to think," I replied. "The whole thing is so over the top."

"Yeah," he said, a note of pride creeping into his voice. "When the realtor showed it to me as a tear-down, I couldn't do it."

I turned to him. "Tear it down? That would be a crime."

His grin was slow to form but no less potent. "Yet another thing on which we agree, Ms. Samuels. I wonder when we'll have our first argument." He pulled out a ring of keys and fit one into the lock. "I'll bet it'll be about something really stupid."

"Careful what you wish for, mister," I said and looked upon the biggest mess I'd ever seen in my life.

"Watch your step," Moe said as he reached up to pull on a light switch. "I didn't know I was having company, or I would have cleaned up." He stood there under the harsh light and rubbed his nose. "That is, if I knew where to put all this stuff."

I could see what he meant. There were hand tools tucked into one corner, and power equipment scattered around the foyer or resting on sawhorses. Plaster bits and paper littered the floor as far as I could see.

"The outside's one thing," he said as he kicked the ends of sawn boards away, "but you kind of need your imagination for the inside."

He took my hand. "I'll go first. I think I have lamps in all the rooms. Just go slow." With that, he tucked my forearm under his. "And stay close." He leaned down and kissed me, the first in what felt like hours.

The large foyer held a sweeping staircase. From there, he led me into a big parlor which was mirrored by a smaller one across the hall. This was a large rectangular room with an impressive fireplace. Oddly, it had a few logs sitting on the grate. The walls were in terrible shape, and the wooden floor was paint-splattered.

From there, we entered the dining room, a spacious area with a bow window. Its parquet floor was in desperate need of refinishing. I could easily imagine the room seating twenty comfortably. I could picture Moe at the head of the table and me at the other end, with friends and family lined up on either side. A big turkey in the center. Oh, this daydreaming habit of mine could be dangerous.

He pointed at the windows. "See those? There's a few panels of stained glass in the basement that I think belong there. As soon as I can arrange it, I'm going to call someone to see if they can repair them. Mostly blues and greens, and some red and gold. Nothing fancy, but I figure it'll be nice with the sun setting in the evening. This is a western exposure."

"That'll influence your decorating," I said as I touched a wall with a paper pattern that could only be William Morris.

It was old and crumbled beneath my fingertips. "Are you taking pictures so you can admire your progress, maybe try to match the colors and patterns?"

"Yeah. I have a notebook going. We'll have to gut most of the rooms, but I took a bunch of pictures the day I bought it. Once I sell it, I figure those will be a big selling point so the buyer can see how much care went into the restoration."

My heart stopped in my chest. "You're going to go to all that work to fix this place up and then sell it?" I spun around to stare at him, nearly in tears. I could hardly explain why. Maybe he'd put it down to an overactive imagination. I certainly wasn't falling in love with him, was I? Or with his house.

"Well yeah," he said, looking confused. "This place is much too big for me. It's a house for a family or a frat."

"Oh." I felt my spirits sink. Had I really imagined myself ensconced here some wintry night, entertaining our family and friends in this wonderful room? Or saw myself sitting on the front porch in a rocking chair one spring evening, surrounded by pots of petunias and geraniums, maybe a dog at my feet, waiting for Moe to come home to me? Sometimes I let my imagination run away from me a little too far. I mean, he might prefer cats. "Of course."

"Come on. The kitchen's through here. There's a butler's pantry between, and another off the back. I'm going to take it all out and restore it exactly as it was. I've never seen a modern design that can match this."

"Sure." My enthusiasm fled, and I looked around with a sense of despair I could not explain. It wasn't as if it were ever going to be my home. He was joking earlier, that talk of engagements and marriage. Some guys run from that kind of talk while others have no trouble spouting it, but then never do anything about it. He must be the latter kind.

I followed Moe though the arched doorway into the kitchen. If I'd thought that the foyer was a mess, this was a mass of confusion. The room had already been gutted down to the studs. There was a folding table with a coffee pot and hot plate. A small refrigerator was pushed into a corner. "I figured I'd best get this room ready next after the bedroom and bath. My mother said that it's the kitchen that will sell a house, so I don't want to blow it."

I nodded and wandered to the back door. It was dark now, but in the moonlight, I could see a huge lawn with a tangle of shrubs. I imagined a gazebo in the far corner, but when I blinked, all I saw was a barren maple.

There was another small parlor and finished maid's bedroom on the first floor that might make a good home office. I could see where Moe and his brothers were making headway with their restoration, could almost picture what it would look like from his enthusiastic description. There was no furniture to speak of.

That's when he took me upstairs. First off was what had been the master bedroom. The airy room was in a corner overlooking the back of the house, with arched windows on two sides. There was a fireplace that leant it a certain charm, and a dressing room that could be converted into a walk-in closet and a luxurious master bath.

There were three non-descript bedrooms on the floor. But when he opened the final door and switched on a light, the breath caught in my throat.

The room was small, but compared to the rest of the house, was in almost pristine condition. The walls were solid, and only a few flakes had come down from the ceiling. Windows flanked the two sides facing the street, but best of all, between then sat a small, round glassed-in turret with a window seat perfect for two.

"The heat's off up here for now. I'll put it back on once

we're ready to work."

He stood back and let me wander around. The only thing in the room was a drop cloth in the corner.

I took a tentative step inside, and the rush of emotion was nearly was my undoing. I turned from him as if to look out the window, but in reality, I needed a moment to gather myself. I closed my eyes and took a deep breath. In this room, I could write a best seller, a string of them. It wasn't just my fancy at work here. I could see myself in this room—in this house.

I could feel him watching me, and slowly opened my eyes to see him look at my reflection in the window. His image wavered in the old glass, and I could not make out his expression.

"How much?" I asked. Holy cow. It wasn't like me to be so impulsive. "How much do you want for this place?" I turned. "I want to buy it."

He frowned at me. "Slow down lady. I hadn't gotten that far." He gave a small chuckle. "If you want it in its present condition, that's one thing, but I really have my heart set on restoring this house to its former glory. That's going to take some money."

"I have money."

It was true. Although I forced myself to live on what I made, I had a trust fund from my grandparents that was mine to control. Surely there was enough to cover the cost of this house. "We can sit down right now and negotiate."

"Darned, I left my two new chairs in the truck," he smiled. "I don't want you rushing into anything, darlin'. Let's think about this a little. I still have to show you the third floor. It's in pretty bad shape from the leaking roof, and you might change your mind. And the basement. Can't buy a house without kicking the tires."

I shook myself. Of course. It's just that the wild rush I

felt was unlike anything else I'd ever felt.

He walked over to me and stopped, staring. Bending at the neck, he pressed his lips to mine gently. "If I knew you were going to want to negotiate, I would have brought you here first thing, rather than make you wait all this time. Of course, it could be all that wine you drank today. I think we both know what happens when you've had more than you should." He chuckled and kissed me again to let me know he was teasing. This time, he brought up one hand that he ran through my hair before it returned to cradle my face. It was warm and rough, and nothing had ever felt quite so good. The yearning I'd felt a moment before to own this house suddenly changed to a yearning of a whole other sort. I stepped closer and wrapped my arms around his waist, reaching up to deepen the kiss and press myself against him.

"Do you want to see the rest of the house?" he asked, his lips against my hair.

I shook my head.

"Then let's go back downstairs," he said. But instead of moving, his arms came around me, nearly lifting me off my feet as he pressed his big, hard body against me. His mouth claimed mine, and I think I forgot to breathe.

Where before his kisses had left me hungry for more, this time, they made me wild. I wanted nothing so much as to crawl up his body and perch there, feeding him kisses and taking more in return. I must have moaned or yelped or something, for he broke away and looked down at me, his eyes half-closed in passion.

"Berry," he whispered. "I want you so bad. Are you going to make me wait six months to have you? I will if I have to, but by the time you're ready, I'll have shriveled into nothing. If I don't die of starvation first."

I shivered and lifted onto my toes to kiss him again. My

mind was mush, but there was one thing I knew. I didn't want to make him wait. I didn't think I could bear it. I knew him well enough to know he was the one I wanted to make love to me forevermore. I opened my eyes again and looked at him. "No. Don't starve," I told him. "I want you too."

Chapter Seventeen

Berry

I could feel the difference in him immediately. Something eased, gentled. His hands still held me, but his touch was lighter.

"I do believe you mean it," he whispered against my lips before he claimed them. And as he did that, the rest of me followed eagerly.

In the time I had known him, Moe never wavered. The man seemed to run on instinct, and now was no exception. There was no dithering or hesitation. Now that I'd made up my mind, I didn't have to think another thought, for Moe was on the job.

"Picture a roaring fire in that fireplace," he urged between kisses. "Imagine there's a huge, soft mattress right at our feet, with soft sheets and warm blankets. No, a bed." His tongue invaded my mouth, and shameless hussy that I am, I opened wider to give him access. His hands ran up my back, and I obligingly shed my jacket and began to tug at the down vest he wore.

Moe dropped to his knees and tugged me down as well. "Pretend we've just had a gourmet dinner. Oysters. Lobster." His hands trembled as they worked the buttons of my blouse and pulled its hem from my pants.

I took up his theme. "With champagne and chocolate-covered strawberries for dessert. Candlelight. And we're sated with food. Our eyes meet across the long table, and you rise and come to me." I worked at the buttons of his thick flannel shirt. "You take my hand and lead me to the bedroom."

"Where I kiss the bejesus out of you," he panted before he began to nibble at my neck.

I frowned and then laughed. He stopped and looked at me before he grinned. "Excuse me. Where I kiss you passionately and convince you without words that tonight is the night I am to become your lover."

I nodded approvingly. "I'll make a romance writer of you yet." I nibbled at his chin.

"I'll settle for being the lover of this romance writer if you don't mind." He then leaned back and looked at me. My shirt gaped open from my shoulders. I hadn't thought much about my bra this morning, but I'd been lucky enough to choose one with a front closure.

He ran one large finger slowly from my chin down my breastbone to the clasp before he met my eyes. "You sure you want to do this?" he asked, suddenly uncertain. It was so endearing I wanted to weep.

I covered his hand with mine. "I am," I assured him, sounding more confident than I'd felt a few moments before. My other hand finished working on his buttons to reveal his chest. I swallowed hard at the sight of that magnificence. Broad and packed with more muscles than a man should have, it was covered with a light tangle of hair. I could feel my nipples pebble at the sight of it, imagined what it would be like to rub myself all over him. My mouth went dry as I pressed close. All my phantom lovers had been hairless. What had I been thinking? I've never seen or felt anything so alluring in all my life. The next time I was at my PC, Captain Conrad was going to get a makeover, and Svetlana an unexpected treat.

"Wow," I whispered as I reached for him to run my hands across him. I touched one dark nipple and felt him shudder. "Do you like it when I touch you there?" I asked.

He closed his eyes and nodded. "Darlin', I like it when

you touch me anywhere." He opened one eye to watch me. "And if you need any help figuring out where to start, I've got lots of suggestions."

I laughed, and any remaining tension melted away. "Don't forget, I'm a romance writer. I've got a few ideas."

"Having read only one of your books, I know that. And I can't wait to try some of them out."

He kissed me again and knee-walked his way closer, until we stood thigh to thigh, chest to breast.

"I don't recall a scene exactly like this in my book," I remarked as he progressed to kiss my neck and shoulder. "I'm glad to see you know how to improvise."

"I'm the improv king," he whispered as he worked his way across my collarbone. "I never know what I'm going to do or say next."

That's when I threw back my head and let go of any remaining control to his capable hands.

Those hands, those talented, tender, creative hands gently caressed my breasts before he moved down to my hips and cupped my rear. He pressed me hard against him, and I felt how turned on he was. I wanted to touch him so badly down there, but my hands were pressed between us, and I could do nothing but caress that massive chest. I could feel my own hard nipples on the backs of my hands, and I think I cried out in pleasure or in pain, wanting to press my flesh against his. I pulled my hands free and caught him around the neck. Capturing his lips, I licked and kissed and sucked them until I caught his lower lip between my teeth and tugged.

"I want you," I hissed. I couldn't help myself. "I don't feel like myself, I feel so wild, so needy."

"Is it Berry here with me, or is it Solange?" he asked with his endearing smile as he took my glasses and set them aside. He kissed me then, and if I thought he'd been thorough before, it was nothing like now when he ravaged my mouth and pressed me down, all the while his hands caressing my rear. The truth was, I had no idea who I was at that moment—Berry, Solange, Trista, Svetlana, or some character I had yet to conceive, or all of them. And I didn't care.

"Undo your bra," he commanded, and I did, finally pressing my skin to his. It was better than what I had imagined, and I did rub myself against him until we were both panting at the contact. Inside my pants, my panties were wet. I wiggled then. I couldn't help it.

"I have to taste your nipples," he said and before I could react, he'd bent his head and sucked one into his mouth, suckling so hard I nearly came then and there. Another jolt of moisture came from me, and I whimpered. It was beyond me to control the sound.

His other hand left my leg and came to fondle my breast, exploring it thoroughly, pinching and weighing and making me crazy for him. He then sucked that one too into his mouth as he began to caress the first, now wet and harder than ever from contact with the cold air.

He draped his flannel shirt over my shoulders, still warm from his body. "Lay down," he urged as he flipped open the drop cloth behind me. "Let's get you out of those pants.

Gladly, I thought. *At last.* I landed with a small plop on the muslin, my legs spread wide, and he kneeled between. I looked at him, from the top of his wild hair (had my hands really done that to him?), slowly down his face, to visually caress that magnificent chest once again. And then, when my eyes lit upon the bulge in his pants, I think I licked my lips. That was so unlike me. Honestly, I have never been so turned on. It was perhaps the most erotic moment of my life.

"You are so beautiful," he said as he cupped my face and kissed me hard. His hands were at my waist, undoing the button and zipper, taking side forays up to caress my breasts and made me crazier with desire. "I want to do everything to you, with you, all at once. You're a feast, and I don't know where to begin."

He began to tug my pants down my legs, and I had to close them to allow it. Then there was the issue of my boots still being on my feet, and we laughed as we scrambled to free me of those. Somehow in the mix, he seemed to have left my panties on. He frowned at the sight, but then gave a little smile as he ran a finger down and around, outlining me with it, feeling how wet I'd become.

Moe leaned forward and kissed me until I lay flat, his hands never leaving me. With his knees, he spread my legs wide and then hitched a finger under the leg of my panties and touched me, really touched me. It felt so good I jumped, and my jumping seems to have urged that finger inside me, and before I knew what was happening, there he was, looking about as pleased as a man can get.

I think I closed my eyes and stilled then. I was so close to the edge. My head was spinning, and I didn't trust myself to think, let alone speak. I am pretty sure I clenched my muscles around that finger then, for he stopped too. I could hear the two of us breathing hard. I opened one eye to find him looking at me, his eyes trailing over my body and coming to rest on my face.

"You going to let us do this?" he asked with a quirk to his brow. "I promise it will be worth it."

I nodded and forced myself to unclench. "It had better be." Oh, that was definitely Solange talking. Berry would never dare. And that grin he gave me—priceless.

He was right. He was good, very good with his hand.

He took his time and made all the right moves. But he stopped as I was approaching the end, and he laughed as he withdrew from me. "Not so fast. I think I can do better than that," he said as he set both hands at my crotch. I was spread out before him, and he was firmly planted between my legs. "You like this underwear much? Spend a lot on it?"

I shook my head.

Before I could think about what he planned to do, his fingers twisted the thin cotton and tore them open. He laughed then and scooted back. "Hang on," he whispered as he set his lips on me. Down there. Oh, heavens.

Now, I'm not a connoisseur of these things. I haven't been with enough men for one thing, and for another—well, I've got a bit of a reputation for being a prude if you must know. Yes, me, the romance writer a prude. Deal with it. What I mean to say is, I didn't have a lot to compare to this experience. What I also mean is, after this, I was thinking that no one would ever hold a candle to what that man was doing to my body. Ever.

I moaned. I thrashed. I whimpered, and I think I even begged. I was on the edge of my seat, so to speak. And he wouldn't let me come. I tried, I really did, but each time I was about to, he pulled away and let me suffer. I swear, the man chuckled evilly a few times when he did. I lost track of time, exhausted from the effort and beside myself with passion.

"Come on," I cried when he left me entirely. He sat up and tugged my tattered panties down my leg. That's when I heard him undo his belt buckle and draw down his zipper. Through half-closed eyes, I saw him sit up and tug his pants down around his big, square knees and rise up above me.

He came down on all fours and kissed me deeply. I

could taste myself on him and licked eagerly, knowing that the end was now near. I picked up my knees, helping him zero in on the spot where I needed him most. I think I may have wrapped a leg around his hip, urging him down. Maybe two legs. Certainly my arms did the same. But he wouldn't budge. Oh, there was a cruel spot to Moe that I would never have guessed. He liked to see me crazed with passion, beside myself with need. I slit my eyes at him and stuck out my tongue. That only made him laugh harder.

"Almost forgot." He reached for his wallet and pulled out a crumpled looking packet. I think I covered my eyes then, not wanting to see the sight of him rolling that condom down his massive length. If I looked too much, I'd be scared and lose this what-ever-had me in its grip.

"Ready now." I felt him press against my body, right at the front door. "You're sure you want this, right?" he asked.

I opened my eyes then. "If you don't make love to me right now, Conrad, you're a dead man."

He found that hysterical for some reason and pressed a little harder. "Okay, I guess that means you're not going to turn me away."

I could see the look of concentration on his face then, the strain. If he wanted me half as much as I wanted him, then all of this must have been as torturous for him. More so, for at least I had the benefit of all his caresses.

He eased into me slowly, carefully, pulling out and pushing in as if he was teasing himself this time. I reached for his neck and tugged him down for another kiss. "All the way in, buddy," I ordered softly. "Playtime's over. You need to get down to business."

Maybe he liked bossy women. Maybe he was tired or frustrated or simply ready, but he didn't need any more urging to sink in all the way.

Nothing has ever felt so right in all my life as the

sensation of having him buried inside me. I wiggled a little to ease his way, and he seemed to like that, so I tried it again.

"Easy now," he crooned before he tweaked my breast and made me jump. "We don't want this to be over too soon."

"Easy for you to say," I managed to whisper. "You're not the one who's been sensually tortured for the past hour."

He laughed and swiveled his hips, making me clench him all over again. "Oh, that's good," he groaned. "And if you think you're the only one who's been tortured, what do you think it's done to me to play with you all this time?" He kissed me rather than let me answer.

"Oh," was all I could manage as I closed my eyes and arched my back. "More," I urged him. "Give me more of you."

Like I said before, I think he liked pushy women, for he did as I asked, pumping his hips harder, changing his rhythm and driving me mad. "Babe," he ground out. "You feel so good."

He pushed against a particularly sensitive spot, and I lifted my hips so he could find it again. That was all it took to finally push me over the edge. "Moe," I cried. "I'm coming. I can't stop."

"Let it flow, baby. Let me see you come. God, but I've never seen anything so beautiful."

His deep voice was what did it. I clenched around him hard and felt my orgasm take my body, not just down below, but all the way up my arms and down my legs. My eyelids tingled. My fingernails would have spasmed if such a thing were possible. It would not stop, wave after wave continued as he pumped into me. I honestly thought I would die from the pleasure of it. He pressed harder and harder, his face straining above me until I brought his lips down for a kiss. I thrust my tongue into his mouth, and then he left me to bury his face in my neck and let out a growl the likes of which I have never heard before.

His hips thrust again and again in a frenzy as he came. He cursed softly as he gathered me closer and kissed me until I was breathless. And then he was still.

"My God Berry, that was amazing," he breathed against my neck a long while later. "You are a wonder, girl."

I could do nothing but hold him close. My body was still twanging, and I tightened around him as each aftershock wracked me.

"Easy sweetheart, unless you want to start me up all over again."

I kissed his ear. I felt wholly unlike myself, and what I was feeling wasn't bad. "I'm game if you are," I challenged.

"You're on." He shot to his feet with a disgusting display of energy, and reaching out a hand, dragged me to mine. "Which room do you want to do it in this time?"

Chapter Eighteen

Moe

Okay, color me surprised. I hadn't set out that morning expecting to make love to Berry that night. I'd hoped, of course, but never let myself expect it. And twice? A man can dream. Sometimes those dreams come true.

We'd made love in the smallest bedroom. I'll never again think of that room as being cramped and dull. Downstairs was a mess, and there were no shades on the windows, but up here, there was a master bedroom that was private.

I grabbed her hand and the drop cloth and made for the largest room on the floor. Berry trailed after me. She'd grabbed her glasses first, then her pants, and held them in front of her. Of course, I'd never lost mine. I can't remember the last time I'd made love in anything but my skin, but it was cold up there. She must be freezing, what with that cute little tush of hers all exposed, not to mention the fact that she wore only a thin blouse over her shoulders, mine over it, and her open bra. I paused as we passed the stairs and tugged my down vest around her shoulders. I can be a gentleman when I need to be.

"This time," I told her as I spread the cloth on the floor, "it's ladies' choice. Now that you've seen what a dog I am, and want more of me anyway, you get to decide what we do and how we do it."

I peeled the condom off and flung it away. I'm not usually that much of a slob, but I was going to gut these rooms one of these days. "And I know I've got another one of these in my pocket, so not to worry. You're not on birth control, are you?" I dug around in said pocket and dropped the packet on the floor beside us.

She shook her head and blushed. Actually, blushed after all we'd done. I could really fall in love with her—more than I was already.

"No matter." I stood there with my hands on my hips, my fly undone, and I was getting hard just looking at her. "So?"

She looked all flustered. "I'm not used to—you know, driving," was what she finally said.

"No?" I had to think. She'd been bossy enough a few minutes ago, turning me on like crazy with her breathless demands.

"My characters are," she amended. "Never me."

"Well, then how about you pretend you're one of them." I pulled her closer and rubbed her chilly posterior with my hands to help her thinking along. "And I'll be whoever you want me to be."

Berry's eyes grew all dreamy then. I would have paid a million dollars to know what was going on in that mind of hers, but I settled for kissing her instead.

"There is one thing," she said as she sank to her knees. "I'm not very good at this, but I'd like to get better."

One of her small hands reached inside my pants and drew me out, half hard and getting harder. She rubbed her smooth cheeks all over the happy fella until he was standing at attention all by himself. Oh yeah baby. If you want to practice, fire away. I'm your man.

"Tell me if I do this wrong," she said, looking up at me as she took me into her mouth.

"Yeah, I'll speak right up," I ground out between my teeth as the sweetest possible sensation engulfed me.

She might have been a novice, but she was a natural. Her lips and tongue didn't need any tutoring, and then she groaned. I swear, I felt it all the way to my toes.

I withstood her sweet torture for as long as I could. But ultimately, I had to pull away. I don't think she'd want me to come in her mouth her first time out.

"Slow down, sweetheart, save something for later," I told her as I kneeled to kiss her. She pouted, and I had no choice but to suck that lower lip into my mouth. I could taste myself on her. I could taste her. I could spend the rest of my life looking forward to being with her. "That was heaven. Now let me give you some?"

I tried to push her down so I could lap up some more of her tasty juices, but she shook her head. "Not again. You made me crazy the last time, waiting. This time it's my turn to do the same to you."

Oh great. Our first time making love, and I created a monster. Did I say, 'oh great'? I meant every word. "I don't think you understand," I tried to explain. "I'm afraid it doesn't work equally between us. You see, women are so much more advanced emotionally than men are, they can take it. Us guys, we're babies. Far too simple-minded for our own good. You give us a little punishment, and it goes a long way."

She cocked her head at me and smiled. It was an evil smile. Believe it or not, I got harder still.

"Bull." She pointed a finger at me and snapped her fingers. "Down."

Oh, I was one happy man.

I suppose I could have turned the tables on her and taken her across my knee to spank her then, but I'd left my two brand-new antique chairs in the truck. Besides, we could get to the advanced stuff another night. I went down to my knees.

She shook her head. "Lie down. I want to be on top."

Thank-you god. I've died and gone to heaven.

"Take off your boots and pants. I want to see you this time," she ordered.

I had to obey, right? It was the least I could do. After all, she was almost naked, and you don't cross a naked woman. "Can I have my shirt back?"

She shook her head but shrugged out of my down vest. "Here."

It was better than nothing.

I lay down, and I think I trembled as she took a long look at me from her stance above. When she straddled me, my little soldier grew harder than he'd ever been before. I'm not a writer, so you'll have to take my word for it that the view from below was worth all the agony of lying on my back in a cold-as-shit room with next to nothing on. I was all for repeating the experience somewhere else another time, say a tropical beach somewhere. My bedroom or hers. A warm cave perhaps. Not to be. I folded my arms under my head and prepared to enjoy whatever it was she had in mind.

It didn't take long to find out. She squatted over me, then sat her cute little rump on my belly before she leaned forward and parted the hair on my chest. Before I could breathe, she started to lick my nipples. Impatient, Jonesy tapped her on the butt from behind to get her attention, but she was otherwise fully engaged. Impatient fella that he is, he tapped again, and she reached behind her to shush him, her hand lingering to caress him, her fingers warm in the cold air.

In case you get the wrong idea, I was enjoying myself immensely.

I guess she got tired of fighting all the chest hairs, for she reached up and kissed me on the mouth, licking my lips and biting them, then moving on to my neck and the skin below my ear. Now, I don't tell this to many people, but that's a particularly ticklish spot for me. I didn't dare laugh. Instead, I found myself curling up and pressing her forward with my legs. She got the message, for she eased up there and began to pay more attention to what was going on behind her.

That's when she started rubbing against me, clenching me hard with her thighs. Yeah, that place where she was sitting was nice and hot and getting wetter by the moment. Mini-Me tapped her again, needing a little of that warmth himself. To help her along, I managed to unbend my arms and reach for her breasts. Have I mentioned how nice those were? Soft, full with the right amount of loft. I was getting kind of anxious to see how much they would bounce in this new position.

I didn't have long to wait. Berry was playing behind herself again, and those two fascinating mounds of flesh were jiggling enough to make me a happy man. She rolled on my protective cover, and when she lifted herself and began to impale herself on me—need I say more?

I'll be a gentleman now and won't give you the blow by blow description. Suffice to say, Berry was as natural and adept at this as she was at her earlier attention to my body. And she was inventive, not afraid to experiment. And her breasts bounced plenty inside my shirt. I couldn't take my eyes off them, except to look at the rest of her lovely body. And darned if she didn't time her orgasm to coincide with my own explosion. How do you like that? I liked it plenty.

In the aftermath, she fell upon me, panting and smiling. I wrapped my arms around her to keep her from sliding off or wriggling away. Most guys may not care for it, but there was little I liked better than the sensation of a sated, drowsy, mostly naked woman draped across me. It also ensured that the little prince stayed warm, tucked up inside her for that much longer.

When she started to shiver, I knew it was my cue to get moving. I rubbed her bum to rouse her. "Hey sleeping beauty. I need to get you home. The rest of the tour will have to wait another day."

She lifted her head and blinked at me with a slow smile. "You promised to make love to me in every room of your house." Darned if Buster didn't perk up at the thought, but the poor boy was tired.

"I intend to keep that promise. But only Superman can do this more than twice in one night at my age." I rolled to my feet and staggered upward, pulling her vertical too. I hugged her. "The next time we do this, we'd both be naked. Maybe on a bed. A carpet at least. It's better that way. Not that I'm complaining."

I picked up her wrist to look at her watch. Going on midnight. "Let's get you and your pumpkins home," I told her as I dropped a kiss on her head. "Unless you want to stop for a beer somewhere?"

She leaned her head against my arm. I love it when a woman does that. A mostly naked woman. Named Berry.

She yawned before she wrinkled her nose. "If I remember correctly, I no longer have any underwear. I'm not sure I feel comfortable going commando in public."

"I don't mind knowing there's nothing between you and me but your jeans," I said in all seriousness. "One less layer to get through next time." I thought a moment more. "Since you're already wearing my shirt, you want to borrow my shorts too?"

She blushed at that. As we reached the first room where we'd done it, she pulled on her pants and started on her socks and boots before she handed me my shirt. "Thanks for the loan." Then she yawned again.

"Forget the beer. I want to see you tucked into bed."

"I won't argue with that," she said with her eyes closed.

I guess I really did wear her out. Hooray for me.

We finished dressing and went downstairs. As I locked the front door and held her arm as we crossed the treacherous front porch, she stopped me. "I really did mean it about buying this house. There's something about it that speaks to me."

"And I'm serious about making sure you get it," I replied. I didn't bother to tell her about the plan that was beginning to form in my brain. It needed a few tweaks before I could comment further.

Twenty minutes later, we were at her front door. I was leaning in to kiss her goodnight as I had done for the past two weeks when she surprised me yet again and reached down to caress my package. "Do you have to leave right away, or do you want to come in for a little while? Warm-up?" she whispered with a husky voice.

"I thought you were tired."

"I napped in the truck," she replied with a saucy little smile.

Despite dire predictions of utter failure, my teammate was willing to give it a go. But there was one problem. "I'm out of condoms."

She unlocked her door and pulled me inside. "I'm sure we can find a solution."

"You keep a supply on hand?" I frowned.

"Nope." She locked the door behind me. "But remember, I'm inventive. And so are you."

She headed for the bathroom and began to take off her clothes. When I hesitated, she started in on mine. "What are you about, woman?" I asked.

She looked at me funny. "I want to warm us up. And we were rolling around your floor. Not to insult your house, but the dust was pretty thick. I'd like to wash it off. Of me, and you."

Oh, you do have to love a practical woman. I reached down to unlace my boots for the second time that night.

I guess she felt she needed more practice on what she started earlier, or she was real hot on cleanliness, 'cause even when I felt reasonably clean, she got down on her knees to inspect me. She must have found a spot of dirt, for in the next breath, she was licking me clean with her tongue. It took a while, and we nearly ran out of hot water, but by golly, once she was done with me, I was clean inside and out.

I staggered out of her tub and nearly fell to my knees in gratitude. Instead, she handed me a towel and asked me to dry her back. One thing led to another, and somehow we ended up in the bedroom. She was sprawled on her back, and her legs were draped around my shoulders. It was my turn to inspect her. She was as clean as can be, but I did a little more anyway, 'cause she seemed to want me to. I am nothing if not an obliging fellow.

I had just enough energy to pull the blankets up over us, but not much more. The lights were already out, and the door locked. There was little left to do but gather her into my arms, smell the sweet scent of her shampoo, close my eyes, and go to sleep.

Somewhere in the early morning hours, well before the sun thought about putting in an appearance, I remembered it was my turn to feed my buddy's dog. He and his woman were off to Mexico for a short vacation, and he'd left the rest of us in charge of his mutt. The dog was used to going out at six AM, and here it was nearly that.

I looked at Berry, sleeping peacefully in my arms. If I could wake up to her face every morning, I'd be a happy man for the rest of my life. I admit I stared a good bit, drinking her in without having to contend with her getting embarrassed about it. And before you ask, yes, I liked what I saw. A lot. Her face was soft in sleep, and she was smiling. She'd probably hate the fact she had a pillow crease in her cheek, but I thought it added to her allure. Besides, her hair was all tangled around and about as sexy as anything I've ever seen. I was making plans to convince her to let her curls have free reign.

Old Repeat downstairs had some ideas and started to thrum with excitement, but I gave him a stern talking-to and, he sulked his way back down. Too bad. She did look especially delectable that morning, but I was still out of condoms. And as eager as the little guy was, I wasn't sure he'd live up to his boasts. I mean, he'd done his best three times in the past eight hours, and he needed a little time to rejuvenate, even if he didn't think so. Maybe tonight we could play some more.

I snuck out of bed and managed to gather my clothes and put them on. I searched for a piece of paper and left her a note. I contemplated long and hard before I started. She is a writer, after all. I didn't want to embarrass myself.

I went back and kissed her again before I left. Not such a good idea because then I was even more reluctant to leave. I forced myself to think about what I'd have to clean up if I didn't get my tail out of her place, and that was enough.

Berry

I woke up to the sun shining through the windows, stretched, and wondered why I felt so good and had sore muscles at the same time. It took no more than a moment before I remembered and smiled.

Moe was gone, but that was okay. We'd never talked about him staying the night. That would have been too much to expect this early in our relationship. Sleeping with him was a bit early too, but never mind that. What was done was done, and I couldn't find it in me to dredge up a single regret. And it wasn't like he'd bolted. That would have been unforgivable. No, he'd stayed and cuddled and snored in my ear until I fell asleep in his arms. What's to complain about that? The thought that his boots had been under my bed for even part of the night made me absolutely gushy.

To be completely honest, the thought of any part of him made me feel squishy, and it would have been nice to have him there to help relieve—or enhance it.

Nope, nothing to complain about on that front.

I threw off the covers and grabbed my robe. Standing, I stretched and felt muscles I hadn't noticed in years. I went in to brush my teeth and wouldn't you know, the toilet seat was up. Not even that bothered me.

When I got to my kitchen, I saw the huge pumpkin Moe insisted on buying. He'd drawn a frowny face on it with an arrow pointing down to the note below. I smiled as I picked it up and read:

> Had to leave to feed my friend's dog. Call me and we can get together later. If I don't hear from you, I'm coming in after you.
> Love, Moe

Love, huh? I smiled again and held the paper to my chest. Maybe not love yet, but if this was pure lust, bring it on.

Conrad looked at the sleeping Svetlana.

Somehow~~, sometime~~ during the night, his anger dissipated and was replaced by a longing that he was at a loss to explain. He wanted her still—that had not changed. Neither was the sting that she had lied to him, had planned to kill him. But the anger—that was missing along with her clothes, her pride, her very sense of self. What he had taken from her more than outweighed what she owed him.

He felt something different. Was it remorse? It was a new emotion for him and one he could not explain. With a gentle finger, he brushed a long curly lock from her face, the better to see her high cheekbones, the pale skin and fine brow ~~he'd come to love~~ he loved so dearly. Her ruby lips were parted in her sleep and in her repose her face was that of an angel. One slender wrist poked out of the bedclothes, and he winced at the red rope burn caused by the bindings of the night before when she would not stop her attempts at murder. It had not been until after she'd fallen asleep that he'd released her, ~~to~~ and rid the room of weapons.

With careful fingers, he picked up that damaged wrist and gently brought it to his lips. The truth was, he had not released her until after he had read the letter her master had sent her, the one where her sister's torture was explained in excruciating detail. No wonder Svetlana had gone crazy in her attempts to kill him. It was the only way she knew to free her sister and herself.

What his darling Svetlana did not yet know was that Conrad had sent his own agents on the road to Moscow months before to free the young girl and had, in fact, succeeded. Anna was now stowed safely with a family Conrad knew, and eagerly awaited a reunion with her sister. Her master had somehow learned that Svetlana did not yet know this detail and continued to torture her through the miles with these letters.

That ~~he~~ the man still lived irked Conrad to no small degree. But he would rectify that problem before ~~much~~ more time passed.

Svetlana did not yet know he knew all about it, that he had freed Anna.

He regretted now his keeping this news from her. It had been a cruel ploy to try to get her to admit her love for him, to trick her into declaring her trust. In the darkest hours of the night, he'd come to realize he'd done little to earn it. Instead of her begging him for forgiveness, the right way of things was for him to go down on his knees before her.

"Crap." **Conrad looked up at me with a scowl.** "This is utter crap. I can't believe you're doing this to me."

I shook my head and corrected a typo or two. "This is what readers want. Handsome, strong, determined men brought to their knees by love."

"But that's not what I would do," **Conrad**

insisted. "I would have tied her up and had my way with her. Then I would have told her, and she would have fallen prostrate on the floor at my feet, forever grateful for my intervention. She would not question it."

"I would." Svetlana woke up from her deep sleep and pushed Conrad off the bed with a hearty shove. "I would have fallen to your feet, but gratitude not last long. Resentment in heart that you keep me in the dark so long. I redouble my efforts to kill you for that. Solange has it better this way."

"You would not." Conrad folded his arms against his massive, smooth chest. Darned, but I meant to rewrite this scene with chest hair.

"Would too," Svetlana insisted as she copied his pose.

"Not."

"Would.

"Would the two of you please resume your places so I can complete the scene? How can you presume to know what I'm going to write next?"

They remained as they were, naked and obstinate as I clicked and dragged up half a page and put my finger on the delete key. "You do as I say, or you'll both be sorry."

The looked at each other and then at me before they scrambled back under the covers.

I found my place and resumed writing, feeling rather smug.

He had to be strong. He would ask her forgiveness, but in his own way. And she would grant it to him, for that was foreordained. Women were to submit to men.

Conrad smirked.

But he wanted Svetlana to forgive him. Making love to her tied to the bed last night had brought him relief and her pleasure, but it had been diminished because she had not been free to love him back. The next time would be like the first when she had given him her body freely, openly, joyfully.

"I told you this," **Svetlana muttered.** "But do you listen?"
"Shhh," I told her.

This time, he would kiss her awake and make slow, careful love to her. And when she was sobbing in relief and joy, he would tell her of his scheming, admit to his plotting, and that her sister was now free. That they would join her soon. As soon as the weather cleared, and they could set sail for her homeland. His crew was waiting. Maybe tomorrow. The next day at the latest. This storm could not last much longer.

Conrad turned to his sleeping lover and whispered, "I love you," before he leaned down to kiss those wine-red lips.

She murmured sleepily to herself and

opened her mouth to his.

I sighed to myself. Would it have killed Moe to kiss me awake this morning? Certainly, my situation with him was nothing like Svetlana and Conrad's, but it would have been nice to kiss him, maybe say good morning and see you later. But he was out of condoms, and we would have needed one. I would have wanted that. Oh well.

His kisses traveled down her face to cover her neck and the top of her chest. Moments later, his lips caressed her breasts, slurping her nipples into his mouth as his hand took to exploring the territory of her lovely body.

"Slurp?" Conrad shook his head. "I don't even slurp my soup."

"I'll fix it later," I promised. "Don't stop me when I'm on a roll."

He shrugged and regained his position at her breast.

His hands found her center of pleasure, and with nimble fingers, he began to comb through her nether curls, his fingers running up the seam of her honeycomb. With a sleepy sigh, Svetlana opened her legs to his questing fingers.

He lay on his side, his head propped on his hand as he set himself to pleasuring her. Her lovely brow furrowed in concentration as he continued to work on her body. Luscious, ripe lips opened on a moan, and she lifted her hips to meet his hand, her body instinctively seeking out the rhythm that they both desired.

A moment later, her deep blue eyes opened to his, the pupils huge in the dim light of morning.

"Good morning, my love," Conrad rumbled in his deep voice. "I trust you slumbered peacefully?"

He could see the warring emotions on her face: lust at what her body desired, hatred of him, and just a wee bit of confusion thrown in for good measure.

He covered her body with his own before she could think much deeper on any of these subjects, and slid down to lap at her honey.

She arched her back and came quickly, but he gave her no rest, for he started in again, his hands reaching up to pinch her nipples lightly, making her cry out.

Slender legs bent at the knee as she cradled him at her very core. She cried out again and again until she begged him to cease swamping her with pleasure.

Conrad suddenly sat up. He looked straight at me. "Something is different. She was salty before. You make her sweet now. I am not a barbarian any longer, but a gentleman. What has changed?"

Svetlana managed to pick up her head too, though her eyes were still drowsy with sensual satisfaction. "She is in love, you dolt. Someone made love to her last night, and not a prototype. A real man."

"No shite?" Conrad sat back on his heels and rubbed his hands together with a gleam in his eyes. "Can't wait to hear all the details."

Chapter Nineteen

Berry

I wrestled with my characters most of the day. They would not cooperate, no matter what I did. Conrad wanted to know how Moe had made love to me, and Svet what I had done to him, and although I could not stop thinking about it, I didn't want to share the details with them. They accused me of lording it over them, and I had to admit that yes, that was the nature of our relationship. I was their creator. I got to tell them what to do. I didn't mind their input in their lives and their story, but in the end, my life was not theirs to know.

Trista and Brad hadn't been as pushy when I was writing their story. Of course, I had no lover then. They had been well mannered, but that's how I'd written them. It had taken quite a while for me to formulate Trista's character just so. In the beginning, before I even wrote a word, she'd fought me to be made tougher, hard as nails. But that wasn't the type of character I wanted. I'd had in mind someone more genteel and sweet. Maybe she never forgave me for that, but look at all I had given her.

Brad, on the other hand, had been grateful for his good looks, his money, and the size of the package in his pants. What he really liked was the fast car I gave him, and the one bar fight I'd managed to dream up where he defended Triss's honor. Talk about fitting something convoluted into my story—the only fights I'd ever seen had been on the screen.

At least Conrad and Svetlana stayed on my computer screen and didn't pop into the room. Maybe that was something that had to wait until after the story was published. I rubbed my aching head. I had yet to explain Brad and Trista's true nature to Moe, and they were 'contemporary' characters. Or had I? A fuzzy memory of our first date resurfaced. I could almost swear I'd confessed my friends' true nature. Well, if I did, he hadn't believed me. Not that he asked about them often, but when he did, it was certainly in the guise of their being real people.

At least they hadn't returned. If they were out wandering the world somewhere, they were doing so without contacting me.

I saved the *To Love a Rogue* file and closed it. I then turned to my other computer, the one hooked up to the internet and turned it on. I quickly went to my website and checked my email. Ever since *You're the One for Me* was published, I tried to answer fan-mail as quickly as I could. There had been a surprising amount of it. I considered it the equivalent of applause at the end of a play. Of course, there had been a few negative comments, but the reviews were positive on the whole.

I had fifteen new emails to reply to and answered them quickly. The last was from a Rosemary Conrad. That gave me pause.

> Dear Ms. Solange DewBerry. My name is Rosemary Conrad. I read your story and thoroughly enjoyed it. I've long admired the modeling profession but was glad you had the heroine turn to a more settled career of interior decorating. That matches her husband's career much better and would allow time for the children that are sure to come from such a passionate relationship.

It never failed to amaze me how people thought that the characters in these stories were real—or could be. It was extremely gratifying. If only she knew.

> The real reason I am writing to you is to ask if you are really dating my son Maurice...

Yikes!

> ...I was quite surprised when one of my boys mentioned meeting you. Another of Moe's brothers hinted that there is a new woman in his life. I realize most writers use a nom de plume but did want to know if you and she were one and the same.
>
> My boy Moe is a good son. He's dated lots of girls in his day, but none of them stuck. None of them were good enough for him to stick around for long. From what my boys tell me though, you're different from the rest.

Okay, major tectonic shift going on here. His mother read my story, with all that hot sex in it? Other writers had told me that meeting fans was great—talking to them about the intimate details of the characters' lives was a snap. But to discuss such things with the mother of the man I was sleeping with? Yuck.

Ha. One night wasn't 'sleeping' with him, was it?

> Anyway, I didn't tell him that I was writing to you. But if you are dating him and want to come by, I would be happy to meet you. Even if you're not, and if you are ever in town, I would love to be able to tell my friends that I had a real, live writer in my kitchen for lunch.
>
> Sincerely, Rosemary Conrad.

If I continued to see Moe, I'd have to meet her sooner or later, wouldn't I? What if when I did, she asked me about the sex scenes for my new book? Eeew. So far, they exceeded the heat if not the quantity of the first one. Not to mention the heat between Moe and me.

I pressed the reply button automatically, but then I hesitated. Do I tell her the truth? Lie? Ignore her altogether?

I deleted my blank page and decided to sleep on the whole thing. Maybe something would come to me overnight.

I contemplated working on revisions for a while longer, but my stomach growled. I glanced at the clock. It was nearly six and I hadn't called Moe. Where had the day gone? I shut down that computer.

My phone rang. Caller ID identified the front desk. "Miss Samuels, Mr. Maurice Conrad is here to see you."

Crap. I must look a fright. I was in sweats and had never done my hair or put on a drop of makeup today. At best, it would take him five minutes to get here, worse, two if the elevators were cooperating.

"Um, send him up."

I ran for the bathroom and forced a brush through my hair. I swiped on some eye shadow before I heard a knock on the door. I glanced at the bedroom. I had yet to make up the bed. I quickly closed the door. Maybe we'd never get that far.

At least the sweats were clean—nothing to be ashamed of. I swallowed hard. Yeah, sure. *The man made perfect love to you yesterday, and today you look like a bum.*

Well, if he cared about what I wore that much, then he wasn't the man for me. That, or we'd have to remove all our clothes as soon as possible.

I put on a smile and opened the door wide. "I was meaning to—"

He reached over and kissed my excuse away. "Let me guess. You were deep in the eighteenth century and lost track of time. You were so caught up, you forgot how a telephone worked." He grinned. "Not a problem. If you didn't want to see me again, you would have told that very nice doorman you weren't at home."

He kiss-walked into my living room, and it suddenly seemed a whole lot smaller than it used to. "By the way, I brought dinner." He held up two bags of what smelled like Italian food. My stomach rumbled again.

"You are a very dear man," I told him as I reached for one of the bags.

He held it over my head. "Not so fast. I'm still waiting for a proper hello from you."

I rubbed my nose as I looked at the carpet. When I met his eyes again, they were flashing in humor. "Hello Maurice Conrad. I'm so glad you came by to see me. May I kiss you now?"

He set the bags down and opened his arms. "That's more like it," he said as he enveloped me. He smelled like outdoors and soap, with a whiff of something that made my heart race.

"God, I missed you today. I wish I could have stayed until you woke up," he said into my hair.

"I wish you'd woken me before you left." I burrowed into his arms, pressing my nose at the vee of his shirt where his skin was showing.

"I was tempted, but if I did, I figured I'd never get out of bed, and that then the damned dog would crap all over the floor, and I'd have to clean it up, not to mention never hearing the end of it. So, my consolation prize was to come back here tonight and try again."

I looked up at him and smiled. "I'm glad. I got a lot done today. I'm almost finished with the first draft. I've got a lot of corrections that I promised to make—"

He looked at me funny. "You promised corrections? Promised who?"

"Ah." How do I answer that? "My characters," I fumbled as I toyed with the top button of his shirt. "I kind of talk to them as I go."

He looked bemused. "Oh?"

Well, he didn't run screaming from the room, so I guess I was okay.

Moe shrugged off his down vest and rolled up the sleeves of his flannel shirt. I think I practically drooled when I looked at his forearms. And his hands—holy smokes, they had me salivating. "What did you do after you fed and walked the dog?" I asked.

"Mostly spent time at the house, taking measurements, tearing up some more of the walls. Cleared away a couple of used condoms. I've got jobs lined up for the next month, so I can't devote too much time during the week until things slow down. Got to do that on my time." He waggled his eyebrows. "I was originally going to spend my weekends doing it. But now," he hesitated as a grin split his face. "Now, I'm planning on spending my weekends doing you."

He sat on the sofa and pulled me down onto his lap so that I straddled him. "How are you with a sledgehammer? Maybe you can help out next weekend if you need a break from your swashbucklers." He kneaded my upper arms and frowned.

"Is that one of those big hammer thingies?" I asked as I brushed a lock from his forehead.

"I guess that's my answer," he sighed and leaned over me. "I'll have to wait and see you in the evenings. You need to keep writing, so you can earn a lot, so I can charge you an outrageous price when I sell you that house. It's going to be perfect, so it'll cost a pretty penny.

I think I must have bit my lip then. I'd almost forgotten about that, what with planning Svetlana and Conrad's sea voyage and all. But the memory brought a rush of emotion, not to mention a wave of desire. "I guess maybe I'll have to learn something about it, so you don't overcharge me. Maybe a little sweat equity?" My voice didn't tremble too much, but it did, a little. His hands were starting to stroke my legs, my back. I was going to turn into a pool of lust before I got any dinner into me. Maybe getting Moe into me would have to come first. Not such a bad proposition.

When he smiled, that warm, knowing look, I began to wonder if he could read my mind. I grew even hotter at the thought. Could I let him know what I wanted and needed through telepathy? I shivered. That would be too much like my imaginary lovers. Not going to happen. Not when I had a live, warm, and very real man right here with me.

We didn't talk much after that. He leaned forward and kissed me, and I didn't have to tell him what to do. He knew, even better than me, what I wanted and needed. How delightful that his wishes coincided with mine so perfectly.

"I want you," he said against my lips. "Now. Hard."

"Oh god," I shivered.

Moe took that as my assent for he started his conquest of my mouth, and the rest of my body followed pretty naturally. His hands were everywhere, touching, probing, caressing, and squeezing. There was no sense of coercion, only pleasure as his large hands touched me, pulled off my top and cast it away. When he saw I was wearing no bra, his eyes lit up before he attached himself to one breast, the other being cared for by his capable fingers.

My head was back, and I think the only reason I was still upright was because he held me so as he kissed my breasts, working on one and then the other until I was in a frenzy for him to get to the rest of me. In my passion, I pulled at his shirt, flicking open the buttons until he was bare-chested. I rubbed myself against him, then, groaning my pleasure as I did.

"Hold on," he commanded as his hands lifted me from my bottom. I shrieked as he stood, and I wrapped myself around him.

"I won't drop you," he chuckled as he made his way to the bedroom. I groaned as I thought of the mess he'd find in there. He must have mistaken it for passion, for he dipped me a little to rub my crotch against his. I felt his hard length then, and groaned again, for a whole other reason.

"I told you I wanted you."

I kissed him then. "And your wanting me made me want you."

He nodded, satisfied with my answer.

I reached for the doorknob, and he strode in and dumped me on the bed. "Get out of those clothes," he ordered and then emptied his pockets onto my nightstand. Most of the jumble there, beside his key ring, were small square packets. "I came equipped this time," he smiled. "I might want to eat you up all the time, but mostly I want to come inside you."

He kissed me hard as he tore his shirt off, then got to work on his boots.

As for me, all I needed to do was kick off my remaining slipper and shuck my pants. He finally sat on the bed and undid his laces, then kicked the boots under the bed. He stood and dropped his pants. I grinned up at him, for it was

Moe's turn to go commando.

"I had this in mind," he said sheepishly. "What's your excuse?"

"I wasn't out in public today," I retorted as he crawled onto the bed and over me.

"Are you wet?" he asked as he reached for one of those small squares.

I nodded. Even if I hadn't been, I would be now.

He tore the packet open with his teeth. "You put this on me," he ordered. He lay back and presented me with all that delicious skin. Oh my god. No phantom lover I'd ever dreamed up could compare to this man.

I rolled the condom on him, and he grabbed me and flipped me on my back. He climbed on and wedged his hips between mine. "I'll fancy things up later. Right now, I don't have the inclination for a lot of foreplay."

I nodded. For my part, I was about as ready as a woman can get.

He pushed in, hard. I groaned, and he pulled out, only to push in again. "You are so perfect," he ground out between clenched teeth. "Wrap your legs around me, Berry."

It sounded like a good idea, and he lifted us both up until I sat on his bended knees. He was in deep, deeper than ever, and I felt him to my very core. My magic button was pressed up against his root, and the sensation nearly undid me.

"Hold on," he barked as his hands lifted me up and let me down."

I cried out in pleasure and felt his smile against my lips. "More," I begged him. "Harder, faster."

He tipped me over and pulled one of my legs up over his shoulder. "You asked for it, lady," he panted. "You got it."

I closed my eyes and arched my back as best I could. He was killing me with sensation. I reached up and clutched the headboard as wave after wave of pleasure rippled through me. Moe's climax came right after mine began, and he pushed hard into me, straining with each pulse from his body.

With gentle care, he lowered my legs and turned me until he held me against his heart. We were both breathing hard, and I was too overcome for words.

I was close to sleep when I heard his stomach rumble. Mine responded, and we both started to laugh. "Stay right here," he said as he rose with a groan and discarded the filled condom. "I want to serve you dinner in bed."

I smiled as I levered myself up and fluffed a pillow behind. I reached for another and set it in place for his return. "Silverware is next to the sink," I called to his retreating back. Oh man, but he had a nice butt. And those long legs. I wanted him again all over. This was so unlike me.

I pulled a sheet over myself, so I could remember what it felt like to be a prude.

Moe returned, bearing the two shopping bags. "I hope you're hungry, cause I bought a little of everything."

He started handing me packages and then ripped the bags open to spread them on the sheets.

"Antipasto," he crowed when he opened a foil bag. "I love this stuff." He grabbed a salami-wrapped asparagus spear and took a big bite as he climbed back on the bed next to me. I dug in and pulled out a morsel, taking my own taste. The flavor exploded in my mouth.

Setting that aside, he opened another package, this time eggplant parmigiana. That dish had never been a favorite of mine, but he deftly picked up a bite and held it out for me to try. The slippery little devil slipped off his fork and landed on my chest. We both laughed, and he then dipped a finger into the container and came up with a blob of sauce. He pulled the sheet down and spread it over my nipples, which he then sucked clean, ending up with the eggplant in his mouth. I closed my eyes in delight.

"That's the best vegetable I've ever had," he declared.

"Me too," I managed to squeak.

"Let's see, what else did I order?" He pulled out a container of meatballs and sausage with onion and peppers.

"That's another one of my favorites," I told him and took it." I carefully picked out a succulent piece and held it up, but it dripped on him. I looked down, and he was half hard already, getting harder. "Oops," I cried in mock concern. "Let me clean you up." And so I lapped up the tangy sauce, making sure I had every last bit before I came up to kiss his lips. "Now let me try some of this beef," I smiled, and took some in my mouth. He watched me chew, his eyes glowing. "Good thing I missed dropping one of those hot peppers on you," I told him after I had swallowed.

"Yeah. It might be fun for me, but you wouldn't have liked it much later when it came in contact second hand."

I closed my eyes, thinking about this. Was this really me? I was not the playful type. I opened my eyes to see Moe studying me seriously. "What is it, Berry?"

I shook my head, keeping tears at bay. "I don't know," I told him. "I've never felt this way before. This—"

"Happy?" he suggested with half a smile.

I nodded. "That must be it. I've never had Italian food in bed with a man before, certainly not naked."

"Me too," he smiled. "Or with a woman."

I gave his shoulder a small push. "What else did you bring me to eat?"

"Well, you already had a good start on me. But you can

finish that up later. Try some of this grilled radicchio. I'm thinking I want some tiramisu a la breast in a few minutes."

After we were sated, we spent time inspecting each other's bodies to clean up any spills we missed earlier. With all the food on the bed, he finally pulled me down onto the rug and made excruciatingly slow love to me before we headed for the shower. I have never had my back scrubbed with such infinite patience and skill. He made me come again with his hands alone before he let me out of the bathroom.

"I'll never get tired of seeing that look on your face," he said as he tied the sash of my robe around me. "That look of surprise followed by pure bliss." He kissed me then. "You are beautiful all the time, but never more so than when I make you come."

"Moe?" I tucked myself into his arms, feeling the towel around his hips begin to slip. "Tell me I'm not dreaming, okay? Promise me this isn't something I've made up for one of my books. I don't think I'm that good a writer."

He lifted my chin and looked into my eyes. "This is real, darlin'. This is what it feels like to be falling in love."

I closed my eyes then. Okay, he said it. Not me.

I blinked them open, and he was still there, still looking down at me, his face open, clear, and waiting for my response.

"Love?"

He held me closer. "What would you call it?"

"I—I don't know. I haven't been in love before, so I don't really have anything to compare it to."

"I have," he said bluntly. "Not like this, not so—so joyful. But this is the real thing, kiddo." He leaned in then and placed a soft kiss on my lips. "You're not dreaming. I won't disappear in a puff of smoke." He placed my hand on his chest. "I won't be gone when you turn the page. Can't put this book back on the shelf. I want you. In bed. Out of bed. On the phone, in my truck. At the grocery store. This is the real thing."

"Okay," I whispered, definitely overcome. "Okay."

"Let's get this food put away. I sure hope you've got clean sheets. I don't want to sleep in tomato sauce, no matter how delicious it was on your lovely ass an hour ago."

"Does this mean you want to stay?"

His brow creased. "I have to be up at five to load up the truck for the day. If you don't mind my waking up that early, yes, I want to stay."

"No dog to walk?" I teased.

"The guy came back this afternoon. Just a living to earn." He took off his watch and set the alarm. "You do want me to stay, don't you?" he asked, sounding suddenly unsure of himself.

I put my arms around him and pressed close. "I want you to stay." *Forever*, I thought but kept that to myself.

Chapter Twenty

Moe

Yes, I was falling in love with Berry. Can you blame me? I'd never before met such a fascinating combination of elements in one woman. She was shy in public, yet forward when we were alone. Quiet in her habits, she was game for anything I wanted to try in bed—or out of it. She was smart as a whip, and her talents were not limited to what she could do with her hands, mouth, even her feet. No, she invented characters that seemed like real people to me (she'd let me read a few pages of one of her first manuscripts that left me panting to read more). She could cook or bake anything I asked of her. She was dear and thoughtful, but her laughter, once it burst from her, was hearty and rollicking.

And don't even get me started about her body with her curves and hidden delights. Suffice to say there wasn't a single thing about her that I didn't absolutely love, other than the fact that she was reticent to admit she loved me too.

I figured I would get her to say it one of these days. She needed the right prompt, and I was just the man to find it or die trying.

It was a fair amount of fun, coming up with new ways to make love to her, to pamper and spoil her. On the weekends when I wasn't working, we went everywhere together, did things I never thought I'd try. I even took her shopping, something I normally can't stand. I made her promise to make it worth my while, so after an afternoon of tromping from one store to another, she finally gave me a sly smile and took me into a lingerie shop. Oh yeah. She let me see all sorts of sexy things on her before she let me make up her mind on what she wanted.

Did you know they frown upon couples making love in dressing rooms? I tried, but Berry said they only allow looking, not touching. Damn.

I nearly got a ticket driving her home, so anxious was I to get her there so I could tell her how exciting I found shopping at the mall that Sunday afternoon. The cop who stopped me was very understanding when I showed him the bag sitting in her lap and her embarrassed smile. Yeah, I owe that guy a beer. All I can say is we barely made it into her apartment. Apparently, there are also rules against doing it in the hallway of her building. But not against the door once we were inside. Yeah, that was a memorable day.

Here's a fashion tip for the ladies: men like skirts.

Do you get the picture? I was crazy about her. I like to think she was crazy about me. I found myself looking at my watch to find out when I could leave a job site so I could get home and cleaned up in time to go see her. I probably stayed over at her place more often than I stayed at my own.

It was about two months into this blissful part of my life when I had my second great idea.

I'd been getting work done on the house. The new furnace was hooked up, and I had one bathroom working, so I was about ready to give up my apartment and move in. But I hadn't done much with the kitchen other than get it insulated. The interior walls were still exposed to the studs.

She was working on that book every spare moment. She never complained about my being at her condo so much, but I was a distraction, and she had a deadline to meet. So, she hadn't been back to my place more than a time or two, and despite my best intentions of getting her to tell me what her dream kitchen would look like, we always got distracted by making love in a room we hadn't tried before. Remember, my house had a lot of them, not counting the basement. Or the attic. Somehow, we never made it to the kitchen.

So, my idea. Her friend Trista was an aspiring interior designer. I needed one of those. I figured since they were friends, Trista would know what Berry's tastes were and maybe work for cheap. Since she and Brad didn't live around here, I figured we could discuss it over the phone and through pictures. She must have a computer, right? Doesn't that make sense? Yup. I thought so too.

The problem was, I had no idea how to get in touch with her. I looked her up online, but the only hits I got were for Berry's book. If the woman was serious about interior decorating, she sure wasn't advertising.

Anyway, I was cleaning out my apartment. Berry told me in no uncertain terms to not come over as she had to get through twenty pages of proofing her manuscript—so I was being good and spent the time packing. In the midst of my cleaning, I found my copy of her book—the one about Trista and Brad.

When I first read it, I admit I was intrigued by all the sexy scenes she'd put in there, but over time, I came to realize they were just filler. The good stuff, according to Berry, were all the romantic scenes that made the characters fall in love. Some preceded the sex, some stood out alone. It was the romance, she told me, that readers liked. The sex was for fun.

Well, sex, as she described it, was entertaining, but it had nothing on what she and I enjoyed. Yes, we did it every chance we had, and a lot of that was inventive. But most of the time it was pretty straight forward I-need-you-I-want-you-take-off-your-clothes-and-lets-have-some-fun. It was pure and simple. And great? Not even close. Mind-blowing, okay? That night I was really missing her.

I thumbed through the book, stopping here and there to read a passage. That's when I remembered that Trista had offered her decorating services to me. The only way I could think of to get in touch with her was through Berry, but she hadn't heard from her friend in months. And if I asked too many questions, Berry would get suspicious. Not so good. Then I thought about my buddy whose wife did the same sort of work, but I didn't want to ask her.

I gave up and tossed the book into a box, then carried it out to the truck. It was a small box, so I set it behind the seat. I got in and drove to my house. I crawled into my bed alone and cursed the cold sheets and lonely pillow that were all I had for company.

The next morning, I got up and loaded the truck for my day's work. As I drove to my job site, I kept wondering how I could get in touch with Trista. It was still bothering me when I went out for lunch with one of my brothers, and on my mind when I got back. We were waiting on the plumber at the other job, and it was going to be a few days, so we figured we'd get some work done at my place while we had the time.

It was a beautiful day, cold but clear with the sun doing its best if you could stay in one place long enough to enjoy it. We don't get that many nice days that late in November, so I wasn't anxious to get back inside. While I was waiting for Joey to finish up a call to his girlfriend, I pulled my copy of Berry's book out of the box in my truck bed and thumbed through it.

Berry and I had been having fun every way I could think of, but I wanted to see if there might be something, in particular, I'd missed that might intrigue or delight her.

Mostly, I wanted tips on the romance part. The sex was great, but I wanted her to know I was really and truly in love with her, and that meant getting good at the romantic stuff like she wrote about. Hell, if a pretty boy like Brad could, I was man enough for it. That was in the back of my mind, but I kept wondering how I could get in touch with Trista. "I wish she was around," I must have muttered.

That's when I saw Trista standing by my truck, tapping her foot. I did a double-take and more or less stumbled out of the cab.

"I was just thinking about you," I said. "Did Berry tell you where to find me?"

"Berry?"

"I mean Solange." I'd almost forgotten they knew her professionally. "Brad with you?"

"Nope." She flipped her hair behind her ears. That's when I noticed she was wearing street clothes, no overcoat. The sun might have been shining, but the day was downright cold.

"He drop you off or something?" I craned my neck to see if he was parking down the street.

"Something," she said and darned if she didn't bat her eyelashes at me.

If I were a smarter man, I'd've paid a whole lot more attention to that question mark forming in my brain, but my notion about the kitchen was still front and center.

"You still in the design business? I sure can use your professional services."

Her smile grew brighter. God, but she was a beautiful woman. Couldn't hold a candle to my Berry, of course, for Berry was not only pretty but also sweet. Trista was—how can I say this? Sex in a bottle. She had definite professional appeal. She should have stayed a model.

"I am, and that's why I'm here...to solicit your business.

Do you need my help?"

"I need to make my kitchen a place that would make a woman drool. I can't even fry an egg without the fire department coming to help, so I need your help."

"You cook for the fire department?"

Why, oh why, did I ignore these signals? "No," I laughed. "I burn everything I touch. Sets off the smoke alarms."

Her smile was tentative as she processed that bit of information.

"I, um, read your book. You seem to know your way around a kitchen since you cooked all those gourmet meals for you and Brad, and your fancy friends back in California. I've got the kitchen roughed out, but need to know what should be included, where to put stuff, things like that." I looked at her as she smiled. "You think you're up for that?"

She nodded.

"Maybe you ought to come inside. You're not exactly dressed for New England in November."

That's when her nipples poked out of her shirt as if they suddenly noticed the chill in the air. I pretended not to notice. "No, I guess I'm not." She laughed as she looked down and took my arm. Maybe it was my imagination, but it seemed to me she pressed my arm to those tits of hers. I ignored her in case she'd done it by accident, and lord knows I didn't want to encourage her if she hadn't.

I hailed Joey to get him to move a little faster as I led Trista into the house. She immediately oohed and aahed over the details of the house, sort of like Berry did, only without the same enthusiasm. I figured that was the difference between someone who loved a house for itself, and someone with a professional opinion.

"The kitchen's through here." I took her the long way so

she could see the grand parlor and the dining room, both now gutted as we reworked the electrical.

We arrived in the open room. I described the layout as it used to be and told her what I had in mind. "So, how exactly does this work? Do you need a deposit, or do I only pay you when you're done with your design?"

She bit her lip. I remember she did that a lot in her book too. Man, it was amazing how Berry got all those details down perfectly. "You're my first client, so we'll have to play it by ear. Maybe we can figure this out as we go." She wrinkled her nose at me as she smiled. "Maybe barter services?"

"You have some remodeling you want done?"

"Maybe some labor." She looked at me with her eyes wide open and winked before she ran a finger down the buttons of my shirt. And she didn't seem like she would stop when she reached my belt buckle. I was beginning to worry that maybe she and I were on the same page of different books.

Damn. "Did your finger slip?" I joked as I took a giant step backward. She really needed to be in the no-fly-zone.

"Silly me, it must have," she purred and took a step closer.

The front door slammed. Someone's been yelling at Joey since he was three years old not to slam doors, but I have never, ever been so happy to hear that bang as I was right then.

"Yo, Joey, back in the kitchen. There's someone I want you to meet."

Joey had been having trouble with his girl. She wanted him to take her someplace exotic for Christmas, and he had college loans to repay. Somehow, they weren't seeing eye-to-eye at the moment, which was typical. Don't know what he saw in her, but that wasn't my business. I will say, his eyes lit up when he saw my company.

"Trista Johnston-Harding, this is my brother, Joey. Joey, Trista here's a friend of Berry's."

"It's just Trista Johnston," she said as she held her hand out to him.

Hmm. What happened to the dash-Harding?

Damned if Joey didn't take that hand and kiss it.

"Tell me, are there any more like you two at home?" she bubbled.

"There are five of us," Joey replied, clearly under her spell.

"Oooh." She blinked, and I could see those blue peepers working on him.

Thank goodness. Maybe now she'd leave me alone. I'm of the opinion that a man should only romance one woman at a time. My choice for the romancing was Berry, no question about that. Still, I might not have liked Joey's girl, but I wasn't sure Trista would make a good replacement.

"Trista and I are working out an agreement for her to help design the kitchen. I want to surprise Berry." I leaned closer to Trista. "Berry and I are working on an understanding, you see. She thinks she wants to buy the house, and I want to make sure it's perfect for her when she moves in."

"Is that right? For Berry—you do mean Solange, right?"

"Right. I call her by her given name, not her nom de fleur. It's a lot less complicated that way."

"And she wants to buy this house from you?"

"She wants to." I winked.

"So, you can negotiate a good deal with her?"

I nodded. "That's the general idea. I want to give her an offer she can't refuse."

Joey's mouth hung open. "You haven't even introduced her to Ma yet."

I scowled at him. "I'm waiting for the right moment. Thanksgiving's too crazy, so maybe Christmas."

Trista looked between the two of us. I got the impression she really didn't get what was going on, but she was smiling to hide her ignorance. As I recalled from her story, she was an only child, so maybe she didn't understand family dynamics. Or men. Real Men.

"I gotta get to work in the living room." Joey held out his hand again. "Nice to meet you, Trista. I can't wait to see what you work out with Moe. If you want a word of advice though, make him sweat for whatever deal you get."

"Oh, I intend to," she replied with a sultry laugh.

The shiver that ran up my spine had nothing to do with the draft in the room, and everything to do with the trouble I suspected I'd stepped into.

"I happen to have the room's dimensions right here." I handed her a copy of the sheet I'd prepared a few weeks earlier. "I want it functional, but nice. Everything has to be quality."

"I understand." She took the sheet from me, her fingers cool against mine. She met my eyes as she slipped the paper into her huge purse.

On her way out the door, she stopped and saw the copy of Berry's book sitting on a sawhorse. She picked it up gingerly and flipped it open before she turned to me with one of those smiles where all her teeth are showing back to her molars. "Mind if I take this? I don't think I was done making my notes."

The hairs on the back of my neck stood up, but I couldn't think of a good reason to refuse her. I had bought it for her in the first place and sort of appropriated it from Berry, who had appropriated it first. "Be my guest."

There wasn't a whole lot more for me to figure out from it that I hadn't already gotten. Berry wanted romance, and romance was what she'd get. I was already making plans for our next big date. I was going to take her to a dinner theater where they perform a murder mystery. I figured that would be right up her alley. And after that, I was thinking we could go up to the mountains for a weekend in the winter. I didn't know if she skied, but I could teach her. Or we could sit around the lodge drinking hot toddies and go lounge in a hot tub, naked. Yeah. I was sure getting creative all of a sudden.

"Thanks." Trista patted her purse before she walked out the door.

Berry

I sat staring at the screen. I'd come to an impasse on my story. I couldn't decide if I needed to make Conrad even more alpha than he was, or begin to scale back the bitchiness in Svetlana's demeanor in the current scene. The two of them were at a stalemate as well, and truthfully, I kind of wanted to chuck the whole thing. My agent was not helping, being away on business, and since my editor was on vacation, there was no one I could call.

Ten games of solitaire later, I was no closer to a solution. I kept hoping Moe would call and save me from all of this. I hadn't seen him for two days, though we texted constantly and spoke every evening. He'd been so good about respecting my need to work, but this once I was hoping maybe he'd break down and beg to see me. Then again, I could call him.

That's when I heard the knock on my door. My building security is very good—they wouldn't even let Moe up without calling me first, so I knew it could only be someone who lived here. I got up from my computer and went to the front door, peering into the spy hole.

I rocked back on my heels, and I think I gasped. Then I

looked again.

"Brad?" I exclaimed as I opened the door. I glanced left and right, but he was alone. "What are you doing here?"

"She's left me." He fell into my arms and sobbed. "Oh, Solange, Trista's left me."

Chapter Twenty-One

Moe

I paced my small bedroom. I made a foray into the parlor, the dining room, even the bathroom, thinking about the renovations I was making, but each time I approached the kitchen, I stopped cold. The idea of working with Trista had me jumpy. I was working my way up to the idea that it wasn't what she'd said so much as the way she'd said it. That and the fact that she'd let her hand wander where her hand had no business being.

And the fact that I had no way to reach her.

Like I said before, I'm a one-woman kind of man. I might like looking—no harm in that, but no touching, no thinking, no nothing but with my babe. For all my faults, I've always been faithful, no matter what.

So, Trista had me unnerved. It rankled, okay?

More than anything, I wanted to make a kitchen for Berry to drool over, one that would make her fall in love with me, assuming she wasn't already. Something that would put it over the top. I wanted to see if I could do that without help. It wasn't like I signed a contract with Triss or anything. She and I agreed to meet in three days when she'd have the plans ready.

But I hadn't seen Berry in a couple of days, and it was driving me crazy. She'd asked me to leave her alone so she could get her work done. Well, two days were up. I picked up my cell and hit my favorite speed dial.

"Hello?"

I'd never heard her so flustered. Were things going badly on the story? "Ber, it's Moe."

"Hi."

My hormones kicked into overdrive when I heard the relief in her voice. "Did I catch you at a bad time? Can I come over?"

There was a long pause on her end. I didn't much like it, but I was trying to be an understanding male. And romantic. "If you're still writing, I promise I'll be there to keep you company. I won't say a word. If you're as tense as you sound, I'll give you a backrub."

"Oh, Moe," she said, sounding so relieved. "That sounds great. I have a bit of—of a situation tonight."

"I'm on my way."

I will admit that I hung up before she could tell me no. Someone once told me—I think it might have been Berry herself—that it was part of my personality that I do things like that—take action without thinking. My dad always said I had good instincts. You can call it what you want. The thing is, when I want something, unless there's a legitimate reason to stall, I go for it. As you might have guessed, I wanted my girlfriend.

When I walked into her building, all I knew was that it was a good thing the doorman recognized me and let me right up without calling ahead—first time ever. I shared the elevator with a sweet old woman who was heading home after a Scrabble tournament in the common room. I tipped my ball cap to her and hopped off on Berry's floor, hightailing it down the hall until I could rap on her door.

I heard some sort of a commotion inside, but she answered quickly enough. "Who's there?"

"It's me." Who was she expecting?

The door was flung open, and she thrust herself into my arms. Now, that's the kind of greeting a man likes to get.

I looked through the open door, and who should be standing there but Mr. Bradley Harding himself. So that was her situation. I guess it was dumb of me to be so surprised. And no, Trista wasn't with him.

I stepped back and looked a little closer at my girl. Her eyes were a little wild behind her glasses and her hair messy. I tucked her under my arm and glared at Brad. He had trouble meeting my eyes. Ah. So that's what was going on. His wife left him, and he wanted my woman? Not so fast.

Things were going to change when I told Berry that I'd seen Trista. Not that I'd figured out exactly how I was going to share that news. The woman might have made me uncomfortable, but she hadn't exactly thrown an overt pass at me. Well, maybe she had. But I still wanted that kitchen for Ber. I also wanted some privacy to talk. I wasn't about to spill my guts in front of the woman's estranged husband. Jeeze, listen to me. Berry's changing how I think.

Speaking of whom, she was holding onto me pretty tight, so I figured she didn't have a guilty conscience. "Hey babe." I kissed her, putting a little more into it than I normally do for company. I wanted to be sure Brad got the message.

"Brad dropped by about an hour ago." She led me back into her living room. "He and Triss are having some troubles."

"Troubles?' Brad practically spat as he paced the carpet. "She left me. Said I was a bore."

Nice. So you make a pass at my girlfriend? Not. "Hey buddy. Sorry to hear that. I'm sure you two can work things out. Berry here giving you some tea and sympathy?"

"She hasn't offered me tea," Brad said thoughtfully before he eyed me. "You haven't seen Triss, have you? She mentioned your name a time or two."

"Me?" I opened my eyes nice and wide to seem as innocent as can be. "I don't know why she'd mention me."

Brad narrowed his deep brown eyes at me. I remember that Berry, when she was acting like Solange, had made a big deal about how soulful they were. To me, they were ordinary brown eyes. Maybe it was a girl thing. She'd never called my eyes soulful. I'd have to ask her about it later. "Just something she said in passing."

"When you two left, you didn't even have a phone number to give me," I reminded him.

Brad slunk over and sank into a chair and threw his arm across his eyes. Do people really do that? It sure was dramatic. "Right."

I looked at my girl. "You okay? Get any work done?"

She and I walked over to the sofa and sat down, close. I kept my arm around her. I wouldn't have done so without Brad being there. No, that's not true. If he wasn't there, we'd have been heading for the bedroom, if not in it by now. She had this aversion to doing it on her couch. Except when she didn't.

"I edited what I set out to do, but there's so much more to do before February. Then Brad showed up, and well, you know."

Did I? "You should have called me. I could have taken him out for a beer and let you get a little more done."

"I didn't think of that."

"How about Brad and I take you out for dinner? Then you can come back refreshed and get a few more hours in." I looked up at Brad. He was still in his forlorn pose. "Sport, where are you staying?"

His arm lowered, and he sat up straight. Christ, but the man's hair wasn't even mussed. Had he cornered the market in hair crap? Do women like men like that? You'd never catch me gelling up.

"Staying?" He looked surprised. "I thought Berry could put me up."

Nope. Not going to happen on my watch. "Well, gee, the thing is she's got a whole lot of work to do, and no matter how quiet you are, it's a distraction having a houseguest. There's a few good motels in town that are easy driving distance."

"Brad's a little short on cash," Berry rushed to say.

Why was she coming to his defense? I was trying to save her a major headache.

"Yeah, that's the problem."

"His credit cards were stolen, and his ATM card."

Brad's eyebrows lifted. "They were? I mean, they were."

What the hell was going on? This sounded a little more than a little suspicious, but I whistled in sympathy. His wife left him, and he was mugged? A big strong guy like that? He was taller than me, and about as fit. Must have been a posse to take him on.

"Now that's a dilemma." I thought another moment. "Here's an idea: how about Brad stays at my place and I stay here? It won't be fun for me, but it's the best I can come up with on short notice."

I have to be honest. I lied. It would be great fun for me.

It was Brad's turn to glare at me. Maybe he wasn't quite such a milquetoast after all. It was hard to tell. "I couldn't put you out like that."

"Sure he could," Berry chimed in. "Moe's place is kind of rustic, but he's got a bed, food, and a working bathroom. You'll have a ton more privacy than if you stayed with me. Remember, my sofa bed's not that comfortable."

"I never noticed," he said. That look of confusion was still on his face. If I were Trista and had seen that look, I would have left him before saying the vows. I wouldn't have cared how good he was in the sack.

"You said so at the time," Berry said through clenched

teeth.

"And where will you stay?" There were definite daggers coming from Brad's eyes this time.

"Moe will stay with me." Berry blushed then, a delightful shade of peach. "Since I saw you last, he and I have—you know, gotten together."

"But I thought you and that Greek guy—"

Greek guy? Berry never said anything about dating a foreigner. She said she hadn't seen anyone for a while.

"Never mind him," Berry said quickly. "This will work out much better." I could tell she was feeling bolder by the way she looked at him. "Until you and Triss work things out. I'm sure it will only take a few days." She stared at Brad. "I mean it. I'll see to it personally."

Whoa. So, there was something else going on here that I didn't know about.

"So, what'll be? Pizza, Chinese, burgers?" I stood up and pulled Berry to her feet. "Honey, you want to go get freshened up?" I ran a hand over her messy hair before I kissed her. And it was a good one too. I could tell by the way Berry's knees sagged. Hot damn. I made sure Brad was watching. Nothing wrong with reinforcing a message, right?

He ignored us as he wandered over to the bookshelf. "I'm in the mood for Thai."

I looked over at Berry for guidance. This was something a little out of my experience.

"I know a great place about fifteen minutes from here," she said before she turned to me. "Do you mind? They've got some pretty spicy stuff." She frowned. "No burgers though."

"I'm game for something new." I'd chalk this up under the heading of 'Romancing my girl under dire circumstances.' If this rhinestone cowboy could eat exotic chow, so could I.

An hour later, I was ready to eat my words, but I could no longer control my tongue well enough to speak. Thai hot's nothing like Tex-Mex or Schezuan. And by that, I mean it's a hell of a lot hotter. I'd have been laughing at myself, but I was in too much pain to try. Brad, of course, took the pain like a man. He and I ordered the same thing, and he didn't even break into a sweat. Berry must have known what to expect, for she ordered something that smelled like heaven and didn't cause her to drink from the water pitcher.

Brad smirked as I sat there, suffering. I was liking him a whole lot less with every passing moment. I couldn't say anything of course, but I was entertaining myself with thoughts of what I could do to make his stay at my place miserable. Turning off the hot water was one idea, but then all my new nice pipes would burst and cost me a bundle. There wasn't much in the way of food of course, except for cold cereal. Even I could manage that, but he might get tired of it.

In the end, I consoled myself with the fact that I'd be in Berry's nice warm bed, and he'd be sleeping alone. I almost convinced myself to feel a little sorry for him now that I'd gotten to know Trista a little better. There was no way a man could be happy with her for long. Way too high maintenance. It wasn't that they deserved each other exactly, but something close.

I tried to remember again how Berry had come to know these two, but I couldn't. It didn't seem like the right time to ask.

When the check came, I was reminded that Brad had no money. I was pulling out my wallet when Berry handed her card to the waiter. "My treat," she said softly. "You always take me out. This time it's my turn."

I frowned, of course, but inside I was proud of her. A guy likes to be treated special every now and again, and not only between the sheets. I kissed my thanks and felt her smile under my lips. For his part, Brad ignored the entire exchange. Figures.

We'd all come in my truck with Berry wedged up close to me. It made shifting a little tricky, but if she didn't mind, I wasn't about to complain. We went back to her place, and Brad got his car. Berry went in, and I had Brad follow me to my place. I took him in and gave him a spare key. No one would be working on the place again until the weekend, so he had a couple of days to himself. "Make yourself at home. watch out for the power equipment and don't go upstairs. The place is a mess. The cable is hooked up, so you can watch TV. It's not the Ritz-Carlton, but it's comfortable."

Brad shook my hand and assured me he'd be fine. He eyed some of the construction manuals I had on a small shelf. "I always wanted to know more about the trade," he said.

I shrugged, looked around and left, wondering if I'd just made the biggest mistake of my life.

Berry

"Where have you been?" Conrad exploded. "I've been standing here, half-dressed, looking at my delectable Slavic wench for hours, and I can't do a damned thing about it."

Great. Just when I'd finally gotten a little time to myself, my characters started in on me. I'd started the rewrites, but unfortunately, the two of them still had memories of the final scenes of the book. It would take all my concentration to make them forget about that and start to live the scenes of the book as if for the first time.

"Sorry. I had an unavoidable interruption. One of my other characters had a crisis. His wife left him—Oh, I don't have a lot of time to explain. Moe's going to be here in an hour."

"Interruption?" Svetlana shook out the arms that had been posed over her head since three o'clock that afternoon. "You start another book before you are done with us? You have our deadline to meet."

"No-no-no-no-no." I wanted to cry. "It's complicated. Someone I knew before. He broke up with his wife and came here for advice. Like a sequel, only not exactly. Then Moe came by. He's coming back. I want to finish this scene and then shut down. I'll start again in the morning.

"Tell more about interruption. Surprise that wives leave husbands after happily ever after."

"This is more like real life," I tried to explain. "There are no re-writes here."

The two of them looked at each other with wide eyes, and I could see them both shudder.

"Then you can keep your world," Conrad declared. "This one might be difficult from time to time, and I may face impossible odds in winning her, but at least I know you will make everything work out for the best in the end." He looked up at me. "No matter how long it takes you." He winked, which blunted the sting.

Svetlana rushed into his arms, and the scene's whole mood was ruined. The two of them were supposed to be at an impasse about her agreeing to set out on a journey with him.

They were supposed to hate each other right about now while desiring each other in secret. In the previous scene, he'd seen her naked for the first time—by mistake of course, and was trying to drive the memory from his brain unsuccessfully. He already desired her. For her part, Svetlana was already lusting after Conrad, but being more of an innocent than he suspected, she wasn't clear on how she was to go about seducing him which she needed to do for as yet undisclosed reasons. But I digress.

"Well, it's mine to keep. I may have to delay finishing this chapter tonight. I have to go back and rewrite something else, to try to figure out where they went wrong and make it right."

"These characters—they are from other story? Come to life?"

I nodded, suppressing a groan. If Svetlana and Conrad knew the others had come to life, would the temptation be great enough for them to also make the leap despite the uncertainty?

"Yes. And it's my job as the writer to try to make sure I fix what went wrong. I'll only be a few days."

Conrad set Svetlana by his side. The two of them stood in the room where they'd met, their hair and eyes wild, but they were hand in hand. "If you need our help, fair lady, you need only call upon us."

I paused. The offer was so heartfelt it made me tear up. "Thank you both. So, if you'll excuse me?" With that, I hit the save button and closed the file. My first editor told me I wasn't ruthless enough with my characters. Didn't make them bleed enough. Of course, it was the same editor that forced me to rewrite Brad so bland that Trista now wanted to leave him, and made her so bitchy that she could do such a thing. How could I have let things get away from me so dramatically?

So, I wasn't ruthless enough? This time, I was hoping to prove her wrong. I set my mind to keep Brad exactly where he was for the moment, no matter how many files I opened. And Trista had better keep her distance until I was ready to deal with her.

I figured I had twenty minutes before Moe returned. In that time, I was determined to find my original version of the story, the one I sent to my agent that convinced her to represent me. I wanted to see how I'd written Brad and Trista before they were transformed into the final version. If Moe was going to be here, I'd have to be very careful about what went on in that den of mine.

Chapter Twenty-Two

Moe

Don't get me wrong, for the next few days, for all intents and purposes, I was living with Berry. Need I explain how fantastic that was? Yes, I could tell that she was stressed by her looming deadline and what was going on with Brad and Trista. Plus, she was working every day. I hadn't met her brother, but I know he ran her ragged, not to mention her boss. Why couldn't Trista have picked him to be her next intended?

It didn't help that I was keeping a colossal secret from Ber. She was so troubled by everything else that I couldn't bear to tell her, and that made me feel like a jerk by keeping it to myself, and a bigger ass for what I knew would only complicate things. Anyway, why didn't Brad do anything for himself except mope around and read books on carpentry and drywall construction? He could at least try to get his credit restored. Maybe even get a job. There must be a need for a cattleman's skills somewhere on the east coast, don't you think? I offered to take him on part-time, but he refused. Said he didn't have the right clothes to wear. Honestly.

The second night I stayed over, I told Berry I needed to be on a job site early the next morning, so she wouldn't worry when she woke up to find me gone. I was supposed to meet Trista at the coffee shop where I usually ate breakfast. I decided that no matter what she came up with, I'd tell her I couldn't afford it. That way I'd get rid of her and not have to worry about it anymore. As I drove over, I kept my fingers crossed that she'd come up with some horrible design, and I'd have reason to let her down easy.

The shop bell rang as I walked through. The owner flashed me a smile. "Hey handsome, got a lady looking for you. I put her in your favorite booth over in the back."

I saluted her and made my way over, nodding to the other regulars.

"Good morning Maurice," Trista smiled. She was wearing two black sweaters, one on top of the other. I seemed to recall Berry calling it a sibling set or something. Berry had worn something similar once, but I'd never seen her wear it again. It didn't suit her the way her regular clothes did.

That was the only style I'd ever seen Trista wear but in different colors. Maybe it was because she was so thin, but it fit her differently than it did Berry. And Trista wore pearls. Those seemed awfully out of place here at the diner.

"I hope I didn't keep you waiting." I shrugged off my coat and hat and slid in across from her.

"Not at all."

The waitress came up with her order pad. "Hey Moe. Haven't seen you here for a few days. How've you been?"

"I'm great. The usual for me, Jenny. Triss, what would you like?"

As far as I know, she hadn't looked at her menu. "One poached egg on a split muffin, no butter. Coffee, black. No bacon, no ham or sausage."

"Coming right up. I'll put this order in and get your coffee."

Jenny spun on her heel and left. I always wondered about her. She and Joey have this bantering thing going. I think he wants to ask her out, but can't get up the nerve, or can't get rid of his current girlfriend, or both. If it doesn't work out soon, he'd have to find someplace new for breakfast. Or I would. The tension was starting to get to me.

"Can I see the plans?" I asked. No need to prolong this, and the shop wasn't far from my house. The last thing I wanted was for one of my brothers to walk in and see us together. Or Brad. But of course, he had no money. What he did have was my cold cereal and milk. He somehow always managed to have gas for his car, and he mooched dinner off Berry every night. It sure was taking him a long time to get his act together.

Anyway, Trista smiled at me. "The plans?" I asked. The funny thing was, I didn't recall seeing anything on the booth seat next to her when I came in other than a huge purse. The roll of papers she pulled out must have been on the floor.

We spread them out, using the salt and pepper shakers to hold the pages open.

I wanted to groan. Somehow, she'd done a great job, at least on paper. Crap. I might have to hire her after all.

Looking closer, what Trista proposed was plenty expensive. It all looked very high-end what with the marble countertops, fancy range hood and all. I seem to remember something about Italian tiles on the floor and backsplash. Dollar signs were popping up before my eyes. The cost of this one room was more than half of what I planned to spend renovating the entire house.

We had to stop when Jenny brought our breakfasts. Triss's looked awfully meager on her plate, whereas mine was ambrosia. Three fried eggs, four strips of bacon, a side of hash browns, and four pieces of toast. On days when I'm really hungry, I add a bowl of oatmeal.

Jenny smiled at us. "We haven't seen much of you. Joey mentioned you got yourself a girlfriend. I'm glad you finally brought her around to meet us."

"Oh, Triss here isn't—"

"It's so nice to meet all the people Maurice knows," Triss replied as she laid a hand over mine. It must have been careless on her part, but the nails seemed to dig into my hand. "And this looks wonderful. Would it trouble you too much to refresh my coffee? And I noticed this cup had a spot on it. Would you mind getting me a new one?"

Jenny looked at her and then at me. I could see what was going on in her brain, but with Triss's nails digging in, I had to wait to correct the misunderstanding.

Trista barely touched her breakfast, though she drank herself through a pot of coffee. I could see Jenny and the other waitress whispering in the back.

I got most of my meal into me before I addressed Trista's plans. "What you've got here would be great if my budget was unlimited, but I can't afford to do this up like one of those shows on TV. Any chance we can scale it back? Maybe some less costly features that could be upgraded later?"

She looked crestfallen. "I thought you wanted the best. To get top dollar when you sell the house to Berry."

"I do want the best I can afford. But you misunderstood my intentions about *selling* to Berry." I wrote down my budget. "You have to make this fit that, or I can't go forward." I turned the plan over again and looked a little more carefully. I may not watch a lot of TV, but when I do, I pay attention to those home improvement shows. Even I know that you've got to make a kitchen workable, not just pretty. Berry struck me as a straightforward gal, and I don't think she'd need two sinks, especially when one was tucked in a corner far from the stove and fridge. That might have been better for storage. And glass-fronted cabinets on the bottom? Wouldn't that be dangerous once we had toddlers running around?

"But I want your home to be a showplace," Trista

exclaimed.

And you want to make your mark as a decorator, no doubt. On my dime. "Maybe you can rework these a little, into something a little more practical. Can we get together again in a few days?

"Oh, and by the way, Brad is staying at my place. He misses you."

She didn't bat an eye. "You and Brad at your place? It's a good thing I didn't stop by there as I planned." She laughed and pushed her uneaten food away. "Tell me, how is my poor, beleaguered husband?"

She said that just as Jenny was walking by. The kid was going to think that not only was I dating a snooty woman, but a married one to boot. Great.

"He misses you. He doesn't quite understand what went wrong," I left out the part about his having made a pass at Berry. Having recently left her husband, I didn't think she was the jealous type.

"Well, if he doesn't know, I can't explain," she went on. "But you can tell him that he really ought to take a little more interest in his wife's profession for one thing. He needs to find something to talk about besides his car and his cattle for another. God, but I'm so sick of hearing about the beef industry."

"I'll pass that along." I put some money on the table. It seemed Trista was as tightfisted as Brad when it came to paying for meals.

"You rework those plans for me, and I'll meet you here in a couple of days. If you can make a nice-looking, functional kitchen for the price I gave you, I'll pay you for your services."

She frowned at me. "You mean it? Two days?"

Damn. I could have wiggled out of this if I'd tried a little harder. "Two."

I grabbed my hat and coat and got out of there as fast as I could. I ran into one of my brothers on the way out. He looked at me, then saw Trista's face peering out from the diner's window. She smiled and waved, then blew a kiss. Joey scowled at me and went in for his coffee to go.

Swell. Someone else I need to explain things to. This great idea of mine was starting to be a lot more trouble than it was worth.

Berry

I did something that week I have never done before. I called in sick.

In all the years I've been employed, I've worked through illnesses, even the flu. I even worked through my vacation a time or two, but I've never called in sick. I thought about it once or twice when I had a raging fever, but I compromised and worked from home those days.

But today was different. And it wasn't only for my story deadline—no, nothing so self-serving. This sacrifice was to try to get Trista back where she belonged, so I could get rid of her and Brad, and stop worrying about what Moe would think when he finally realized we hadn't seen them in years. Without my telling him the truth about them. With any luck, I'd never have to explain to him what really happened or have him think that he was sharing my delusional fantasy. There were many things I didn't mind sharing with him, and the more I got to know him, the better I liked doing that. But my psychoses were my own.

I focused on figuring out how to lure Trista back into the fold. In my innocence, I figured once I found the original story, it would be a snap to get her to comply with the program. In the original, she had a fabulous life: a career as a world-renowned fashion model, a jet-setter's life, piles of money, and the adoration of millions. Add to that one hunk of an alpha male who had long loved her from afar, and she had it made. Brad was anything but dull in the original.

I didn't know if this would work to make her want to come 'home,' but I spent the day beefing that up, piling on all the stuff that made her who she was, augmenting those scenes that made her tick and fall in love with her husband. I made sure he was hunkier and sweeter than ever, that their black moment of despair was more desperate than ever. When I read it again, I wept harder than I had the first time.

I even threw in a bonus round of phenomenal sex, patterned after but not exactly like the last time Moe and I made love. My toes were still curled from that night. He'd pretended to tie me up before he made love to me. It drove me absolutely wild, and I think I deafened him when I screamed that time. He repaid the favor by roaring when I pretended the same thing on him. I think I liked that even more.

Brad and Trista never shied away from anything I'd thrown at them in the bedroom. How could they not love this?

I hoped that Moe wouldn't be tempted to snoop around my files. I knew he was sensitive about his private life being exposed. But really, he's so creative when it comes to sheets and blankets and horizontal surfaces. It made me feel downright selfish for keeping all that fun strictly to myself.

In short, I did everything I could think of to make sure Triss and Brad were absolutely perfect for each other all over again. But that was beside the point.

The actual problem was, Trista wasn't falling in with the plan.

I looked at her character sheet a little more closely.

Despite the makeover, she was more shallow than I remembered and obsessed with her appearance, but that made sense as her career depended on her looks. When I first wrote this story, I thought I'd have a lot of fun describing her outfits, each more fabulous than the next, but it became a chore. I mean, how can one work those into the storyline and have it believable? The changes my editor had me make to her had added depth to her character, made her pop on the page into someone a whole lot more real. At first, I don't think I could have been prouder of her if she'd been my flesh-and-blood child instead of a brainstorm. But some of the conflicts I had with the original version of Trista, was creeping into the woman she'd become. I didn't know what I could do to counteract that.

Brad, on the other hand, was totally hot in the original. He was cute and sexy and very charming. Not to mention rich. I could hear his Texas twang from day one, what with all his 'darlin's and 'shucks'es' and all. I'd test-driven him more than once (he had another name then, and as far as I know, no memory of those evenings) and found him entirely to my liking. When my editor had me tone him down, I'd been heartbroken. She'd been kind. "Larger than life, Berry dear, just not super-sized."

All afternoon, I reworked that story to death, to no effect. By the end of the day, my fingertips and wrists were sore from pounding away at the keyboard, but Trista didn't pop out of the laptop to see me.

When Moe got back that evening, it was way after dark. I hadn't even showered. I think I ate at some point, but I wasn't sure. To say he looked concerned was an understatement. It was all I could do to save and shut down the program before he walked into the den.

"Are you feeling okay?" His large hand went to my

forehead. "You don't feel warm."

I smiled, stood, and stretched myself into his embrace. The truth was, I felt a little dizzy and more or less fell into his arms.

"Never better. Hard at work. Now I know what it would be like to be a full-time writer." I kissed him then, hoping for a little reciprocal action, but he wasn't to be distracted.

"Are you sure? We haven't known each other that long, but you don't strike me as the type to forget about getting dressed. Again"

I shrugged. "Let me get something going for dinner. I'll shower and dress then. Really, I was so wrapped up in my story, I forgot all about the time. Unlike you, I didn't have to impress anyone today. Not my boss, or my brother, or any sexy prospective clients."

He stepped away from me then and turned away. Was that a hint of a blush on his face? My suspicions were immediately aroused. Had I hit a nerve with my comment about sexy customers? I was determined to ignore it. I didn't want him to know how jealous I was feeling. "How did your early morning meeting go with the designer? Did he have what you wanted?"

"Uh, sort of." Moe left the room and went to hang up his jacket. "Got to make a few changes. The plans were too expensive. Gonna meet again in a few days."

Wow. Now I was really getting worried. In the background, I could hear Conrad and Svetlana whispering. Could they hear what was going on? Were they able to read between the lines better than me?

I sat at the computer, determined to shut down the program when Conrad hailed me.

```
"Mistress DewBerry, I beg you listen
before you consign us to the darkness."
```

"Make it quick—I've got things to do."

"Svetlana and I are aware of your dilemma. We have watched with interest as you changed your other story all day."

"You saw that?" God, but this was getting weird. Weirder.

He nodded, and I saw Svetlana push him as if to say more. "Yes. We understand that a character has gone rogue. The one time you got up to pee, Brad came by to check out my ship. He told us that his wife left him." Svetlana gave him another gentle shove. "We, ah, we'd like to help."

"I can't imagine what it is you can do," I hissed. I could hear Moe in the bathroom washing up. I was running out of time.

"We, well, we wish to step out of our story and go search for Trista. Perhaps we can convince her to return."

"How?"

"We feel she does not know of your efforts on her behalf. If she learns of them, perhaps she will repent and return."

I shook my head. Moe's footsteps were coming closer. "Let me think about it. I'll talk to you tomorrow."

I did a cold shutdown of my PC and hoped I hadn't destroyed anything in the process. There was no way I could let Moe know what was going on. He'd think me a crazy woman. And the truth was, I had more than fallen a little in love with him. If he left me now, I'd die of a broken heart, for sure.

Chapter Twenty-Three

Moe

I knew something was seriously wrong when Berry called in sick a second day. It made sense that she was worried about her deadline, but from what she said, she was keeping pace with her planned rewrites and was even a few days ahead. Still, I was only the boyfriend and a relatively new one at that. I wasn't in a position to criticize her, and as she was so upset, I did everything I could to ease her way. I wished she would confide in me about whatever it was that was bothering her. The night before, she'd been distracted, staring idly toward her office as we snuggled on the couch and watched TV. She totally ignored her glass of wine. It wasn't until I started to get her out of her clothes that she seemed more normal. She was plenty focused then, thank-the-lord-Amen. I don't think it was purely research on her part either.

And you know what? When we were done and she was snuggled up close and looked ready to fall asleep, she pulled my arm around her and said, "I love you, Moe." More of a mutter, but she said it. I know she did. Finally. I'll tell you, I took me a long time to fall asleep after that. A hell of a long time. But in a good way.

That morning she got up with me, and I knew as soon as I closed her front door, she was heading right back to the den. Well, I'd done what I could to make sure she'd gotten a good night's sleep. And she loved me. Hell, I didn't care that I had a shit-eating grin on my face. Nothing was going to go wrong that morning.

I headed over to my place. This business with Brad was

starting to get on my nerves. I loved staying with Berry—that was great, but I needed some clean clothes, and I hated the feeling I was intruding when I walked into my own home.

I unlocked the front door and called out. There was no answer, so I walked through the place, making as much noise as I could. As I neared the kitchen, I could hear something. It was kind of like connubial bliss coming from the bedroom. Had Trista returned to her husband or had he found himself another woman? The first made me hopeful—the second pissed me off. It's one thing to loan my bed to a stranger, but another thing if that stranger is getting it on in my house. He damn well better plan on washing the sheets before he left.

When I came to the kitchen, I found the bedroom door wide open. There were Brad and Triss getting it on, rolling around the floor, and having a fine old time.

I wanted to duck out as soon as I saw what was going on, but I was so surprised, I was kind of paralyzed. Besides, I was pretty certain they'd seen me too. I guess I figured they'd stop or finish up in a hurry, knowing that they had company. Instead, they somehow managed to roll right into the kitchen and keep going. I shouldn't be shocked, right? Any couple who agreed to have their lives portrayed in a fictional setting would have to be exhibitionists, don't you think?

They finished with a bang. Brad was holding her down by the wrists and pumping his hump for all it's worth. She screamed, he bellowed and then they were one. I couldn't believe what I was seeing and hearing.

"Oh, hi Moe."

Trista blinked up at me, all smiles. Brad was still heaving above her, getting the most of his lay.

What else could I do? I had to be polite. "Hi," I said in

return.

"You need something?" Brad rolled off Triss and left her exposed. I looked away, but not before I got an eyeful. Holy. Crap. And I have to admit he was pretty impressively hung too, not that I'm comparing, mind you. Yes, guys do look. And no, I don't think he had me beat in that regard. Oh, and for the record, Trista was as beautiful naked as she was in clothes. She didn't rush to cover up either, despite how cold it must have been down there. I mean, it looked like her body was reacting, but she didn't seem to feel it.

I can tell you this. If Berry and I were interrupted, you can bet I'd make sure she was covered as soon as I was cognizant. Before. And there was no way I'd let her lie there letting another man ogle her. Not that I was. Ogling her that is. Yeah, I looked at her. Hell, she seemed to want me to. And let me tell you this: Triss looked like a woman from one of those magazines, so perfect it looked as if she were airbrushed. Truthfully though, I kind of liked all the interesting, imperfect parts of Berry's body a whole lot more. Besides, I was soon to be a happily married man. I just needed to ask her. And have her say yes, was all.

"I came for some clothes. If you guys don't mind, I'll grab some stuff and get out of here."

Brad finally tossed Trista the sheet that had trailed off with them, and she took her time to fold herself into it. He didn't bother and sat down in one of my new antique chairs with his naked butt. Man, I'd have to scrub that thing before I ever used it.

"Help yourself." Triss went and sat on Brad's lap and began to nuzzle him. Naturally, the sheet slipped off.

"So, you two back together again?" I asked over my shoulder. And before you criticize me, could you come up with something better under the circumstances? "I'll have to call Berry and let her know the good news. She was worried about you two."

"No." Triss bit one of Brad's earlobes. "I'm just here for the sex. Something happened yesterday, and I got so turned on, I figured I'd see if Brad was free."

"Oh." *Crap.*

"Yeah. She wanted me to tie her up," Brad said as he captured Triss's bottom lip in his teeth. "It sounded like fun." He kissed her deeply before he stopped and looked up at me. "You didn't have any rope, so we pretended. Then she pretended to tie me up. Man, you've got to try that. We were at it all night."

I had a sick feeling in the pit of my stomach. I'd just done that with Berry. Could there be an epidemic of fake bondage in the city? Was it a full moon or something?

"Yeah, well, maybe." I stood to go. "If you'll excuse me?"

I don't think the two of them heard me as they fell to the floor and were at it again. No wonder Berry had tired of them as houseguests.

But where exactly did this leave me?

Trista looked up at me from what she was doing to Brad. "See you in a few days, Moe? Same place?"

I nodded, grabbed my stuff, and got out of there.

Berry

```
"She knows what you do. Is not working."
```
"What?"

```
"Trista. She knows of what you plot. She
found Brad last night and made love to him
as you described. But she does not want to
return. Prefers freedom."
```

I narrowed my eyes at Svetlana. I squinted so hard it hurt. "And exactly how do you know this?"

"Brad tells me."

"You talked to him?"

She had a guilty look on her face. "We not leave book. Computer not shut down last night. We talk all night. He and Trista are still making love now. Even arrival of your Moe does not stop them."

"WHAT?"

"He goes for clean clothes. Catches them."

"And he didn't leave?" My heart was racing. Bad enough *I* watched them, but him? He didn't strike me as that kind of guy. But who knew?

"Ah, he goes now. Brad has stopped talking. They are like, how you say, bunnies?"

"I don't believe this," I sputtered.

Svetlana shrugged. "You write us today? Yes? This tack of yours not work for Trista. You think of other plan. Conrad and I help if we can."

"Where's Moe now?"

She scrunched up her face. "Cannot tell. Only know what Brad say, and he is fully involved. But will not last. Trista only wants him for the screw. Brad thinks it is Moe she really wants." Svetlana listened again. "Said that Moe and Trista met, will meet again."

"I beg your pardon?"

"I only tell you what Brad tells me. You write now. Me and Conrad. Deadline approaching. Work on part about sister. Needs added oomph."

I was seething inside. Moe met with Trista and didn't tell me? And he was going to meet with her again? How was this even possible? How was any of it?

I hung my head in my hands. It was barely seven in the morning and I already had a raging headache.

"So, what do you propose?"

Svetlana looked nervously over her shoulder. Conrad stood in the background and nodded at her. `We think we need come out in your world and hunt her down. As soon as she exhausts the body of Brad, she leave him, go looking for others.`

"Can you stop her?" I asked.

`With the might of my arm,` Conrad cried as he flexed his bicep. `I can snatch up that feisty wench and return her to where she belongs.`

"And can you get Brad too? And keep him there?" I asked. "Exactly how can I trust that the two of you aren't going to go rogue on me as well?"

Ah. The look of shame on their faces spoke volumes.

"I think not," I told them. "Maybe we'll leave it for the day. I want to hear what Moe has to say for himself." I saved the document, straightened them out, and thrust them back into the scene I'd last revised. "Now, let's get some rewrites done."

I managed to get a decent day's work in and was back on track for my deadline. By the time Moe arrived that evening, I was showered and dressed, and making dinner. But I was seething. Had he really seen Trista and said nothing to me? What was worse was that I knew she was no more than a figment of my imagination. How could they even function without me? The only thing that kept me from screaming at him was that knowledge that even if he was attracted to her, it was proof that he cared about another aspect of my persona. She was the product of my imagination, after all. Right?

Somehow, I wasn't doing a great job convincing myself.

But Triss and I were nothing alike. Physically, she had every advantage in terms of height, weight, skin, and hair. I wrote her beautiful, with all the attributes I wish I had but could never hope to achieve. And I tried to make her smart but had to keep her somewhat naïve to make the plotwork.

More than anything, I wrote her bold. She could talk to people in ways I never could, fly around the world, wear beautiful clothes, and show off that body. Me? I hid behind drab colors and unflattering styles. In my everyday life, I strove not to be noticed. The one time, the one and only time I made a point to dress up—and ironically dressed just like her, look what happened—I met Moe. And now I was dying of jealousy.

But to write her—or to write an ass-kicking character like Svetlana, I had to have some of that inside me, didn't I? If I really wanted Moe, why couldn't I fight for him? Besides, what kind of life would he have with Trista? She wouldn't age. I was fairly certain of that. She couldn't have children unless I wrote them in for her. She wouldn't be able to function in the world unless I gave her the skills to do so.

Once upon a time, I'd spoken to my agent about writing a sequel in which Triss and Brad featured prominently. I'd written enough other characters into their story, so I could have Triss and Brad play a role in another romance, maybe give my readers a glimpse of how much more fabulous their lives had become.

But that was impossible if she remained AWOL. And no, I wasn't about to do her any favors, the two-timing, backstabbing you-know-what.

Moe would be here at any time, and I still didn't know how to broach the subject with him. I could pretend I'd spoken to Brad…that might work. Whatever it was, I would have to bide my time. I didn't want to ambush him, after all.

"Honey, I'm home," Moe sang out a half hour later.

I laughed and came into the living room to see him. "Dinner will be ready soon," I said, to complement his comment.

"I see you got dressed today." He leaned down to kiss me. I got a good sniff of the brisk fresh air that always seemed to be around him.

"Did you get a lot of work done?" he asked.

I nodded. "Back on track. I'll go to work tomorrow. I have to remember to sneeze a lot. Or was it a pulled muscle I told them?" I frowned. I couldn't recall what lie I'd used.

He nodded and headed for the bathroom. "How much time do I have before we eat?"

"Half an hour," I told him. "Maybe more."

"Good." He came out of the bathroom with his shirt off and his grin on. I started to salivate. "Do we have time for a little nookie?" he asked, waggling his eyebrows before he nuzzled my neck. "I've been in the mood for you all day."

"You have?" I swallowed hard. It was difficult to maintain my cool demeanor when he was making my bones weak with lust. Besides, I'd been thinking of him when I'd been writing about Svetlana and Conrad earlier.

"Um hummm," he said as he started pulling things apart, like buttons and zippers. "It started as soon as I walked out the door this morning." That was a surprise since he woke me up by making love to me. "What do you think about the bedroom, or maybe the sofa? I wouldn't mind a little rug burn if you want to go for a ride," he said, with that cute wiggle of his eyebrows. "Lady's choice."

I didn't have to think very long. Conrad and Svetlana had engaged in a healthy bout of lovemaking with me as director not an hour before. The thought of getting a mouthful of him was too appealing. I reached for him, making slow progress. He had to wear his button fly jeans today, and he was already bulging. And despite his having seen Triss, glory be, it was me he wanted.

I may be a shy, retiring type most of the time, but there are times when I want something, and I want it bad, I'm not afraid to go after it. Or him. I picked the rug, just as Svetlana had done with Conrad. I soon realized that my imagination was working fine, thank-you-very-much. I sure do know how to write a realistic love scene.

We finished up as the oven timer went off. Somehow, we'd both kept on our tops. While Moe's pants were at his ankles, mine had ended up across the room. I did have the benefit of the apron I had donned earlier. Moe gave me a light smack on the rear that made me want him all over again, but dinner was calling from the kitchen.

Moe

I watched that cute tush of Berry's as she scurried into the kitchen. Man, that woman slays me, she absolutely does. When we first met, I never dreamed she'd let me do the things to her that she does, let alone enjoy them. And that's not even going into the things she does to me. And she's perfect in the sack. I don't know how Trista thinks she can ever win me away from my honey. I mean, we hadn't known each other for very long, but I was seriously thinking wedding bells. Despite my teasing her on one of our early dates, I've never thought that way before. With the holidays coming up, I knew I'd be looking at diamond rings. There was no question in my mind.

It was chilly in the condo, so after a quick trip to the

bathroom, I pulled my clothes together and went to get her pants. I noticed the computer was on in the den. I'm not a nosy guy by nature, but I'd already read one of her books. She never exactly told me she *didn't* want me to read her work in progress—not that she strictly told me I could. But I didn't think she'd mind that much if I peeked.

I had a general idea about this one. She called it a historical, taking place in Europe. Hell yes, I was curious. As I buttoned my fly, I wandered over to check out a page or two.

Damned if I wasn't sorry that I had. Based on where the cursor was, it looked like she'd just finished working on a love scene, and wouldn't you know it was one where the woman seduced her lover by doing him exactly how she and I had just played. Worse, it seemed the dude's name was Conrad. Coincidence? I found it hard to think it wasn't.

I stood there sputtering for a moment or two before it occurred to me how I was feeling. Betrayed. Deceived all over again. Her own personal guinea pig.

And the hell of it was, I was turned on all over again. Crap, I didn't like this.

Chapter Twenty-Four

Berry

I couldn't believe what I was seeing. The man I'd just made love to, the man to whom I had given my heart, my body, my soul, the man I'd just told I loved… was snooping around my stuff. He stood there, calmly reading my unfinished story, slowly paging down. The nerve of him, holding my pants in one hand and my mouse in the other.

And when he looked up at me, his eyes were so cold.

"What are you doing?" My voice sounded dead to my ears.

"What am *I* doing?" He straightened, "I was going to ask you the same thing. Using me to test out your theories? Practicing your sexual technique?"

I have never been slapped in the face, but I don't believe it could hurt more than his words did.

We stood there looking at each other for a heartbeat or two. I think I needed a deep breath before I spoke, but when I did, I didn't sound the least bit like myself. I wasn't certain who this man was that I was talking to either.

"As I recall, it was you who initiated things in here a little while ago, not the other way around." Did I really sound so self-assured? Did I really sound like Trista? I lifted one brow. "Lady's choice?"

He shrugged. "If not now, then later. Were you saving this to try the next time I looked your way?" He leaned against the desk. "Tell me, are you going to give me credit at the back of the book, your experimental stud?"

I was suddenly dizzy. I'm not sure. I held on to the door to keep me on my feet. "So much for the dedication I planned."

"And what's with your hero's name? Tell me that's not a coincidence," he said softly.

Oh crap. I never did get around to explaining that, did I? Something told me it was too late now. I could literally feel my heart breaking. "You wouldn't believe me, no matter what I said, would you."

"No. I don't suppose I would."

All my adult life, I've worked hard to keep myself protected, covered. I've made an art of not being noticed. Until Moe. He made me come out of my shell, made me feel beautiful when I knew I was not. He made me feel sexy, cherished. Damn it—he made me feel loved. Because of him, I could go out into the world and hardly think twice about the risk that posed.

Now all I could feel was that new world shattering around me, crashing to the ground without a sound.

At this moment, I felt more exposed than I'd ever felt before in my life. The apron covered me to my knees in front, but my backside, legs, and feet were still bare. I'd rarely felt so vulnerable—and this from the man whom I'd trusted more than any other, ever.

Despite my crumbling world, something inside would not allow me to grovel. I could salvage this. Well, I could try. This time, I was not going to cry. "It's not the worst thing in the world to be used as an example of supreme sexiness," I said. "I'm sure the partners of other writers aren't squeamish about it."

He winced. Crap. Not the right approach.

"I'm not other men."

He sure wasn't. I could practically hear Conrad and Svetlana shouting at me, but they were too far away. He didn't seem to be able to hear them, thank goodness.

"It's not like I'm sleeping around. It's all imaginary.

Come on, Moe. I was just working on that scene. You told me I got to choose how we made love. It was still on my mind. It's not like we did it first, and then I wrote it down." *Not like the other day.* "I'm not lusting after some fictional character." *Not anymore. Now I'm only lusting for you.*

"And I am?"

That's when I noticed exactly how angry he really was. That broken heart I imagined in my chest? It wasn't breaking. No, it was shriveling up and turning to dust.

"I'm not the one who sits around in pajamas all day writing about things that aren't real, making stuff up. I'm out there, doing real work, talking to real people, building real things. I date real women, or at least I thought I did."

Oh, that hurt. But I didn't crumple. No. I straightened my back, naked rear and all. "There are many ways to make a living, you know. I work in an office and push paper all day. I don't make anything real, but I get paid for it and paid well. So, what if I use my imagination on my own time. Don't you do the same thing when you rehab a building?"

He stomped around the small room, his arms waving wildly, behaving like no man I'd ever met before. "It's not the same at all. I would never betray you. Hell, I don't even talk about what we do in bed with the guys, not like some do. What goes on between the sheets is between you and me, babe. Until you go and blab it all on paper."

"It's not like that at all," I shouted. "You're wrong about this. I know it looks bad, but you're angry, snapping to judgment without thinking about it."

"Yeah, well, I've thought enough," he said as he brushed past me. "I'm out of here."

My eyes burned then. My heart was the size of a speck of dust. "Then go. Go to that tramp Trista. I'll bet you gave her that book, didn't you? See how welcoming and warm she is on a cold night like this," I yelled.

That stopped him. He didn't turn, but his voice was clear enough. "What? How do you know about her?"

Aha. Guilt. Oh, this evening was getting better and better.

"I know you've met with her behind my back, and you're planning to meet her again." I was feeling wild inside. "If you want her so bad, go to her. Go see how much she can offer you that I can't. You and I don't owe each other a thing. I guess we don't mean anything to one another, after all. You want her, go after her. But don't think you can have me and her at the same time. I'm not putting up with any competition, real or otherwise."

His brow lowered. Oh damn, I'd said it. I was in trouble now.

"What do you mean real or otherwise?"

"Why don't you ask her," I said. "You think any woman can be that perfect all the time? Feel no cold, no hunger?"

"She's a little odd," he admitted. "But she's a hell of a lot nicer to me than you are right now."

"Then go, you bastard." *Before the tears can fall.* "Go to her and get the hell out of my life."

Pants or no, I marched to my front door and held it open. "Get out of my house."

He pulled his coat from the closet. "I'm going. And I'm kicking your friend Brad out of my place too. See how much you like having him sleeping on your couch. If that's where he'll sleep. He's already proven he doesn't mind having his love life smeared across the printed page."

I slammed the door after him. I imagined my neighbors popping their heads out their doors along the long hallway. I didn't give a damn, but rushed into the bathroom to throw up.

That man was far from a perfect lover. He'd left the toilet seat up. Again. Good riddance.

Moe

What the hell just happened? I asked myself as I punched the elevator button. It was too flipping slow, so I took the stairs, all eleven flights. Had I really just walked out on the greatest thing that ever happened to me? After getting the best loving of my life, did I treat her like dirt?

It was tempting to pound my head against the cinderblock walls of the stairwell, but it didn't seem like that would solve anything. I couldn't go back up either. Not tonight. She was probably so mad she wouldn't want to speak to me for a week.

I am a jerk. Just don't tell anyone I said that.

The last thing I wanted was to go back to my place to find Brad and Trista still at it, or worse, find no one there but some stained sheets. Oh crap.

Did I mention that I turn into an idiot when I'm in love?

Of course, Berry was right. There's nothing wrong with what she does for a living, or what she wants to do for a living. Instead of yelling at her, I should be grateful she sits around her place all day and thinks up interesting ways to have sex, make love, do it, get it on—you can call it what you want. And she was right again about tonight. It wasn't like she was writing about what we had done. We did what she'd written about. If anyone read her stories and put me in the same category as all that hot sex, I should be proud. Instead, I was feeling guilty as hell.

And I was feeling like a skunk. An idiotic skunk.

I walked out into the bracing November air and called to apologize. She didn't pick up. I tried again. And again. No luck. The last time, I left a message.

"Berry, it's Moe. Listen girl, I'm sorry. I was wrong. I'm an idiot, and you can even tell my brothers I said so. I know it wasn't what I said. I got scared. And jealous. It was like a flashback with Carly all over again. I didn't think I could face that, but for you, I will. Call me honey. I love you darlin, I think."

I pressed the end call button. If that wasn't romantic enough for her, I don't know what was.

I stood there in the parking lot, looking up at her building and hoping she'd come to the window and wave me back up. Instead, I saw the lights in her den go out, then the light in her living room do the same. I stood there, freezing my ass off, waiting against hope that I'd see her silhouette in the window, but it wasn't meant to be.

I only moved when the security guard came out to yell at me to get out of the lot. I was making the residents nervous.

I couldn't face going to my place. I'd be there in the morning to start working again. Instead, I was going to spend the night at mom's. She never minded if one of her boys slept in her spare bed.

Berry

He almost had me with that message. Almost. If he'd come out and said 'I love you, darlin', that would have been enough. He did say the three words my heart ached for, but it was those two little words he tacked on at the start, 'I think' that blew it. Those fueled my anger that night. I needed a little more certainty. I wanted him to grovel a whole lot more before I could forgive him.

I put on my pants and headed into the kitchen. Dinner was ready, and it was a damn fine meal too. That idiot ruined it. I was tempted to heave the whole thing into the trash, but I'm too frugal for that. I cut the chicken into meal-sized chunks and froze them along with the peas and biscuits. I was going to be awfully sick of chicken by the end of next week. I'd taken to buying the big ones since Moe had such a hearty appetite. He could easily eat twice what I could in one sitting. I wiped away a traitorous tear as I looked at the phone one more time.

Call me again, I silently begged. *I'll pick it up this time.* But he didn't.

I cleaned the kitchen until it was spotless and headed back to the den. I needed to do something about Trista and Brad before they showed up on my doorstep, either singly or as a bickering pair. What Svetlana told me didn't sit well, and I was beginning to despise this creation I had been so inordinately proud of a few months ago.

"Get back in line," I whispered to Trista under my breath. "Brad will follow you. He'll forgive you," I promised. "I'd make him. Let me move on. I promise you a great cameo in my next book."

But I didn't hear a peep from either of them. For all I knew, they could pop back into my living room at will. I was sure as long as Trista had a copy of my book, she was a free spirit in this world. What I couldn't figure out was why Brad didn't just evaporate since he was away from it. Was it enough that it was in her possession, or did it have anything to do with so many people having met him and believing him real? What were the rules of physics in that damned universe I'd created? How in the world could I counter all that?

I stared at the screen where Moe had so recently looked. That scene I'd written had been hot all right. I regretted not telling him about my character's name, but there was little I could do about that now, short of showing him drafts I'd written long before we met. He'd need to be here for that, though.

I loosened my hair and fluffed it up to try to relieve my headache. I sat in the chair and placed my fingers on the keyboard.

Now what?

`"You did not listen to us,"` Conrad scolded. `"We could have prevented this from happening."`

"Yeah, sure," I replied. "Exactly how? Moe has no idea you two can talk to me. *I* can hardly believe it. Trista and Brad didn't talk back nearly as much as you do."

The two of them shrugged. `"We're better written, I guess,"` Conrad replied. `"A testament to your skill, fair lady."`

Oh, I really did make this hero too charming for his own good.

"So, what would you have done?"

`"If you'd printed out a few of our pages, we could have stepped out to meet Moe."`

"Right," I snorted. "And what would you have said to him, once he woke up from his faint."

They looked at each other in confusion.

"Moe doesn't know Trista and Brad aren't real. I mean, real like me, as opposed to real like you."

`"Are we not the same?"` Svetlana asked.

"No," I replied. You're fiction. I am not."

`"Ah,"` said Conrad.

`"Oh,"` said Svetlana. `"This changes things."`

"Not to mention, you two are written for another century. If you've been looking into the other story, surely you've noticed that things are a bit different than what you're accustomed to."

`"We were going to ask,"` Conrad said, looking down. `"But we still wish to help."`

`"Feel responsible for breakup,"` Svetlana added. `"You're unhappy about this. Not write` happy for us."

I nodded. "I don't know what to do. He hasn't groveled enough, but I want him back anyway."

"But there will be a happily ever after," **Svetlana assured me.** "All good stories end so. Hero and Heroine must suffer first, make it all worthwhile. Great passion needs contrast. Wonderful sex alone does not make for happily ever after."

"We want to get Trista back where she belongs, so the natural order of life can continue," **Conrad added.** "If one character goes rogue, what's to stop the rest of our world from falling apart? And we're not published yet. We want our happily ever after."

Svetlana came to stand by him, and the two of them stood there, arms wrapped around one another, looking at me with hope and fear.

I took a deep breath.

"I appreciate your wanting to help, guys, but here's the deal. Out here in my world, there are no guarantees. People get old. They get hurt. Sometimes they die before their time. There's hunger that goes on for days and weeks and months, not just a few pages."

"Impossible," **Svetlana cried.** "We know of no such thing."

"Because I haven't introduced that to your world," I reminded her. "Out here, unpleasant things happen that can't be corrected in a revised draft. There are no rewrites in my world. People get cold and can't find heat to warm themselves. Sometimes they get unreasonable for the sake of being unreasonable and not simply to move the storyline forward."

"Not like your world so much," Svetlana grimaced. "This one much better, despite the hardships. I know, even if I don't let on, that you will make everything come out okay."

Her faith in my abilities warmed me.

"But we still want to come out there and help," Conrad added.

I wasn't sure I'd convinced them. What if I suddenly had four characters go rogue on me? I wasn't certain Trista knew this new reality yet but damned if I couldn't find her to tell her.

"There's one more thing about my world you have to understand," I told them. "Here where I live, there is no guarantee of a happy ending."

Svetlana shook her head. "This is hard to believe. Everyone has a happy ending unless they are the villain of the story. Your Moe will come back, no?"

A tear fell then, and then another. "No, Svetlana. In my world, I can't force my will on him the way I can with you two. If he's through with me, that's that. I could beg him to return, but I will not humiliate myself for the sake of a love he no longer feels."

That had the desired effect. I saw them both shiver and realize how good they had it, despite the painful turning points in the plot I had yet to refine.

"This is true then?" Svetlana asked, her face pale.

I nodded.

"Moe won't come back to you?" Conrad sounded like an indignant big brother. I wished Rocky were a little more like him.

I shrugged. "I don't know. Maybe. But he might change his mind about me, or he'll say something else that's even more stupid than what he said tonight. Or I'll say something that he finds unforgivable. For all I know, he might end up with an old girlfriend."

"And you, with an old boyfriend, or a new lover who is even better and brawnier?"

I thought briefly about the one failed romance in my past and shuddered in revulsion. But then about Moe's big body and how well he used it. I thought about his smile and how it warmed me up inside. I closed my eyes and imagined myself back in his arms, his warm lips pressed to my forehead as we slept.

"There is no one better than Moe," I said. Another tear leaked from my eye. "So, you see why I need to get Trista back into her book."

"So she does not steal Moe from you as she intends."

"Not only that. I think it upsets the balance between your world and mine if she and Brad stay here too long. They're not of this world. You—all of you, are written bigger than life, better, more beautiful, stronger. You don't age or grow warts. Your feet don't smell, and your breath is always sweet. Damn it, and you never need to change the oil in your cars or hunt for food unless it will move the story along."

"This is true," Svetlana agreed. "Only villains have ugliness and smell bad. And my breasts do not sag no matter how big they are." Naturally, she had to demonstrate to a grateful Conrad. "I like this. I do not wish to bind myself as you do."

I had to concede her point.

"Okay, fair lady. We agree to help you

contain your rogue heroine, and once we do, we shall come right back so you can write us our happily ever after ending. We solemnly promise this to you." **They looked at me with pity.** "And we do what we can to improve your chances of one as well."

Then those two dear characters placed their hands on their hearts and bowed to me. I couldn't have written the scene better if I'd tried.

Chapter Twenty-Five

Moe

I groaned as I awoke to the alarm. I stretched, rolled over, and promptly fell out of the cot my mother put me in the night before.

That woman's wily. All her boys are over six feet tall, but the only bed she'll loan us is a small twin. She says it's for the grandchildren she's been waiting for. I think it's to discourage us from invading her domain longer than one night. Besides, not one of us has yet brought home a girl that she's approved of. Berry would have been the exception, but now it looked like that might not happen after all. Crap.

I was up before mom was awake. I'd have to figure out what to do today or face another night on this bed. Besides, I had to meet with Trista that morning.

The truth is, after having seen her and Brad go at it like a couple of porn stars, I wasn't certain I could look her in the eye. And what was the point? If Berry had really and truly kicked me out, she probably wasn't still interested in buying the house. More than that, I couldn't even dream of giving it to her as a wedding gift anymore.

Ah, hell. A man sure can make of mess of things without even trying. Scratch that. I can't blame all of mankind for my failings. It was all my fault.

Still, a man's got to face the day no matter how dismal. I rose, showered, and shaved, and was out of there before six. I showed up at the diner to Jenny's disapproving stare.

"That woman's back," she said with a sniff. "I don't understand how you can date her."

"I'm not," I hissed. "She's an interior designer."

"But she said—"

I frowned. "I don't care what she said. I'm not dating her, and I don't plan to. Now, if you don't mind, please unpoke your nose from my private business and get me some breakfast?"

"Sure, Moe." Jenny walked disdainfully to the back of the shop to place the order. Man, I never used to think up crap like that until I met Berry.

I sat down across from Trista. She looked as beautiful as she normally did. Her skin was pale and flawless—her big blue eyes sparkled in the dim light. When she smiled, I noticed how white her teeth were. With all the coffee she drank, she must use one of those whitening products. And she had on another one of those twin sets. This one was grey. I can't explain how, but it was a whole lot more revealing than some of the other ones she'd worn. A lot. Or maybe it was because I'd seen her naked. Hell.

"Hey," I said, trying not to notice. "Order yet?"

She nodded. "Do you want to go over the plans before or after we eat?"

I suppressed a yawn. "After. I can't think until my stomach stops rumbling."

"I heard you missed dinner."

That got my attention. "Really? Did you talk to Berry?" I sounded like a flipping kid with that hopeful tone.

"No. Svetlana." She sipped her steaming coffee. How did she do that without burning her lips?

"Who?"

"Svetlana. I spoke to her last night. She said you and Solange made love, had an argument, and you left before dinner. Of course, she doesn't know what happened after that. I assumed since you didn't go to your place, you didn't eat."

Wait a minute. That snippet I'd read on the sly, was that one also about another couple who Berry knew? It had a woman named Svetlana. I didn't figure Trista knew them too. How the hell did Berry meet these people? Didn't anyone have any modesty anymore?

And how did Trista know I didn't go back to my place unless she and Brad were at it all night long?

The truth was before I went to mom's, I'd gone to a bar and had a few beers on an empty stomach and heard a lot of useless talk about what trouble women were. I might have contributed to the conversation. Just a word here and there. Then I'd gone to my mother's and heard plenty from her about what idiots men could be. I was starving now. My head was full, and I wanted nothing more than to go back to where things were yesterday morning when I woke my honey up with a bit of lovin'.

"How's Berry?"

"Svetlana didn't say." Trista grabbed a couple packages of artificial sweetener and dumped them in her coffee. "I didn't ask." She stirred briskly. She looked up with narrowed eyes. "I find Solange to be a bit controlling. Don't you? I mean, she's always got an opinion about everything. And she's not happy unless you do everything exactly as she says." She shuddered delicately.

I hadn't exactly noticed that, except a few times when Berry was giving directions like, 'more,' or 'harder' or 'right there,' or 'kiss me you fool'. I didn't mind those at all. "I guess my relationship with her is a little different than yours."

Jenny brought my coffee along with a glare. I didn't mind the distraction.

"So you and Brad working things out?" I asked purposely within Jenny's range. I might be a jackass some of the time, but not always.

"Oh no," Trista shuddered. "I left shortly after you did. I didn't need him last night, so I didn't go back."

Great. I could have slept in my own bed, after all. Except that Brad was probably still in it.

"It sure seemed like the two of you were heading full bore toward a reconciliation," I offered. "Not that it's any of my business, but the guy's crazy about you. He doesn't seem to be able to function without you either." He certainly hadn't made much headway about replacing his lost credit cards or money. I was getting a mite impatient with him.

"That's the problem. He's so dull," she told me. "Oh, he's a wild man in bed, but once we've done it four, five, or six times, there's nothing to talk about."

I nearly spit out my coffee. Four to six? Maybe at nineteen, but at their age?

"Maybe he needs to be encouraged. You must have had plenty to talk about when you were dating. You did marry him, after all."

She looked into the distance, and all I could see was her naked body. I didn't want to. I mean, she was fully clothed and not even a turn on for me, but it was as if... well, never mind, other than it was very strange.

"Back when we first met, we had plenty to talk about," she said. "But after the wedding, it seemed like we ran out of things to say. He kept repeating himself all the time."

"Bummer."

She looked at me up and down as I gulped my coffee. Then she looked at me again, her eyes half-closed as she leaned forward. "I want to have sex with you. Mind-blowing sex. Not like that humdrum ordinary sex you have with Berry."

I stopped mid swallow and burned my throat. In fact, I think my heart stopped beating there for a minute or six.

"Ummm, Trista..."

"As far as I can remember, I've only ever had sex with Brad, and he only can do six things. I know there was a man before him, but I have no memory of sex with him. It couldn't have been good, or I'd still be with him."

I managed to swallow my coffee. Then I sputtered a time or two. "How do you know what sort of sex Berry and I have? You haven't been talking to her..."

Trista scowled. "Of course not. I haven't seen her, well—that she's known—for months. But I've seen the two of you. I can teach you how to have more fun than that."

Which was kind of funny, had I stopped to think about it at the moment, 'cause up until this time I thought I'd been having plenty of fun. "Wait a minute. How the hell do you know..."

"I've been spying on you, darling."

Damn, but that woman had a smug smile. And how? Did she have a camera at Berry's place? More than one? What about the sex we'd been having? "How the hell..."

Saved by the fried eggs and another glower from Jenny. I tucked into my meal, happy to have an excuse not to talk. Trista ignored her breakfast. Did the woman live on coffee alone?

"So, if you and Solange are done, I'd like to date you."

I give the woman points for being straight forward, but what the hell was it with her never using Berry's real name?

"Really? It was only a small spat. I'm kind of hoping we'd make up."

Her brows rose, and I could see a smile around her coffee cup. "That's not what Svetlana says."

Svetlana? How does she know so much? "I'm not sure who she is or how she knows so much, but I intend to set things right with Berry."

"Really?" she said again. Those plucked brows arched higher.

Who did she think she was? "Really," I replied.

"Best of luck to you with that," she smirked. "When you realize it's a lost cause, come back to me. Unless I find someone else more interesting than you in the meanwhile."

Trista was one cool customer. I was beginning to wonder why I had ever thought her attractive. What had Berry said about her last night—that she wasn't real? I didn't know about that, but I was beginning to reformulate my opinion of her.

I concentrated on my meal until it was gone. Just as I pushed my plate aside in order to look at the revised plans Trista had drawn up, the bell of the diner tinkled. In walked a couple who seemed vaguely familiar. The man was tall and had a peculiar swagger. The woman was beautiful in an exotic way, with a full ruffly kind of skirt. They spotted Trista immediately and came to our table.

The three of them kissed the air near each other's cheeks. We moved further into the booth so the two of them could sit.

"Maurice, I'd like you to meet Captain Conrad and Svetlana Pickering. These are friends of Solange."

I stared at the woman sitting next to me. Her dark eyes looked deeply into mine. Svetlana? From the pages I'd read last night? She who sucked Conrad's Johnson until he roared in pleasure, just like I did when Berry did that to me? The same Svetlana who then rode him until they both fell into a sweaty puddle of satisfaction? Jeeze. how many couples did Berry know who were willing to put their most intimate lives on public display? Where the hell did she meet them?

And the dude's name was Conrad? That meant that she really hadn't borrowed my last name at all. Oh hell.

"So pleased to meet you," Svetlana told me, her knowing eyes twinkling. "I know you know all about Conrad and me. It's our turn to get to know you." She held her hand across the table for her husband's. "We're on a mission, you see. Solange sent us."

Berry

I was sure I'd just made the biggest mistake of my life. I'd just set two unfinished, unpublished, out of time characters free in the world with only their promise they'd return. Both had proven themselves cunning and manipulative when they needed to be. But what choice did I have? They could get close to Trista, and I could not.

In the meanwhile, with every spare moment I had, I had to keep working on their story to meet my looming deadline. It was creeping ever closer, and I had at least one more draft to write before I'd be satisfied. And there was that pesky little bit of research I had yet to do on eighteenth-century sailing routes so that my readers wouldn't slam me for continuity problems. At least Conrad and Svetlana cooperated. No backtalk from them as long as they were out in the world. True, they didn't seem as well rounded as they normally were, but that's what third drafts are for.

And I had to figure out how I could reach out to Moe without making a complete fool of myself. I would settle for seeming an incomplete fool if I had to. I'd even get up the courage to tell him I loved him. Face to face, when I wasn't mostly asleep.

I have to admit, I was getting nervous about this whole thing. What if he and Trista did get together? She was so beautiful, so sexy, so perfect. How could he ever want to look at someone like me after having had her? But worse, what would happen when he found out she wasn't real?

Would he commit himself? Would he commit me or shun me the next time we met? I could hardly bear to think about it, but it was a problem of my own making.

When I arrived at work, both Rocco and Duncan were after me all day. There was a pile on my desk, not to mention a filled email inbox. Heaven forbid someone else should pick up the slack while I was out. And they wanted me to work straight through until it was all cleaned up—three days' worth in one. I told them both, as politely as I could, to go pound sand. Duncan looked scandalized. Rocco smiled at me, but it wasn't a smile to make me all warm and fuzzy. Would he fire his own sister over two sick days? Could life get any more difficult?

As it turns out, it could.

Brad was waiting for me when I arrived home. He must have popped into my condo during the day, bypassing security. He was looking relaxed, fit, bronzed, and buff, and his smile had the megawattage that made him prime romance hero material. He was relaxing on my sofa with the TV on. Apparently, he had a taste for daytime talk shows.

"Hey," he waved as I walked in, my computer bag slung over one shoulder, a stack of papers in my other arm.

"Don't tell me. Moe kicked you out." I dropped my keys into the tray by the door and allowed the computer strap to slide down my arm. "When are you and Trista going to reconcile?" There. Put the onus on him.

He shrugged as if he really didn't care. "Don't know. Right now, she's set her sights on your boyfriend. I figure I'll let her wear herself out on him before I do anything. But I guess he's not your boyfriend anymore, from what I'm hearing."

"Oh?" My goodness, but my characters were all a bunch of gossips. I don't remember writing them that way.

"Who says?"

"Svetlana and Conrad had breakfast with Triss and Moe this morning. I managed to eavesdrop without being seen. Right now, Triss thinks of me as more of a booty call until she can get him in bed."

"And you're okay with this?" *What happened to all those rewrites I did?*

He slumped into his seat. "To be honest, they weren't much good."

Could he hear me think?

Brad lifted an eyebrow as if wondering why that was so strange. Oh, crap.

"I gotta be honest with you, girl, those rewrites were kind of desperate. Until Triss changes her mind, I don't have a lot of choices, do I? Other than you. I started to remember the time before you hooked me up with Triss. Before I was who you remade me."

He eyed me in a way that made me feel a little twitchy.

"I thought, maybe since you and Moe are done, you and I could pick up where we'd left off," he said.

My heart started to pound, and not in a good way. "Hold it right there, buster. Nothing doing."

He frowned. "But I thought—"

"You know, Brad, I think Trista was right. You'd better leave the thinking to her. Or me."

He bowed his head. "Okay." After a while, he added, "I didn't think it would work. Same with Moe. He really doesn't seem too interested in Triss."

That was the best news I'd heard since yesterday.

"How about some dinner? I've got this great chicken I made."

He stood, rubbing his hands, and made his way to the kitchen. "Sounds terrific."

Moe

Have you ever wondered exactly when you lost control of your life? Not me. Until then, that is. One minute I'm loving up my babe and feeling like everything's going my way, and the next I'm sitting across the table from another woman who was scowling at me like I don't know what the hell I'm doing.

Actually, at that moment, I didn't. I've never been to a restaurant where they had a waiter just for the wine. The guy gave me the cork, so I put it in my pocket. Then he pours me a tiny little sip. I think the guy's being a cheapskate. I was buying the whole bottle—I wanted a full glass. So I drank it and held my glass out for more.

Triss gasped. Conrad sniggered, and Svetlana closed her eyes and shook her head. I haven't been embarrassed like that for a good long time, and I didn't even know why I was.

I have to say the meal was really good. The food was tasty, but there wasn't a lot of it. It came out on these huge plates and was arranged like in a magazine, but for the life of me, I felt like I was a boor for cleaning my plate. And the dessert—I really would have liked a slice of pie instead of the sculpture they put in front of me. I couldn't figure out how to eat it.

My companions managed to deconstruct their meals without problem. I tried to watch how they did it, but I kept getting distracted by something else, and by the time I looked again, it was done.

Naturally, I was stuck with the bill. As well-dressed as the three of them were, you'd think between them they could have coughed up some cash to contribute, but no. When the check came, the waiter placed it in front of yours truly, and I had to whip out my credit card to pay for it all.

None of them even said thanks.

All in all, Conrad was a good guy. He knew which fork and which knife to use and didn't mind helping me figure that out. I knew Berry would know, which made me sad. He was into sailing reproduction eighteenth-century ships. I mean, it was interesting and all, but after a while, it kind of got on my nerves. The part about the reenacting naval battles was cool, but once you hear one story about a sea battle, they all start to sound alike. He didn't know jack about sports either, not even who the favorite local teams were. I mean, I would have liked him fine if he followed the Sox or even the Yanks so we could argue, but it was as if he'd never heard of either of them.

The ladies spent most of the meal whispering to one another. I heard the name *Solange* hissed more often than I could count. I could tell that Triss was getting pissed off at Svetlana. Triss scowled at everything that one had to say. And Triss kept running her hand over my arm, all the way up to my bicep, and she kept smiling at me, wrinkling her nose. It really got on my nerves. Funny how her fingers were so cool. Even with all that rubbing, the friction never warmed them up. And Svetlana was getting cross, as she put it. Isn't that quaint? Apparently, Triss found her just as bossy as she found Berry.

After dinner was done, when my credit card was quietly sobbing because there was no credit left, we all walked outside. True to form, none of them had anything resembling a winter coat. Conrad was wearing a suit, as was I, but the ladies each had on fancy thin dresses with only shawls. They didn't seem cold.

I wasn't exactly in a position to invite them back to my place for a nightcap. For one, I didn't have any liquor in the house, and the last I remembered, I only had two chairs to my name. I still needed to clean one of them. Make that two. I couldn't remember which one Brad had sat his naked ass down on, and I wasn't taking any chances.

Speaking of whom, Triss never mentioned him. He'd certainly made himself scarce at my place. When I got there a few days ago, the bed was made up with clean sheets. Somehow he'd restocked all the food with exact replacements. All my books were back on the shelf as I'd left them. It was as if he'd never been there at all. Kind of like what happened when Berry and I got back from our first date. He hadn't left a note either.

Truthfully, all that expensive wine had given me a terrible headache. I prefer beer. The only thing I wanted was to crawl into a nice warm bed with a nice warm Berry beside me. I don't recall exactly how it happened, but before I knew it, I was saying goodnight to the three of them and getting into my truck alone. I don't know how they came, but they were leaving the same way.

On a whim, I headed over to Berry's building. I looked up and found that the light was on in her den, but no other rooms. That didn't tell me much other than that she was probably pounding at the keys to finish her story. That was better than the alternatives that had plagued me all evening—thinking of her with that good-looking, rich boy sponge. He was no better than the rest of them. I prayed he wasn't with her, that he'd taken his fancy sports car and headed out for parts unknown. I wished the rest of them would follow.

There was something off about all of them, but for the life of me, I couldn't figure out what it was. Maybe it was their having grown up in places far from here. Maybe it was that they apparently had no shame when it came to what I considered private matters. I knew that I didn't want any part of it. Trista and Brad might have been a lot of fun to read about, but knowing them in real life was a whole other story. I didn't want to get to know the others any better for the same reason.

I wondered how Berry was feeling about them right about now. Betrayed, perhaps? It was time to call her. Maybe I would tomorrow. I looked up at her window again and wondered how she'd react if I called her right now—if I parked and rang her doorbell.

But I was dressed in my best clothes. I'd have a hell of a time explaining to her that I had taken Trista out for a fancy meal—far fancier than anything Berry and I had done. Nope. Not going to happen.

I hit the gas and headed home to my cold, lonely bed.

Chapter Twenty-Six

Moe

Berry wasn't answering her phone the next morning. Maybe she was visiting family or friends. Maybe she was sleeping in after working late the night before. Maybe she was out with Brad, choosing a turkey for Thanksgiving dinner.

Maybe she was still mad at me.

I hung up without leaving a message.

The holiday was four days away. I'd be spending it with my mother and brothers, as I always did. One or two of the guys were bringing dates. I hoped it was enough to distract mom from badgering me. I never noticed her ragging on the rest of the boys about it the same way.

That's when I heard a knock on the back door.

There was no curtain, so I couldn't very well pretend I wasn't home. Besides, Triss was standing out there in the cold, looking very annoyed and glaring at me.

I opened the door, standing there as I was in my jeans, socks, and thermal undershirt.

"Good morning."

She brushed by me without a greeting. "I have never been so embarrassed in all my life," she said without preamble."

"I beg your pardon?"

"Last night at the restaurant. Were you brought up in a barn?"

That sounded a little like an insult to my mother. She happened to work very hard to bring up five boys on her own, and the older I got, the more I appreciated what an effort that was.

"I was not. Nor do I go around insulting people or their mothers first thing in the morning before they've had their coffee." I closed the door behind her.

"Well, I haven't had any either. Go make some." I could swear her toe was tapping.

"I'm afraid that's impossible. I was heading out." I indicated my boots in my hand.

"I'll go with you." She sat herself down and crossed her legs. She had on another one of those twin sets. Orange this time. This one was skintight. I hoped she was sitting on Brad's butt-chair.

I heard a car drive up outside—probably a neighbor's.

"Triss, I've got things to do today, and after last night, I don't think it would be a good idea for us to see each other anymore. We're from different worlds. I don't think we're well suited for one another."

"Nonsense."

Trista cocked her head before she stood and walked over to me. Before I could react, she'd pulled my head down and kissed me, hard. I kind of lost my balance and dropped my boots on the floor and grabbed her so I didn't pitch over. Triss pushed up against me and mashed her body to mine at that. All it took was a second or two.

That's when I saw Berry's face through the same glass door Trista had walked through. I watched as her eyes grew as big as saucers and then she was gone. I could hear her shoes clacking on the planks of the porch floor as she ran away.

Shit.

I tried to break from Triss, but she had me in a headlock. Christ, she was strong for a skinny woman. I managed to pull my head away, but she wouldn't let the rest of me go.

"What the hell do you think you're doing?"

"I thought it was time you knew how I felt about you." She smiled as I heard car tires screech away. "You were taking your time making a pass at me, so I thought I would do you the favor of letting you know I'm available."

"Do you realize that Berry saw us?"

Her smile grew cat-like as she seated herself. "Solange? Did she? Tsk, tsk. What a shame."

Why the hell did this woman always use Berry's nom de guerre? "I have to go after her."

Triss shook her head at me. "And what do you plan to tell her?"

I glared at her. "I thought I'd start with the truth."

I swear that woman just looked at me and smiled. "Do you really think she's going to believe you?" she said at last.

"Why wouldn't she?" I replied with a sinking feeling in my stomach.

"If the roles were reversed, would you believe her?"

Oh, crap.

"So, now that you're rid of her once and for all, how about inviting me to Thanksgiving dinner?"

Berry

I could not breathe. And it's a good thing I knew my way home because I could barely see. My stomach hurt so badly I thought I was going to hurl the breakfast I hadn't managed to eat.

After I'd kicked Brad out last night (I knew he wouldn't freeze), I'd gone to bed, talking myself into going to see Moe the next morning. I don't know why I didn't do something simple like call him first—it seemed a little more spontaneous to show up. So much for a carefully planned impulsive move.

The last thing I expected was to see him in a lip lock with Trista. She wasn't exactly a virgin when the story opened, but her experience with men was limited, and she was one-hundred-percent in favor of monogamy. She believed in honoring her vows. I didn't write her to be a tramp. She wanted to be one, but I'd put my foot down. I wanted hers to be a sweet, sexy romance, and that's what I'd published.

I am such an idiot. Just because I wrote her one way didn't mean she was still that way. She'd apparently gained all sorts of knowledge in the weeks she was on the loose. And from what Svetlana and Conrad had told me, she was no longer anything like the character I originally envisioned.

I wanted to cry, but I couldn't catch my breath long enough to do that. How could she do that to me? How could he? I didn't know which betrayal hurt more.

I managed to get myself home, and I rushed into my condo and shut the door before the sobs wracked me. That's when Brad walked out of my shower without a care. Or a towel.

"Oh, for crying out loud, can you at least pretend to be modest?" I cried.

"Whoa. What's got your boxers in a twist?" he said as he reached into the linen closet. He must have grabbed the first thing he touched, for he tried to wrap a pillowcase around his body without much success. It was one of my oldest ones, and with the moisture on his body, he didn't leave much to the imagination.

"What the hell are you doing here?" I wiped the tears away. "I thought I told you last night I didn't want to see you again until you got your wife back. And brought me that book."

"I was going to Moe's, but Trista was heading there. I

didn't want a confrontation with an audience. The last time, she and I were rolling around on the floor in front of him. He didn't seem too pleased about it, so I came here." Brad looked at me sheepishly. "Is that where you were?"

I slowly nodded.

"Were they rolling around on the floor?" He sounded sad.

"Not exactly. Maybe the prelude. Or whatever the hell comes after. After-after," I amended with a gulp.

"Oh."

I blinked, and he was dry. The pillowcase was on the floor at his feet, and he was—how shall I put this politely? Rigid.

"So, do you want to roll around on the floor with me...?"

I closed my eyes. I thought I'd eliminated the ellipses from his syntax. "No, Brad, I do not."

"I figured," he sighed.

I dared to peek at him to find he'd dressed in his usual outfit of Oxford shirt and khakis. "It was worth a shot," he shrugged and smiled. "So. What do we do next?"

What indeed.

I'd hinted to my mother that I might want to bring a date to Thanksgiving dinner this year. I didn't give her the details—in case this thing with Moe didn't last. If I had and it didn't, I'd never hear the end of it.

Maybe I could make Brad over into someone more like Moe, at least for a few days. I looked at him as he stared into space. This wouldn't be easy. The published version of him was proving very hard to over-write. But it was worth a try.

I swore to myself if I was ever lucky enough to have *You're the One for Me* re-released, I was going to have a field day rewriting it to match my original vision. Brad was going to be a hell of a lot more alpha, and Trista would have a real comeuppance. I gritted my teeth hard. Planning my retribution was going to be a lot of fun.

Moe

I faced off with Trista on my back-porch Thanksgiving morning. "Okay, these are the ground rules." For the life of me, I couldn't figure out how she got from one place to the next. I never heard or saw a car. Did she take taxis? Uber? I didn't even know where she was staying, and we never spoke on the phone. This was the spookiest relationship I was ever in against my will.

"You will be nice to my mother and my brothers."

"I'm always nice," she protested.

"My idea of nice, not yours. No snarky comments when someone's left the room. Offer to help when we get there and as often as you need to."

"What do you mean, help?" She was tapping her toe again. God, I hated that.

"Mash the potatoes or something," I replied. "Just offer to help and do whatever mom tells you needs doing."

She arched a brow. "But I'm a guest."

"No such thing. Everyone pitches in."

"What if she asked me to clean the toilet?" Her perfect nose wrinkled. I hated that more than the toe-tapping.

"She won't," I said between my teeth. "She'll have cleaned her place within an inch of its life. Just cooking and washing up afterward. You know how to do all that stuff."

"Very well." She folded her arms. "Anything else?"

"No swearing. My mom hates that."

She pouted.

"Just be normal and natural. Ask questions if you have them. This may be different from Thanksgivings where you come from."

She hefted her enormous purse higher on her shoulder. "Can we leave now?"

I heaved a silent breath. I was dreading the next few hours. "Yeah. Let's go."

Berry

Brad was in my den, my computer was mysteriously on, and he looked as if he'd gotten a shock. "What do you think you're doing?" I shrieked.

"I was only looking," he murmured, rubbing his fingers together. "Is that thing always so painful?"

"What?"

"When you touch that machine," he said, pointing to the laptop. "Does it hurt you?"

Great. Was my computer shorting out on me? At least I'd backed everything up last night, but I couldn't afford the delay computer repairs were going to cost. For the past several days, I'd worked on nothing but Brad's script for meeting my family. I was now four days behind in my schedule to submit my latest draft, and there was no way I could call in sick again. I'd have to put in some long nights. Damn.

I sat in my chair and gingerly placed my hands on the keyboard. Nothing but the familiar smooth keys, the raised bumps under F and J. I looked up at him. I scrolled up and down the file without problem. "It's fine. Are you sure you weren't touching something else?"

He reached over and with a tentative forefinger, touched the silver top of the keyboard. I could see a spark jump from it to him, and he whipped his finger away, sucking on it.

"I've never seen that happen before." I think I narrowed my eyes at him then. "Were you planning some mischief? Like rewriting something?"

He looked guilty. Maybe it was some sort of cosmic feedback loop or something that backfired if he was trying to rewrite himself. I had no idea how it worked, but I was grateful. I was starting to worry about myself that I was taking all this for granted. At least the forces of nature, or un-nature, seemed to be on my side.

"I told you it would be disastrous for you to rewrite this script," I told him. Brad was getting as willful as Trista. "Besides, this is only for today. Once dinner is done, you can go back to being the way you were."

"Do you mean it?" One brow lifted meaningfully.

I gritted my teeth. Not for the first time, I wondered why Trista had put up with him for as long as she had. I couldn't figure out why the book was selling so well, for I was thoroughly hating both my hero and heroine at this point.

"Yes. And then maybe you'll help Svetlana and Conrad?"

So far, Brad had done nothing but sit on his butt all day. The other two were out there doing what needed to be done. So far, it hadn't worked, but I figured it was a matter of my coming up with the right strategy. Con and Svet were taking a well-earned break. Trista wouldn't tell them what her plans were, and I figured it was best for all concerned that I didn't know. The only thing I did know was that Trista had yet to spend the night with Moe. Oh, and that the kiss had been staged for my benefit. That soothed some of the pain, but not entirely.

I still hadn't heard from Moe, but I did check my caller ID every day to find he'd called. It was something at least. But why didn't he ever leave a message or call when he knew I'd be free? I was determined that he make the first move. I may not have had much pride, but what I had, I clung to.

Brad came up to me and hugged me. "I know you're doing your best." His lips began to travel from my cheek to my neck. At the same time, his hands wandered down to my hips. He pulled me closer.

I stilled. "Brad, if you make one more move in that

direction, the next time I sit at my computer, I'm going to delete all your male parts. No, not good enough. I'll shrink them. Understood?"

His body went from lax to rigid in a moment, all except that part that had been rigid a moment earlier. He carefully lifted his hands from me. "Yeah. I get it."

I stepped back. "I'm glad we understand each other. Now, let's go."

Chapter Twenty-Seven

Moe

So far, so good. Trista seemed nervous as we walked up the two flights of stairs to mom's apartment. Or maybe it was annoyance that the elevator was out of order. The noise level alone would have made a sane person think twice about entering. That excluded me right off the bat.

We carried the four pies I'd bought the day before. That was one good thing about Ma. She knew my limitations and didn't mind that I didn't make anything from scratch for the meal—was, in fact, grateful I gave up trying.

"Maurice." Ma greeted me with a big hug and pulled my head down for a kiss on the cheek. "You're the last to arrive. Dinner's almost ready."

"Ma, this is Trista Johnston-Harding."

"Just Johnston," Trish said with a wrinkle to her nose and daggers in her eyes.

Ma looked from the boxes in my hand, clearly printed with the store name, to my date done up in a golden twin set along with her pearls. "What, you don't bake?" she asked.

The next thing I knew, Trista was holding a perfect, golden-crusted apple pie in her hands and presented it to my mother. My mouth dropped open. Ma blinked. I blinked and shut my pie hole.

"Of course, Mrs. Conrad. But Maurice had already bought those, and I was so busy, I didn't have time for more than the one." She looked down, almost demure. "I hope you like it."

"That's more like it." Ma took the offering with a grim

nod. She smelled the pie and looked up at Triss with a smile that alerted all my panic sensors. "I'm sure it will be fine."

Ma is nobody's fool. She took another look at Trista all dressed up in her sweaters and pearls. "You remind me of someone." She looked again at the impossibly high heels Triss wore. "Someone from a book."

Triss laughed her tinkly laugh. "How flattering."

"I didn't mean it that way." Ma turned around and walked back into bedlam. "Make yourselves comfortable. Maurice, offer your guest a drink."

"Can I help with anything, Mrs. Conrad?"

Ma heaved the pie in her hands. "This will do for now. Joey's smashing the spuds. Once he's done, we'll sit and eat. I'll need help with the cleaning up later." Ma took off, leaving the two of us in the doorway.

Triss wrinkled her nose. "Dishes," she whispered. "I hate doing dishes."

I cringed at the face she made. "Yeah, well, there's no dishwasher, so you'll have plenty to hate," I laughed. Never let it be said I'm a nice guy *all* the time.

We walked into the living room where every inch was covered by a hodgepodge of tables and chairs. My brothers were all there, save for Joey in the kitchen. Their dates were sitting sullenly next to my brothers. A few cousins had also been invited, including various spouses and children. All in all, I think there were about twenty-five of us squeezed into that tiny apartment.

Next year, I vowed, I'd host the meal in my remodeled Victorian. The kitchen would be done, and with any luck, Berry would have forgiven me and would preside over the meal with my ring on her finger. I closed my eyes, picturing her at one end of a long formal table, me at the other. Was that a bulge of a baby under her apron I saw? The last time she'd worn an apron in my presence, she hadn't had a whole lot on under it. I grinned to myself. That had been great. Until it wasn't.

That lovely image was cut short with a sharp pain in my shin. "Aren't you going to introduce me to everyone?" Trista hissed.

I cleared my throat. "Hey everyone. This here's Trista, my kitchen designer." I didn't want any mistaken ideas today. "She didn't have anywhere to go today, so she's here with me." I put my hand on the back of her waist. "Triss, this is everyone."

"Idiot," she said under her breath before she graced the room with one of her brilliant smiles. "Hi everyone," she beamed. "I'm so glad to be here." She sat down next to my next youngest brother. "I think we've met before." She held out her hand. "Tell me, do you like turkey on Thanksgiving?"

Sammy looked up at me as if he couldn't believe this one. Of all of them, he's the one who'd been most taken with Berry. He shot me a dirty look as if to say 'you gave up that one for this?'

"Yes, we've m-met. And no. I hate turkey." He folded his arms across his chest. "And stuffing, cranberry s-sauce. I especially hate apple pie."

Not that you'll be surprised, but I have to report things went downhill from there.

Berry

"I'm so pleased to meet you, Mr. Samuels and Mrs. Samuels."

Brad was wearing his best smile as we walked into my parents' home. "Berry's inviting me to your lovely home means the world to me."

Thank goodness he used my real name. He handed

mom the two pies I'd baked that morning, no help from him, of course. Brad had been enchanted by the parade on TV and was far too engrossed to help.

"We're so pleased to have you." Dad shook his hand, and I was glad for all the practicing we'd done. Gone was the lily-livered handshake Brad started with. This was a firm, warm, two-handed shake that would do any he-man or politician proud.

"Hi, Princess." Dad finally tore his attention away from Mister Wonderful to beam at me. At least with Brad there, I wouldn't hear anything about my unmarried, childless state. Those remarks would come the next day, but I planned to let voicemail do the heavy lifting.

"Hi, dad." I kissed his cheek and then followed mom into the kitchen. Rocco was already in the living room with Darlene. I nodded as I passed through. Heaven forbid either of them do anything to help.

I'd quizzed Brad all morning and all the way over today. If he messed up, he'd do it on purpose because I knew he had his script memorized. No staring into space, no inane questions. Smile, but not too much teeth. Make eye contact. Sit up straight. Keep your clothes on. Do not talk about religion, politics, or sex. Talk about your ranch, but only when asked. We met through mutual friends. We were only friends. Do not mention that you are a fictional character from a romance novel.

For the first time, I was grateful no one in my family had read my book.

"Hi, honey." My mom hugged me and blew kisses near my cheeks. Her hands were full of butter and cream for the potatoes. Everything else stood on the countertop: a perfectly golden-brown turkey, string beans, cranberry sauce, and I could see the sweet potato casserole browning in the oven. "Your young man seems very nice.

Dad likes him."

"Um-hum." I didn't bother to correct her impression that he was mine. I was just minding him until I could unload him.

"How did you meet?"

"Oh, through a friend of a friend," I said, hoping that would be the end of that conversation.

"That's nice. Does he write in his spare time like you? What a lonely hobby that is."

"Brad owns a ranch in Texas," I told her. "He'll be heading back there soon."

"What a shame, just as the two of you are getting to know one another. Maybe you can go out there to visit him."

"Maybe." I poked around the cabinets to get glassware. "What can I do?"

"If you can start to carry things out, that would be great. Rocky and his girlfriend were all set to help, but they must have gotten distracted. Brad is very handsome, by the way. And so tall!"

"That he is," I agreed. I'd toned down his sun-streaked highlights for today, so he'd look a little more normal, but he still towered over everyone else in the room, and was so broad, I hoped he'd fit at the table without crowding. Maybe I'd overdone it, but Moe was as big as Brad was. Mostly. Moe was right-sized. I blinked and focused on what my mother was saying.

"...and he seems so gentlemanly."

"He has perfect manners." I'd seen to that in the first draft. It was one of the things Trista first noticed about him when they were reintroduced years after being separated as childhood playmates. He knew his dinner fork from his salad fork. He was probably the only modern romance hero who knew asparagus could be eaten with the fingers in polite company.

As I carried the green bean casserole into the dining room, I watched him interact with my family. He was so perfect. I wondered how in the world could they possibly think he was real?

No doubt the same way Moe could be fooled by Trista. I wondered how they were getting on.

Moe

"Can you pass the t-taters? Please," Sammy called down the table. Triss was oblivious as she pushed the food around her plate. I swear, I don't know if I'd seen her take a bite of anything.

"Triss, the potatoes?" I asked under my breath. "Can you pass them?"

"I had no idea what he was talking about," she whispered back as she lifted the bowl and passed it to me. "Is he always so rude?"

"Rude?" My youngest brother had asked as nicely as I'd ever heard. "That's just his way."

She shuddered delicately. "Well, his manners leave something to be desired. Where I come from, the please comes first, and proper names are given to objects."

Where exactly did she come from anyway? I could feel the heated stares of the rest of my family as we spoke. I guess when I told her to not talk about anyone behind their backs, she didn't get the unspoken part about not talking about them to their fronts either. There were some uneasy glances shared around the table, and more than one pitying look cast my way. If I'd been in one of their chairs, I'd have done the same.

I have to admit, I was feeling plenty sorry for myself. Things would have been so much better if it were Berry sitting to my left instead of this harridan. I had Ber to thank for giving me words like that from her historical romance. Damn.

"Are all your family meals like this?" she stage-whispered.

I figured I might as well go in over my head. "Like what?"

"So—boisterous?"

I had to laugh. "Boisterous? Everyone's on their best behavior tonight 'cause you're here."

I caught a brotherly wink or two at that. Maybe they would find a way to forgive me one of these days.

"You're joking."

"Afraid not. This is as good as it gets." I shoved another forkful into my mouth in the hopes of ending the conversation.

"Why, even that Slavic slut Svetlana has better manners than these boors."

The rest of the table grew quiet. Even the kids.

I glanced around and smiled at everyone in the hopes they'd ignore her. I leaned closer. "I thought Svetlana was a friend of yours."

"Oh, no." She shook her head emphatically and wrinkled her nose when she smiled.

You know, if I liked Trista more, I'd speak to her about that bad habit of hers. I wondered if she thought it was charming.

"She's a friend of Solange. We're just acquaintances."

"You mean, I just dropped over two hundred bucks on dinner for people you don't even like?"

She turned those big blue eyes on me. "It's only money."

"And how is Berry, anyway?" asked Paul. "Man, I sure wish you'd brought her along tonight too. I really like her."

"Me too," the others chimed in.

Ma's head popped up from her conversation with my cousin Julie. I could practically see the question marks popping out of her head.

Just like I could hear Trista's toe-tapping under the table.

"I haven't been able to connect with her," I replied honestly. I didn't need to mention that I had neglected to leave messages each time I called. For the life of me, I couldn't figure out why. I've never been such a coward, but I didn't know what to say to her, but not saying much would have been a whole lot easier if she were on the other end of the phone.

"Who's Berry?" mom asked, and the room went quiet. "You have another girlfriend besides this one that you haven't told me about?"

"Triss is not my—"

"They were dating before," Trista said. "Now he's seeing me."

"Not for long," I whispered under my breath. "Ma, it's kind of complicated. Berry is the writer I met at the bookstore. I told you about her. We had a misunderstanding. I'm trying to make amends with her."

"You are not," Trista hissed. "You're mine now. That's the way it works."

What the hell was she talking about? What works what way? "Don't I get a choice?"

"I made the choice. It's always for the woman to do," she insisted. "Solange explained that to me."

This was news. "Exactly when?"

"When—when she first wrote—I mean, when she created—Oh fuck it all. When she and I first met."

Not even the grandniece sitting on my mother's lap made a peep at that Very Bad Word spoken at my mother's table. Was Trista delusional? I didn't hardly breathe, let alone look at anyone. I am not, and never will be, that brave.

I rose and grabbed Trista's arm, hauling her to her feet. "Excuse us, please."

"Excuse me." Trista smiled blandly. "Maurice and I need to finish this conversation in private."

"I'm a little afraid to," I admitted. My brothers laughed, but my mother narrowed her eyes at me. I could read into that. *Get rid of her before I do it for you.*

"Everyone, if you'll pardon us?" I escorted Trista to the front hall without waiting for a reply.

As I left, I heard Joey complain, "It figures they'd leave before the cleaning up starts."

We walked out into the stairwell. "What the hell are you talking about?" I shouted, not caring that anyone could hear. I wasn't technically in my mother's home at the moment, so I could use words like hell and damn. But I would never, ever drop the f-bomb. Nope, not ever going to happen. "You're here only because you invited yourself, Triss. We're not dating. We don't have a relationship, and I don't appreciate your implying to everyone that we do."

"Of course we do. Didn't you kiss me in your kitchen the other morning?" She ran a cool finger down the front of my shirt, but she didn't stop there. That hand of hers kept going until it cradled my crotch.

You know, there's desire that a man feels in his head. There's love a man feels in his heart. And then there's sex. The pirate in my pants didn't give a damn about the first two. All he knew was stimulation, and that's what he was getting. Damned if the traitor wasn't starting to stand at attention at the worst possible time.

"See," she cooed in my ear. "You want me. You know you do. We don't need anyone else. Just you and me, handsome. We could go back to your place, and I can show you a thing or two. I know you saw Brad and me go at it, but that was nothing. wait until you find out what I've got in mind for you. I'll give new meaning to the words 'all night long'." She stretched and sucked my earlobe into her mouth. "You and I could get it on right here, right now if you wanted. I know how to be quiet when I have to." She cupped me again, and my turncoat throbbed. "But I don't want to be," she whispered in a husky voice.

I can honestly tell you, I have never, ever been in exactly this position before. It wasn't nearly as much fun as it might sound, either. I removed her hand as gently as I could. "Triss, I think somehow you've gotten the wrong idea about me. I've been trying to be nice about this, but it's time for some plain talk."

She didn't seem to be listening, for she'd moved on from my ear and was breathing hard against my chest, rubbing herself all over me. I hate to tell you that it felt good, but... well, it did. Except for one problem. She was the wrong woman.

"Stop it. Listen to me." I stepped away and banged into the wall. "I'm only going to tell you this once. I'm not into you. You're a beautiful, sexy woman, but you and I are not meant to be. You need someone like Brad. Someone rich and famous. Someone who can treat you the way you deserve to be treated. I'm never going to have the kind of money he has or the connections. I don't think I'll ever be able to go into a fancy restaurant and know what kind of wine I want. When I go out to eat, all I want are burgers and beer."

"I can teach you all those things," she purred.

"But I don't want to learn them. I've fallen for Berry. I love her."

She stopped. "You love her? Berry? Are you serious?" She threw back her head and laughed. "That small-minded hermit. She's so imperfect. All talk and no business. She lives in a dream world."

"I don't know about that. I found her world to be plenty interesting," I said.

"She's timid and kowtows to everyone."

I seemed to recall a few times when she got plenty bossy and bold. In fact, the rest of me—every part of me remembered that as well. "I'm not so sure..."

"You don't really know her." She struck an indignant pose. "Did you know she sleeps around?"

My heart stood still there. "I beg your pardon?"

"She sleeps with all her male characters. She did Brad before he became Brad. Not that I mind, of course. And she was doing Conrad too. In fact, before you came along, she was test driving some tall, dark, and handsome lover for her next novel, the one where Brad and I are supposed to be supporting characters."

That did it. Trista had lost her mind. "Berry isn't the type to sleep around."

Triss bit her lip. Maybe it was occurring to her that if she treated Berry this badly, Berry might find another person to play a role in her next book. If I ever got to talk to that little woman again, I'd make a point of telling her to stay as far away from Triss as she possibly could. I'd even strike a bargain with her. It might kill my ego and strain my patience, but she could test-drive any romantic or sensual scene she wanted, as long as it was with me. So long as she didn't use my name. In print that is.

"Do you have any idea how little sense you're making? Berry doesn't sleep around. She's got a vivid imagination, for which I am very grateful. Maybe in her mind..."

"Exactly," Triss crowed. "That's where she does it. But in her mind, she's a tramp."

I rubbed my neck. A guy might not think that such a bad

thing. This guy, for instance.

"You know Triss—this evening is over. I'll get my coat and make apologies to everyone, but I think it's time I took you home."

"You really want that little hussy more than me?" she huffed.

I rubbed my chin. A warm, imaginative hussy who doesn't have a mean bone in her body, compared to an uptight sex-crazed meany? "Yes."

She looked like she could not believe what I'd just said. She stood there, glaring for so long, I thought I'd fallen asleep. Maybe I had, for the next thing I knew, I was standing in that stairwell alone. To be honest, I didn't even hear the door slam when she left. It all made me a little dizzy. Maybe I was losing my mind.

I went back into the apartment. "Triss, uh, Trista decided she had a headache and went home."

I lied badly, but no one challenged me. I might be mistaken, but there seemed to be a collective sigh of relief. My mother smiled at me for the first time in hours.

Pete kicked back a chair. "Come try some of this pie. It looks great, but it's tasteless. It's like eating nothing at all. The next time you go for an ice queen, make sure she really knows how to bake." He took another bite. "I'll bet Berry knows how to cook."

Yeah. In the kitchen and in the bedroom. And she's inventive with the moo shu leftovers too.

I took home Triss' pie pan. I figured she'd show up sooner or later to claim it. Berry had once said that Triss wasn't like a real woman. I was beginning to believe her. But the women I knew were protective of their cooking gear. She'd be back.

Chapter Twenty-Eight

Berry

My parents and Rocco couldn't get enough of Brad. They wanted his opinion on this, that and the other thing. My father even asked him how he voted. I had a bad moment there, for I had steered clear of politics in my remake of the man. I needn't have worried. Brad had listened carefully as my family spoke of the recent election, and he managed to parrot most of their ideas right back at them and make them sound fresh. It took the attention off me and my cringes. My own ideas ran contrary, but I wasn't about to announce that in this company.

Brad would have stayed all night to bask in their adoration. I, on the other hand, was exhausted. I had the next day off and planned to get up early and make some progress on my novel. I would turn my phone ringers to silent, make a big pot of coffee, and focus, focus, focus. Brad would disappear or face my wrath.

It was late when I finally dragged him out of there after promising my mother I would bring him back if I could. I could see the wedding wheels turning in her head. Crap. On my way out, she whispered to me, "Oh honey, he's perfect. I don't even mind that he's been married before. As long as there are no children to worry about, we can pretend it never happened."

Like that could be arranged. I mean, the book was published. And Brad wasn't real.

My parents might love Brad, but I wanted a real man, not a perfect one.

The next morning, I woke up early as planned, but

instead of a nice, quiet day, there was a ruckus in the living room.

I stumbled out in my flannel nightgown to find Svetlana sulking on the sofa and Conrad holding Brad hostage with his rapier. Ah. The perfect way to start a long holiday weekend. I wish I didn't know who in the world these people were and why were they in my living room. But no, me and my imagination. I took a deep breath and did my best to glare at the three of them.

"What the hell are you doing?" I squealed.

"He was trying to steal my woman," Conrad said, the tip of his sword never wavering from Brad's Adam's apple. "He was sweet-talking her into some madness."

"Oh, stuff it, Conrad," Svetlana mumbled. "He was being polite. Is scene where I am hit by you by mistake and have black eye. He wants to know if it pains me."

"Oh, really?" I walked into the room and took Conrad's arm, forcing the weapon down. "Brad, is this true?"

He had the grace to look guilty. "I wanted to know. My backstory has me getting one, but since I never lived it, I didn't know. I thought if you were going to fill in the details of my life in your next book, I should get prepared."

"Right, cowboy," Conrad sneered.

He sheathed his blade and turned to me with a deep bow. "Svetlana and I have done our best. We tried to reason with her, to force her. Even blackmail. We threatened to tell Moe she is not real. She only laughed at us. Told us he'd never believe it. We have discussed it at length and realize it is impossible to force that woman back into her story." He hung his head as he fell onto the cushion next to Svetlana. "I fear she is right. We have nothing on her."

Brad sank onto a chair, his head in his hands. "What am I going to do? I love that woman. Don't ask me why. I'm just written that way." He raised his head and glared at me. "It's all your fault."

"Me?" Were they forgetting who the injured party was here? "Trista's not the heroine I created. When I first imagined her, she was sweet and innocent, not this wanton know-it-all."

My knees felt weak, so I shoved my company over and sat down next to them. "Imagine how I feel?"

"And because of this, you keep tight rein over Conrad and me." Svetlana made a face at me. "We have no fun out in the world."

"Indeed," Conrad agreed patting Svetlana's knee. "Until we are published, we have not the same freedom as Triss. She tried to convince us, but these pages you wrote—" he pulled them from the leather bag hanging at his belt. "While they give us the freedom to wander about your world, these are too structured for us to break free."

Svetlana stood and posed for me, her breasts thrust forward in her linen blouse, pretty much the way I imagined she would on the cover of her book. "Come, Conrad. We do no more good here. Let us return to our book. Solange, open file so we return. You finish story. Until we have happy ending, we do nothing else. Maybe once we have the same freedom as Triss—"

"Not on my watch," I muttered.

"—then we can do some good in the world."

"I agree with my lady," Conrad said as he swept to his feet and made me a fine bow. "Return us. Make us famous. Give us the happily ever after you promised."

"Maybe if you'd made my happily ever after a little happier…" Brad started.

"Maybe if you'd shut up for a few minutes," I snapped back at him, but then stopped. The poor man looked ready to cry. That did it. He was my last metrosexual sensitive male hero. From now on, I was only going to write alpha males, flaws and all.

"I'm sorry. We're all doing the best we can. Maybe if you'd give me a little time, I'd think of something."

"You haven't yet," he moaned."

Thanks for the vote of confidence, buddy.

"You are unkind." Svetlana shoved Brad on the shoulder. "She has been hurt by all this. She lost the man she loved because you not control your woman. Does she complain to you? Does she berate you for this?" She sneered at him. "No. She is strong. She keeps doing what she does. She has no happy ending waiting for her at the end of this tale."

"Now wait a minute here," I cried. "My story isn't exactly over yet."

Svetlana glanced at me and whispered, "I try to tell this ungrateful wretch to be patient. Not time to defend him." She winked my way.

You wonderful creature, you. I winked back.

I rubbed my hands together before I placed them on my hips. I faced them like a drill sergeant. "Well, unlike all of you, I have to invent my own happy ending."

I held out my hands. "Conrad, Svetlana, give me back your traveling papers. You're going back where you came from."

Conrad handed me his. With a sly grin, Svetlana pulled hers from her bodice. I saw Brad's leering stare as she did so and knew if I could write her well enough that a fictional character was lusting after her, my reading public was likely to appreciate her as well.

I took the two packets and with a flourish, ripped them to pieces. Conrad bowed, and Svetlana grinned, and with a small pop, were gone.

I turned to Brad. "As for you." And then I was at a loss

for words.

"Yes?"

"I—" I sat back down with nothing to say. "I don't know. I'm fresh out of ideas."

"Is it true that you won't have a happy ending?" he asked tentatively. "I know I sounded kind of ungrateful, but it really is all your fault."

"Gee, thanks."

"I mean it. Is it true? Out here, you don't have happy endings?"

I shook my head. "Some do. Not everyone. Certainly no guarantees. I wasn't counting on anything with Moe, but it seemed as if we were headed in that direction."

"And because of me and Trista... things fell apart?"

I looked up at my first published hero and found a look of genuine concern, almost sadness on his face. "I can't say that with any certainty. Maybe things would have run their course anyway. It's hard to tell. No rewrites in my world as much as I'd like them."

I tried to smile at him, but I'm not sure how successful I was. "Now, how about you make yourself scarce for a few hours and let me get some work done. I really need to focus. I did promise I'd get Con and Svet published on time. Maybe while I'm working, I'll figure out the puzzle of your conundrum and mine at the same time. Maybe I can write my own happy ending after that."

He stood and nodded. Then he did the strangest thing. He leaned down and hugged me, kissed me on the cheek the way a friend would. No passion, just something that felt like genuine, warm emotion. "Okay. I guess I've been a little selfish."

He stood up. "Maybe I'll head south for a few hours. My tan's fading what with this New England weather of yours. I have to make sure I look good for the sequel."

I took his hand. It was warm and rough, and felt amazingly real. "That's very kind of you. I hope there is a sequel for you, but I'm not sure how I'll do that as long as Trista is a renegade. I'm not familiar with another contemporary romance series that kills off the heroine from the previous volume. Maybe I could make her a drunk or something."

I felt a smile come on, then a laugh. "Wouldn't that get the romantic press atwitter?"

"Then, you could write me a new heroine; someone patterned on you." He smiled at me, that thousand-watt smile that first caught my attention when I was auditioning leading men two years ago. "Someone smart and cute and all-powerful."

Ha! Wouldn't that be a kicker to have someone featured in a novel who was more like me. Lumpy bodies and dual colored eyes were not in the normal script. It would never sell. "You're on, pardner," I said anyway.

He kissed my cheek again and then vanished without a sound.

I thought for a moment about what he'd said, and what I'd said before that. If only I could rewrite Trista as she'd been before she was published. But it was too late. All the ideas I'd had for the sequel were now rubbish, but if I tweaked them, maybe had Triss come to a bad end so that Brad could find someone new... I shook my head. It would never work. From my fan mail, I knew my readers had loved Trista.

Still, the idea would not die. I tucked it away for a later moment of reflection. This day was going to be devoted to what I needed to do, not to wishful thinking.

The den and my PC awaited me, but first, I would treat myself to a cup of freshly ground café de cocoa. It had been a rough few weeks, and I deserved a treat. Then I'd take it on a brisk walk to get my blood pumping.

Maybe I'd think about something other than Brad and Triss, Con and Svet. Maybe a new pair of lovebirds was what I needed. A fresh heroine, a brand-new hero...

Ideas for my next novel were starting to pop into my head, so I grabbed a stack of index cards and a pen, and headed into the kitchen. I was feeling the first tentacles of hope in many days. Today was going to be a productive one. I was sure of it.

Moe

I knew I'd left the pie pan on my table the night before. I'd washed the damn thing as soon as I got home, and I sure didn't put it away. There was no place to put it. But it was gone.

I was staring at the spot when there was a knock at my back door. At this time in my life, I suppose I should have been past the point where things surprise me, but there stood Brad Harding.

He looked different. Maybe it was because the last time I'd seen him, he'd been sitting buck-naked in my kitchen with an equally naked Trista perched on his lap. But it was more than the clothes. His tan had faded, and he looked somehow more thoughtful, more mature. There were lines on his face that I hadn't noticed before, and when he smiled, it wasn't his usual phony smile. This one had a hint of remorse to it.

I opened the door and leaned on it. He might look apologetic, but it didn't mean a damned thing. I folded my arms against my chest and felt my hands close into fists.

"Yeah?" I said.

"Mind if I come in? I've, uh, got a few things I wanted to talk to you about."

"You can do your talking right here."

He lifted one brow. I wasn't certain why, but seeing Brad do that irritated the hell out of me. "And let all that warm air out of your kitchen?"

Being the ornery SOB that I was that morning, I stepped outside in my socks and shut the door behind me. "You can talk out here."

He kind of smiled then, and I seem to recall I sort of scowled. I didn't like that pretty boy wasting all his charm on me. Why didn't he use it to hold on to that troublesome woman of his and save us both a lot of aggravation?

"Okay. I'll keep this brief. I just left Solange—I mean Berry."

I said nothing but hoped my frown said it all.

"She misses you." He held up his hand. "Not that anything happened between us. That was all wishful thinking on my part. I was looking to hurt Triss, and Berry was convenient."

If I'd had hackles, they'd've risen. "Are you telling me she's not worth your time?"

He had the nerve to smile then, and then to laugh. "Not at all. If I'd have met her when I was first in my right mind, she's the woman I'd have gone after. But I'm afraid I married someone else. Now I need to do what I can to convince my wife to return to me. I've been letting everyone else do my dirty work. I think it's time I manned up and did something on my own."

"Would you? And hurry? My family all think I'm insane for dating her, which I'm not. She's damned manipulative."

Again with that apologetic smile. "I know. It's a habit I intend to break her of," Brad shook his head. "I need to take a firmer grip on the reigns of matrimony, I suppose."

"You need a firmer grip on something. That woman's just about driven me crazy, what with her popping over here when I least expect it." I stared at him before I glanced over at his fancy sports car parked behind my truck. "Sort of like you. I didn't hear you drive up."

He shrugged. "Part of my makeup, I guess. You'll have to talk to Berry about that. It's how she wrote us."

"Man, that's a crock. She might have written your story, but you still have free will. You don't have to be like she wrote you. She jazzed it up to sell books. That's fiction."

"Is it?" He smiled again, like he knew something I didn't. I really hated that. "Life sometimes imitates art."

"I don't believe this," I said.

He shrugged. "You can believe anything you want to. Like happy endings. Berry believes in them, despite herself."

"I can't believe this conversation is even happening." The wind was blowing, and I was getting cold.

"Suit yourself. Some mornings I wake up and can't believe I'm here, yet I am." His smile faded. "Aren't I?"

"Oh, get real." *And get to the point. I'm freezing out here.*

He looked downright solemn at that. "It's my fondest wish."

"I don't have time for philosophy this morning. I have a life to live, things to do." *Nuts to thaw.*

"A woman to woo?" he asked.

Okay, that stopped me in my tracks. "Berry's okay?"

"Kind of quiet, but she's a strong woman." He leaned in. "She misses you."

Something inside me stilled. "You and she..."

"You should know I had designs on her. Serious ones. She's awfully pretty, good-natured too. And she's a hell of a writer. That's important to a man like me. And that body... nothing like Trista's to be sure, but man, those curves..."

I probably shouldn't admit this, but I hit him then.

Hauled off and hit him good right in the face. I think I wanted to knock some of those perfect white teeth out of his mouth or give him a black eye, at a minimum.

It'd been years since I was in a fight. Yes, he reeled back on my porch, but he didn't fall down. He did look surprised, and I got some satisfaction from that, but mostly, all I got was a sore fist. "If you touched her…" I threatened.

Brad shook his head as he faced me. There wasn't even a trickle of blood. I really hated that son of a bitch right then. "Nothing…" he said. "I tried to seduce her… She said no…"

"Did she?" Now, this was interesting. "Did she say that, or are you guessing? Or are you lying to me?"

I give the guy credit. Most of the guys I know would've thrown a punch right back at me at the first suggestion they were lying, even if they were. Especially if they were. Especially if they'd already been punched in the face. He just stood there and gave me that grin of his. I really hated that.

"I'll tell you what Berry said. She said that there's no guarantee of a happy ending in this world. But she's determined to make the best of it. She wants to write her own, but she's still trying to figure how the plot will flow. That's why I'm here. She wrote my happy ending, so I want to help you with hers."

I shook my head in disgust. "You talk like guys in those books Berry writes, not like a real man."

"If you're asking if I'm a little more in touch with my own feelings, then the answer is yes. It was one of the lessons I learned in *You're the One for Me*."

I was getting a creepy feeling from this guy. Halloween was over but he might have missed the memo. "You aren't for real, are you?"

"That's what I've been trying to tell you, Moe. I'm not, at

least not in your world. Neither is Trista. Or Conrad and Svetlana."

"This conversation is over," I said, reaching for the doorknob. I'm pretty certain I had some heavy metal pipes somewhere in the kitchen. If he got any weirder, I figured I could grab one, even if it was still connected to the wall.

He nodded pleasantly. Back to the old Brad. "I understand. Berry thought you'd take this badly. I'm using conjecture there, as I didn't tell her I was coming to talk to you. But for the record, she's very real. Very human. And she's alone now. I know she's got, as she so quaintly put it, a shit-load of work to do today, but something tells me she wouldn't mind if you were to interrupt her." He stepped from the porch and strode to his car, but then turned around to wave. "I'll be back sometime soon. I think we're going to need your help to round up Trista once and for all."

As I watched, he and his car disappeared with a loud pop.

Or was that the sound of me falling through my door?

Chapter Twenty-Nine

Moe

I know what you're thinking. 'Big strong contractor spooked by a phantom cattle rancher. Ooooh, scary.'

And you'd be right.

After Brad's disappearing stunt, my knees were genuinely wobbly and my hands shook. It took a good five minutes before my heart stopped trying to jump out of my chest to hide in the basement.

Trista disappearing last night, her pie pan gone this morning, and now Brad going poof before my eyes? Either I was having the weirdest daydream of my life, or something bizarre was going on. Something that started and ended with Berry.

But that didn't mean I didn't take Brad's advice to heart. He might not be real—it was hard to believe, but at the moment, I had no other explanation. I might have imagined the entire thing, but if Berry was missing me and I was missing her, maybe, just maybe, I had a chance to make things right with her.

And you know what? Once Brad disappeared, my fist stopped hurting. It was the damnedest thing.

I stepped into my boots, shrugged on my jacket, and was in the truck heading for her place before I stopped shaking.

That guy creeped me out big time. I didn't want to spend too much time thinking about it, so I turned the stereo up, loud. Good old Lyle was singing about sleepwalking, and that suited me fine. I was off to storm the castle and win Berry, the fair princess. Or Solange, the lady writer. I didn't care which. I wanted them—I mean her, more than ever. And I was hoping like hell that she was as real as I remembered.

I pulled onto her street and found it was filled with people out and about. Everything looked so darned normal it almost made me feel better. The sun was shining between the November clouds. There were a few dog-walkers, some kids on bikes, and a huddle of chilly-looking souls waiting for a bus. And in the distance, walking like she had someplace to go, was my Berry. She was moving along at a good clip, but then stopped for a moment and fumbled with something in her hands. I slowed down to watch her making a note on a card. Another idea for her story, no doubt. I smiled. I hoped it was something juicy that she and I could practice later.

I rolled down my window. "Yo, Berry," I called.

She nearly tripped on the sidewalk but recovered soon enough to frown at me. "Are you trying to kill me?" she yelled.

A car behind me beeped. I pulled over and let him pass. "Not exactly," I hollered back. "Mind if I park this thing and walk with you?"

She had a bemused look on her face. "Suit yourself."

I took as a good sign that Berry didn't tell me to get lost, so I put the truck in gear. There was a break in the traffic, and I swung a hard U-ey and pulled into an empty spot right in front of her.

She started walking again as soon as I was out, and I had to hustle to catch up to her.

"You're going to trip if you walk with your boots untied," she commented, not slowing down a bit.

"So, hold up and let me tie them," I complained. I took her by the arm and hauled her in.

She looked so darned pretty, her cheeks all rosy from

the cold. I could see the puffs of her breath in the air. She was wearing pink and looked about as sweet as a piece of candy. I forgot all about being spooked by Brad and wanted nothing more than to tug her in and kiss her. But I didn't. We were on a busy street, and something told me she wouldn't take to public displays of affection. At least not until I was done groveling. I'd hardly gotten started.

"Have a good Thanksgiving?" I asked as casually as I dared while I tied my laces.

She looked at me and took off walking again. "I've had better," she replied over her shoulder. "You?"

I sprang to my feet and took off after her. "The same. I had Trista over at my mom's."

She looked at me for a long moment, still walking fast. "That must have been interesting."

"Interesting doesn't begin to cover it," I agreed. "For the record, my brothers all missed you."

"I'm glad someone did."

"She makes a terrible apple pie."

That cute nose of hers turned up a notch. "I'm not surprised."

This was not going as well as I'd hoped, but better than I expected.

"My mother hated her."

"That's nice."

I couldn't tell anything from her tone. "Berry, the pie plate disappeared."

She stopped suddenly, and I was three steps beyond her before I knew it. How do short people control their momentum so well? I nearly fell on my face.

She squinted at me. "Exactly what do you mean, 'the pie plate disappeared'?"

I took a deep breath. This might be make-or-break time for me, and I didn't want to mess it up.

"She made this pie. Only she didn't have it when we drove over there. It just sort of appeared in her hands when we walked in. Then she got mad at me when I told her I wasn't interested in becoming her stud muffin, and she left in a huff. We all ate the pie anyway because we're gluttons, but it was tasteless."

"And?" Her toe was tapping, but it didn't bother me half as much as it did when Trista did it. Maybe it was because Berry was wearing pink sneakers instead of stilettos.

"Well, in addition to not even tasting as good as cardboard, the pie wasn't all that filling. I took the pan home to give it back to her the next time she popped up." I scratched my head. "She does that, you know, appears when she wants. She never did give me her phone number."

"Get to the point," my Berry frowned.

"So, I took the pan home and washed it last night. I left it on the table to dry when I went to bed."

She folded her arms.

"This morning, when I woke up, it was gone."

"You probably forgot to lock your door, and someone stole it," she said.

I was heartened by the fact that she sounded only half convinced. Berry turned to walk away, but I held out my hand and touched her.

"I locked my doors," I said. "All of them."

"So some stranger—or the former owner has a copy of the key and broke in during the night. You don't have much there, so they took the only thing of value."

"Ber, I changed the locks when I bought the house. I've got thousands of dollars worth of power tools in my place, and those were exactly where I left them." I think I smiled then. She was trying hard to convince herself that I didn't know what I knew.

"Well, maybe you left it in your truck," she said exasperated.

I shook my head. "You can check for yourself."

She whipped off her hat and squeezed it. "So, what do you think caused the big mystery? Other than the obvious, that you're delusional? And why so much fuss over a pie plate? You can pick up a new one for four bucks."

I took her arm and turned her around so that we headed back for her building. "I don't think I'm delusional. I know for a fact that I took it home with me. My mother insisted. She said, 'I don't want anything of that woman's in my home. And don't bring her back here if you know what's good for you.'" I kind of made up some of that, but Berry didn't need to know. She's not the only one who can make up stories when she wants.

"I think you know more about this than you let on," I told her.

She hadn't yet objected to my holding her arm, so I chanced taking up her hand in mine. There was a layer of mitten between us, but it was a whole lot better than nothing.

"There are a few other anomalies, like why Trista has about a thousand twin sets, and never goes anywhere without her pearls unless she's buck naked. Like the fact that neither she, Brad, Conrad or Svetlana seem to be aware that it's cold outside. Svetlana, maybe I can understand, being as she's not from these parts, but the others—not so much. And that none of them really drives anywhere, or seems to have a permanent or even temporary place to live. And then there's the fact that none of them ever, and I mean ever, has any cash on them."

I saw her gulp. It wasn't quite a nod, but her chin dipped as if she were thinking about nodding.

I held my breath. "This here sidewalk might not be the

best place to discuss this."

She did nod then and looked up as if her building had come into view. "Do you want some coffee?" she asked.

"I would like nothing better." I squeezed her hand. "Nothing better, than to have you tell me the whole story about how you came to know those four. And exactly how we're going to put the genie back in the bottle."

I don't think I'll ever forget the look of surprised relief in her eyes, or the way it made me feel all warm inside.

Berry

He knew.

I don't think I've ever been quite so dizzy before. But even knowing the truth, Moe came back to me. He hadn't gone running to the authorities. Didn't send the men in white coats after me. He came. Himself. With that grin of his. But how did he figure it out?

I don't think Trista would have told him unless she was really angry. I'd come to understand her well enough to figure she wanted to pass as human and wouldn't have said anything upon pain of death, which of course, to her, meant nothing. More or less. It's what I would have wanted had I been in her place. And what was she, but a reflection of my imagination?

Did Moe figure it out on his own?

Brad.

We didn't say another word until we were behind the door of my condo. While what I really wanted to do was pass out on the couch, I knew I needed to keep moving, so I hustled into the kitchen to make coffee. Anything was better than talking. I didn't know where to begin, so I took the long route, getting coffee beans from the freezer and pulling out the grinder before I even began to heat the water.

Moe stood there watching me with a little smile on his face as if he knew what I was going through as if he was feeling the same thing.

"I wanted to tell you," I said once I had run out of things to do.

"I seem to remember your trying to, once or twice." He looked at his feet. "I didn't want to know," he replied quickly, then smiled again. "It is kind of fabulous if you think about it."

I groaned. "Maybe for you. Do you have any idea how crazy it's made me, knowing that the two of them were out running around, then Con and Svet too? Trista was wildly out of control, and Brad became a pain in the ass, but Conrad and Svetlana? I wrote them to be ruthless. Who knows what they could have done in the real world. And I'd be responsible."

"From what I can tell, everything is pretty much self-healing, if that pie is any indication," Moe said. "I mean, I wasn't even stuffed after I ate it, and I should have been." He looked down at his boots. "I get the feeling you tried to stop this from happening in the first place."

I nodded. "Yeah, well, best laid plans and all that."

We took our coffee into the dining area and sat down.

"How did it begin?" he asked.

So I told him, and I mean everything. That Trista used to balk when I was first writing and wanted to be someone other than the heroine I always dreamed of writing. That Conrad and Svetlana still talked to me and that I'd gotten better at listening. I explained how I needed to go meet with Duncan and couldn't figure out what to wear, so I opened the file to remember what Triss wore when she first met Brad because it sounded so sophisticated. How I never, ever expected them to pop up like that as if they were flesh and blood. I even told him how I named Conrad in the first place, and fortunately, he laughed.

I told Moe about how I like to write because it allows me to escape to a place where I'm smart, where I have all the answers. There is no problem too large, so complex that I can't figure out a happy ending for it. There are no emotional situations that are too dire for me to address. It's the only part of my life where I felt some control.

Mostly, I told him how I kept hoping that once I got them away from the bookstore, they'd fade and never come back.

"How did you think them up in the first place?" Moe asked at last.

My finger found a little imperfection on the handle of my coffee mug and worried that bump. "Promise you won't laugh?"

"I promise." He looked so solemn that I almost believed him when he nodded.

"I was in the grocery store looking at cheap picture frames for my desk. I saw this perfect looking couple—"

"Shopping? You mean they *are* real?"

I shook my head, rubbing that little nub on the mug. "No. Well, not like you mean. They were in the photo that was part of the frame's packaging. The guy was wearing a cowboy hat, and the woman looked like a fashion model. As far as I could tell, they *were* Brad and Trista personified." I looked up at him. "You didn't notice when you went in there, but that frame with their picture is still on my desk. Kind of coffee-stained now." Boy, that was a tough confession, but he didn't even seem to notice.

"And then when you bought her a copy of the book, I kind of figured I was doomed." I couldn't look at him. "I was so intimidated by you, I could hardly tell you to back off, or that you were enabling a fictional character to cause mayhem upon the world."

"You'd already captured my attention," he told me, that old twinkle in his eye. "If you'd come on that strong, I might have backed off."

"Naw. You were already under Trista's spell. She was fascinating. I wrote her that way."

He shrugged. "Maybe. And she's beautiful. But it was you I wanted to get to know better."

"Because you knew she was married," I countered.

"Because you were the one who was so interesting," he corrected. "You were the one with the mismatched eyes trying to impress your boss. You were the smart one who didn't want anyone to know." He reached across the small table and took my hand. "Don't mistake my intentions or try to rewrite that scene. It was you all along." He lifted my hand then and kissed it. Held it next to his heart.

"So you can accept this? I mean, it's part of me, as much as I've come to hate it."

He swallowed hard. "I think so."

"Because if you can't, you'd better go now. I don't think I have a whole lot of control of the situation anymore, not that I ever did. If you want me, you get these characters too. Part of a package deal. At least until I figure out how to recapture Trista and Brad and put them back where they belong."

"I want you." His big brown eyes looked into mine. "I'll take them if I have to, but no mistake about this either. I love you."

I kind of melted then.

He must have known, for the next thing I knew, he'd hauled me onto his lap and was kissing me. And after that, I was kissing him back. It didn't take long for us to stumble our way to my bedroom and really come to an understanding of how much we loved and missed one another over the past few days. And because we'd been apart for so long, I thought we both needed to reach a deeper understanding, you know, to make sure there were no hard feelings left? So we made up all over again.

I love long weekends. It was like waking up all over again and having the whole day in front of me. I must have snoozed a little after all that activity, and Moe did too. I woke up to the oddest sound of laughter, and it wasn't coming from the man in whose arms I was lying.

"So, I don't totally suck as a matchmaker."

My eyes flew open, and I felt Moe startle beside me. I had to smile at his instinct of making sure we were both covered. I opted for the blanket too, for that morning, I had made my bed with my oldest, softest, most transparent sheets.

"What the hell are you doing here?" Moe grumbled. "Just because you and your wife are exhibitionists, it doesn't mean we're all feeling so fancy-free."

Brad flashed his million-dollar smile. "Whatever. But just so you know, I've flushed Trista out of hiding. She'll be here soon. You two may not get another chance, so you'll want to be ready."

"Ready for what?" I asked. I still didn't have a clue as to how to recapture her and stuff her back between the pages where she belonged. I barely believed I had Moe back.

"Better think fast. She heard you two were reconciled, and she's worked up a good head of steam."

"How did she know that?" I asked. "We haven't told anyone."

Brad gave me a knowing smile before he popped out of sight.

I looked at Moe, and Moe looked at me. We smiled and scrambled for our clothes.

"Got any brilliant ideas?" I asked as I zipped my jeans. For the life of me, I couldn't find my panties and didn't know if I had time to get another pair.

"Yeah, but not about this." He leaned over and kissed me. "I think this is your area of expertise."

"Thanks for nothing," I grumbled.

"Can't you rewrite her or something?"

"Tried that. I figure as long as she's got that copy of the book you bought her, she's impervious."

"So, you need to distract her while I take it from her," he reasoned.

"Maybe you can distract her, and *I* take the book from her," I replied. "I think she might be a little more willing to be distracted if you're the one she's looking at."

"Nope." He shook his head. "I was pretty convincing the last time I saw her that I wasn't interested. I'm not that good an actor."

"Damn," I whispered under my breath. But then an idea popped into my head.

"Okay, I've got it. Just follow my lead, and don't let surprise get in the way."

That's when we heard the sound of angry feet in the hallway. Trista had arrived.

Moe looked askance at me but nodded.

I met her at the door before she had a chance to knock, or blow it down, or whatever it was she wanted to do. She looked more perfect than ever, not a hair out of place, her big blue eyes shining. And her twin set was silver today, shot through with sequins. There wasn't a speck of lint on her, damn it. I don't recall writing them quite so snug. Nor did I ever write them so that her nipples showed through. Was that a nipple ring poking out? Ewww.

I took a deep breath. Having Moe at my back was literally and figuratively comforting. This might be my one and only opportunity to set things right. I didn't know if it would be enough.

"Hello, Trista," I said. "I've been wanting to talk to you."

"Really?" she sneered and pushed her way into my living room. "Well, now's your chance."

She gazed at Moe, looked him up and down with eyes so hungry, I only wish I could do them justice in a description someday. "I see the two of you are together again." She flicked her fingers at us. "You don't know what you're missing, handsome," she purred at him before shooting me a dirty look. "If you think this one's hot in bed, you haven't seen anything."

Moe smiled as he placed his warm hands on my shoulders. "I've read your story. I think I know your tricks."

"Tricks." She huffed. "I've become a whole lot more than what you read. I've seen a lot of the world since then. Other books where the hero and heroine do all sorts of *interesting* things poor little Solange can only dream about."

Oh crap. She had me there, but Moe laughed. "You have no idea at all if you're only reading about sex in books." He looked at me then and placed a quick kiss on my lips. "So many people mistake romance novels that way. See, the sex is just the mechanics. What Berry and I feel in here," he patted his heart, "that's not something that can be captured in mere words."

She huffed again. "Talk. Talk. Talk. I know men. You only want one thing. As much as you can get, as many ways as you can get it. Brad told me he told you we're not real, but I can tell you, we're better. We don't age. No wrinkles, no odors. We can go anywhere in the world we want in the blink of an eye."

"And a mere mortal like me could never hope to follow you. Why do you want me anyway?" he asked. "*I'm* going to age. *I'll* get wrinkles, and believe me, when I get home from work, I have to take my boots off outside for all the odors I've got."

She sauntered up to him and ran her hands up his chest. "But don't you see, that's why we'd be perfect for each other. I can't really smell," she purred.

"And as for you getting older, I'll leave you before that happens, so no one will mind."

Trista looked around as if it were all settled. She repositioned her purse on her shoulder. I could see a corner of the book from where I stood. Moe, being taller, probably had a much better shot at it.

Not so fast. She turned, and it was out of reach for both of us.

"So, Triss. In all that reading you've been doing, what's the most exciting thing you've encountered?"

She resettled herself to show her body to its best advantage. "Oh, I don't know. There are all sorts of positions that you never had us try. I'm anxious to get it from the back for one."

Interesting. It seemed as though sex intrigued her more than the romance. I'd have to keep that in mind. Not that she was my typical reader. "What about a threesome?" I asked, not daring to look at Moe. "You and two men?"

She shifted, suddenly uncomfortable. Moe looked like he was going to choke. *Don't lose it now, buddy*, I thought.

"If Moe doesn't mind—"

He shook his head. "Nope. Nothing doing. One man, one woman. That's it for me. Now, a threesome where there's two women and me—I might be able to round up some enthusiasm for that."

You'd better be acting buster... But it was the opening I'd been hoping for. I had her attention, and her back was to Moe.

"So, how about that Triss? Ever think of doing it with another woman, letting Brad—or Moe—or both of them watch?"

"Well, I don't know." She frowned. "I'd have to think about it."

"No time for that," I said as I pushed up against her and hauled her head down. "I say right now. There's Moe, there's you, and there's me. Let's try it."

That's when I kissed her.

Chapter Thirty

Moe

Damn, but did Berry surprise me. It must have been the Solange side of her.

Lots of guys find it a turn on to see their woman kiss another woman. Not this guy. I didn't want her to kiss anyone but me. Still, I spent a long moment being dumbfounded before it occurred to me she wanted me to do something. I don't know if Berry was getting into the kiss with Triss or if she was a fine actress. My money's on the second. It kind of unnerved me to be honest, but hell, you've got to admire the woman for making an opportunity like that. I hoped our having possession of the book would be enough.

I would never make a living as a pickpocket, but I did my best. It was really pretty simple since Triss had that huge gaping purse over her shoulder, and the only thing in it was her book. I held my breath and tucked my hand into that bag and grabbed it.

She knew the moment I had it. She broke from the embrace with an angry shriek and clawed at me. "*That's mine*," she hissed.

"Not so fast." I hid it behind my back. "We needed to get your attention."

Berry was standing there, enjoying this immensely. She wiped her mouth on the back of her sleeve. It wasn't the most ladylike thing I've ever seen her do, but it was gratifying.

"Maybe we all ought to sit down and talk this thing through," she said.

"I will not," Triss whispered angrily and almost headed for the door, but thought better of it. Brad popped into the room then and made himself comfortable.

"Do you want coffee? A snack?" Berry asked just as casual as can be. It would be the third time she made it this morning. I grinned, seeing our now cooled cups still sitting on her table. And I hadn't eaten anything yet today—okay, not exactly true, but you know what I mean.

"I want nothing from you," Trista sneered. She turned to me and gave me a sultry smile. "But from you, handsome, I want it all."

I shook my head and slipped the book into my back pocket before I sat on a chair. She'd have to go through me to get it, and even I could see she was losing strength.

"I already told you, I'm for Berry, and she's for me."

"Even after she kissed me like that?" Triss teased. "That was a hell of a kiss. If you give me back my book, I'll put on a show for you. We both will."

Brad sighed. "Come on, Triss. Sit down and listen to what Berry has to say."

She ignored him, but when I smiled and shrugged, she folded her arms and made for the sofa, as far from her husband as possible.

I could hear Berry making coffee, but I thought it was a little more important for me to sit on the book than to help her. I'd make up for it later by cleaning her kitchen.

Moments later, she came out with a tray with four steaming cups and a plate of cookies. They were vanilla swirls with candied cherries in the middle. She smiled and winked at me, and I dug right in. Now these tasted like something. I took another, just in case Brad made a pig of himself before I got seconds.

Berry sat on the arm of my chair and didn't seem to mind when I put my hand around her hip. Just one layer between her and me. I grinned at our company.

"Now, isn't this nice?" Berry smiled at her guests. "I've been wanting to talk to you, Triss, to see what you think of the world."

"You've got a funny way of displaying hospitality," she sulked. "Kissing me like that, then having your boyfriend steal my book."

"I do believe he purchased it."

She folded her arms a little tighter against her chest but said nothing.

Berry took a sip of her coffee. "Brad, what do you think of the real world? Care to stay in it?"

He smiled at the assembled company and fixed the crease in his jeans. "It's got some interesting parts. I will sure say that. You just scratched the surface, Solange, when you described stuff in our book. It's a mighty interesting place."

"There's only so much you can do with one hundred thousand words," Berry said, her voice low. "I wasn't writing a travelogue."

"No, you sure weren't," he laughed. "But I sure liked seeing how you folks live out here. This place for instance. Nice and homey. And your parent's place—like a palace. Nothing like Moe's. That was plenty charming on the outside, but what a dump on the inside."

"I'm just getting started," I muttered. "Come back in a year." Oops. Wish I hadn't said that.

Berry chuckled and patted my knee. "Triss, you've been awfully quiet."

"I want my book back," she moaned. "I can't go anywhere without it."

"That's kind of the point I wanted to make," Berry said, her voice sad and kind. "That book isn't going to last forever. Paper and glue. One good rainstorm, and it could all fall apart. Real people don't last either. But you, you have the chance to last forever in people's hearts the way I wrote you. This book is selling far better than I ever dreamed it would. People love you."

"All the more reason for me to stay," she cried.

"All the more reason for you to go back where you came from. The way you've been carrying on doesn't fit the profile of the Trista our readers love. You've become mean spirited, stealing other women's men, saying rude things. Swearing." Berry shook her head. "That's not the character I wrote."

Triss tossed back her hair and narrowed her eyes. "But the way you wrote me is a sap. A goody-two-shoes. That's not me. Not anymore. It never was. Just look at your earlier drafts. I was a lot more interesting before you listened to your agent and editors. I mean, even you—you're not as much of a goody-two-shoes as you want everyone to think you are."

Berry gave a little jolt at that remark, but I think I was the only one who noticed. "It can be you again," Berry said softly. "If you try. As soon as I'm done with Conrad and Svetlana, I was all set to start another book. I've been making notes about it all morning. You and Brad were going to be featured as a matter of fact. I've got you pegged as the neighbors of the hero when they all buy new vacation homes in Vermont to go skiing in the winter."

"Make it Colorado," Brad asked. "Closer to home in Texas."

Berry shrugged, "Okay. I don't know that area, but maybe I can take a trip, so I know what I'm writing about."

"January's a slow time for me," I said quietly. "It might be a good time for the two of us to get away together."

She turned to flash me the prettiest smile, and my heart melted all over again.

"On the other hand," Berry said as she turned back to Trista. "If you insist on staying out here in the world as you are, I'll have to write about Brad all by himself."

"That would never work," Trista laughed. "What type of story would you have without me?"

Berry grew quiet. "Well, for starters, I could feature him in the next volume instead of making him a supporting character. I could save the sequel for later. Think of it, tragic hero loses the love of his life in a terrible skiing accident." She pursed her lips. "No, that doesn't sound quite right. Maybe to a drunk driver?" She shook her head. "No. It would have to be stronger than that, to really break people's hearts."

She closed her eyes and put her head back. "I've got it. You're are at a dinner party, and you had one too many. You came in separate cars. When it's time to leave, you refuse to let Brad drive you, even though he's sober."

Berry gave a little wiggle then, sitting on the arm of my chair as she did. I patted her rump affectionately. God, but I love her.

"He's going to regret that for the rest of his life. Oh, this is perfect. You see, you're the drunk driver, and you take your own life as well as that of another young family. Only the beautiful young wife is left, grieving for her husband and twin babies."

There was a gasp. I might have been me who made it.

"Brad is heart-broken too, and after a tender scene or two where their hearts individually mend, the two of them fall in love." Berry smiled. "That's it. Quite dramatic, of course. There would have to be lots of guilt and pain naturally. You were drinking because after three years of marriage, you were barren. The obstacle of falling in love with the husband of your husband's killer for my new heroine? Very dark. Lots of internal conflict. People are going to love it. Especially in the epilogue when the happy couple discover she's pregnant."

"NOOOooo!" Trista cried. "You can't do that to me. You can't kill me off. You can't make me out to be so awful."

Berry lifted one brow. "No?" She smiled gently. "What can you do to stop me?"

"People will hate you for that," Triss moaned.

"Not if I write it the right way," Berry said quietly. "I can make it last just one chapter. A prologue—it'll be over in three pages. The readers will cry, which they want, but in the end, they won't like you for what you did to Brad, breaking his heart like that, and worse, for what you did to those children. I'd even make you pregnant, but they don't find out until the autopsy. No, that would be too gruesome. I'll write you barren. People would hate that. I hate it. I'll probably cry for a week when I write it. Heck, I feel a tear or two coming on now just thinking about it."

"Can you make the young widow a redhead? Brad asked. "I think I really like redheads now,"

"You're torturing me because I took Moe from you, aren't you? You're jealous of me and my beauty."

To her credit, Berry simply shrugged, but I couldn't sit back and take that. "For the record, you didn't take me anywhere. You forced yourself on me and spent a lot of my money without a single thank-you." I shifted in my seat. "I never stopped wanting Berry the whole time."

My love turned and smiled at me before she faced her foe once more.

"I guess it comes down to this. Either you willingly go back into the story, or I write the sequel the way I want to."

"That's blackmail."

"Sure sounds that way to me, darling," Brad said as he put his arm around his wife. "I wished I'd'a thought of that sooner. Would have saved us all a lot of grief."

Trista sat on the sofa, her eyes narrowed and squinty, her fingers furled into fists. But she sighed and said nothing. It was as if the fight went out of her with a whoosh.

It seemed as if the tide had turned. I couldn't tell if Berry relaxed if even a little. She was sitting up as straight as ever. She'd hooked her fish, but had yet to reel it in.

"What if I'm not ready to be a supporting character?" Triss asked as she reached for Brad's hand. "I'm not ready to give up the limelight."

"Hmm." Berry rested her chin on her fist. "That might be kind of hard to arrange without creating a huge, *believable* misunderstanding between the two of you." She thought a moment. "What if I wrote the book as I said, with you being neighbors and all. It can be those two who were married and then lose their families. You two can be the helpful neighbors who pave the way for them to fall in love."

Brad looked like he liked the idea, but Triss was skeptical. "Only if you don't kill off any babies. I don't think I could stand that."

"How about a beloved pet dog?" Brad suggested.

"Only if it was already old and sick," Trista insisted. "Put out of its misery."

"I didn't figure you to be quite so tenderhearted, sweetheart." Brad cuddled her closer.

"It's the new me. More vulnerable than before," Trista said with a sniff. "But I still want at least three scenes where I'm featured. And I want to try something kinky with Brad. No more boring regular sex. Maybe something where I can wear high-heeled boots, and a collar and leash? No. A whip."

Berry smiled. It seemed she'd won the day. "I can't make you too saccharine or outlandish or no one would believe in you."

"I'm sure you'll figure it out." Trista's eyes went all

dreamy. "And make the misunderstanding over the fact that I can't get pregnant and Brad feels like he's only half a man because no matter how hard he tries, he can't knock me up. He feels terrible about it, and the whole time I'm blaming myself. We break up over it, but can't stop falling into bed with each other anyway." Trista was warming to her subject. "He thinks it's because we're doing all sorts of kinky things, like tying each other up, but it's really a matter of his tighty-whiteys being too snug, and as soon as he's changed to boxers, that's it, and we live happily ever after with twins.

"No. Triplets." She turned her eyes to Berry. "And I want a full sequel, not that supporting character shit. You can save the redhead's story for later. Have someone else kill her family, not my Brad."

She beamed, happily planning her future.

Berry rose and put her coffee cup down on the tray. "You've given me lots of ideas to work with. Let me think about it for a while, maybe talk to my agent. I want to make sure she thinks we can sell a sequel so soon. Maybe begin to hint that there's trouble in paradise in the next book, then come out with it in a year or two?"

She stood up. "Now, are we all in agreement? You two will go back and continue your happily-ever-after until I contact you. It seems Brad's taken an interest in interior decorating after all. And landscaping to complement it. Maybe the two of you can discuss that while you're waiting. Design and plan your vacation home, or redo the ranch?"

Triss clapped her hands together in glee. "What a great idea. We can compare notes. You wouldn't believe the dump that Moe's mother lives in. There were tables and chairs everywhere. Nothing matched. And paintings on velvet—it wasn't to be believed."

I must have moved, but Berry put a hand to my chest to

slow me. "Down, boy," she whispered. "We can't expect she'll change that much in an hour."

Berry was right, of course. Everyone was exactly where she wanted them, me included. Ten minutes later, she had Trista practically begging her to be let back home. "I haven't had a decent night's sleep or a good tumble for weeks," Trista said. "Come on, Brad. Let's go straight home and into bed. I've heard about all sorts of things I think we ought to try."

Berry reached around and grabbed the book from my back pocket and flicked it open. A soft pop and Trista was gone. Brad stood up and smiled at the two of us. "You won't let us wait too long, now will you?" he asked wistfully.

"Just as long as I need to," Berry promised. "But it won't seem like any time has passed where you'll be."

Brad nodded once. He leaned over and kissed Berry's cheek, then held out his hand to shake mine. I allowed it, and then there was another soft pop, and he too was gone.

Berry collapsed onto the sofa, her eyes closed, body lax. The volume fell to the floor. "Am I dreaming, or are they really gone?" she whispered.

I admit I had to look around the condo before I replied. Their two cups of coffee were back on the tray as if they'd never drunk them. Even the cushions where they'd been sitting were once again smooth. I checked the closets and under the bed. Even the toilet tank. "They're gone," I said.

She opened her eyes and held out her hand. "Let me see that book."

I picked it up with the tips of my fingers, afraid if I opened it, Trista and Brad would spill out exclaiming that they'd changed their minds.

She had no such compunction, for she flipped it open. All the notes Trista had made were gone, the pages clean once again. Only Solange's signature on the front cover was there.

Berry blew out a huge sigh of relief. "It's like they were never here," she breathed.

Of course, it occurred to me that they still were. In a sense. Berry had imagined all four of them. So in a way, they were still there, only contained in one delightful, delectable bundle. I didn't want to imagine myself holding all of them when I held her in my arms...

She opened the drawer of her coffee table and pulled a rubber band off a deck of cards, securing the book. She examined it carefully before she tossed it on the table with a happy sigh.

I lifted her legs and sat next to her on the couch, draping them over me. "They *were* here, weren't they?" I asked. "I mean, this wasn't a group hallucination or anything, right?"

She covered her face with her hands. "I don't even know anymore," she said. "If anyone we know mentions them, we're safe. I mean sane."

"But we broke up because of them, in a way. It's not like Trista seduced me. Or succeeded."

Berry peeked at me then and smiled. "And Brad never got anywhere with me either."

I blew out a relieved breath at that. "So. Where does this leave us?" I asked.

She reached for my hands and hauled herself up until she was sitting in my lap. She wiggled until she straddled me. That's when she put her arms around my neck and leaned in close. "It leaves you and me alone, together," she said with a smile. "Here in my place with nothing to do for the rest of the day but to enjoy ourselves."

"After I wash all those coffee cups, I was planning on getting some work done at my place. I have a new kitchen to install." That's when it hit me. If every trace of Trista and

Brad had disappeared, did that mean the kitchen plans had too?

"And you'd rather be doing that?" Berry asked, resettling herself more pointedly.

Come to think of it, there really wasn't much of a choice. I kissed her then and pulled her even closer. "I think those cabinets can wait until tomorrow." After all, Thanksgiving was a whole year away. We'd get plenty done before then, when we sat down in our newly refurbished dining room together and presided over the first annual joined family holiday celebration.

"Naw," I said as I made it to my feet and carried her into the bedroom with her in my arms. "I'd much rather stay here and celebrate the start of our hard-won privacy."

Chapter Thirty-One

Berry

A year has passed since Brad and Trista were last here.

    A few months ago, when we moved our stuff into the refurbished Victorian, Moe found that old copy of my book. He wanted to throw it out, but I wouldn't let him. The book sold well, and the royalties were still coming in. Sales were about to bump again, now that my latest story was about to be released. Conrad and Svetlana's story was a lot grittier and risqué than *You're the One for Me.* The advance copies that had gone out were getting wonderful reviews.

    Needless to say, I was hard at work on my newest. True to my word, it was the follow-up to Brad and Trista's story. The working title was *It's Better the Second Time Around.* I'm not thrilled with it, so I'm keeping an open mind. I'm also tinkering with some new characters, and Moe thinks my new hero and heroine are almost too realistic. They haven't popped in to visit us, but I'm afraid it's only a matter of time.

    Anyway, I'm half focused on Brad and Trista. They're both behaving very nicely this time. Due to the storyline, I was able to let Trista loosen up and have some fun. Brad grew up and had developed an interest in carpentry, but wanted Moe's help. He built a special little gazebo for Trista as an anniversary gift. Moe refused to talk to them directly, and I wasn't about to let either character loose in the world again, so I did quite a bit of conveying messages this time around. It helped that Moe happened to have been building me a gazebo at the same time, so he could give me the information firsthand.

But on the other hand, I don't quite know when it will see the light of day. I'm kind of nervous about it, and there's another story that's been taking up a lot of my writing time.

I'm not sure why I wanted to keep Trista's copy. Maybe it was a lesson in maintaining control of my writing and my characters. Maybe it was a reminder about how I found my power at a time when I was feeling powerless. Or maybe it was a reminder of the first time Moe and I met, for if we hadn't, nothing else would ever have happened, and that would have been a tragedy to end all tragedies.

I have to admit I'm a little bored with their story, so I'm thinking of putting it down for a month or two, so I can work on something else that's been chasing around my brain.

Moe conceded to let me keep the copy, but instead of putting it in a shadow box frame as I wanted, he installed a wall safe in my tower—my writing room. In that safe, I store all the flash drives where I keep my manuscripts, as well as other precious things I own. Despite the fact that we've been a year now without any of my characters coming for an unexpected visit, Moe isn't letting down his guard. If they want to pop out of the book, he wants them to do so in a cramped, dark space so they won't be tempted to stay.

Can't say I blame him.

At the moment, I was basking in the glow that all newlyweds must feel after they've hosted their first big party. I was proud to show off my new home to my family. Moe and his brothers did a terrific job restoring this old house, and I've had a lot of fun making it into a home. When we got back from our honeymoon, and Moe showed me that he'd added my name to the deed, I burst into tears. There's no more talk about him selling it as a spec house. Instead, we show it off for potential customers. We've had some offers, but I've made it quite clear that this is my home, and I'm not leaving it. I can go straight from my bedroom to my writer's nook. Moe built me a desk and a window seat in there, so I can look out my turret windows when I'm in need of inspiration.

As you might expect, there was a spot of resistance in the Samuels home to my marrying a laborer, as my father put it. But Moe has a way of growing on people. I think the first time my father softened toward him was when Moe dressed up for a family function, and it wasn't some off the rack rag, but a nicely tailored suit with a designer label. It didn't hurt that Moe was able to quietly discuss his business model and modestly brag about his income from last year.

Of course, my brother fired me for some infraction after I announced my engagement. I laughed at him. Duncan quit in protest, leaving Rocky high and dry. He turned out to be an okay kind of guy after all, almost kind of heroic, making that last stand for me and all. Maybe someday I'll pattern one of my heroes after him. I'll need to add about eight inches of height first, and a little more muscle to his physique, plus a twinkle in his eye. Oh, and a personality. But underneath, I'll know it's Conrad Duncan.

But back to my family. My mother was wowed the first time she saw our house, especially when Moe showed her the 'before' pictures. And when Moe was able to converse intelligently with my grandfather about the stock market, my brother was finally won over as much as he's ever won over by anyone, though I think he was more than a little pissed when Darlene made a pass at Moe.

I put an end to that pretty quickly and set Darlene straight about who was who in the family hierarchy. In fact, she didn't make more than a peep all night tonight, despite the big new rock on her finger. I think my announcement about my impending state of motherhood trumped news of her engagement. I'm not the same quiet mouse I once was, thank goodness.

And no, this pregnancy isn't just so I could have the experience to write about it when I finally allow Trista to get pregnant. This was for Moe and me. After all, we have this huge house and all those bedrooms to fill. Not that we are going to fill all of them, I warned him and his mother. Trista might foolishly think she wanted triplets, but I was going to have one baby at a time, thank-you-very-much, and I was cutting off at two. Three if Moe asked me really nicely.

And speaking of nice, as a husband, my Moe is all a woman could ask for and more. Yes, he is still big and strong, and my breath still catches in my throat every time he walks in the door. But it's more than size and brawn. It's his sweetness, his humor. It's the love I felt for him, and he feels for me.

I know how trite it sounds to say that every day is better than the day before, but that's exactly how it was, and how it is. Waking up in his arms in our big bed makes me start every day with a smile, even when the morning sickness starts before I open my eyes. He's so sympathetic, the first time I barfed because of his baby, he barfed right along with me so I wouldn't be embarrassed. I told him that one of us being sick was enough, and he could stop. He's done his best to hold it in ever since.

Some days, I think he's even more excited about this baby than I am and keeps coming up with cute little names like Bix or Guy or Lyle. Naturally, he never comes up with any girls' names. I smiled to myself. We have quite a few months before I win this round with him. What's the point of ruining his fun?

So, as I said, we haven't been troubled by Brad or Trista, Conrad or Svetlana for a year. We sometimes tease each other that it was a shared dream we had and not real at all. I dream about them though, and sometimes new characters too, the ones whose stories I have yet to tell. Whenever that happens, I cuddle up to him and tell him "Moe, "I'm having such a hard time separating fiction from reality, I don't even know if you're real."

Whenever I do that, he grins at me and says, "Babe, let me show you just how real I am." And he does.

But we both feel the same way. There are no physical reminders of them, no photos, and of course, anything they created disappeared into the ether when they did. Personally, I'm glad. When Moe described the kitchen Trista designed, I was aghast. The way I had him build it, it's so much more functional. All that fancy tile can wait until after the kids are through with college. Mine is a kitchen I can cook in.

Still, imagine the relief we both felt the first time someone mentioned meeting Trista or Brad. In fact, I think it was the first time I met Moe's mother. The day after Brad and Triss disappeared for good.

"Ma," Moe said as we walked through her front door. "Ma, this is Berry. I'm going to marry her. She's the one for me."

Now mind you, he hadn't precisely been asked me to marry him yet—not since that second or third date when he kind of announced it. But that's what he said.

Rosemary looked me up and down. She's a big woman, tall and substantial. Her eyes are shrewd, and her arms were crossed. One could say she's imposing. I guess she'd have to be to raise five strong boys on her own. "You the writer?" she asked me.

I nodded, too intimidated to speak. I'd never replied to her email.

"Good. He needs someone who can think, and keep him in line, not to mention make him happy." She swatted

Moe lightly for no good reason.

It wasn't exactly a ringing approval of me, but she hadn't come at me with a cleaver either. She looked at her son. "Thank goodness you had the sense to drop that other one—who thought she was a character from a book."

Moe and I looked at each other then, and he looked like I felt, as if the wind had been sucked right out of me.

"Yeah, that's who she reminded me of," Rosemary continued. "She was a dead ringer for your heroine, Berry, even the name. But once she opened her mouth, it was all over. What a waste of protein that one was. I think your character was a lot more real than that piece of trash." She took our coats. "So, are you writing anything now?"

I remember swallowing hard so I wouldn't squeak when I opened my mouth. "I'm finishing a swashbuckler. Moe tells me you like to read romances. Maybe you'd do me the favor of reading my manuscript and give me your honest feedback."

Rosemary stopped in her tracks. I think there were tears in her eyes. I didn't know if I should give her a hug or run.

"You mean it? That's the nicest thing anyone's asked me." She hugged me then, and Moe grinned as he looked on until she cuffed him again. "She's a keeper. You understand?" Rosemary turned to me and leaned in close. "Anything you can do to help my other boys along?" she asked under her breath. "They all go out with tramps. I'm glad the two of you are setting a good example, but I think they all need some help. Joey especially."

I have to say I was touched. My own mother won't read my stuff, even with my success. And no one's ever asked me for help in fixing anyone up. In fact, Moe introduced me to a nice woman who would be perfect for Joey. She works in a donut shop, but she's much more than just some random waitress. I've got some ideas. That hero and heroine I mentioned earlier—they're both kind of wrapped up in that whole idea. I need to think about it a little more. Wait for the right moment.

It's also nice it is to have someone else to talk to about my writing other than Moe, who thinks everything I write is a prelude to sex. When he's around, I guess it is. Certainly to romance.

He's been very helpful about acting out scenes with me to make sure they work. All that foolishness about being embarrassed has gone by the wayside. Any time he's been asked about that, especially by other men, his chest kind of puffs up. I try not to let him see me smile when he tells men that the sex is well and good, but it's the romantic scenes he inspires. Those, he says with great confidence, are the most important part. And who am I to contradict him?

But what I like most about being married to him is the love. The acceptance, and the pride. He's more man than I ever dreamed existed, a better hero than any I could make up, stinky feet and all. And he loves me, my dreamy interludes, my moments of stress, and those occasional days of elation.

Which is not to say that love is not returned full force. I've found my own happy ending, especially late at night, when I'm having trouble falling asleep. That's when he takes me in his arms in our big cozy bed. He'll say, "Let me tell you a story."

And then he'll press the start button on this cute little tape recorder and play me this story he made:

"Once upon a time, there was a beautiful woman who lived far too much in her own head. She invented wonderful characters and made them come alive.

"One day, when she was taking a break from her work,

she met a man with no imagination at all. But as luck would have it, he was looking for a woman who had enough for two. They met and fell in love. There were some troubles and some very odd characters in between. The lovers parted, but then they found each other all over again. And then they got married on a beautiful sandy beach in the early spring, and they love each other very much. Oh yeah, and they lived happily ever after. The end."

The End

A Waitress in a Doughnut Shop

A novel by Solange DewBerry

June

Jenny

"Joey and his girl are at it again." The waitress smirked and hurried to the kitchen with her load of dirty dishes.

Jenny Ellsworth's shoulders slumped as she heard the words, then turned to watch as Joey Conrad and his girlfriend argued. Again.

To be honest, it was the girlfriend who was going at it. By the time Jenny saw her, she had an empty champagne flute in her hand and was looking around for another to toss. Joey sat at the head table and wiped his face, then stood and shed his soaked tuxedo jacket. He turned emotionless brown eyes upon his date. That didn't stop *her* jaw from flapping the entire time.

Why did he put up with that harpy? Did insanity run in the Conrad genes? Jenny didn't want to consider that possibility.

But to watch Joey get ragged at again...it was almost too much.

She stood by the side of the dance floor and shifted from one aching foot to the other. Between her and the drama across the room, the glowing bride danced with her handsome groom, happily oblivious to the sideshow. All around, guests were laughing and clapping and generally having a ball. Yes, Jenny's feet were killing her, but as she was at this wedding as a guest, not simply as the caterer, it was worth the discomfort. Even if she'd rather be wearing her soft-soled white shoes instead of these killer stilettos, they wouldn't have gone with the amethyst silk sheath she wore. Regardless, it beat dressing up as a cowgirl, medieval tavern wench, or space invader, as she'd done, depending on the job.

The bride and groom, Berry and Maurice Conrad, were well connected, and if she made a good impression, it would mean more jobs for her as manager of The Sweet Shop's catering division. She'd rather cater a wedding than a carnival any day. Except at the moment, with the drama going on up on the dais in front of two hundred and fifty people, it might be hard to differentiate.

"I never want to see you again."

The harpy's shriek cut over the DJ's PA system as Joey's date slung an oversized, poison-green leather purse over her shoulder and stomped off in clunky high heels, shoving her way through the crowd.

Jenny watched as Joey shook his head silently. He gave an apologetic smile to the others at the table. That was Joey... urbane, serious, polite, and so hot she wanted to fan herself.

Why did he put up with that woman, she asked herself for the thousandth time, before she sighed. All those Conrad brothers were too handsome for their own good— Joey more than the rest. And seeing him in his damp shirt... Jenny had to bite her lip. There was nothing fake about those muscles. Hot damn, he was so good looking all dressed up, she had to look away. Bad enough she got tongue-tied when she saw him in his usual flannel shirt, jeans, and work boots. She always got a funny feeling in the pit of her stomach when she looked at him too long, and she didn't have time for a fit of unrequited lust. She might be a guest, but she had work to do.

Besides, dreaming about Joey would do her no good. It hadn't yet. No, she needed to stop daydreaming and check in the kitchen. Her staff should be ready to roll out the pastry buffet and serve the cake. She'd been up until midnight setting the last of the rosettes on five tiers of buttercream frosting. Everything had to be perfect for every job she did... but this one had to be even better.

In the center of the dance floor, Berry swirled in Moe's arms as a song ended. Jenny couldn't help her small wistful sigh. Who in their right mind wouldn't be envious? To watch them, no one would guess that they'd ever been anything but deeply in love. The trouble they'd had with that other couple—those strange people last year—that was all in the past.

Why couldn't *that woman*—Jenny grit her teeth—*Colette* appreciate the fine man Joey was? Why did she always have to pick an argument, and why always in public? Didn't she understand the bride was supposed to be the center of attention at her wedding?

The DJ was blathering on about slowing down the dancing for a romantic ballad. The opening strains of Foreigner's *I Want to Know What Love Is*, filled the hall. It was a clear signal it was time to leave.

Pushing away from the wall, Jenny made to turn when a touch on her hand startled her. She spun to see none other than Joey looking at her, his hand held out in an invitation to the dance floor.

Her mouth dropped open, and she shook her head. She didn't have time for this now. "I have to..."

He quirked one dark brow upward with a crooked smile to match and tugged lightly on her hand. A shiver ran through her that she was powerless to stop. Oh crap.

"Come on, save me from embarrassment," he said in

his deep voice.

Great, a pity dance. Or was he trying to teach Collette a lesson with the first unattached woman he saw? Maybe it was all a dream. Maybe he broke ranks tonight and was drunk—although she'd heard Joey never got drunk. There had to be an explanation for why he was there. In front of her. Looking as good as a man could look.

How could one man be so damned appealing? Before she could think of running away, before her brain kicked into a higher functioning mode, her hand slid into his, and he pulled her onto the floor. The music kept playing, and she moved into his arms as if she'd done it a thousand times.

His arms tightened, and she held on, promising herself she wouldn't enjoy this, wouldn't get used to it, wouldn't think it would continue beyond tonight, beyond this song. Joey belonged to Collette. Tonight, tomorrow, next week, they'd get back together as they always did. This moment wasn't real, just part of the fairytale that belonged to Berry and Moe.

A traitorous idea slipped into her mind. Maybe for once, a bit of enchantment could fall on her, if only for a little while.

Jenny closed her eyes as the chorus filled her, and Joey swept her around the floor. Maybe pretending was okay. Who besides she would know if she instilled in her memory what it felt like being in Joey's arms? It wasn't as if she'd cornered him. He came to her. And it was him, not her, who danced them off the floor and away from the crowd. This wasn't real, just her overactive imagination out for an unexpected vacation. What was a wedding if not to dream upon?

Joey said something to her. She must have replied, for he fell silent, pulled her in closer. She opened her eyes to see Collette far away, cornering one of the other Conrad brothers, Sammy perhaps, or Paul. She hoped he told her to take a big old flying leap. Jenny closed her eyes again.

And then Joey had danced her through the kitchen doors. The music was muted, and the clattering of the kitchen assaulted her ears. Joey stopped and looked down at her. The look in his eyes was something she never thought she would see in this life, but there it was. Longing. Hope. Perhaps she was the one who'd had too many glasses of champagne.

She blinked to clear her sight. It wasn't possible that Joey could be looking at plain Jenny Ellsworth with such desire. He smiled, the back of one finger caressed her cheek, and then the smile was closer, and his eyes were closing. She felt the gentle press of his lips on hers and then, finally—finally, she stopped thinking and let herself fall into the moment.

It was too sweet, this kiss like raw honey. This dream of hers—she'd wake from it any moment and find herself back in the real world, serving coffee and doughnuts instead of dancing in a castle of spun sugar. Jenny opened her eyes to prove it to herself, only to see Joey smile down at her, his hands holding hers between them. Was that throbbing sound of the dishwasher, or her heart sloshing around in ecstasy?

"I've been wanting to do that for the longest time," he said softly before the kitchen doors banged open. That tender look in his eye...

"So, this is where you've gotten yourself. Quit slumming in the kitchen. Oh, hi, Jenny." Collette's astringent voice broke through the spell. Normal kitchen clatter resumed. The closing strains of the ballad could be heard through the swinging door, loud, soft, loud, soft.

"Joey. I want to go home. Now," Collette said. "Your dumbass brothers all told me to call a cab, but I don't have any money."

No, the little voice inside Jenny screamed. *No!*

Joey closed his eyes, squeezed her fingers before he dropped Jenny's hands and turned to his date.

Did this woman have magical powers over him? Jenny tucked her hands up under her arms as a chill engulfed her.

"What'cha waiting for? Jenny's got everything under control here in the kitchen," Collette demanded. "Let's go. I don't wanna wait for Berry to throw her bouquet. I never catch the damned things anyway."

Joey turned back to Jenny; his brows furrowed.

She couldn't bear to watch her sugar cube fantasy melt before her eyes. She shook her head and turned away. "What *are* you waiting for? I've got things to do," she said over her shoulder as she picked up a tray full of dirty dishes. Damn, but it was hard to balance it wearing heels.

He looked between the two women one last time before he hung his head and followed the blonde from the room.

The doors were still swinging as Jenny took a deep breath and set down her tray. Well, that was over before it began. She looked around the kitchen. "Everything okay here?"

"No worries, Jenny," her chef said carefully. "Go back out there and have a good time. We'll get the desserts out there."

She forced a smile as she glanced about the kitchen. It didn't seem a good time was in the offering, at least for her. Best to face reality.

Did Joey really look as miserable as she thought when Collette came in? Or was it resigned? Or simply her imagination running overtime? Did it matter? Regardless, he'd left Jenny and followed her. Joey was too much a gentleman ever to break it off with a woman. It had to be insanity, or maybe a hit to the head when he was a kid. None of the other four brothers seemed so touched.

So much for her grand romance. It had lasted what, five minutes? Four?

She took another deep breath, kicked off her shoes, and Jenny the guest, became Jennifer, the caterer. Back to business. It was time to cut the cake.

She would not think about what might have been. Magic? Impossible. She wasn't the type to suffer from a broken heart. That was best left for fairytale princesses or people like Berry—a writer with imagination to spare.

Jenny had a job to do, and damn it, she was going to do it.

If you enjoyed this story, please leave a review to let other know how much you liked it. You can also contact the author at SolangeDewBerry@Gmail.com.

Made in the USA
Middletown, DE
26 February 2020